In Twilight's Shadow

D0003763

Tor Paranormal Books by Patti O'Shea

In the Midnight Hour
In Twilight's Shadow

In Twilight's Shadow

Patti O'Shea

tor paranormal romance

A TOM DOHERTY ASSOCIATES BOOK
NEW YORK

This is a work of fiction. All of the characters, organizations, and events portrayed in this novel are either products of the author's imagination or are used fictitiously.

IN TWILIGHT'S SHADOW

Copyright © 2008 by Patti J. Olszowka

A Tor Book
Published by Tom Doherty Associates, LLC
175 Fifth Avenue
New York, NY 10010

www.tor-forge.com

Tor® is a registered trademark of Tom Doherty Associates, LLC.

ISBN-13: 978-0-7653-5580-5
ISBN-10: 0-7653-5580-9

First Edition: June 2008

Printed in the United States of America

0 9 8 7 6 5 4 3 2 1

For my writing buddy, Melissa Lynn Copeland. There aren't enough words to convey how much I appreciate your help, so I'll simply say thank you.

In Twilight's Shadow

Prologue

Creed wasn't sure what he'd expected the forbidden dimension to look like, but this wasn't it. The forest was filled with old-growth trees rising eighty, even a hundred feet into the air, with branches only at the very top. Bushes and grasses covered the ground and the path he walked was uneven, roots coming up to trip the unwary.

Nothing about the woods was pastoral or idyllic. There wasn't a sound to be heard—not the chirp of a bird, the buzz of an insect, or the rustle of a small animal scurrying away. The silence was unnatural, wrong, as if every living creature held its breath, trying to outwait danger.

That was unnerving enough, but what really put him on edge was the fog of residual black magic hanging like a shroud over the land. It interfered with his ability to scan his surroundings, and because of that, Creed kept his presence cloaked—he wasn't invisible, but nothing or no one else could read his energy. It took a lot from him to hold the shield, though, and he needed to get out of here before he burned through his power. He had no way to recharge, not when the earth was as fouled with remnants of dark magic as the air was.

The call of . . . *something* made him hesitate. The sudden noise was worse than the silence, but when nothing happened, Creed continued forward. It was dangerous to stand around, and he had to reach the portal out of here before he ran into trouble.

He should have stayed put.

As Creed entered a more thinly forested area, something about four feet tall swooped down and landed in front of him. He didn't know what the hell it was, but it only took a split second to decide that with a monkey's face and the elongated ears of a donkey, the thing was damn ugly. Then it bared teeth that would make the shark in *Jaws* envious. It wasn't a friendly gesture. Creed gathered his power and shot a rope of fire at it.

Jaws staggered under the wave of flame.

The instant he let up, the creature took to the air. It didn't appear to be too injured. Creed searched for cover, diving behind a boulder just in time to avoid the first fireball.

With a screech, it circled above him, seeking a better angle. Creed shifted, shooting up at it. It was risky. If other dark-force beings were in the area, his shots pinpointed his position, but he hoped the fog dampened the brightness.

One volley connected with his opponent and did some damage. But not enough.

Coming around, the thing laid its ears back and let loose with its own stream of fire. Creed rolled to avoid the blast. He felt the heat at the soles of his feet and jerked his legs clear. He barely had time to reinforce his protection spell before Jaws let go from the other direction.

On his back, Creed fired with both hands directly up at his diving opponent. It pulled away and he retreated behind the stone again. Maybe it wasn't much of a bulwark, but it was all he had.

At least it was all he had until the creature spit out some kind of sonic blast. He couldn't hear it and he couldn't see anything, but Creed sensed the wave hitting the rock.

It broke into tiny pieces.

Holy—

He rolled to his feet and took off. From the corner of his eye, he saw a second surge pulverize what remained of the boulder. He zigzagged among the bushes, trying to keep clear of any shots aimed at him. The creature shrieked again, telling Creed how close it was, and he twisted to the side. The blast winged him.

This couldn't continue. His protection spell wasn't going to last much longer and the strength of his magic was waning. Fire didn't seem to be doing anything except momentarily slowing Jaws down. It was time for plan B.

Creed gathered his power and tried to focus. It wasn't easy with a moving target, but he worked to thicken the air molecules above the creature's wings. With birds, air needed to travel faster over the top of the wing so that the pressure was lower beneath it—it was what kept them aloft. If the same principle held true here, maybe he could knock the thing out of the sky.

Jaws hit the ground with a satisfying thud.

Opening a chasm in the earth, Creed telekinetically pushed his attacker into the hole before it could recover from its landing and closed the fissure around it. He took a deep breath and waited, half afraid that he'd be fighting again and he'd already used too much magic.

Things remained quiet, though.

He made tracks out of the area. With no idea if he'd killed the dark-force creature or just delayed its reappearance, Creed couldn't afford to linger. Besides, he needed to get out of this dimension before he ended up facing something much more deadly—this *was* one of the demon realms, after all.

Demons. He still had a job to do. Creed wiped his hands over the seat of his jeans as he walked, dislodging some of the foliage stuck to him. After he crossed back, he'd have to clean up before he headed to Minneapolis, the destination of the demon he was hunting.

He scowled as he considered the type of reception he'd get there. Ryne Frasier was the troubleshooter in charge of that territory and she was pissed at him. Hugely pissed. Four months ago, he'd withheld a small piece of information from her. And as it turned out, it had been vital.

Of course, he'd intended to tell her eventually, but it wasn't as if he could have known she'd need the info in a matter of days. He'd figured there was plenty of time to pass it along.

And he was lying to himself.

Ryne had every reason to be angry at him. He'd deliberately held back a critical detail because he'd been feeling vindictive. Creed grimaced. If he showed up on her doorstep, she'd clock him.

Scrambling over a row of boulders blocking the path, he considered things. He needed someplace to stay, somewhere away from humans, and though Ryne wouldn't be issuing any invitations, there was another option. Maia Frasier lived in Minneapolis, too. Staying with her wouldn't offer any advantages, but it was better than a hotel.

Safer.

Decision made, Creed picked up his pace, not slowing until he spotted a giant tree that had fallen across the path. He muttered a curse, but as he grew closer, he noticed the trunk was high enough that he wouldn't need to duck to get under it.

He took a minute to wonder over the size of such a tree, then shook it off and continued underneath it and around the bend.

Creed stopped short. Hell, a zortir, and it was gorging itself on another of its kind. He took a step back, hoping to get away unnoticed, but the creature lifted its head and looked him in the eye. With blood dripping from its maw, its pale orange horns deepened in color as it amassed its store of venom. *Shit.*

Drawing magic, Creed braced himself for another battle.

1

CHAPTER

Maia tapped her fingers against the steering wheel as she waited for the garage door to open. All she wanted to do was retreat inside and let her frustrations melt away.

The day had been a bitch.

It began when she'd overslept. Instead of taking that as an omen and going back to sleep, she'd been foolishly grateful that she'd woken in time to grab a quick shower and stop for some coffee.

Traffic had been awful, but it always was. She'd had to brake hard to keep from rear-ending the idiot who'd cut her off, which made her cup topple out of the drink holder, drenching her linen trousers from knee to ankle.

She'd punched in at eight on the nose . . . which meant she was tardy. Tardy! Like she was a flipping eighth grader. She was never late, but did that matter to her new boss?

Every other manager she'd worked for had allowed her a little leeway because she was a good employee. Not this one.

Maia took a deep breath and forced herself to relax—her knuckles had gone white from how tightly she squeezed the wheel. Next, she worked at unclenching her jaw, but the headache was bad enough that it was going to linger even after she took aspirin.

As soon as the door was up, she pulled her sedan into the garage, turned off the engine, and headed inside. At least it was Friday. For two days, she could kick back and unwind. No more traffic. No more fires to put out. No more jerks to deal with.

The coolness of the air-conditioning washed over her, making her home feel like a sanctuary. In a minute or two, she'd change clothes, make herself a salad, and head out to her garden.

Her peace was short-lived.

Maia picked up the murmur of voices and opened her eyes. It only took a second to realize the television was on. She frowned. The only person who might show up uninvited was her sister, but Ryne knew the hours she worked. That meant—

Her temper ignited. After the day she'd had, the last thing she should have to put up with was a burglary. That would just be the perfect ending—filling out police reports and dealing with the insurance company. Damned if she was letting anyone make her life more miserable than it was already. Balling her hands into fists, she headed for the living room to see if the bastard was still around.

Halfway across the kitchen she stopped in her tracks. It would be stupid to face down an intruder now that she didn't have her magic. The smart thing to do was leave and use her cell phone to call 9-1-1, but that went against the grain. She'd been trained to confront problems, not run from them.

If there were thieves, they were probably long gone by now anyway. What were the odds that a burglar had decided to take a break to watch *Jeopardy*?

To hell with it. Looking around, she spotted the pepper mill and grabbed it. It wasn't much of a weapon, but it was heavy enough to cause some damage. Taking a deep breath, she went to challenge any unexpected guests.

He wasn't a thief.

The man sitting on her couch, feet propped up on her coffee table, was Gineal. She'd lost almost everything when she'd given up her magic, but she still had the ability to sense what someone was. "Excuse me," she drawled.

With a casualness that told her he'd been aware of her presence, the man looked over his shoulder at her and she was able to identify him. Creed Blackwood.

Maia had never worked with him—she'd never even talked to him—but everyone knew who he was.

Blackwood's reputation for being cold and lethal was well known, but if they'd met last year, Maia would have been prepared to like him. He'd been one of her sister's closest friends, but something had happened to change that. Ryne had refused to say what, but she was loyal to a fault, and if she was on the outs with this man, he'd been the one to cause it.

"What the hell are you doing in my house?" Maia demanded, irritated that he hadn't bothered to offer any excuses for his intrusion.

"It's about time you got here," he complained, and she tightened her grip on the pepper mill.

"If you don't like waiting, don't show up uninvited."

Blackwood clicked off the TV, tossed the remote on

the couch, and got to his feet. For an instant, she thought he seemed unsteady, but as she tipped her head back to hold his gaze, she decided she'd been mistaken.

He had a jacket on. It was hot outside, unbearably humid, and her AC wasn't set that low. His banged-up tennis shoes should have been thrown out months ago and the faded blue jeans that hugged his muscular thighs were so worn, they were white in a few interesting places. When she realized where she was staring, Maia hurriedly lifted her gaze.

With her height, she rarely had to look up to meet a man's eyes, but he was taller by about half a foot. She didn't like it. She didn't like his looks either. He was gorgeous—too gorgeous—and she didn't trust that, not after—

Maia cut off that thought and studied the man before her, trying to find a flaw. His face was sculpted perfection—high cheekbones, full lips, and a chin with a bit of a cleft in it. His black hair was longer than hers—shoulder length and slightly wavy—and it made her itch to run her fingers through it. Even the dark stubble on his chin added to his good looks. He didn't say a word, merely stared at her. Uncomfortable with the fevered intensity in his dark brown eyes, she asked, "What kind of idiot wears a leather jacket in August?"

"Troubleshooters are usually more welcoming to their brothers-in-arms."

"I'm not a troubleshooter." Not anymore, and that made her heart clench. He knew this—there wasn't a Gineal alive who was unaware that Maia Frasier had ceded her powers seven years ago. "Why are you here?" she repeated.

For a moment, Maia thought he was going to deliberately misunderstand her question, but instead he said, "I need a place to stay."

She immediately became suspicious. Troubleshooters followed protocols, and this was Ryne's territory. "Why didn't you check in with my sister?"

Blackwood shifted, planting his weight evenly on both feet. "What makes you think I haven't?"

"You're a visiting enforcer and the custom is that she offer lodging and assistance if you need it." Maia stared hard at him, daring him to lie. No one was more likely to follow the rules than Ryne.

"I plan to tell her I'm here."

"When?"

"Eventually."

His candor threw her off stride, but she regrouped quickly. "The code says you announce your presence upon arrival, not on your way out of town. Or are you afraid that you'll have to deal with Ryne's anger over what you did to hurt her?"

"That's part of it."

His admission stunned her; it was the last thing she'd expected. "And the rest?"

He didn't say anything for a long moment, then one side of his mouth quirked up. "Summers doesn't like me."

Now *that* Maia believed. Deke Summers was Ryne's fiancé, and if gossip among the troubleshooters could be trusted, Blackwood had been interested in Ryne himself. Despite talking to him for all of two minutes, Maia could tell Creed didn't back away from a challenge. Neither did Deke. Add a highly pissed off Ryne to the mix and things could go to hell fast.

Still, she didn't think a little thing like turmoil would stop him, so what was the real story?

Sweat dampened his forehead, his hair, and she watched a bead roll past his temple. "Take your jacket off before you pass out."

"I'm fine."

Something was going on. Did Creed look pale beneath his dark tan? All she needed was a Gineal troubleshooter with some exotic fever infecting her. He might be able to contact a healer and be back on his feet in no time, but *she'd* have to deal with her HMO.

"If you need someplace to sleep and are too cowardly to face Ryne, go find a hotel," Maia ordered. She couldn't allow herself to worry about him.

"And endanger humans?"

The tone of his voice put her back up. "*I'm* human now."

He shook his head. "You might not have your magic, but you're not human. You were raised among the Gineal and trained to be a troubleshooter. Our tenets are ingrained in you."

"That doesn't change the fact that I'm an outsider." And Maia hated that. She hated all the damn secrets, all the things Ryne couldn't tell her.

"I didn't say I wanted to consult with you. I said I needed a place to stay."

His tone aggravated her even more. "Blackwood, this isn't the Frasier Inn. Go away and find a hotel without a lot of humans in it, one where you can come and go without raising any questions about what you're up to."

Maia pivoted to leave the room, but he moved fast enough to grab her arm. She turned, ready to blast him, but when he stepped back, Creed staggered, nearly falling. Grabbing him to help him keep his balance, she demanded, "What's wrong?"

"Nothing."

"Bullshit. You couldn't convince a five-year-old that you were fine, not even a gullible one. Want to try again?"

Instead of answering, Creed stepped away from her

hold, as if to show her that he was perfectly fine. The look he gave her dared her to contradict him.

What was it with men? Gineal or human, they were all the same. Either they were big babies who whined about a paper cut or they could sever an arm and still insist they were ready to wrestle alligators. Blackwood apparently fell into the second category.

"If nothing's wrong, then you can leave." Never give a troubleshooter an inch. She'd had the training, knew they looked for weakness in an opponent and exploited it.

" 'I will never turn from a laoch solas who comes to me. My home, my bread, my assistance is theirs, have they but need—' "

"I told you before," she interrupted, "that I'm not part of our society any longer. The oath doesn't apply to me!"

"You'll always be a troubleshooter on some level."

Creed swayed—just slightly—but Maia noticed and clenched her hands around the pepper mill to keep herself from rushing to his side. She didn't think he was faking it, but she couldn't let herself be dragged into his assignment—whatever it was.

"Go to Ryne. Even if she'd like to punch you, she'll help, and she's got the magic to be of assistance. I don't, and if you bring trouble to my door, I'll be a sitting duck."

Blindly, she turned, needing to escape. This time he didn't try to stop her, and on trembling legs, she retreated to the kitchen.

The guilt hit as she took a bottle of water out of the refrigerator. He'd been Ryne's friend. Maybe they were on the outs right now, but that didn't mean they'd never make things square. Besides, Creed had stood beside Ryne when few others had. Maia owed him for being there for her baby sister when she hadn't been able to do anything for Ryne herself.

But damn it, she didn't want to get involved in this mess, and it would be sticky, Maia didn't doubt that for a minute. Creed Blackwood was a roving troubleshooter—he specialized in hunting demons, no matter where in the world they might be. They were the most dangerous adversaries an enforcer could face, and without her powers, she should definitely steer clear.

Still, he was sick or hurt, and troubleshooters always looked out for each other, sort of like Special Forces soldiers and their principle to never leave a man behind. No matter how much she wanted to, Maia couldn't turn her back on him.

"Hell," she muttered and put the water down on her counter with a thump. She stalked back to the living room, hoping Blackwood was gone and she wouldn't have to deal with him or his mission.

No such luck. He was lounging on the couch, eyes closed, and he looked worse than he had a few minutes earlier. Maia approached cautiously, but when he met her gaze and seemed foggy, she stopped hesitating. It was second nature to reach out and rest a hand on his forehead to check for fever. He was burning up. She didn't know why he hadn't summoned help himself, but he definitely needed a professional. "I'll call Ryne and ask her to send a healer this way."

Creed caught her wrist. "No healers."

"You're not thinking clearly. You need someone who can take care of you."

"No." The word was tough, implacable, and left no room for discussion. That didn't stop Maia.

"If you think you're going to die here and leave me with a mountain of red tape, you better think again."

His lips tipped up at the corners. "It's not that serious."

Maia almost called him a liar, then she realized that he might not understand how bad off he was. "Blackwood—" She stopped, then restarted. "Creed, listen to me. You're running a fever. I don't know if you've picked up some virus or you have an infected wound, but either way, your temperature is high—probably dangerously high. You need a healer."

Without saying a word, he met her gaze and she could see the stubbornness. "Idiot," she muttered. More loudly, she added, "Fine, then I'll drive you to urgent care. An hour waiting there should make you more amenable to the Gineal way of taking care of this. I'll get my purse and be back for you."

She was nearly to the kitchen when he caught her. Maia never would have believed he could move that fast, not as bad as he looked. Loosely clasping her forearm, he said, "You can't bring humans into this."

Great. That meant whatever was wrong with him was something the doctors wouldn't be able to explain and might lead to questions that could reveal the existence of the Gineal. "No humans," Maia agreed, but his hand felt clammy against her skin, and standing this close to him, she could see he'd gone from pale to ashen. "You do need help, though."

"You heal me."

"No." Her tone was every bit as obstinate as his, but she didn't care. Sure, she could still heal—even humans were able to do that—but no one understood how working with energy tore her up inside. It was too reminiscent of when she'd been Gineal.

Maia pulled her arm free and the soft tug was enough to leave Creed off balance. "If you don't want me to involve Ryne, fine. I'll ask someone else to call a healer."

Blackwood made a grab for her as she stepped away.

He missed and his body thudded into the wall, but Maia caught him, lowering him until he sat on the floor.

"Promise me," he rasped, "that you won't call anyone, human or Gineal."

"I can't swear to that. You need help."

His hand squeezed hers hard. "Promise me."

The urgency in his voice, the intensity in his gaze despite the glassiness of fever, had her saying, "I promise."

Creed's eyes closed and his grip relaxed. An instant later, he was unconscious. Maia didn't know if he'd fallen asleep or passed out, but it didn't matter—*she* was the idiot. Because she'd given her word, she was the one who had to take care of him, and if that meant working with healing energy, she'd have to use it. His body slumped into hers, and biting her lower lip, she eased him down until he was laying flat on his back.

The first thing Maia did was visually assess his physical condition. She saw no outward signs of trauma, and to her disgust, she found herself thinking again about how gorgeous the man was. Shaking her head, she reached for the zipper on his leather jacket. She needed to make him comfortable and check him more closely for injury.

Maia didn't have to go any further to find the problem. On either side of his torso just above the kidneys were two dark red stains on his white T-shirt. "Hell."

She hesitated, then left him. Maia collected her first aid kit, a few towels that had seen better days, and a washcloth. She placed them on the floor next to him, then went to fill a pan with warm water.

His T-shirt was tucked firmly into his jeans, and because of his injuries, she didn't dare yank it free. Gingerly, she reached for the button at his waist and opened it before lowering the zipper. Leaning over him, Maia first pulled the shirt free in back, then carefully eased one side up in front. She kept a close eye on her progress, but fortunately, the fabric wasn't stuck to the wound, and she inched the other side up, too.

Two ugly punctures continued to seep blood—and some kind of orange gel. Something about it teased her memory, but she couldn't quite bring it into focus, and until she did, she couldn't risk touching it. She leaned closer and took a whiff.

Maia jerked backward so fast she fell on her butt. The odor was horrible, but didn't travel far. "Zortir!" Good God in heaven, he'd tangled with a zortir.

Taber, her mentor, had been wounded by one of those creatures. One of the first things the poison affected, she remembered, was telepathy. That explained why Creed hadn't summoned help himself.

What mattered was trying to recall how the healers had dealt with the venom. It was potent enough to hurt her if it touched her skin. No wonder he hadn't wanted humans involved. Not only could the orange toxin kill them, it would also raise questions and they'd undoubtedly test the substance. Maia didn't know what answers their labs would come up with, but it couldn't be good for the Gineal.

With a sigh, she pushed her hair out of her eyes and considered what to do next. She'd been twelve when Taber had been attacked, and twenty years was a long time—too many details had faded from her memory.

What she did know was that she couldn't sit here. Her magic was gone, and even if she still had it, her talents hadn't earned her a spot in the healing temple. The question was what could she do right now to help Blackwood?

Slowly getting to her feet, Maia went to her shelves and pulled down her home remedies book. It was written by humans for humans, but they dealt with their own venomous creatures; there might be something in here she could try.

She found it in the section under bee stings. The paste was a mixture of baking soda, vinegar, and meat tenderizer. There was a papain enzyme in the tenderizer that might break down the toxins in the zortir venom. Until that was taken care of, she couldn't touch the punctures, and she had to be able to put her hands on them to do an energy healing.

Using her finger to mark her page, Maia made one last check on Creed. No change. She went into the kitchen to mix up a big bowl of paste.

Grabbing an old silicone spatula and a pair of rubber gloves, she returned to the spot where she'd left Blackwood. Maia used the spatula to scoop the paste out of the bowl and smoothed it over the wound nearest to her. Creed didn't move.

From her position, she couldn't see the left side of his body clearly enough to put on the application, and he was too close to the wall for her to kneel on that side, so she came up with an alternate solution. She straddled his thighs and leaned forward. For a moment, she was distracted by the overt sexuality of the position, but she ignored the way her body tightened and concentrated on carefully covering the second puncture.

As she waited for the poultice to work, Maia moved off him and tried again to recall what she knew about zortirs.

Think, she exhorted, forcing herself to focus.

Okay, zortirs walked on four legs and they were fast. The venom was delivered through two horns on their heads. They had some basic magical abilities, but nothing more than that. What else? There was more she should remember, Maia was sure of it.

As she removed the first layer of paste from Creed's torso, an important fact came back to her. Zortirs lived in a dimension that centuries earlier had been declared forbidden.

He'd probably been in pursuit of something, like Taber had been. Probably. Except if that were the case, why didn't he want her to get him a healer? It raised questions she didn't like to consider. The only Gineal who traveled to that environ were longtime users of black magic.

Had Blackwood turned?

2

After nearly twenty-four hours of caring for her patient, Maia was exhausted. She glanced down at his face. He was still out, but she thought this was a healing sleep. Dipping the cloth she held into water, she wrung it out and ran it over his chest. Her arms ached from the hours she'd already spent performing the task, but cooling him with lukewarm water and giving him regular doses of acetaminophen were necessary to bring his fever down.

Last night, Creed had managed to walk to the bedroom by leaning on her, and when she'd gotten him into bed, Maia had stripped him down to his briefs. Luckily, he'd been aware enough to help her, because she didn't know how she would have brought it about on her own. As she dragged the cloth across his torso, she tried not to notice how well delineated his muscles were. For heaven's sake, the man was sick.

The doorbell rang, saving her from her thoughts, and

with a weary sigh, she put down the rag and went to answer it. As she neared the front of the house and could see out the window, Maia groaned. It was her sister.

Reluctantly, she unlocked the deadbolt and opened the door. Deke was standing off to the side, half turned to watch their backs, and Maia almost smiled. Once a cop, always a cop.

Without waiting for an invitation, Ryne came in, her fiancé right behind her. Maia had a small house; there was no foyer, and once they were inside, they were in her living room. She automatically backed up, bringing them deeper into the house so Deke could close the front door.

"Maia, what's up? Is something wrong?" Ryne asked.

"What makes you think something's wrong?" she countered calmly.

"You're not ready."

"Ready?"

"To go out. I've never seen you leave the house without being put together."

"I don't look that terrible." At least Maia hoped she didn't.

"We both know you couldn't look bad if you tried," Ryne said quietly. Deke's arm slid around Ryne's waist and he pulled her against his side. "I just meant that you never go out without your hair being styled, but tonight it looks as if you washed it and let it air dry. And the way you're dressed. I know we're just going out to dinner and a movie, but you're never this casual except around the house. I wear tanks in public, you don't."

Oh hell, Maia had forgotten about the movies. Ryne, the little sister she'd had to forcibly drag out of her house

at times, had done a one-eighty in the four months since
Deke had moved in with her. Now, the shoe was on the
other foot and it was Ryne initiating outings. "I'm sorry.
It slipped my mind."

Her sister closed the distance, and before Maia could
figure out what she was up to, Ryne had her hand on her
forehead testing for fever. Irritated, Maia scowled and
stepped out of reach. "What did you do that for?"

"Because you're compulsively organized. You must
be sick if this slipped past you."

"I'm fine," Maia reassured her and she managed to
keep most of her impatience out of her voice.

"You did feel a little warm."

"That might be because the air isn't working," Deke
pointed out. "I could take a look at the unit for you.
Maybe I can save you a service call."

"Thanks, but that isn't necessary." Maia had turned
off the AC so Creed wouldn't catch a chill.

If she'd only remembered their plans for tonight,
she could have called and canceled. It wasn't as if
she was hugely excited about going out with Ryne
and Deke anyway—she always felt like a fifth wheel
with them. It wasn't anything they did deliberately, but
they were a couple, and it showed in the way they
could communicate with a glance, a shared smile, or a
quick caress. And it reminded Maia of how alone
she was.

"I don't mind doing it," he assured her.

"Deke's good with his hands," Ryne offered earnestly.

"Babe, that's kind of personal to be sharing with—"

Ryne turned and scowled at him. "Knock it off."

He donned an innocent look and Maia knew it meant
he was up to no good. Her sister obviously recognized
that, too, because when he started to say more, she put

her hand over his mouth. "Don't start, okay? Maia's sick and I want to focus on her."

"I'm not sick." Maia realized an instant too late that claiming to be under the weather would be the best way to get Ryne and Deke to leave without having to go through an inquisition. The fact that she'd thrown away the opportunity drove home how badly she needed some sleep.

"Then what is going on?" Ryne asked. "And don't tell me nothing, because I know you too well for that."

Rubbing her forehead, Maia tried to recall what exactly she'd promised Creed. Had she told him she'd conceal his presence or had she merely said she wouldn't contact Ryne to get him a healer? All that prevented Maia from telling the truth was her word—she owed Blackwood nothing more than that.

But she might have said she'd stay quiet—and it was important to Maia to keep her promises.

"I had a really bad day at work yesterday," she offered with a grimace and ran through what had happened.

There was a long pause, then her sister said, "This crap happens all the time, Maia. I find it hard to believe that it's still bothering you a day later."

Ryne did know her too well, and it was a weak story anyway. "It isn't only what happened yesterday, it's an accumulation of things. I've been there six years and it keeps getting worse."

"If you don't like it there, quit."

Resentment welled. It was easy for Ryne, but then she had the salary that came with being a troubleshooter. "I can't quit. I have a mortgage and bills and I need health insurance. It's not as if *I* can call a healer."

Ryne stiffened and Deke's other arm went around her in a loose hug. Maia sighed and rubbed her forehead again. "I'm sorry," she apologized as she lowered her arm. "I didn't mean to sound snotty or resentful, but you don't have any idea what it's like to be powerless, and leaving that job is harder than—" The sound of a thud cut her off.

Both Ryne and Deke were past her and down the hall before she could form a word. Maia hurried after them, but she was too late—they'd found her guest. Blackwood, the idiot, had gotten out of bed and fallen face first onto the floor.

Ryne turned and glared at her. "You're letting Creed stay here? After what he did to me?"

"What *did* he do to you?" Maia demanded.

The look of frustration on her sister's face appeared close to what Maia herself was feeling. Something inside her, though, was glad that Ryne chafed against the restrictions as much as Maia did. The law was clear, Gineal didn't share information with outsiders, but she was damn tired of being kept in the dark.

"You have to believe it's serious. I don't turn my back on people for no reason."

"I know that."

"Then how can you let him stay in your house?"

"Extenuating circumstances?" Deke suggested, and bent down to roll Creed over, revealing the two wounds on his body. "I rest my case."

"I'll summon a healer."

"No!" Maia interjected.

"Zortir wounds can't be self-healed because the venom affects our powers," Ryne pointed out with such exaggerated patience that it set Maia's teeth on edge.

"I'm aware of that," she said stiffly. "He made me promise not to have anyone call a healer."

Ryne scowled. "That means *I* have to heal him and I'd rather give him a good, swift kick."

With no more than a muttered curse, her sister surrendered and knelt beside Creed. Closing her eyes, she took a deep breath and put her hands on him.

Maia felt another pang and this one was strong enough that she nearly gasped. Ryne was doing the same type of healing Maia had done, but with one addition—magic. When she finished, Blackwood would probably be close to 80 percent healthy and able to refill his internal well with enough power to heal himself the rest of the way.

She watched Ryne work. Deke stood behind his fiancée and slightly to the side, arms crossed over his chest. The stance was both protective and possessive, and Maia felt oddly ambivalent about that. For much of her life, she'd defined herself in two ways—as a troubleshooter and as Ryne's defender. Maia had lost her identity as a Gineal enforcer, but she'd still had her sister to watch over. Now that job was gone as well.

Blackwood and Ryne both opened their eyes about the same time, and when her sister pulled her arms back, the puncture wounds on his torso were nothing more than a pair of angry pink circles. The two of them stared at each other for a moment, then Ryne stood and moved back until she could take Deke's hand.

Creed's gaze found Maia's. "You broke your promise," he growled as he sat up.

Maia went rigid. "I did not break my word! My sister and I had plans for tonight, and if you'd stayed in bed where you belonged, she probably never would have been aware you were here. When you passed out, you gave your presence away."

Slowly, Blackwood got to his feet. The man wasn't entirely steady, but he was light-years ahead of where he'd been ten minutes ago. He rubbed a hand over one of the wounds, and for the first time since Ryne's arrival, Maia became conscious that all he wore was a pair of briefs. That hadn't bothered her while they'd been alone, but now that there were spectators, it seemed intimate.

"Why are you in my territory?" Ryne demanded, voice low. Maia immediately became wary. Her sister only spoke in that tone when she was so furious that she had to hold herself under tight control to keep from going ballistic. "And why are you imposing on Maia?"

"I didn't think she'd turn me away."

"Protocol says you come to me."

"Protocol also requires that you ask me to stay with you, and we both know that invitation wouldn't have been extended. I'm sure the council would be displeased at your lapse." The words were purely meant to goad Ryne.

"I don't have to allow you in my home if I have cause not to trust you," Ryne told him, her voice even more controlled than it had been a moment ago. "You gave me that reason. Do you want to take this to the ceannards and see whose side they come down on?"

"I don't have time for that."

"Yeah," Ryne drawled, "that's what I thought."

Creed ignored the comment. He walked over to the chair where Maia had tossed his jeans and yanked them on. "So, Summers," he said almost conversationally, "you went from thinking you were human to discovering you were a dormant to becoming Gineal, and now you're learning to be a troubleshooter. That's a hell of a transition to make."

"I told you he'd be one of the few who remembered," Deke said quietly to Ryne.

Maia was so shocked, she froze. It was a rare occurrence for a dormant to discover he was Gineal, but apparently that had happened with Deke. One thing made sense, now—she'd wondered why she hadn't recognized him when Ryne had introduced them. This explained why he was an unfamiliar troubleshooter.

Blackwood pulled on his bloodied shirt before he said, "Did she agree to marry you before you did the spell or did she stall until after you came into your powers?"

Maia's temper hit the red zone. Bunching her hands into fists, she stalked over to Creed. "Okay, Blackwood, that's it. I have no idea what the hell happened between you and Ryne, but I've had enough. Say one more inflammatory thing and you're out the door, do you understand me?"

For a moment, she thought he was going to challenge her and Maia was briefly disquieted. If he pushed, Ryne would step in, and it could get ugly.

"I hear you," Creed bit out. His capitulation was grudging, but he stood down, and she released a silent sigh of relief.

"Maia," Ryne said, "can we talk privately?"

What now? But Maia nodded and followed her sister out of the room and down the hall. She didn't stop until they were in the kitchen, then Ryne said, "You aren't seriously going to let Creed stay here, are you?"

Oh hell. She should have realized this was going to be a point of discussion. Maia pulled out a chair from the table and sat down. She needed to be seated for this. "He was hurt and I couldn't throw him out."

Ryne took the chair across from her. For a moment, she stared and Maia found it hard not to squirm under that steady regard. "I can understand that," Ryne said at last. "He's not hurt any longer, though, and by tomorrow morning, his powers will be back to full strength."

"Are you going to invite him to stay with you?" Maia countered.

Her sister didn't try to hide anything and Maia could

see she was torn. She could even guess what Ryne was struggling with. Clearly, she didn't want Creed to stay with Maia, but she was just as determined that he not stay with her and Deke.

"Do you think he's that dangerous?" Maia asked quietly.

"I don't know, Mai. It could have been the circumstances or a spur-of-the-moment impulse that he didn't think through. It's even possible it was an honest mistake."

"But you don't think that it was."

"No. It's unlikely it was premeditated, but I do believe what he did was deliberate."

Of course, Ryne couldn't tell her what it was he'd done, and that could make all the difference in Maia's decision. "Do you believe that my life is at risk?"

Another hesitation, then a reluctant, "No, I don't think you're in physical danger from Creed, but don't forget, if whatever he's here to hunt turns and goes after him, you might get caught in the crossfire. Dark-force beings don't care about civilian casualties."

"I know that." Maia kept her voice even with effort. Did Ryne think she'd forgotten everything once she'd given up her magic? "He mentioned his reluctance to go to a hotel because of the human occupants."

"Yeah." With her index finger, Ryne traced the symbol for eternity again and again on the table top. About the time Maia was ready to reach out and stop the motion, her sister looked up to meet Maia's gaze. "If I invite him into my home, it means I have to give him free access for the duration. I don't trust Creed enough to allow that, not any longer."

Maia heard the apology in her sister's voice, but the bottom line was what Ryne wasn't saying—her sister believed the other troubleshooter posed a risk to her.

"As long as I don't have to sleep with a knife underneath my pillow," Maia said quietly, "I'm okay with him staying here."

"But—"

"Ryne," Maia interrupted, "if anyone knows what a Gineal under the influence of the dark forces is like, it's me. Believe me, if I see any signs that worry me, I'll tell you immediately and you can report it to the council, okay?"

After a long pause, Ryne said, "You don't want him here."

No, she didn't, but more than that, Maia didn't want Ryne to fight Creed, and she didn't want to see any humans die. She could live with the man for a brief period of time. "Odds are, we'll hardly see each other. I have my job and he'll be out doing whatever it is that roving troubleshooters do when they have a mission."

"I don't like it."

Maia did reach out then and lay her arm on the table palm up. She waited until Ryne took her hand. "I know you don't, sweetie, but it's the best option."

"If I'm wrong about Creed—"

"You're going to give yourself wrinkles if you keep worrying like this," Maia teased, trying to lighten Ryne's mood. She sobered. "Trust me to take care of myself."

Ryne didn't look happy, but with a sigh, she said, "Okay, but remember to call me if you're concerned."

"I will," Maia promised.

With a grimace, Ryne extricated her hand and said, "I better get back there and make sure Deke's behaving. He doesn't like Creed much."

When they reached the bedroom, the tension was palpable, but since Deke was smirking, Maia didn't think the two men were close to trading blows. Creed, she noted, was completely dressed now, including his shoes.

Maia frowned at him. If that man thought he was physically able to go out and start his mission, he had another think coming. A few minutes ago, he'd been passed out on the floor, and even though he felt better, he wasn't ready to go anywhere.

"We'll have to reschedule the movies," she said to Ryne, but Maia didn't stop scowling at Blackwood.

"We could stay."

"Yes, you could, but I was up all night taking care of him, and now that he's not in need of constant medical assistance, I want to unwind and go to bed early."

"I have a name," Creed pointed out.

"Any idiot who gets out of bed and faints on the floor has earned an assortment of names," Maia pointed out conversationally. "You're lucky I'm sticking with pronouns."

"I didn't faint," he growled.

"Faint, pass out—same difference. You get back into bed and I'll walk the two of you to the door."

No one argued, and Maia had Ryne and Deke at the front entry before anyone balked at her orders. "I'll be right there, babe," Deke said. "Why don't you wait for me by the car?"

Ryne looked suspicious and reluctant, but after a couple of moments of silence, she left.

"Don't trust him," Deke said, voice serious and very soft. "You don't know what happened and I guess I can't share it with you either, but I can tell you to watch your back. Blackwood nearly got Ryne killed."

3

CHAPTER

Maia turned from her left side to her right, growled as the blankets bunched up, and tried to adjust them. She pulled too hard, though, and that left her feet sticking out. With a quiet curse, she did another rearrangement.

She was exhausted, but she'd woken up just past midnight and hadn't been able to fall back asleep despite trying for nearly an hour. The longer she tossed and turned, the more the walls seemed to close in on her, and that was making her crabby. She switched back to her left side. Damn it, why couldn't her brain stop whirling? She didn't want to think. Not now.

Blackwood's presence exacerbated her restlessness. His intensity seemed to fill her house and that kept her on edge. Why the hell hadn't she kicked him out after he was healed? There must be plenty of hotels with low occupancy rates; tomorrow she'd have to tell him to find one and stay there.

But what if he wouldn't leave? She could see him refusing, and it wasn't like she could force him to go, not on her own.

What did Deke mean, *Blackwood nearly got Ryne killed*? That sentence encompassed any number of scenarios, from inciting a dark-force creature into attacking her sister to something relatively benign, like inadvertently showing up too late when Ryne was on a call-out and needed assistance. Maia doubted, though, that Blackwood had merely been careless—she knew her sister, and Ryne stood behind her friends. Nope, he'd done something that couldn't be explained away.

Groaning her frustration, she surrendered. Throwing back the covers, she got out of bed and dug through her drawers for shorts and a T-shirt. Until her mind settled, she doubted she'd be getting any more sleep. When Maia was dressed, she slipped into a pair of sandals and quietly opened her bedroom door. The house was dark, and except for the hum of the air conditioner, dead silent.

As she opened the door to her back patio, oppressive humidity immediately surrounded her. Maia didn't care—she needed to be outside. For a moment, she paused and tipped her face up to the sky, letting the starlight bathe her face and allowing her senses to drink in the night. Tranquillity settled over her, and only then did she ease the door shut and take the steps down onto the wooden decking.

Crossing the length of the patio, Maia sat in one of the wrought iron chairs, and leaning back, extended her legs and closed her eyes. The sound of crickets chirping and the gentle play of the breeze through her hair calmed her further. Her neighborhood was peaceful at this hour and she let the quiet sink into her. She definitely needed this.

Her brain still wouldn't shut down, though. Her sister had immediately recognized what kind of injury Blackwood had and she hadn't turned a hair over his traveling to that off-limits dimension. The casual acceptance relieved Maia. She sure didn't want to deal with a Gineal who'd embraced the dark forces.

Something about Creed, however, made her react—and she didn't like it. She knew what intense attraction felt like and Maia had no intention of going through that again. She'd learned her lesson. If fate was kind, he would finish his assignment quickly and move on.

Creed's presence pervaded her home and he hadn't done anything. After Ryne and Deke had left, he'd followed her orders and returned to bed. He'd been out in minutes, but that was good—sleep was the fastest way to replenish his magic.

If only hers could return so easily.

She was jealous—of Blackwood for getting his powers back . . . and of her sister. Maia had done the healing on Creed that he'd asked for, and while it had improved his condition a little, it had been an incremental change. She would have had to do long healings over a period of a couple of days to do half of what Ryne had done in mere minutes.

She longed for her magic, wanted it to the very depths of her being, and it was gone forever. Sometimes she wished she hadn't done the spell to give it up, but there'd been no other option—she'd been a lost cause. If she hadn't ceded her power, the council would have assigned Ryne to bring her in.

When the pain grew too great, that's what Maia remembered, that she'd shielded Ryne—she'd taken care of her sister. Besides, if Maia had been brought before the ceannards, not only would they have stripped her of her powers, they'd have taken all her memories of the

Gineal as well. Voluntarily giving up her magic had allowed her to hold onto her past—to hold onto her only family.

In the distance, she heard a car door slam. The wind kicked up again, and she sighed heavily. Why had she fallen? For years, she'd tried to analyze what had made her go so far into black magic, but she'd never come up with any concrete answers, only theories.

Deciding she didn't want to spend another night examining her actions and motives, Maia turned her thoughts to her current problem—Creed Blackwood. He was going to be trouble, and not only because of his assignment. Why couldn't she keep her mind off him or how he got her all hot and achy? Maia felt herself tensing and rolled her shoulders to loosen up. Maybe she just had a thing for pretty men; after all, she hadn't reacted like this to any male since—

No, don't go there! As she was trying to battle back the memories, Maia felt a stare that drove the past out of her head. With as much casualness as she could muster, she opened her eyes and looked around the yard. Nothing.

She visually scanned again, being more thorough this time, and spotted a tan and black cat sitting under her maple tree. The anxiety left her body like air flooding out of a balloon. Mister Jenkins. The name was silly, but her neighbor lady was eighty-five, and at that age, the woman should be able to name her cat whatever she wanted without getting grief.

"Hi, MJ," Maia greeted softly. "What are you doing out here? Hmm?"

The cat sashayed toward her and she straightened in her seat, planting her feet flat on the patio. As soon as he reached her, MJ jumped onto her lap and flexed his front paws into her thigh until Maia ran her hand down his back and over his tail. "You realize if Mrs. Olson wakes up and finds you're gone, she's going to be scared. You have to stop sneaking outside."

Disdainfully, MJ pulled his tail free from her loosely curled hand. The look he gave her carried the contempt royalty would level on a serf.

Maia chuckled softly. "Sorry, I forgot who I was talking to."

She ran her hand over MJ's back again and he allowed it, a sign she'd been forgiven for her lapse. Mrs. Olson would be frantic when she discovered her cat was gone. Unfortunately, MJ was the feline equivalent of Houdini and regularly escaped from his house. Maia bit her lip. Her neighbor's eyesight was failing and it was becoming easier and easier for the cat to sneak past her. She tried to check on the woman a few times a week, but maybe she needed to stop by every day.

With a purr as loud as an idling tank, MJ put his paws on her shoulder and kneaded to get her attention. Maia complied with his wishes and resumed stroking him. The touch of smooth fur and warm body comforted her, and made the whole world seem a little less lonely. She turned her face into his side.

Maybe she should get a kitten of her own, a companion to ease the emptiness.

The cat's noisy rumble stopped abruptly and he gave her another look. "Don't tell me—you read minds and you don't like the idea of my being unfaithful to you." Maia scratched behind his ear. "No need to worry, where would I find another cat as special as you?"

That mollified MJ and he turned his head into her hand. Maia followed his instructions. No, it probably wouldn't be a good idea to get a pet. She'd end up being the crazy cat lady, the one with twenty animals taking over her home. When Ryne and Deke had kids, they'd cry and plead with their parents, begging not to have to visit Aunt Maia because her house smelled and she was weird.

As if sensing he didn't have her full focus, MJ jumped off her lap, gave a swish of his tail, and without a backward look, ambled away. Maia moved fast, scooping him up before he could get far. "Sorry, guy," she said as he hissed in complaint, "but I can't let you roam free. You're a house cat; that means you belong indoors and your personal servant will be in a tizzy if you're not there when she wakes up. You're going back home."

She headed next door, trying her darnedest to hang onto fifteen pounds of squalling, twisting animal. Maia had a feeling the next time MJ snuck out, he wouldn't be so quick to head her way, but what else could she do?

As it usually was, the screen door to Mrs. Olson's porch was unhooked and Maia put the cat inside and grabbed the knob for the wooden door behind it. She closed it quickly, but even so, that damn cat nearly managed to bolt past her. No wonder the older woman was having trouble keeping him indoors.

Maia could still hear his outrage when she returned to her seat on the patio. Wincing, she tried to ignore him, figuring he'd give up if his feline temper tantrum brought no response, but he continued for a really long time. She was about to shush him, afraid he'd wake Mrs. Olson, when MJ went quiet on his own.

Her relief was short-lived. She noticed that the crickets and other night creatures had also gone silent as suddenly as if someone had flipped a switch.

The hair at her nape stood on end. She did another scan of her yard, but again, she didn't see anything. Something was out there, though; Maia didn't doubt it for a minute. With a casualness she didn't feel, she stood and headed for her door. Depending on what was lurking, the wards Ryne had put around Maia's home might be enough to keep her safe—if she could get inside.

Adrenaline pumped through her body in a way it hadn't in years, and her hands and legs trembled. She was human now, and not only had she never fought without her powers before, she also had no magical protection around her body. One shot and she was done. Her only chance was to get in the house and let Blackwood handle it. In the next instant, Maia realized that he wouldn't have enough power amassed yet. Hell.

It seemed an awfully long distance from where she was sitting to the door and she hated being this exposed, this vulnerable, but more than that, she hated that she *was* this vulnerable. If she had her powers— But she didn't and it scared her to realize how completely she'd once relied on them.

She was in no-man's-land when she caught motion from the corner of her eye. Immediately, Maia whirled, vainly trying to draw power as her arms instinctively came up to block the blow. She winced as the force sent pain shooting through her. Blinking hard, she sized up her opponent.

Olteil, she identified from the short purple horns on its forehead and greenish skin tone. Probably a male, although it was damn difficult to be certain with one of these creatures because both sexes were heavily muscled.

Maia spun out of the way of a second strike and the miss had him roaring in outrage.

Hell, another vocal male. Between MJ and the Incredible Hulk, half the neighborhood was going to be bitching in the morning. Or calling the cops tonight.

Her momentary distraction allowed him to deliver a glancing blow to her shoulder and Maia gasped. His bellow had been a diversion, but at least he hadn't hit her dead on.

Blocking a kick with her thigh, Maia tried to remember an olteil's strengths and weaknesses. She'd never fought one as a troubleshooter and it had been a lot of years since she'd studied anything to do with magical beings. *Think.* She had to think.

Quick reflexes saved her from taking a strike to the face, but it was close enough that she felt the breeze as his hand went by.

The olteil brought his knee up, driving for her midsection, and Maia used her palm to shove his leg to the outside. It left him off balance, but she couldn't shift around quickly enough to take advantage of it.

She used her elbow to block another fist and attempted to come up with some info about her enemy that would help. Her mind stayed stubbornly blank, and that scared her as much as being without her powers did. How could she attack something so much stronger than she was without magic? She couldn't.

Maia tried to ease the fight to her left. All she needed was an opportunity to dash into her house and slam the door in his face. He shouldn't be able to enter, and if he did, Creed would hear the fight and could use a mind link to summon help for them.

The Hulk lunged at her again and Maia barely leaped away. Now she was farther from the door, damn it.

If she were still Gineal, she could incinerate him with one short spell. Maia shook off the thought and focused on staying alive. She needed to move the other direction and—

She raised her forearm to blunt the force of his strike, but this time, the olteil grabbed her.

Maia bit her lip to keep from squeaking at the bruising pain. She'd known letting an enforcer stay in her house would cause nothing but trouble. The olteil drew her near and she twisted and squirmed, much as MJ had when she'd scooped him up. Her movements were about as successful with the Hulk as the cat's attempt had been. He managed to catch her other arm and smiled, revealing a set of purple snaggleteeth.

She brought her foot down hard on the olteil's, but her sandals were insubstantial. Still, she managed to get an arm free, and with as much force as she could muster, she brought her elbow back into his stomach.

It did nothing.

Where was the cavalry when she needed it? She'd lost her telepathy, but Maia sent out the call anyway. *Creed!*

One minute he was sound asleep, the next he was alert. A scan of the room showed no threat present.

Creed muttered a soft curse. He used to be able to trust his instincts, but they'd been fucked up for a while now and this was probably another false alarm. As much as he'd like to ignore his gut and go back to sleep, he couldn't—he wouldn't be able to relax until he'd verified it was clear. Just in case there really was something to worry about, he did a quick assessment of his condition—physically he was near 100 percent, magically maybe 10 percent. Shit, he better hope it was another misfire because he was in no shape to battle much of anything.

He tried to scan beyond the bedroom, but his low power level limited him to a distance of about fifteen feet. Tossing back the blankets, Creed got out of bed and started pulling on his clothes. He didn't waste any time, but he'd had this happen often enough in the last few months that he felt no real sense of urgency.

Crossing the hall, he checked Maia's bedroom. As soon as he opened the door, Creed reached for the light switch and flipped it on. She'd be pissed off, but he'd handle her wrath. The first thing he saw was that the room was light gray in color, classy and elegant, much like his hostess. It took him a second longer to realize she wasn't tucked safely into bed. His heart began to pound a little faster when he noted the door to the master bathroom was open and it was dark.

Her moving around had probably been what woke him up to begin with. That realization had the adrenaline flow slowing. To be thorough, Creed made a check of the bathroom, but as he'd expected, it was empty.

He flipped lights on as he went. The living room was empty, too, but he studied it for a minute. Pale greenish-gray walls and wide, white crown molding again spoke of quiet elegance. Creed frowned. If her house were for sale, easily 99 percent of the people who looked at it would find the decor inoffensive, but her home wasn't on the market. It told him that Maia Frasier made safe choices.

He continued to the kitchen. This room was the epitome of bland neutrality—cream walls, blond-wood cabinets, and pale beige tile around the sink. Boring. He had a hard time imagining someone this cautious being a troubleshooter.

Maybe the house had been painted like this when Maia had moved in and she hadn't cared enough to change anything. That would explain a lot.

Creed was about to go downstairs and check the basement when he heard a growl outside. It could be a dog, but he doubted it. He turned the lights off in the kitchen and gave his eyes a few seconds to adjust to the dimness before looking out the window. The sense of trouble *hadn't* been a false alarm. Not this time.

Maia was outside fighting something. His adrenaline barely spiked when he got a look at her opponent. An olteil. The hormone surge dissipated. With her training, she should be able to handle things without him, and Creed didn't rush to the back door, guessing it would be over before he got there.

It wasn't.

He leaned against the jamb and watched her use her elbow to stop a strike. Instead of going on the offensive, she leaped out of the way of another blow, and then brought her forearm up in another blocking attempt.

The olteil anticipated it, though, and he closed his large hand around her arm. Creed straightened, but expected Maia to break free. Her response was to stomp on her attacker's foot. Shit, he was going to have to wade into this.

As he went down the stairs, Maia's gaze met his and he read the relief in her eyes. Creed strode across the distance, but he was confused about why she hadn't taken out her opponent long before this. Olteils were strong, but they weren't all that quick and that made them vulnerable. With the training she'd had in martial arts, the fight should be over already.

The olteil faced the opposite direction and didn't realize Creed was there until he grabbed the assailant's arm and twisted it up behind his back. To prevent himself from being pinned, the creature released Maia and pivoted, tugging free as he spun.

Creed turned to block a kick, and before his foe could lower his leg, he grabbed the ankle and yanked. The olteil hit the dirt with all the grace of a hundred-year-old oak tree crashing in the forest.

Following him down, Creed forced his arm high behind his back, effectively ending the fight. The olteil bellowed his fury, but he ignored it. Creed had enough magic to send the creature to the dimension where he'd been gored and keep it there for a while. Silently, he chanted the spell and closed it.

His opponent disappeared.

With a frown, Creed got to his feet. Maia stood at the top of the stairs next to her house and she smiled wanly as he looked her way. "Thanks," she said and ducked inside.

For a moment, he stood there, staring at where she'd been. Maybe it was because he'd woken from a sound sleep or maybe it was because of fighting the poison in his system for so long, but Creed didn't understand what had happened. Maia hadn't appeared to be injured, and barring that, she shouldn't have required any assistance from him, not with an olteil.

Wanting his questions answered, he followed her inside. She wasn't in the kitchen or the living room. He continued through the house until he reached her bedroom and found her kicking off her sandals.

"What went down out there?" he asked.

She gave him a glance over her shoulder. "You can probably guess."

"You're misunderstanding my question. Yeah, I can figure out that you were outside and the olteil showed up, but what I want to know is what the hell were *you* doing?"

Maia stiffened and turned to face him, her arms crossed at her waist. "There's no reason why I shouldn't go outside. This is a safe neighborhood."

He felt his own muscles become rigid. Creed was getting damn sick of trying to pin her down on a question that wasn't very hard. "You know what I'm asking. Why didn't you take him out as soon as he attacked?"

"My magic is—"

"What does magic have to do with it? I didn't use any

to fight him and I didn't need to. It was an *olteil*. They hardly have any power, and what little they do possess doesn't help them in an altercation."

"He was bigger and more muscular than me."

Creed closed the distance until he was an arm's length away. "Yeah, but you're faster, and with the training you have in martial arts, you should have put him on the ground before I made it out of the house."

It was difficult to tell because he was blocking the light, but Creed thought some of the color had drained out of her face. "You don't know what you're talking about," Maia said.

"The hell I don't," he growled.

"I've never faced an olteil until tonight."

"You trained."

"I've never initiated an attack without magic before—not even once."

"You have a million excuses." Creed shook his head. "I'll defend the weak until I draw my last breath, but in this situation, you shouldn't have been one of them, and I resent like hell that you acted helpless. Ryne would have been mortified if she'd seen you tonight."

Maia's chin went up and she closed the distance until she was toe-to-toe with him. "Leave my sister out of this."

"Then don't embarrass the Frasier name."

"I defended myself."

"Defense, not offense."

"It worked, didn't it?"

She tried to spin away, but Creed took hold of her shoulders and gave her a gentle squeeze. "What would you have done if I hadn't woken up and gone outside? The olteil was stronger than you, and without going on the attack, it was just a matter of time until he won."

"You were here, so it's not an issue."

"Next time I might not be around. Don't you get it? You have to be able to take care of yourself."

"I know that." The tenseness left her muscles. "Don't you think I know that? It's not easy living without magic."

Maia had sounded defensive as she tacked on the last and Creed shook his head as he joined her next to the door. "It's been seven years, that's long enough to adjust."

"That's easy for you to say."

"Maybe so," Creed agreed, "but you made the decision to cede your powers. And yeah, I do know why. A lot of troubleshooters in your position would choose to go down in a battle with the enforcer sent to bring them in."

Looking away for an instant, Maia ran her hand through her hair, then met his eyes again. "Ryne would have been the one they sent after me," she said quietly.

As he dropped his gaze, things clicked into place for Creed. Maia hadn't given up her magic because she'd wanted to, she'd given it up because she didn't want to force her sister to kill her.

4
CHAPTER

Maia swiped her badge through the time clock and breathed a sigh of relief—back from lunch with two minutes to spare. The new manager required that they punch in and out if they left the building, and she'd needed to get away from the office before she became violent.

The time spent calming her nerves, though, was shot to hell fast. She could hear Herb and his incredibly loud voice before she made it past the fax machine. Didn't the man ever work?

She opened her bottom desk drawer and put her purse away. Maybe he was irritating her more than usual because she was angry at Creed.

The longer she thought about what he'd said, the more furious she became. How dare he judge her?

She'd stewed about it all night and had been ready to confront him Sunday morning, but Blackwood was gone when she got up and he hadn't returned before she headed to bed. Maia had wondered if he'd come back at all, but when she'd opened the guest bedroom door to check before leaving for work, he'd been there, dead to the world.

Bringing up the sign-in screen, Maia logged back into the system. "Adjust," she muttered. She'd like to see how well Blackwood did without his magic. None of the Gineal realized how much they relied on it, and they wouldn't understand unless they suddenly became powerless. "Embarrass the family name, my ass."

Maia shifted her papers so they were closer and started adding data to the spreadsheet. Blackwood wasn't a complete idiot, he had to know the council would have sent her sister after her. Yet he'd essentially said she should have let a troubleshooter kill her rather than cede her magic.

Or had he?

She bit her lip. It might have been more of an observation than a suggestion. Her typing slowed a little as she thought about it. Creed's tone had held absolutely no inflection. Perhaps she'd jumped to conclusions.

Many Gineal believed that if they turned, it was noble to allow an enforcer to take them out. In a way, it made sense. The longer one of their people used the dark forces, the more dangerous and unpredictable they became.

Her e-mail beeped and the notification window told her it was something she needed to look at. She opened the note and the attachment, then hit the print icon. The laser printer was done with the document before she reached it. She stapled the papers, turned to go upstairs, and nearly walked into another woman.

"Maia, hi. You don't happen to have my—"

With a smile, Maia handed the packet to the secretary. "I was just on my way to drop this off."

"Thanks! I don't know why IS won't set me up to receive this directly."

"Corporate bureaucracies, you have to love . . ." Her voice trailed off when she noticed her manager standing there, waiting.

He tapped the face of his watch with his index finger and asked, "Are you girls on the clock?" Without waiting for a response, he walked away.

Maia gritted her teeth. *Girls.* She was thirty-two years old.

Taking a deep breath, she smoothed her hands over her taupe-colored skirt. She'd outlasted the other managers, she'd outlast this guy, too. Maia stalked back to her cube, took another deep breath, and began typing. If she hit the keys with enough force to make them clack loudly, so what?

You can't change other people, you can only change your reaction to them.

With a deep sigh, Maia went still. That voice might have sounded like Taber, her former mentor, but the words had come from within her own head—and it was an apt reminder. She couldn't change anyone. When would she learn?

She'd tried to alter her parents' behavior, first for herself, then later, for both her and her sister, but that had never worked. She'd wanted Ryne to moderate her gung-ho intensity, but that was like trying to tame a hurricane. Maia lived in dread that one day she'd lose her sister. Being all alone in the world was probably her biggest fear, and that was something else she had no control over.

If she were still Gineal . . .

Maia resumed typing, but made herself hit the keys as softly as possible. She didn't fit in anywhere. There were large sections of her past that she couldn't discuss, and for that reason, she kept humans at arm's length. The Gineal had suffered horrendous persecution throughout their history and now they hid their existence by blending in. Secrecy was ingrained from childhood and she wouldn't risk her people.

That same secrecy had put distance between her and the Gineal men and women she'd once called friends. Most had simply dropped her, and while a few of her closer confidantes kept in touch, there was a reserve between them that hadn't been there before she'd ceded her magic. It hurt, but she understood. Mostly.

Which brought her thoughts back to Creed. There were more reasons to stay away from him than just his pretty face. If she were stupid enough to let the attraction she felt get the best of her, she'd end up being hurt. The powerless were for casual relationships only and she'd never been able to take sex lightly.

She was deeply engrossed in her task when she sensed someone standing behind her. Biting back a sigh over the interruption, Maia swiveled her chair. Her eyes widened, then the blood drained from her face before it rushed back, flooding her cheeks with heat. "How did you get in here?" she demanded, voice low.

Creed tapped the sticker on the left pocket of his navy blue T-shirt. "Visitor's pass."

"They don't just hand those out. How did—" She stopped short. The man could do magic; there were a dozen ways he could have gotten one of those temporary badges. "Never mind. Why are you here?"

"You forgot to give me a key to the house."

"Why don't you—" Maia cut herself off again, aware that the normal background noise had gone silent. She looked past Creed's shoulder at the textured cloth wall. No doubt the clerks on the opposite side were leaning in her direction, straining to hear every word. "Let's go somewhere with some privacy," Maia suggested and got to her feet.

Blackwood blocked most of the entrance to her cube and he didn't move. Maia hesitated, but it was the challenge in his eyes that made her attempt to sidle past him. Her breasts brushed his arm, and damn it, she felt her body react to the inadvertent touch.

With an almost imperceptible note of sarcasm, he asked, "Air-conditioning too cold for you, angel?"

"Shh!" Didn't he realize people could hear him? As she headed down the aisle, she looked over her shoulder and the expression on his face told her he'd done it on purpose.

She glanced to her left when she passed the next row. Her coworkers were standing there, watching. Okay, it was slightly embarrassing to have him trailing behind her like she was royalty, and the discomfort grew worse when she passed a pair of secretaries in the hall. She slowed so Creed could catch up, but he didn't pull alongside her. With a scowl, she walked faster.

Maia didn't stop until she reached the alcove next to the elevators. It held the floor's mail satellite, but this was about as private as it got unless she dragged him into the conference room, and there was no way in hell she was going to deal with the kind of gossip that would incite.

"Why do you need a key?" she asked when he joined her. "Just use magic to pop the locks. I assume that's what you've been doing?"

"Yeah, I have been," Creed tucked his thumbs into the front pockets of his jeans, "but when I was coming in last night, I almost got caught by your neighbor, an old lady."

"Mrs. Olson. She was probably looking for her cat."

He shrugged. "I convinced her that she missed seeing me unlocking the door because it was dark, but now it's a bright, sunny afternoon and I don't want to take chances."

Maia rubbed her forehead, trying to ease the tension that had settled there. She should have thought of this herself and left her extra key on the table for him. It was a small thing, but it was the little stuff that could reveal the existence of the Gineal. "My spare is at home."

"I figured. Give me an idea where it is so I can zero in on it and call it to me."

Scrunching her eyes shut, Maia tried to remember where she'd last seen the set of keys. They were probably in a drawer somewhere, but it had to be years since she'd run across them and she couldn't be positive where they were.

"This isn't rocket science," Creed drawled.

She glared at him. "Yeah? Why don't you tell me where your spare house key is?"

"I don't need one."

"In other words, you don't have a clue. Well, I don't either. It's not like I routinely have guests that need to borrow it. Why don't you blur the area while you pop the locks? I'll do a search when I get home this evening."

He was shaking his head before she finished talking. "Waste of magic," Creed said.

Maia wanted to give him a good solid kick. Yeah, the Gineal didn't use their powers unnecessarily, but this seemed excessive. "What do you suggest then?"

"Let me have your key and I'll have a copy made."

She didn't like that idea at all and opened her mouth to tell him that when she caught movement over his shoulder. "I'll take care of that for you," Maia said to the employee standing outside the alcove. She reached past Creed to take the co-mail envelope. The woman only hesitated an instant before handing it over and leaving. "Fine," Maia capitulated, not wanting to risk someone else coming over. "You just make sure you're at my house when I get off work."

"I can't afford to sit around waiting for you."

"Let me get this straight—it's okay for me to be inconvenienced by you, but you can't scrape up fifteen or twenty minutes to let me in my own home?"

He made a low grumbling sound.

"What was that?" she asked. "I couldn't quite make that out. Was that 'thank you, Maia, for putting me up in your house'? Or maybe 'thank you for sitting up all night taking care of me while I was sick.' Oh, wait, surely that meant 'after all you've done for me, of course I'll be there when you get home.'"

There was another grumble, then, "Fine. What time can I expect you?"

The lack of graciousness in his voice had her hands curling into fists. Not here, she reminded herself. It damn near killed her, though, not to respond to his abrasiveness. "Usually between quarter after and five-thirty."

"I'll be there," Creed agreed without enthusiasm.

"The key's at my desk." She gestured toward the hall, and this time, he stepped back to let her pass. She was conscious of Creed lagging behind her again and wondered what kind of questions that would raise, but she couldn't worry about it now. Getting him out of here was of paramount importance.

Bending over, Maia opened her drawer and dug through her purse until she found what she was looking for. She carefully removed her house key, handed it to him, and returned her car keys to her purse. "I'll be home around 5:15," she reminded him.

Creed slipped her key into his front pocket. "No problem. See you later." He sauntered away and Maia couldn't help herself—she stared after him.

With a loud sigh, she got back to work, half surprised that no one was at her cube, quizzing her. The reprieve didn't last, and as she fended off questions, she began counting the minutes till she could get out of there.

As she walked to her car after clocking out, Maia made plans. The first thing she'd do when she got home was change into casual clothes. Maybe she wasn't wearing nylons, but her skirt and sweater were restrictive in the August heat. Next, she'd have something light for dinner, then she was escaping into her garden. Most people probably considered weeding a chore, but Maia found peace when she had her fingers working the earth, and she craved the serenity.

She opened her car door and sucked in a sharp breath as heat burst from the interior. Reluctantly, she climbed in, and the metal of the ignition switch nearly burned her fingers as she turned the key. Maia put the air conditioner on max and lowered her windows, then gingerly placed her hands on the steering wheel and pulled out. As she drove through the parking lot, cool air finally started coming from the vents and she closed the windows again.

A glance down at the dashboard while she was waiting for the light to change made Maia groan. She'd forgotten she was low on gas.

When she reached a station, she turned in, chose an available pump, and opened her car door. The hot, humid air seemed twice as oppressive as she waited for the tank to fill.

To entertain herself, she watched the heat shimmer off the asphalt, but the sound of a strident voice had her glancing over at the library across the parking lot. A teenage girl going into the building was loudly protesting to her mother about having to read on her summer vacation, and Maia smiled. She could have voiced the same sentiment at that age, but she'd been an apprentice troubleshooter. Not only had she needed to read for school, there'd been half a million books on spells and magic and Gineal history and assorted other topics she'd been expected to study as well. God knew, the tests Taber had given her were a lot more difficult than anything a human teacher had expected of her. If she'd known then what she knew now . . .

Maia sighed and almost choked on her own breath when a man exited the library. Her heart leapt into her throat before it began throbbing at a hundred miles an hour. The hose from the gas pump made a thunking noise, signaling her tank was full, but she didn't take her eyes off the guy.

The way he moved was familiar—the fluid grace, the absolute arrogance—they were things she'd never forget. Maia stared until he opened the door to a sports car and got in. The glare from the sun as it hit the windshield blocked her view, but she still didn't look away, not until the car drove past the station and out of sight. Only then was her paralysis broken. With shaking hands, she placed the nozzle into the pump and put her gas cap back on.

It wasn't him. Maia knew it couldn't be. This man's hair was much darker for one thing, and even if the guy had moved the same way, there was absolutely no chance it was Seth.

After all, what could a demon need at the public library?

5
CHAPTER

Creed parked the car, but didn't turn off the engine. It had happened again. Fuck. He tightened his hands around the wheel. Someone was breathing harshly, almost gasping for breath, and an instant later, he realized *he* was that person.

He tried to slow his respiration and calm the wild pounding of his heart, but he was more frightened now than he'd ever been battling demons, monsters, or any other dark-force creatures. Even in the air-conditioned interior of his rental, sweat born of fear beaded his forehead and trickled down his left temple. Creed wiped a hand across his face and tried to ignore his tremors.

Of all the shit he'd dealt with in the last eight months, he hated this the most. For the third time, he'd fallen into some kind of somnambulant state and regained awareness in an unfamiliar location. He looked around. A graveyard, and judging from the uniform white headstones and the precision of their layout, it was a military cemetery. Releasing the steering wheel, he leaned back in his seat and took another deep breath. Of all places, why had he driven here?

Creed's breathing quickened again and he fought for control. He was a troubleshooter, damn it. It was his job to face down threats and overcome them—even if the enemy was his own mind.

He knew what he should do. The Gineal believed in honoring their emotions, embracing them and then releasing them. To do otherwise meant they took on a life of their own, hiding within and growing until they became a formidable obstacle that could no longer be ignored. He understood. This was different, though.

As an enforcer, Creed had been scared many times, but that had been a good fear, the kind of fear that sharpened instincts and honed reactions. What he felt now was different. This was ugly and blunted his senses. The most frightening part, however, was that he didn't know if he could release it once he embraced it. That might leave him paralyzed, unable to do his job. He couldn't and wouldn't risk it.

Now, more than ever before, the Gineal needed their troubleshooters—every last one of them—to be at the top of their game. He knew it. The council knew it.

Movement caught his attention and he watched a line of cars turn onto the grounds and slowly wend themselves to a gravesite. He focused on counting the vehicles, anything to help him find his peaceful center and thrust the shakiness away.

By the time the last of the mourners had driven past, Creed had regulated his breathing and cleared his head. Maybe he'd come here for a reason. Maybe there was something he was supposed to discover in this cemetery. When he'd zoned out before, he hadn't been able to find any higher purpose in his destination, but that didn't mean there wasn't one now.

Reaching for the ignition, Creed turned off the engine. He hated cemeteries. It was stupid, a phobia left over from when he'd been a child and watched his grandmother interred. Too young to understand the concept of death, he'd only known that his grandma was in a box and they were throwing dirt on it, burying her. From all accounts, he'd caused one hell of a scene. Age had dulled the sick feeling in the pit of his stomach, but it hadn't eradicated it.

Reluctantly, he opened the door and stepped into the thick, humid air. He shivered despite the heat, but Creed ignored his reaction and took another deep breath. Looking around, he tried to decide where to begin his search. The roar of a jet engine distracted him and he glanced up in time to see a 747 climb above the canopy of trees. That told him his location, and now he had a good idea of how long it would take him to get to Maia's house.

The thought of her had Creed checking his watch. It would be tight, but there was time to explore before he had to head back to unlock the door for her.

His pulse picked up its pace again, but this had nothing to do with fear. Despite her professional attire, Maia'd looked sexy as hell when he'd seen her at the office. The grayish-brown skirt she'd been wearing had ended below her knees, but it had lovingly followed the contours of her hips and thighs. Not clingy, but close fitting, and he'd had a great view of her ass as he'd walked behind her. Shit, he'd been lucky she hadn't turned around and caught him leering.

Maia had looked just as good from the front. She'd been wearing an orange sweater over some shiny orange thing with lace. It had left a lot of her chest bare, but had more than adequately covered her. He wasn't sure how a woman could look hot and businesslike at the same time, but Maia had managed it. She'd had him fantasizing about opening the four buttons on her sweater, pushing it aside and cupping her breasts. Creed shook his head.

She might have gotten him more steamed up than anyone had since he'd been a teenager, but he wasn't a boy any longer. At thirty-five, he had control—more or less—and he knew how to keep his mind on his job.

Returning his focus to the cemetery, he mentally quartered the area. There wasn't time to cover all the grounds, but Creed had to trust that if there was anything for him to pick up on, it would be on the side where he'd parked the car.

He started in the corner closest to the road. For a moment, he closed his eyes and extended his senses. When he detected nothing of note, he moved on, careful to walk lightly in respect of those buried here.

It was near the central flagpole that Creed picked up a trace of something. He went nearer to the marble wall surrounding it and reached out mentally again.

The energy was so ugly, he physically recoiled.

Cautiously, he probed again and this time Creed got a more accurate read. It was a remnant, a persistent stain from a dark-force creature that was no longer present. He unclenched his hands and allowed himself a deep breath. As strong as the lingering aura was, this thing must have been incredibly powerful. And incredibly evil.

Did this dark entity have ties to the one he hunted? Was that why he'd been guided to this cemetery?

He was canvassing the area, trying to find the strongest trace of the creature, when his cell rang. Muttering a curse, he reached for the phone. Creed looked at caller ID, then glanced at his watch. It was damn close to five o'clock and Maia was going to have his ass for being late, but there wasn't much he could do about a call-out. "Yeah," he said without enthusiasm.

It was a member of the council. A ceannard only issued an assignment when it was a serious situation, but while Creed's attention sharpened, he'd been through this too many times in the past to work up much excitement now.

Taber was succinct, passing along just the bare bones before he sent Creed a telepathic transmission with the details necessary to handle the assignment. "Got it," Creed said and disconnected the call.

He returned the phone to his waist and perused the area. The burial was still taking place about fifty yards away. No way would a transit go unnoticed. He did a second search, this time for somewhere he'd be concealed. The stone building he spotted wasn't ideal, but it might work. It didn't surprise him to find the door locked when he tested it and he went behind the structure to see how much cover it offered.

Adequate, Creed decided. He wouldn't be completely shielded, but there was no one in view. He began the spell to open the transit. Magic worked by focusing energy, not by using words, but speaking aloud helped him concentrate, something he needed now.

The gateway appeared, glowing in the late afternoon sun, but Creed hesitated. The portal's sheen was mirror-like, preventing him from seeing what waited on the other side. Once, not that long ago, he'd have walked through it without thought, but those days were gone.

He couldn't stand here long, he knew that—if anyone saw the transit, it would raise questions—and a costien demon wasn't all that powerful; it was only about midrange and he'd taken out tougher opponents. Something inside him, though, balked, and Creed fucking hated the self-doubt more than any of the other changes he'd suffered.

Shaking off his reluctance, he strode forward, crossing through the transit before he could second-guess himself.

It was night in southern Germany, but he'd been prepared for that. Waving a hand to close the portal, he waited for his eyes to adjust to the dark.

The terrain was uneven, with large boulders strewn around as if a giant had tossed a handful of dice. Creed scowled. Footing would be uncertain at best. Moonlight hit the mountains, illuminating the rocky faces and casting long shadows in the valley where he stood. Large evergreens offered protection and cover, but there were also expanses of open meadow, and he'd have nowhere to hide if he was caught crossing one of them.

Battle calm descended. Finally.

His telepathic scan was quick, but it pinpointed the demon's location. Something felt off and Creed probed again, more carefully. As soon as he figured out what had him wary, he pulled back fast, not wanting to risk being detected.

Shit. This wasn't a costien; it was a groige, and there were damn few demon branches that were more powerful or more dangerous than this one. They usually kept to themselves, though, so what the hell was this one doing in the Bavarian Alps? And why had he grabbed a human?

Normally, the Gineal monitors were sensitive enough to pick out what kind of dark-force creature was using black magic. They passed the signature on to a tracker who pinpointed the location of the being in question and then a troubleshooter was dispatched to take care of it. The accuracy rate for monitors was phenomenal—unless it involved the strongest groups of demons.

Creed mentally stepped back to reassess the situation and his plan of attack. A groige could control the four elements as effortlessly as an enforcer, and that branch had incredible stamina. If he was lucky, his odds of surviving this encounter were maybe fifty-fifty—and luck hadn't been on his side lately.

Withdrawing wasn't an option, not when the demon was holding at least one human hostage, and for that same reason, he wasn't going to have a lot of time to think things through. At least he'd opened the transit far enough away from the groige that it wouldn't have been detected in the few seconds it was active. For whatever good that would do.

Part of a poem he'd been forced to memorize in school echoed through his head: *Into the jaws of death, into the mouth of hell, rode the six hundred.* Creed's lips quirked. Nothing like thinking positive.

A shriek ripped through the night, sobering him instantly. Time had run out. He muttered a protection spell under his breath as he loped toward the demon—not that it would help for long against one this strong, but it was better than nothing.

He slowed as he neared the top of the hill, not wanting to give away his presence—or the advantage of surprise. Cautiously, he peered through the row of trees.

Hell, the groige was female. As vicious and nasty as male demons were, they couldn't hold a candle to their women.

The demon was tall, probably close to six feet, but Creed had seen damn few short demons. Her hair was long, the color impossible to guess in the moonlight, and she was strong enough to easily handle the human struggling against her hold. It took nothing more than a quick glance to see the boy was about thirteen or fourteen, but Creed didn't understand why she wasn't using her powers to hold the teen in thrall and end the scuffle.

Like most troubleshooters, his affinity was with fire and his first inclination was to draw upon it, but a groige would be familiar enough with the Gineal to expect flame. Given the situation, however, Creed didn't dare open the earth or send a torrent of water down the hillside. Not with the boy right there.

There was no other choice. Drawing on the element of fire, Creed waited, unable to risk a shot while the teen was writhing. Then he spotted the makeshift altar, the dagger, and the statuette of a grotesque beast— Ahriman, Creed identified, the ruler of all Persian demons. He grimaced. Great. This was just fucking great. If this demon followed that leader of evil, the fight was going to be even uglier than he'd anticipated and he'd—

A sudden memory stopped him cold. It was worse than he'd first thought. The demon didn't worship Ahriman; the idol was part of a ritual involving human sacrifice. No wonder she wasn't controlling the kid with magic—the rite wouldn't work if the boy was under a spell.

If the council had any idea what was going on here and what branch of demon was involved, it would have arranged for backup. It was too damn late for him to request help now. As close as he was, the demon would pick up any telepathic request he sent. Creed lowered his odds of survival.

Although he'd studied it, he hadn't heard of a demon performing this ceremony in his lifetime. Hell, the last instance recorded by the Gineal was at least three centuries old. Most considered the cost far too high for the

momentary benefit, so why was the groige planning to
use it?

The teen continued to battle, and while he appreciated the boy's determination, it left Creed unable to en-
gage the demon.

Shoot anyway. It was an enticing suggestion and
every muscle in his body went stiff as he fought the
urge. The Gineal protected humans.

*The Earth is filled with billions of people; what dif-
ference does the death of one child make?* He fought
harder to ignore the inner voice, but logically it made
sense.

There was another scream as the groige slashed the
boy with her razor-sharp talons. The sound jerked
Creed away from the abyss. He wouldn't risk the human.

As the boy fell to the grass, Creed shot a rope of fire
and moved quickly into another position. It didn't
matter—the demon tracked him effortlessly and released a burst of magic strong enough to make his head
jerk backward.

The metallic taste of blood filled his mouth, but he ignored the pain. Creed called on fire again and let loose
with both hands. He ran, not waiting to see the result,
and tripped over a stone jutting from the ground. The
demon's shot sailed harmlessly over his prone body.

Quickly, he rolled to his feet, ready to face the
groige's next attack, but she was strolling after the teen.
The boy was scuttling away on his hands and knees and
losing ground.

Creed preferred to fight demons at a distance, but it
was having no effect on one so powerful and he had to
protect this kid. "Into the valley of death," he muttered
and charged down the slope.

She ignored him, more intent on grabbing her victim

than on a Gineal troubleshooter. Or at least he *thought* she was paying no attention to him until he saw the bòcan appear in front of him. Creed stopped short. There were an even half dozen of the hobgoblins armed with staffs, and while he was a good three feet taller, they were much quicker.

In the split second it took him to appraise the situation, he was surrounded, and directing a shockwave of energy in a circle didn't drive them back.

He grunted as he took a blow to the back of his right knee. Even with his protection spell, his leg buckled. Catching his balance, he called on the wind and sent it gusting strongly enough to knock them over like whitebearded dominoes. The yelling brought him satisfaction, but it was short-lived.

Two bòcan on his left flank came at him, staffs held at the ready like samurai swords. Creed jumped, adding a spell for levitation. He heard the whistle of the wood as they swung through where he'd been standing. This time he brought the wind in a downdraft powerful enough to send his attackers to the dirt.

Propelling himself through the air, Creed landed close to the demon. His sneakers had barely touched down when she turned, and with a casual wave of her hand sent him flying a good twenty feet.

His breath left him in a rush as his head hit the rocky ground. He was dazed, but he knew he had to move.

They were on him before he could get to his knees. Whatever the demon had thrown at him had stripped away most of his protection and he felt every blow the bòcan delivered. With his thoughts scrambled, Creed couldn't focus his magic, and he worked on clearing his brain.

The creatures wielded their staffs like major league batters swinging for the fences, and every time he attempted to regain his feet, they brought him down again.

It was the teen's pleading tone that forced Creed to try harder. He grabbed one of the staffs and yanked with all his strength. It came loose. The unarmed bòcan bared crooked yellow teeth and Creed teed off, catching him solidly on the side of the knee.

The flunky went down screaming. With one of their brethren incapacitated, the rest came at him with new ferocity. Creed met them with his own slams, but because he couldn't get to his feet, he wasn't swinging with much power.

He took out another of the attackers, redoubling his efforts to clear his head. The kid had gone damn quiet and Creed had no idea what the demon was doing to him.

Another bòcan made a run at him and Creed met him with a burst of fire. It didn't kill him, not with his magical shield in place, but it did stop the assault.

With control of his powers back, Creed made the earth shake and buckle until the five remaining creatures were unable to stay upright. He kept it up until all of them tumbled down the rocky slope.

With the minions out of the picture, Creed staggered to his feet, looked around, and found the kid strapped down to a large boulder, the groige standing over him. In the moonlight, it appeared as if the leather bonds went all the way under the large stone. Great. That meant the boy wasn't going to free himself and make things easier. Creed was still considering how to handle this, when she raised a hand and called forward her dagger. He moved then; he had no choice.

He only made it half the distance before the demon sent him flying again. Creed hit the ground hard enough to knock the wind out of him and he gasped for air.

Once he was taking in oxygen, he pushed himself into a sitting position. How the hell did he fight something this powerful when he couldn't get within ten feet of her?

The demon began chanting, and though he wasn't ready to stand yet, Creed struggled to his feet. She was too close to the kid to take a lot of risks and he went with fire, releasing a quick shot. She didn't react.

Doggedly, he approached, but this time the groige snarled at him. He didn't understand the language, but he understood the tone—she was pissed. Before he could shoot again, she directed a burst of magic that sent him sailing with such velocity, his vision went black when he struck the earth.

Shit, he hated dealing with strong demons.

Since he couldn't do anything until his eyesight returned, Creed ran through what little he knew about her breed. All demons had a weakness. What was a groige's?

His mind remained stubbornly blank, but his eyes were clearing. Biting back a groan, he stood. He hurt. Everywhere. Creed didn't think anything was broken, but if he kept annoying the demon, fractured bones would be the least of his worries. Why was he putting himself through this for one human? The kid had probably gotten himself into this mess through sheer stupidity anyway.

Walk away.

That was exactly what he should do. It wasn't like the demon was threatening the Gineal, and the ritual she planned to perform would cost her big time. Sure, she'd boost her powers, but that was short term—maybe a month—and when the time was up, she'd lose double what she'd taken.

The argument could be made that he'd be doing more to help his people by letting the teen die rather than dying himself in a futile effort to save the boy. Not only were troubleshooters vital, but the groige would end up weakened. Creed didn't have a doubt that he could put that spin on his departure for the council.

It was the crying that stopped him from leaving. He hadn't slipped far enough into dark magic yet to abandon a human. With a grimace, he repeated the protection spell—for all the good it would do him—and went to save the boy.

The demon heard his advance and her eyes glowed red as she turned to look over her shoulder. A smart man would heed the warning and back off. He didn't slow, even though he didn't know what the hell he was going to do to stop her.

In an instant, Creed ran through methods of attack. Fire hadn't fazed her and anything he did with earth, wind, or water had the potential of hurting the boy as well. She growled, and this time he did draw to a halt. He needed a plan, damn it.

A desperate idea came to him. What if he bound her? Not just her powers, but physically as well.

She'd break loose in a nanosecond. It would take a full binding ritual to hold her, and even if he were strong enough to conduct it, he'd never finish before she blasted him halfway to hell.

But Creed measured the distance between them anyway. It wouldn't take more than an instant to cross it if he had an incantation ready to go. That would mean juggling spells, not an easy thing to do, especially when he was this beat up, but it wasn't impossible, and his gut said this was the best way.

As she stared at him, daring him to interfere, Creed silently repeated the proclamation that would put him directly in front of her. It didn't take long until all it needed was the words to close it. He partitioned it off in his mind.

The boy fought his restraints, the sudden movement startling both him and the demon. She turned to look at her hostage. This was his chance. Creed hurriedly recited the binding spell and closed it.

Just as quickly, he closed the first incantation, and before he could blink, he stood in front of her. She didn't move.

He reached up, ripped the dagger from her grasp, and in one smooth motion, drove it under the ribs and into her heart. For a moment, the groige simply stared at him, then she fell.

Creed ignored the kid's whimpers, and kneeling down, intoned the proclamation to transform the demon's body into energy and sent it into the universe. Only then did he look at the teen. He started crying harder and Creed sighed.

"Relax, you're safe," he said, but he had no clue if the kid spoke English or not. Still crouched, he reached out and tugged at the leather straps, but they were secure. Creed stood and examined the fastenings at the wrists and ankles—he was going to have to use his powers to free the boy. Not good, not when he was running low because of the strong blows the demon had delivered.

Before working on the straps, Creed did a spell to heavily blur the teen's memories. What happened tonight would be more ethereal than a dream, and not even hypnosis would shake the truth out of his brain. The proclamation left the kid asleep. Next Creed did the incantation to free him, then another to send the boy back to his home. Only then did he sit down. Hard.

Leaning against the boulder the demon had been using as an altar, Creed began to recharge his powers as he
ran through what else needed to be done.

He'd have to check and make sure the bòcan were
gone. The last thing he needed was to have them hang
around, creating problems, and since they were known
to eat humans who offended them in some way, the
trouble could be huge.

It took about five minutes before he felt up to scanning the area. Luckily, the minions had departed on
their own, so he wouldn't need to have the council send
another troubleshooter. Creed figured he required at
least an hour before he'd be strong enough to tackle
them again.

With the biggest items resolved, he slumped back and
closed his eyes. He could feel energy flowing from the
earth into him and he embraced every wave.

His peacefulness was shattered, though, when he felt
the other. Creed wasn't sure who it was; all he knew was
he was a demon—a dangerous one—and he was male.
For months now, without warning and without his doing
anything, Creed had been able to read him. It was both a
blessing and a curse.

A blessing because it had allowed Creed to learn his
enemy was headed to Minneapolis and what he planned
on doing here, but a curse because there was no control.
Creed couldn't force the connection and he couldn't
delve deeper.

For example, he knew this demon was reading right
now. Creed needed to know what held his prey's attention, but he couldn't see or sense more. He remained
mentally quiet and kept himself open as he recharged
his magic.

He didn't get any helpful information, but he knew
when the demon was on the move again. Creed tried to

stand, realized there was nothing he could do, and sat back down again. He had no clue where his quarry was or what he was really up to. Hell, for all Creed knew, he was reading the want ads. He snorted.

The other wasn't in a hurry, but before Creed could relax, he sensed something, some sharp emotion. And in that instant, Creed picked up something else from the demon. One word. A name.

Maia.

6

CHAPTER

Maia stared at the toe of her T-strap pump as she toyed with the clasp of her bracelet. *It wasn't Seth. It couldn't be Seth.* But she had a horrible feeling that it was. Her argument that demons didn't go to libraries was lame. Beyond lame. Just because she didn't understand why Seth was there didn't mean there wasn't some logical reason. Besides, he'd never been a typical demon.

A shiver went through her and she abandoned the gold chain at her wrist to wrap her arms around herself. She was sitting on her back patio, the late afternoon sun beating down on her, and she should be sweating, but she wasn't. Maia was freezing, the cold coming from somewhere deep inside.

When she'd known him, his hair had been golden, his eyes the blue of the deepest ocean, but this man's hair had been just a few shades lighter than Creed's nearly black color. That, too, was weak logic. The Gineal could change their hair color at will, and there was no reason to assume demons couldn't do the same. At the very least, dye would take care of it.

When she'd known Seth, she'd believed he was human. That alone made him extraordinary. Gineal could always sense what someone was, and even without her powers, Maia could still do this, but he'd fooled her right up until—

She'd been an idiot. Men gravitated toward her because of her appearance, and though she knew looks meant little, by the time she'd been twenty-five, she'd taken the attention for granted. When Seth had shown interest in her, Maia hadn't questioned it, but had merely accepted it as a given. That had been her first mistake.

In the years since that final night—the night she'd given up her powers—she'd spotted a lot of men who looked more like Seth than this one had. Hell, Minnesota was filled with blond-haired Scandinavians. She'd seen guys who reminded her of Seth in other ways, too, but she'd never reacted this way before. That was the bottom line—something deep inside knew it was him and she had to trust her instincts.

Which brought her to the big question. What in the name of heaven was *he* doing in Minneapolis? Revenge?

He'd been enraged with her that night and she didn't doubt that he'd like to get even for what she'd done to him, but it should have been difficult for him to find her here.

Maia brooded on his presence and what it meant until the sound of someone speaking her name jerked her from her thoughts. Her cheeks heated as she realized her eighty-something neighbor had snuck up on her. She could just imagine what Creed would say about *that*.

"I didn't mean to startle you," Mrs. Olson apologized. "Are you all right?"

"Fi—" Maia cleared her throat, sat up straighter, and tried again. "I'm fine, thank you."

The older woman didn't try to hide her skepticism. "I thought you might like a lemonade," she said and held out a frosted glass.

Reluctantly, Maia took it. No one made lemonade as good as her neighbor, but since Mrs. Olson was carrying two glasses, Maia had a feeling she was in for some well-intentioned meddling. And sure enough, the woman pulled out a chair, placed it next to Maia's, and settled in. Mrs. O might look frail, especially when the flowered housedress she wore appeared to be two sizes too big, but Maia knew firsthand how indomitable her will could be.

Maia sipped her cold drink and tried not to be the one who broke first. Tried and failed. "Mrs. O, you shouldn't be sitting in the sun like this. You'll get heatstroke."

"You've been out here nearly an hour and haven't keeled over yet."

"I'm fifty years younger than you."

"If you want me in the shade, you'll have to move first."

It was manipulation pure and simple, but she couldn't help but smile at the older woman's feistiness. Maia put her lemonade on the table, stood up, and opened the patio table umbrella, adjusting it until her neighbor was shielded. As she started to sit, she noticed Mrs. O's stubborn expression and shifted her own chair until she was shaded as well. "There."

"That wasn't so hard, was it, dear?"

Feeling a tad petulant, Maia shook her head and

reached for her glass. "You don't need to fuss over me," she said gently. "I can take care of myself."

"Everyone needs a little fussing now and then—even mother hens like you."

"I'm not a mother hen."

"You are. Do you think I haven't noticed the way you take care of me? You check on me more than my own children and grandchildren."

That was probably true and it angered Maia. What was wrong with Mrs. O's family? Did they think she'd be around forever? Already, Maia could see her slowing down, and she hated to think of a day when her neighbor would need to go into a nursing home.

"There's nothing wrong with being a nurturer," Mrs. Olson said, "but you need to learn to accept help as well as give it."

Maia shrugged, not wanting to argue. She could take care of herself. The bravado drained away quickly, though. Without magic, she wasn't as self-sufficient as she'd like, not in all circumstances. Of course, she was a noncombatant now and would have remained on the sidelines if Creed hadn't shown up. Unless Seth was here to—No, that was ridiculous.

A sudden thought jumped into her head. "Did the pharmacy deliver your medication?"

Mrs. Olson laughed. "And you tried to deny being a mother hen," the woman scolded with a smile.

"High blood pressure is dangerous."

The older woman sobered. "I know it is. Yes, I have my medicine and yes, I took it. Sometimes I wonder if you're trying to attain sainthood."

It was Maia's turn to laugh, but there wasn't much humor in it. "Maybe I'm atoning for my past sins."

"Bah. You're a good girl."

Shaking her head, Maia said, "With all due respect, Mrs. O, you didn't know me before I moved here."

"You couldn't have been much different than the sweet person you are now."

Maia was unable to meet the woman's eyes. She shifted, put the glass on the table, and stared out into the yard. A montage of some of her actions while she'd been using black magic flashed through her brain and she gripped the chair arms. The heat of shame drove away the icy cold and she could feel sweat begin to pool at the small of her back. When she was able to force the words, Maia said softly, "You'll have to take my word for it."

The silence dragged out long enough to be uncomfortable before Mrs. Olson asked, "Why are you sitting outside?"

After a brief hesitation, Maia turned to her neighbor again. "Creed, my houseguest, has my key. He was supposed to get it copied and meet me after work, but he must be running late." Something for which she was eternally grateful. She'd needed time to get over the shock of maybe—probably—seeing Seth again.

Mrs. O put her own glass on the table. "I don't trust that boy."

"Creed?" she asked incredulously, and when the other woman nodded her head, Maia nearly choked. There was absolutely nothing boyish about Blackwood. When the amazement subsided, Maia asked, "Why not?"

"There's something about him . . . I can't put my finger on it, but it makes me uneasy."

Maia mulled that over for a minute. It could be Creed's edge. Troubleshooters all seemed to develop one to some degree, and because he'd been doing the job for sixteen years, it was pronounced in him. Maybe that was what Mrs. O had sensed. Or maybe it was something else.

Blackwood nearly got Ryne killed.

Deke hadn't elaborated, but he wasn't someone given to exaggeration either. Had Creed begun to turn? Was that what her neighbor had sensed?

With most Gineal, the slide into black magic was gradual, almost imperceptible for a while—to both the one falling and those around him. To defeat dark-force creatures, enforcers had to routinely use gray magic and it left them at greater risk than anyone else. Maia herself hadn't realized she'd succumbed until she'd been deep into murky territory. Too deep to ever go back.

"Maia? I'm sorry if I offended you. Certainly, you know your boyfriend better than I do." Mrs. Olson took a short sip from her glass. "After all, I only talked to him for a few minutes the other night."

"He's not my boyfriend," Maia answered absently.

"Lover, then."

That instantly brought Maia's thoughts back to the conversation. "There's nothing romantic going on between us."

Mrs. O looked skeptical and Maia swallowed a sigh. If she insisted, it would be a case of protesting too much. She'd dealt with this before; it was a by-product of her appearance. Despite the fact that she'd hardly dated since moving to Minnesota, her neighbor still couldn't believe that someone who looked like Maia had a platonic relationship with her houseguest—especially one with Creed's gorgeous face.

"You don't need to worry about him." It was easier to return to the original point.

"If he's not the problem, then who is?" Mrs. O asked.

Oh hell. "What makes you think—"

"My eyesight might not be what it was thirty years

ago, but I could see the broody expression on your face from my kitchen window. No woman looks like that unless a man is involved."

Maia ran through her options. She could lie or politely point out that it was no one else's business, but she found herself saying, "I think I saw an old lov— boyfriend today."

"You still have feelings for this man?"

She twisted her fingers together in her lap. "Not the kind you mean."

The older woman put her hands over Maia's, stopping the motion. "He scares you."

She could hardly deny that. "Yeah, he does. He's evil, but I didn't realize that until it was almost too late."

"Is he with the Mob?" Mrs. O whispered the last two words and Maia nearly smiled.

"No, he's not Mafia." If only it were something that benign. The most vicious organized crime boss couldn't hold a candle to a demon like Seth.

"Have you contacted the police? If this man is as bad as you say, they'd want him behind bars."

The police wouldn't have a clue how to handle him. Besides, humans would be no match. That was why the Gineal had taken it upon themselves centuries ago to stop dark-force beings and protect the powerless. "They wouldn't know about him," Maia said cautiously. "He's always kept a low profile."

"But if he's come to hurt you—"

"I don't think he's aware that I'm here," Maia interrupted. "I knew him when I lived in Las Vegas."

Mrs. O gave her hands a squeeze. "If he knows your sister is here, he might have guessed about your presence."

That gave Maia pause. Seth had blurred parts of her memory and she couldn't be absolutely certain that she hadn't told him about Ryne, but protecting her sister was second nature; she didn't think she'd shared anything. Maia wished, though, that she could be positive about that. "Ryne lived in Chicago during the time I knew him. It would be a stretch . . ."

A stretch, but not impossible. If she'd slipped and told Seth about her sister, she could have mentioned the Twin Cities. Ryne had done her training here.

What if he'd decided to get revenge by going after her kid sister? Seth had been beyond furious that night. If Maia hadn't cast him to an alternate dimension, he probably would have killed her then and there. She'd left Vegas the instant she'd had her life sorted out, afraid he'd return sooner than she'd thought possible, and she'd run for Chicago. The Gineal Company was based there and more of her people lived in the Windy City than anywhere else.

Seven years. It was long enough for him to have learned about her new home. Seth would know that killing her would be too easy. If he really wanted to make her suffer, he'd hurt Ryne and let Maia live with the knowledge that it was her fault.

"Drink this," Mrs. O said, pushing her glass back into her hand.

Maia did as ordered. The bite of the lemonade helped her calm down, and when she put it aside, she'd regained control. "Sorry, my imagination ran away from me."

"You went white, dear. If he scares you this badly, you have to go to the police."

She nodded. Her pride would smart, but she'd call Taber. He'd been her mentor when she'd trained to be an enforcer and he sat on the council; he'd know the best way to handle this.

"Make sure you tell your young man, too."

"He's not—" Maia cut off the protest. "I don't—" Oh hell. She didn't want to tell Creed anything, but what if Seth was his assignment? It could be a coincidence that they were both here at the same time. After all, there were too many dark-force beings on the loose now to say conclusively that the two events were connected—except this was exactly the kind of assignment the council would give to the legendary Creed Blackwood.

"Maia?" Mrs. O pressed.

"I thought you said you didn't trust him," she countered.

"I don't, but I *do* believe that he can take care of himself and keep you safe, too. Promise me you'll talk to him."

She hesitated. Yeah, she probably would tell Creed about Seth—even if it wasn't the whole truth—but Maia balked at giving her word on it, and that's what her neighbor wanted.

"Speak of the devil," the older woman murmured.

Maia turned and saw Creed striding along the side of the house. She had to make a decision now or Mrs. Olson might say something to force her hand. "I will talk to him," Maia promised quietly, "but in my own time and in my own way."

The tension left her muscles when the older woman nodded; Maia had expected more of an argument. With that worry off her mind, she returned her focus to Creed. The man could move, there was no doubt about that. He had an athletic grace that she could watch for hours, but since he'd give her grief if he caught her gawking, she looked down to adjust her bracelet.

Creed nodded once when he reached them and said, "Sorry I'm late."

He didn't sound sorry. What he sounded was tired and that had Maia studying him more closely. She'd missed it—too enthralled by his body to pay attention to anything else—but exhaustion was evident on his face. There were fine lines in the corners of his eyes that weren't usually so apparent and he was pale under his dark tan. "Not a problem. Things happen; I understand that."

As his gaze met hers, she knew she'd been right—Creed had gotten a call-out. Not an easy one either, judging from the flatness of his expression.

"It's time for me to go home," Mrs. O said, breaking the unspoken communication.

"You don't have to rush off," Maia said. "Right, Creed?"

"Of course not," he agreed, but she heard politeness, not sincerity, in his voice.

Mrs. Olson shook her head. "*Wheel of Fortune* is on in five minutes and I can't miss my show." The woman put both her hands on the chair arms and pushed slowly to her feet. Maia itched to help, but she knew her neighbor's pride would have her fending off any attempts at assistance.

But when the older lady stood, she swayed precariously and Maia leaped to her aid—only to be vigorously waved away. "Don't be such a fussbudget," Mrs. O snapped and Maia backed off.

When she had her balance, she reached for the glasses and Maia said, "I'll wash them and return them to you." She saw the protest forming and nipped it before it could bloom. "It's the least I can do to say thank you for the lemonade."

"That's okay then." Mrs. Olson stepped away from the table and teetered slightly. Her second step wasn't any steadier and Maia twisted her fingers together.

"I'll see you home," Creed offered.

"I can walk fifty feet on my own," the woman said.

"I'm sure you can, but my grandfather would haunt me if I didn't escort a lady to her door."

Mrs. O stared suspiciously at him for an instant, but he must have passed inspection because she nodded. With more savoir faire than Maia would have guessed he possessed, Creed offered the older woman his arm. That earned him a glare, but she did take it. Reluctantly.

Maia kept an eye on them, but Creed accommodated Mrs. O's much slower pace and his body language showed his attentiveness. Confident that her neighbor was in good hands, Maia sat down again. This facet of Creed was a surprise. She never would have expected solicitousness from him, not when she'd only seen his aggravating side, and it was . . . sweet. Now *that* was a word she never thought she'd associate with the man.

Leaning back in her chair, she continued to observe the duo. She should be thinking about how she'd raise the issue of Seth and how much she should reveal, but instead she found herself wondering about Creed's assignment. He wouldn't tell her anything. She wished she could get used to the secrecy, but despite dealing with it from her sister, Maia still let curiosity get the best of her.

The pair reached Mrs. O's home. Her neighbor dug a key out of the pocket of her housecoat and unlocked the door, but it was barely open when MJ came streaking out.

Maia started to stand. It wouldn't be easy to run in her heels, but she'd have to execute an intercept mission.

She didn't make it to her feet, though, before Creed swooped down and captured the cat. Maia had just began to relax when something odd happened. MJ was genial and liked everyone, even strangers. In fact, she'd never met a friendlier cat. But he didn't like Creed.

With growls and hisses loud enough for her to hear on her patio, MJ bit and clawed at Creed, trying to get free. He hung onto the animal, but it couldn't have been easy with all the twists and gyrations.

Mrs. O took him and MJ quieted immediately, but his ears remained flat to his head. The glare he gave Creed was almost scary.

Maia felt that cold feeling return to the pit of her stomach. Many animals were sensitive and they reacted violently when they came into contact with negative energy. MJ's behavior left her wondering again if Creed had delved into black magic.

7
CHAPTER

Maia pulled on her white and navy-striped polo shirt and zipped her navy Bermuda shorts. Creed had gone to pick something up for dinner, but instead of using the time to call Taber, she'd taken a quick shower.

She needed to think before talking to a member of the council. If she stated her concerns about Blackwood, he'd face an incredible amount of scrutiny and it wouldn't end quickly; he'd be closely monitored for months. It was a terrible thing to do to a troubleshooter if he was innocent. In battle, there was no time to second-guess decisions; if an enforcer needed to go very gray, he had to make the call in an instant, not wonder what the ceannards would think.

Leaning forward to look in the mirror, Maia ran a comb through her hair. Although she'd tried to keep her head out of the water, the ends of her chin-length cut had become damp. Did she need to freshen her makeup?

When she realized she was primping for the man, she dropped the comb and took a step back. Was she out of her mind? Sure, he looked like a fantasy, but the personality was straight out of a nightmare. Blackwood was abrasive, arrogant, condescending, intense, and maybe using dark magic.

Maybe.

Unfortunately, MJ's reaction didn't prove anything. If it were that easy, the Gineal would regularly test themselves with cats. Creed had been on a call-out and had most likely been fighting a demon. If some of that energy was still clinging to him, MJ could have been responding to that.

With a loud sigh, Maia opened the door to her walk-in closet and looked for her sandals. Nothing had ever been simple when it came to identifying Gineal who had fallen to the dark forces. The cleverer someone was about hiding his actions, the longer it took to discover him—and the more dangerous the fight was for the troubleshooter sent after him.

She'd hid her own use of black magic for quite some time, and if Seth hadn't shown up, she might have concealed it for a while longer. For a brief instant, she remembered the power, the sense that she could do anything. Then she forced herself to recall that it was a lie—no one was invincible. No one.

Maia heard the front door open with a sense of relief. She didn't want to spend another night dwelling on her fall, wondering why she'd succumbed. There were no answers, only more questions—only more doubts. Sliding into her sandals, she hurried to meet Creed and see what he'd found for dinner.

She caught up to him in the kitchen and stopped short. He was walking toward the table; the evening sun rode low in the sky, making his nearly black hair gleam.

Maia had never gone for guys whose idea of dressing up was putting on a shirt with a collar, but she had to admit, Blackwood was giving her a new appreciation for jeans and faded T-shirts. It was only when he put the bags down that she was able to pull her attention from him. "Fast food?"

"You got a problem with that?" he asked.

"There was a family restaurant," Maia kept her tone even with effort, "right across the street from that place that does curbside to go. Their menu is a lot healthier than this." She gestured toward the bag.

"Sorry," he apologized. "I felt like french fries and didn't think beyond that."

He really did sound apologetic and that made Maia suspicious. She'd found his original offer to pick up dinner hard enough to believe, but this? It wasn't Blackwood. She decided to give him a push. "You're getting too old to be eating this stuff. I know using magic burns a lot of calories, but at your age, you have to worry about cholesterol and your heart."

"I'm only thirty-five." Creed's voice was tight.

"It's all downhill from here," she said with barely suppressed glee. "I bet a healer has already used the phrase *now that you're over thirty* at least once."

Color touched his cheekbones—anger, she'd bet the bank on it—and Maia knew she'd hit a bull's-eye. The healers could fix just about anything, but they didn't like expending their energy on something that could be easily prevented, and they weren't shy about pointing that out.

"You're over thirty yourself," Creed said.

"Yes, and thank you for mentioning that." The color on his cheeks darkened. "But at least I don't eat that junk."

A muscle jumped in his jaw. "Would you like me to go out and get you something else?"

Now Maia knew for certain he had ulterior motives. "What do you want?"

"I could go for a pop, but if I ask for one, you'll probably lecture me again. I'll drink water."

He'd deliberately misunderstood the question, but instead of calling him on it, Maia took a bottle of water out of the refrigerator and plopped it on the table in front of him. "I don't keep any soda in the house."

"That figures," he muttered.

"What was that?" Maia asked, although she'd heard him plainly.

"I said, that must be why you have such a great figure."

"Uh-huh," she said, skepticism lacing her voice. He definitely wanted something from her and Maia decided to see how much fun she could have with Creed before he either lost his temper or got to the point. "I suppose one meal that's unhealthy won't kill me." She pulled out a chair from the table and sat. "The plates are in that cabinet," she said, pointing.

"Plates? That's what the wrappers are for."

"Never mind," Maia said, sounding greatly inconvenienced. "I'll get them myself."

She began to push away from the table, but before she had the chair back more than a few inches, Creed said, "No, I'll get them. Just relax. I know you worked all day."

He'd worked, too, and not behind a desk, but Maia decided he deserved this for trying to manipulate her. When he put the plates on the table, she waited just long enough for him to think she was happy and then asked for silverware; after that it was a glass, and finally orange juice.

"Anything else?" Creed asked, and though he tried to sound solicitous, she heard the note of irritation.

"Napkins."

"In the bag," he growled. Maia simply beamed up at him, making no attempt to get them herself. After a long moment where they stared each other down, Blackwood reached in, grabbed the stack, and tossed them on the table. "Happy?"

"Yes, thank you." She waited until he'd pulled his own chair out from the table and sat down before she said, "You know, I think I'll have water, too, instead of orange juice. Would you mind getting one for me?"

He did mind, that was obvious. She waited for him to tell her to get it herself, but Creed stood, stalked to the fridge, yanked it open, and retrieved a bottle. "Anything else?"

"No, I'm good."

"Are you sure?"

"Absolutely." He sat down again. "What's for dinner?" she asked, making no move to reach for the food.

Instead of answering, Creed took the sack and handed her a regular bag of fries. He'd gotten the largest size, she noted. "Wait a second," Maia protested. "You get that huge box of french fries and I get this measly little bag? What's up with that, Blackwood?"

"You said this stuff was bad for you." There was a growl in his voice that almost made her laugh.

"It is, but that doesn't mean I want to go hungry." He stared at her. "You could give me some of yours," she suggested sweetly.

With a frown, Creed shook out some fries onto her plate.

"Five? That's all you can spare, Mr. Scrooge?"

His scowl deepened, but he shook out a few extra. Maia raised her brows and waited. He added more, checked her expression, and kept going. When she had nearly half his fries, she said, "Thank you."

Blackwood grumbled softly and reached back in the bag for the burgers. He handed her a regular, put two gigantic ones on his plate, and began unwrapping his meal.

"You're kidding, right?" Maia asked. "You're not really giving me this tiny single and eating both of those yourself."

He stopped, and wordlessly handed her one of his burgers. Maia put hers in his hand, and humming happily, dug into her meal. The burger and fries were too greasy for her and she knew she wouldn't be able to finish everything, but that would just anger Creed all the more.

"As small as you are, how can you eat so much?" he asked after he'd downed his first burger.

"I have a fast metabolism." That used to be true, but now she'd have to double the length of her workouts all week to try to burn off this one meal. The idea didn't make her happy, but Maia knew the memory of the look on Blackwood's face would be enough to keep her going without complaint.

"So your call-out this afternoon was a demon?" Maia asked, pushing on another front.

"Yeah, a groige. Shit, she was a bitch to take down," Creed answered absently as he dipped a fry into a pool of ketchup.

His offhand reply shocked her. She'd expected him to tell her brusquely that she was an outsider, or if he wanted to stay on her good side, to try to fob her off gently. The one thing Maia hadn't been prepared for was that he'd actually answer her with no apparent qualm.

"That's a pretty dangerous branch," she commented

when she regained her equilibrium, "but I thought they usually kept to their own dimension and didn't bother humans."

"They do, but not this one and not today." Creed unwrapped the second burger. "She was doing that rite to take a human's energy and I can't figure out why."

Maia had to search her memory to come up with which ritual he was talking about. "You mean the one where she'd lose part of her own power at the end of a few weeks?"

"Yeah." Creed looked up. "It doesn't make any sense. You can't think of any reason why she'd do it, can you?"

Maia uncapped her water and filled her glass to hide her absolute shock. Roving troubleshooters had always picked up the bulk of the demon call-outs and she couldn't believe he was asking her for enlightenment. "No, I can't, but then I'm still trying to get over my surprise at your candor."

His lips quirked. "The law about silence was put into place during one of the early persecutions when some Gineal who'd ceded their powers bargained with humans to save themselves. The information they passed on ended up costing others their lives. Since we're not being hunted and since you didn't give up your magic to save your ass, I think it's safe to talk—to a point."

"How do you know the reasons for our code of secrecy? I don't remember learning that in my lessons," she said.

That got her a shrug. "I'm interested in our history."

Since she had no clue what to say, Maia went back to her food. It was hard to picture someone who looked like Creed—someone who acted like him—having any kind of scholarly bent, but she should know better. How many times had people judged her by her appearance and been shocked to find she had an IQ higher than her shoe size? Part of it was that he was a troubleshooter and they were men and women of action, but when she'd been a member of the cadre, she had read every book she could find on art. She was doing to him exactly what others had done to her.

"What turned you on to history?" she asked. If she'd had to guess what interested a man like Blackwood, she'd have gone with sports or weapons.

Creed quit eating to study her for a minute. Whatever he was looking for, he must have found because he said, "My grandfather was one of our librarians, he worked in the tasglann. He used to tell me that the best stories were the ones that really happened."

His grandfather had been a dìonachd? And not just any librarian, but an archivist? Maia nearly choked on a fry. There was something strange about their magic. She didn't know how it was different, just that it was. "I didn't think enforcers could be descended from librarians."

"There've been a few of us, but no one other than me in the last five or six generations." Blackwood wiped his hands on a napkin, then reached for his water. "If it makes it any easier for you to believe, my grandmother was a troubleshooter."

"It helps," Maia admitted. "Don't take this wrong, but one of the laoch solas married a dìonachd? Wow."

Creed's lips actually curved. "Yeah, I know, and despite my heritage, the librarians put me on edge as much as they do any other troubleshooter."

"That must have made the holidays interesting."

With another shrug, he picked up his burger again.

Subject closed, Maia thought and bit back a sigh. She shouldn't complain; the amazing thing was that he'd said as much as he had. Since she understood protecting family, she let the topic drop and returned to their original subject. "Is there a particular area of our history you focus on?"

"You mean like troubleshooter fighting techniques in the time of ancient Rome, or the first Gineal persecution during the dark times?" She nodded. "No, I don't concentrate on any one era." Maia scowled at him until he glanced up. When he caught her expression he grimaced, but she didn't cave in under his glare, and he said, "I like to read archived personal journals—any time period."

"Why?" As far as she was concerned, the only thing more boring than history was reading about the day-to-day lives of ordinary Gineal.

"Why do you like to read about art?"

He'd checked out her bookshelves; she should have known he would. "Art history is fascinating. I can see how styles developed and changed, for one thing, and how different movements influenced artists. That doesn't explain your interest."

"We have millions, maybe even billions of spells, yet we use only a small fraction of what there is because of the overwhelming numbers. It's almost impossible to find anything."

Maia nodded. Most of their books were handwritten and few had an index. Even if someone knew exactly what he wanted, it wasn't easy to find. The dìonachd themselves didn't know everything that was available, although most were better versed than the average Gineal—including the troubleshooters. "What does that have to do with journals?"

Creed finished his burger before he said, "Sometimes they wrote about magic. I've read entries that led me to incantations that I never knew existed."

It made sense now—he'd found a shortcut that had

probably saved him months, if not years, of studying texts. Smart. Very smart. She'd have to be careful if she talked to him about Seth or she might find herself revealing more than she intended.

The reminder of her demon sighting made Maia lose her appetite and she pushed her plate away.

"That's all you're going to eat?"

"Yes."

He growled, muttered something she couldn't quite hear, and helped himself to her fries.

"Your arm's still bleeding." Blackwood looked down, wiped his right hand on a napkin, and then dragged his index finger along the scratch on the inside of his left forearm. Maia watched the wound heal and felt a pang of longing. She shunted it aside. "You shouldn't have done that. Mrs. O is going to wonder what happened to the slice."

"She didn't get a good look, but I didn't heal it completely anyhow. If she says anything, I'll just tell her that her hellcat didn't gash me as deep as she thought." Creed reached over and snagged what was left of her hamburger.

Maia shook her head. "How much magic did you burn through fighting the groige anyway?"

Creed polished off the burger before he said, "A lot." Without another word, he began clearing the table.

The message was unmistakable—don't ask anything else. Maia didn't heed it, though. "You almost drained yourself, didn't you?"

He looked at her long enough to cock an eyebrow, then turned back to the sink. She clasped her hands in her lap. In battle, a troubleshooter could use magic much faster than he was able to replenish it. Most of the time, it wasn't an issue, but then there were the assignments that couldn't be resolved quickly. Since Creed fought demons regularly, this wouldn't be his first near miss, but it was the only one Maia knew about.

It was tempting to tell him to sit, that she'd finish cleaning up, but she refused to fuss over him. He wasn't doing this to be nice; he wanted something from her and she couldn't forget that. As he began loading the dishwasher, Maia left the table and went into the living room.

The distance helped put his close call in perspective. She wasn't sure why she was worrying about him; if anyone could take care of himself, it was Blackwood. The rovers were the strongest of the troubleshooters, and he wouldn't appreciate her concern anyway. Agitated, she checked her plants, decided none of them needed watering, and sat on the right side of the couch. She had a feeling she'd want to be comfortable when he finally broached whatever it was that had him acting agreeable.

Reaching for a magazine on her coffee table, she flipped through it, but found nothing that held her interest. She exchanged it for another, but her thoughts wouldn't settle and she gave up on trying to read.

Maia was leafing through an issue of *Smithsonian*, looking at the pictures, when Creed joined her. "Did you want coffee?" he asked.

She closed the magazine and leaned over to put it on the end table. Something about his demeanor had her nerves shrieking and her entire body tensed. Since it would only be worse the longer this took, Maia confronted it head-on. "Why are you being nice?"

"Maybe I'm trying to apologize for leaving you outside in the heat." He looked at the chair opposite her, frowned slightly, and settled on the couch.

The chair was squarely in front of the window, she realized, and Blackwood didn't want his back to the street. Maia shifted, putting more room between them. "I doubt it. You figured I'd understand there was nothing you could do about a call-out and I do. So I repeat— why are you being nice?"

His hesitation tensed her even further. "I want to ask you some questions."

Fortunately, her muscles couldn't become any more rigid, because if she hadn't already been strung tight, her reaction would have put Creed on red alert. "What do you want to ask about?" she managed with calmness she didn't feel.

Another pause. "Demons."

What were the odds that it was nothing more than co-incidence that he was asking her about demons on the same day she'd seen Seth? Slim and none, she decided, but what did Creed know and what was he guessing at? Maia took a deep breath and linked her fingers in her lap before she spoke. "What about them?"

"It's common knowledge that Gineal who use black magic regularly associate with dark-force creatures."

"Most do," she allowed.

He leaned forward. "Did you?"

Maia glanced down at her hands and had to force herself to relax her fingers before he noticed that her knuckles were white. For a microsecond, she considered lying, but it wasn't worth it. "Yes," she said, refusing to elaborate.

Creed stared at her without speaking, but she didn't try to fill the silence. This was a trick all troubleshooters learned, and it was particularly effective on humans, but she couldn't believe he thought she'd fall for it. If he was irritated by her lack of response, it didn't show. At last, he asked, "Did you interact with demons?"

She felt her cheeks heat. Seth didn't count—she hadn't known what he was for a long time—but she had connected with other, weaker demons. A few had even been regulars in her entourage. "Not all of them are pure evil, you know." Maia nearly cringed as she heard the defensiveness in her voice.

"They're all dark and dangerous."

His neutral tone made the way she'd lashed out seem glaring in comparison. She took another deep breath and said more quietly, "Yes, I was friendly with some. Why are you asking? Does this have something to do with your assignment?"

Blackwood ignored her questions. "Was one of them darker and more dangerous than anything you'd felt before?"

Her heart pounded faster and her pulse sped up. He was asking about Seth, he had to be, because when the demon had dropped his mask, Maia had never sensed anything that malevolent before in her life. She'd spent years wondering why he'd latched onto her. There were other Gineal who'd turned and who'd gone deeper than she had. When she noticed Creed was waiting and watching, she pushed her thoughts aside. "Why? Is this the demon the council sent you here to hunt?"

"Just answer the question," he growled.

Her temper started to rise. "Why don't you answer a few of mine?" Maia leaned forward until she was nearly nose-to-nose with him. "This isn't a one-way street."

"I'm the troubleshooter."

"That would be more effective if I hadn't been one myself."

Creed pushed to his feet and made a circuit of the room; his muttered curses had her fighting back a smile. Enforcers were trained to maintain control of their emotions and it pleased her immensely that she'd driven him past the bounds of his restraint. She sobered when it dawned on her that this had merely postponed their discussion. What did she tell him? It sounded as if he was here to hunt Seth, but if that were true, he likely knew more than she did about his quarry.

That left the big question, though. Why did Creed think she had any information about the demon he was after? There was no cause for him to associate Seth with her. None.

Creed stopped in front of her, hands resting on his hips as he glared down at her. "Is there some reason why you don't want to answer me?"

Maia crossed one leg over the other, shooting for nonchalance, and countered, "I could ask the same of you."

After a long moment of consideration, he dropped back on the couch. "I've been a rover for fifteen years and fought a lot of demons in that time, but I've never been after one as dark as this one. He makes the groige seem like Mary Poppins."

She waited for more, but that was apparently all Creed planned to say. Maia considered things, then decided she had to risk it. "Why do you think I know anything about him?"

A flash of something crossed his face so fast, she didn't have time to identify it. Slowly, Maia put both feet flat on the floor and turned to face Creed squarely. "Start talking," she ordered.

It was obvious that he didn't want to, but Maia also read his resignation. Creed knew she wasn't going to back down. To his credit, he didn't turn arrogant and try to insist it was troubleshooter business, but he didn't leap right into an explanation either. Instead, he scowled and stared out the window. She waited, giving him time to collect his thoughts.

At last he said, "I heard the demon use your name."

"My name?" Maia feared her heart would leap from her chest it was pounding so hard. It had to be Seth. He must have seen her and recognized her despite the changes in her appearance. Hell, what was she thinking? Seth could read energy; he'd most likely picked up her signature and identified her from that.

"Yeah, and Maia isn't that common. He must know you and have a reason for using your name."

Like walking out of a library and spotting her pumping gas. Creed wanted an answer and it flustered her. What did she say? How did she explain? How did— Wait a second. If Seth was in that parking lot, how had Blackwood picked up anything?

"Just where were you when you heard him?"

"What do you mean?"

"You know exactly what I mean. Did he show up after you fought that other demon? Did he come up to you on the street corner, say 'Maia,' and run off? What were the circumstances?"

It was nearly imperceptible, but his muscles stiffened, raising red flags in her mind. If they were talking about Seth and if Seth had said her name when he'd spotted her, the only way Blackwood could have heard it was telepathically, because she knew he hadn't been in the vicinity. But while the Gineal were natural telepaths, they couldn't read most dark-force creatures. There was no way he should have been able to pick up on a de- mon's thoughts. Unless he was using black magic.

If she was smart, she'd act normally until she could report this to someone. That wasn't what she did. "How deep are you?" she asked soberly.

"What makes you thi—"

"Cut the bull, Blackwood. I know you didn't physi- cally hear that demon speak, and the only way you could form that kind of mental connection was if you were using magic you shouldn't be."

He turned his gaze on her, his dark brown eyes so intense, Maia almost gasped. "I haven't fallen," he told her.

"But you crossed the line."

"I haven't fallen and I won't."

Only an idiot would argue with him, but that didn't stop her. "You can't be sure you haven't already passed the point of no return. Unless someone deliberately calls the dark forces to himself, the slide is gradual enough that you probably wouldn't notice it happening."

"I know that." Each word was razor sharp.

"I'm reminding you," Maia said quietly, "because it's easy to lose sight of it when you're using black magic."

He locked down, she watched it happen—his face, even his eyes, went blank. "All I get from him is a stray sense every now and then. It's not constant and the connection is nebulous when it does happen. I'm okay, you'll have to trust me on that." After a short pause, he said, "Let's get back to the main issue—how does he know you?"

Maia weighed her options. Blackwood was adamant that he hadn't fallen, and he was convincing, too. She hated the uncertainty, but it had always been difficult when it came to the dark forces. With a sigh, she decided to wait and see. If he had gone over, she'd know— sooner or later. She measured him for another moment, then said, "I've only met one demon that matches your description. He called himself Seth when I knew him. I can't tell you much about him, though, because he hid his true nature from me."

"Where would he go? What would he do? Where would he hide?" The questions came at her rapid fire with no time to formulate a reply. "Well?"

"I don't know. I don't know. I don't know. I think that answers everything."

"Come on, you have to know."

Irritated by his tone, Maia stood and walked out of the room. Tried to anyway. Creed caught her arm before she made it halfway across the floor. "Let go of me," she said coolly.

"No. Don't you understand how important it is to get him?"

Maia raised her free hand and pushed her hair off her face. "I'm aware that Seth is dangerous, but I never learned anything about him that will help you."

"How long did you know him?"

She shrugged. "Five or six months."

"Then you probably know more than you realize."

"Maybe, but I'm not going to rehash every minute I spent with him on the off chance that something might click for you. Hunt him the way you normally do with demons and leave me out of it." She pulled her arm loose and headed for her bedroom.

"Maia," Creed called.

She hesitated, then shaking her head, continued walking. "I can't help you."

"He's after Ryne."

8
CHAPTER

Seth loved the energy of the mall. There was irritation and petulance and anger and a myriad of other roiling emotions that were manna to be savored. He'd have to remember this and return when he could simply enjoy.

A group of men wearing gang colors neared and he drank in their barely leashed violence. All too soon, though, they reached an intersecting corridor and turned off. As much as he wished he could follow them, he had other obligations. Seth searched the crowds, found the two auras he was interested in, and realized they'd stopped to gaze in a store window. He looked around, saw a kiosk selling T-shirts, and pretended to examine them while he kept tabs on the couple.

It was difficult to believe this woman was Maia's sister, but the energy patterns didn't lie.

Maia. Walking out of the library and seeing her unexpectedly . . . Even with her hair cut so short, she was still beautiful. He didn't like the pull of attraction that had gripped him when he'd spotted her earlier this evening. After what she'd done, he shouldn't be remembering the feel of her beneath him or the taste of her skin. And he shouldn't be wondering if she was remembering him tonight as well.

He shook off the thought and refocused on the sister. This woman was pretty enough, but not a beauty like Maia. It mattered not. What he wanted from her had nothing to do with her appearance and everything to do with power.

Seth lightly probed, felt the incredible strength of her magic, and his eyes slid half shut in bliss. He wanted to reach out and grab it, but knew that would do him no good. For now, she was protected—he could be patient. Soon enough her power, and that of the man she was connected to, would be his.

To his disgust, she dragged her companion into the store and Seth knew he'd be in for a wait. He glanced over at the grouping of T-shirt samples he stood in front of, then threw his head back and laughed.

Even as he conjured some money, he was searching for the clerk. It was too perfect to resist. Seth wondered if Maia would find the slogan as humorous as he did, and decided she probably wouldn't. Ah, well, her amusement didn't matter, only his own.

Creed watched Maia come to an abrupt halt and turn to face him. He'd known that would grab her attention. She might be unwilling to take action for her own life, but from everything he'd seen, she'd battle to the death to protect her sister.

"What do you mean, Seth is after Ryne?" she demanded, stalking closer to him with each word. She kept going until the toes of her sandals nearly touched his sneakers.

Her scent teased him. If he'd had to guess, he would have thought Maia would prefer a flowery perfume, but she'd surprised him. Whatever she wore was light, but there was a hint of spice that Creed found intriguing. He wondered where she'd dabbed it—at the pulse point of her throat? Between her breasts? In the hollow behind her knees? Damn, he wanted to discover all those places, and explore them thoroughly.

When he realized he was leaning toward her, Creed crossed his arms over his chest and tried to regain control. Instead of looking away, he studied Maia. She had a sexy mouth. Her bottom lip was fuller than the top and it made him want to nip it, then lick away the sting. He was fighting the urge to do it when she pulled him out of his fantasies.

"Don't you dare go all stone-faced on me now, Blackwood. Talk," she growled. He had to shift away, afraid he'd reach for her if he didn't.

"You want it spelled out?" he asked once he had some distance. "The demon is out for Ryne's blood—get it?"

Fireworks went off in her chocolate-brown eyes. Creed wasn't sure why he'd been deliberately antagonistic, but it wasn't smart. Not only did her temper make him hot, but he needed her cooperation.

"Why?" Maia asked. "There's no reason Seth should know she exists. I never mentioned her. Ever."

He followed Maia's thought process easily. "The demon's not after her because of you. He wants power and she's strong; maybe the strongest among us. Better yet as far as he's concerned, Seth can get to Summers through Ryne and take his magic as well."

Confusion clouded her face before anger returned. "What are you trying to pull?" Maia crowded nearer and raised her chin. "Demons can't take Gineal powers. If they could, we'd be at war with them all the time, but we're not, and when they do make an appearance, they usually bother humans."

"They can take human energy," he reminded her.

"For a short period of time, and the price is much higher than they're usually willing to pay. The groige you fought today was the exception. Are you claiming that they can get the same temporary boost from one of us?"

"Not temporarily. Permanently," Creed corrected.

For an instant she looked worried, then she shook her head. "You're such a liar." Maia stepped back. "I nearly bought your story, but I'm not naïve enough to believe any demon can take our powers, not and be able to use them indefinitely. If that were the case, we'd all know about it."

Creed let her take about a half dozen steps before he said quietly, "There's information stored inside the central library that's been lost to the Gineal for centuries—that's a fact. You want another dose of reality? The council knows more than they tell their soldiers. You *are* naïve if you think otherwise."

Again, she stopped and faced him. Maia measured him, but Creed knew she wouldn't read more than he wanted her to see. "The council is aware that demons can take Gineal magic?"

Shifting, he tucked his hands into the pockets of his jeans before he shrugged and said, "I doubt it."

"Then what are they keeping to themselves? I want an example. Prove that you're telling the truth."

The request didn't surprise him; he would have been disappointed if she hadn't demanded evidence, but it was a no-win situation. "And how do you verify what I tell you? Do you think if you walk up to the ceannards and ask them, they'll confirm or deny it? You're an out-sider." Her cheeks went red at the reminder and he waited a moment. "You'll just have to trust me."

"You're wrong, I don't have to do anything of the sort."

"You'd put Ryne at risk?"

She scowled at him. "I have nothing except your word that she's his target."

This was tricky ground and he had to be careful. "You know Seth. Does he have a reason to be obsessed with gaining power?"

"All demons want more."

Although she sounded sarcastic, the color had drained out of her face and Creed knew he'd hit on something. "Yeah, but how many of them have attempted to go after a Gineal troubleshooter? Your Seth is fixated on Ryne."

Instead of denying any claim to the demon, Maia turned her head and pushed a hand through her hair. When she looked at him again, she said, "You men-tioned that Seth could get Deke's powers through Ryne. That shouldn't be possible."

He noticed she wasn't arguing that the demon couldn't take Gineal magic any longer and that was one step forward. "That's one of those things the council doesn't share with our people."

"Start explaining."

As Creed shook his head, he tugged his hands out of his pockets and gently clasped Maia's shoulders. For an instant, he was distracted by the heat of her skin through her shirt, but he pushed it aside. "No. You keep asking me questions, but you haven't given me any information."

"You're looking to make a trade?" she asked.

To a degree, but he wasn't stupid enough to say that. "Quid pro quo."

"What do you want to know?"

Maia sounded suspicious and Creed tried to pick something relatively innocuous to put her at ease. "Is Seth his real name? That seems strange for a demon."

With a grimace, she took a couple of steps to the sofa and settled on the arm. "What I said was that he told me his name was Seth. He also managed to appear human and I had no idea he was a demon for a long time."

There was something in her voice that made him suspect she was withholding details, but he wasn't certain enough to call her on it. Instead, he asked, "Do you know who he really is?"

Her sigh was almost inaudible. "His true name is Sutekh, but he's better known as Set."

"Set?"

"You know—Egyptian mythology. The evil god of chaos; the one who was reputed to be the slayer of Osiris."

"Fuck. Are you sure?" He held his breath.

Maia shrugged. "Not a hundred percent, no."

Creed felt some of the tension leave his body. "You must be wrong. We were taught that the demons who were powerful enough to be worshipped as gods left this dimension millennia ago."

"True," Maia agreed and linked her fingers in her lap, "but it's not as if our troubleshooters banished them; the demons left of their own free will and who's to say one or more didn't decide to come back? Maybe they never really left in the first place. After all, the whole theory comes from our scholars' interpretation of human lore."

"Hearsay and conjecture," Creed murmured. He leaned his shoulders against the wall and closed his eyes. Maybe Maia was right and they had returned. If Earth was hovering in the shadows of Twilight Time as he believed, then it would make sense that the most powerful of the dark-force creatures had returned in preparation for the final battle. Damn, that meant things had escalated more than he'd realized, more than he'd feared.

"Okay, I shared, now it's your turn to talk."

Slowly, Creed opened his eyes. She appeared militant and there'd be no way to avoid telling her something. "So ask," he said.

Maia pursed her lips and the desire to feel her mouth under his roared back. Creed tightened his hands into fists as he fought the urge to cross the room. His control should be better, but it had been too damn long since he'd gotten laid. He had the demon to blame for that, but even if good old Seth wasn't a factor, Maia was off-limits. He needed a woman with a lot of power and he didn't have time to waste on someone without it. Ryne had been perfect, but she'd gone and fucked up every-thing by falling for Summers.

"You're scowling and I haven't asked anything yet," Maia pointed out.

"I was thinking about something." She opened her mouth, but he brusquely cut her off. "It's personal."

"Well, excuse the hell out of me."

She sounded offended and Creed knew he should apologize—he needed to stay on her good side—but he didn't feel like playing nice anymore. He was tired, frustrated, on edge, and didn't want to be attracted to her. "Are you going to ask a question or do you plan to just pout because I'm not spilling about something that's none of your business?"

Her entire body went ramrod straight. "You're such an ass."

"And your point is?"

Maia was halfway to the hallway before she came to a dead stop. "If you think you're getting out of it this easily," Maia growled, "you better think again. I see your ploy and nothing you do is going to derail me from protecting my sister."

Creed shrugged. It didn't make any difference to him if she stayed or left. He wasn't telling her anything he didn't want her to know, no matter how insistent her questions.

With a low snarl, Maia got in his face again, and with his back to the wall, there was no way for him to put some badly needed distance between them. He started to reach for her, wanting to pull her hips to his, and it took all his restraint not to do it. Was she provoking him deliberately? When he looked into her eyes, Creed realized she was too pissed off to have a clue that she drove him to the edge of his control.

"Here's what I want to know: how did Seth find Ryne?"

"What?"

"You heard me. If he didn't go through me to find my sister, then how did he pick up on her? I doubt he trolled the entire world looking for a strong Gineal."

"I can't answer that." Maia looked suspicious, so he added, "I said I had a vague sense of the demon now and then; it's not like our minds are joined and I can read his every thought." Nothing he'd said was a lie.

"Does the council know why he chose my sister?"

"They're in the dark." Completely in the dark. Maia had made the assumption he'd expected—that his hunting Seth was an assignment. It wasn't. He was doing this on his own time and the ceannards had no idea what he was up to. With a little luck, it would stay that way.

"How—"

"You've had two questions," Creed interrupted. "It's my turn to ask another."

"You haven't told me anything yet."

"Is it my fault you didn't ask the right things?"

Creed wouldn't have thought she could get any closer without touching him, but Maia went up on her toes, going nose-to-nose with him. "Uh-uh, that's not how it works. Quid pro quo means information for information, not question for question. Now, how can Seth get to Deke through Ryne? That doesn't make any sense."

He debated challenging her definition of their deal, but decided what Maia wanted to know was innocuous in the scheme of things, and it was time to rack up some goodwill points. "They have something called a true soul pairing. It's when two troubleshooters connect on every level," Creed explained without being asked. "If Seth overcomes Ryne, he'll have free access through her to Summers' magic because he's barely begun training to be an enforcer."

Maia eased down until both feet were flat on the floor. "If Deke is the weaker link, why doesn't Seth go through him to get Ryne's power? That would be more logical."

"I don't think he can," Creed said, "but that's a theory, not fact. Besides, the demon would be fighting Ryne either way, because she'd sense the instant he tried anything like that and go after him. You saw how protective she is of Summers; she'd fight more fiercely for him than for herself."

"Yeah." Maia took a step away. She started to say something, stopped herself, then asked, "Why haven't I ever heard of this soul pairing thing?"

She sounded so dubious, Creed had to fight to keep his expression neutral. Smart not to trust him, but he was telling the truth about that. "It's something that the council has deliberately kept from the Gineal, but it's real. It can only happen between two troubleshooters, and it allows the couple to not only share their magic but to increase it—the sum of the whole is greater than its parts. Plus, they develop a mind shield strong enough to block the enticement of the dark forces entirely. Those are the biggest benefits."

"Why is it a secret then?" Maia asked. "You'd think the council would encourage these pairings."

"You'd think," he said dryly and shifted to give himself more space. "The problem is that it doesn't happen with every set of enforcers just because they form a relationship. Your parents had that bond, but Sinclair Duncan's parents don't."

Maia scowled and Creed knew why. Sin Duncan was another troubleshooter and he'd been her sister's best friend—until it became known that Ryne's mentor had been playing on the dark side. His desertion had hurt Ryne more than any other and Creed guessed Maia wouldn't be forgiving of that.

Creed shrugged when she didn't comment. "Troubleshooters are predisposed to seek more power anyway. What would happen if this were common knowledge?"

"I get it. Enforcers would be so busy trying to develop a pairing with each other that they'd ignore the other Gineal and maybe miss who they're supposed to be with. Even worse would be the issues it might raise with our people. There's some jealousy anyway, but if we isolated ourselves from the general population in that way, it would cause trouble."

"Yeah," he agreed, "and we can't afford that right now."

"The Gineal can't afford it at any time," Maia corrected. "What are you doing to find Seth?"

Creed had known he wouldn't divert her for long, not when Maia was all about protecting Ryne. "I've been canvassing the area, trying to pick him up. I haven't had any luck and I can't risk continuing this strategy, it's too time consuming. That's why I want intel from you about his likes and dislikes, where he used to hang out when you knew him, and things like that."

Maia stepped back and returned to the couch. As she sat down, she said, "If I could help you, I would, but I honestly don't know anything that will do any good. I thought he was human and that he had a job. What was he doing for those hours every day?" She held out her hands palm up. "Who knows?"

"What did you do when he was with you?"

She went still, then her lips quirked. "Often we did whatever I wanted—dinner, a show, hanging out at nightclubs with the group. He was charming and agreeable."

"Unlike me," Creed tacked on for her. He didn't wait for Maia to comment. "Nightclubs? You drank?" That stunned him, since even a tiny amount of liquor made control of their magic uncertain.

"Of course not, but they were places to see and be seen. And I'd gone deep enough by then that I liked the atmosphere."

He understood what she was telling him—her perception of events wasn't completely clear. Dark magic changed people and they reached a point where it was all about them. If someone or something didn't have a direct impact on her, Maia was unlikely to recall that it had happened. Like attracted like, so probably Seth wouldn't have gone near her if she hadn't been so far gone, but it was a bitch now when Creed needed information.

"It's more than that," Maia said quietly, following his thoughts without him saying a word. "Seth blurred my memory." Her smile held no amusement. "I don't know how much is affected, but enough that there are things I can't be sure of."

After mulling that over for a moment, he asked, "Did you ever feel the full extent of his power?"

"Once. Briefly. There's no way you can begin to imagine his strength." She locked her gaze with his. "I'll work with you every minute of every day until we bring him down. I don't want him anywhere near my sister."

"Whoa! Wait a sec. Define 'work with you.'"

"I mean that I'll take vacation time from my job and be at your side offering whatever help and advice I can for as long as it takes you to neutralize Seth."

"Are you out of your fucking mind?" Maia went rigid, but Creed didn't give a shit. "You're powerless, remember?"

"So?"

"So? *So?*" He went over to her and leaned over, glaring into her eyes. "I don't have time to babysit you."

Neither his size nor his tone seemed to intimidate her. "No one is asking you to watch over me. You worry about Seth and I'll worry about myself."

"Right," Creed drawled sarcastically, "that's going to work. He could decide to use you against me, then what? Do you think if you flash that smile, Seth will be so bowled over by your beauty that he'll leave you alone? You can't be that stupid."

He wanted her angry, so pissed off that she wouldn't look beyond his words. Her lack of magic was a genuine concern, but he had other reasons to keep her out of it—like the fact that his bond with the demon was deeper than he'd led her to believe.

Except she didn't become mad. Maia's lips turned up. "Why not? Seth has been ensnared by my appearance before, who's to say it won't happen again?" She sobered. "It doesn't matter, though. I was a Gineal troubleshooter—I know the risks. You do what you need to do to eliminate Seth and I'll do what I have to in order to stay alive and out of your way."

"No."

"Yes. This is my sister he's after." She leaned forward. "You either include me or I'll work on my own, but I'm not sitting on the sidelines."

He pivoted away from her, so frustrated he couldn't stand still. As he paced the room, Creed tried to figure out how the hell to dissuade her. Maia was deceptively soft. She looked all pliable and sweet, but beneath the surface was a spine made of steel. He glanced over, saw her amusement, and swallowed a growl. It took another couple of circuits before it occurred to him that she was bluffing. She believed her threat would encourage him to keep her at his side, but she certainly wouldn't act alone no matter what she claimed, not when she hadn't even taken down that olteil.

Creed stopped in the middle of the room, hooked his thumbs through the belt loops on his jeans, and said, "You do what you have to do."

When Maia nodded her head and didn't argue further, he breathed a silent sigh of relief. She *had* been bluffing.

Before he could formulate more questions about the demon, she spoke. "You haven't said anything to Ryne yet, have you?"

"What makes you think that?" Creed replied cautiously. This was another field full of land mines. One wrong step and Maia could cause his plans to blow up in his face.

"Because Ryne is too furious at you right now to listen, and since you're not a complete idiot, you'd realize that."

Despite himself, Creed's lips curved. "Thanks. I think."

"But you have to tell her, even if you have to sit on her to get her to hear you out."

Shit, this was exactly what he'd been afraid of, and if he didn't do some fast talking, he would lose control of the situation. "And what's the first thing Ryne's going to do if she knows about Seth?"

"She'd work with you—"

Creed cut Maia off. "Like hell she would; you know your sister better than that. Ryne would go after Seth herself." There was silence. "Wouldn't she?"

"Yes," Maia agreed softly. "But if she's as strong as you say, and if she's got extra power from her soul pairing thing with Deke, then maybe she should be the one to—"

He interrupted again. "Summers is untrained as a troubleshooter. Shit, he's untrained in magic, period. Until four months ago he was a dormant, and Ryne's got a lot of teaching left to do. How do you think he'd fare against a demon like Seth? And if you believe your sister could keep him out of it, you better reconsider. You've seen the two of them together; one's as protective as the other."

It was his turn to bluff. Summers wasn't as vulnerable as Creed wanted Maia to believe, and if Ryne had explained her lover's talent to her sister, Creed was sunk. He was betting, though, that Ryne hadn't said a word. It was against Gineal law to share anything about their people with an outsider, and when it came to the rules, no one was more hidebound than Ryne.

Creed didn't breath easily until Maia nodded. "Does she have any experience fighting demons?"

"Not much," he said. "I think the council assigned her to take down a pair from one of the weaker branches about three years ago, but the rovers get the demons with any real power."

Maia stared at him for a moment, then said, "Okay, for now, we'll keep Ryne out of it. She *would* go after Seth if she knew about him, and you're right about Deke being right there with her. Besides, if Seth is after Ryne's power, the last thing we need is for her to put herself directly in his sights."

The words *for now* made him uneasy, but Creed decided he'd worry about them later. Maia stood and began to walk out of the room, everything apparently settled as far as she was concerned. In a minute, he'd go after her, but right now, he needed to clear his mind and ensure she didn't suspect that he was withholding information.

Maia would slit his throat if she learned he planned to use Ryne as bait.

9
CHAPTER

Maia went down to her basement, flipping the light switches on as she proceeded. Creed was going to be chasing after her in a minute, asking questions, and she'd have to answer them. Somehow. She headed straight for her built-in and dug through the drawers, looking for a particular crystal. Moldavite helped latent memories come to the surface, and after what Seth had done to her mind, she needed any boost she could find.

When she'd ceded her powers, she'd left everything that accompanied being Gineal behind. Ryne had gotten Maia's half of the family library, her other tools and implements had been given away, and she'd only done energy work twice in the last seven years—the night her sister had nearly been killed, and for Creed when he'd been hurt. Maia had held onto her stones, though, unwilling to part with them. But while she hadn't wanted to lose this piece of her past, she'd had no desire to handle the crystals either. Instead, she'd dumped them in this drawer and hadn't looked at them again.

As she shifted the rocks, she caught a glimpse of olive green, and in an instant, had her hand wrapped around a hunk of moldavite. The vibration of the stone was intense, almost more than she could tolerate after years without touching it, but she let herself sink into the resonance anyway. Ryne was in danger and Maia would walk into hell itself if she had to.

She strained to hear if Blackwood was moving around, but it was silent. He should have been right behind her, demanding answers. Why wasn't he? If he didn't come down in a minute, she'd have to go upstairs and find him.

Maia was determined to help bring Seth down. If she asked for official permission, the council would tell her to stay out of this and let Creed take care of his assignment. She understood that. In normal circumstances, her involvement could endanger Ryne further.

This situation, however, wasn't usual.

Blackwood couldn't be trusted. If he was using dark magic—and she'd had more than one indication that he might be—Seth would find it easy to influence Creed.

Reporting him wasn't a viable option. Who else were the ceannards going to give the mission to? Another rover? It was widely known that Blackwood was the strongest of the ten—Ryne called him the biggest badass troubleshooter the Gineal had—and he had the best chance to defeat Seth. Besides, he and Ryne had been friends for years. Maybe things weren't rosy now, but on some level, that might make a difference. She couldn't leave her sister's safety completely in his hands, however.

Not until Maia was certain that he hadn't strayed too far.

Her fingers clutched the crystal she held. Why did

everything surrounding the dark forces have to make life so damn difficult? If only there were some way to measure how deep Creed had gone, some way to know whether he'd protect Ryne or hurt her.

With a sigh, Maia shut the drawer and crossed the room to go back upstairs. It would make everything much simpler if she could tell her sister that Seth was after her, but Creed had been right about Ryne's response—she'd initiate a confrontation. Damn Ryne and her kick-ass mindset and damn Blackwood for not being above suspicion.

Maia closed the door to the basement sharply behind her. It was only then that she realized how dark it had gotten and that neither she nor Creed had bothered to turn on any lights upstairs. Maybe that was for the best. It would offer her some privacy as they talked about Seth.

Her temper climbed when she saw Creed standing exactly where she'd left him. Didn't he care enough about stopping that damn demon to follow her downstairs and demand answers? This was *her sister* in danger, and even if Blackwood was pissed off about Deke acing him out for Ryne's affections, Creed should still work hard to protect his friend.

Before she could blast him, common sense returned. If Maia wanted to stick close, she couldn't put his back up. "Are you ready to talk about Seth?"

"I thought you said you didn't know anything."

She picked up the light mockery in his voice, but opted not to call him on it. "I don't think I'm aware of anything helpful, but I'm willing to tell you what I can recall." Maia showed him the crystal she held. "And I have some assistance."

He snorted and she gritted her teeth to contain the torrent of words. A lot of troubleshooters looked at stones as a crutch for those who were less powerful, but most kept their thoughts to themselves. Maybe she hadn't been as strong as Blackwood, but she'd had more than enough magic to be an enforcer. Maia's personal opinion was that some people had an affinity for gems and some didn't. Obviously, this man didn't.

"I was thinking," she said, voice tight, "about what Seth liked to do, and I realized that he often steered the group toward nightclubs. There were times he talked me into going when I hadn't been interested."

"What kind of clubs?" Creed asked, but he didn't sound particularly excited.

"The upscale kind. Very upscale."

Talking about it brought back some memories. How many times had she and Seth sat in one of those bars, surrounded by her entourage? It wasn't that she'd never been alone with him, but she'd had her followers along more often than not. One side of her mouth quirked up. She'd been a different person then and that hadn't been because of black magic. Once, she'd been vivacious, friendly, outgoing, and certain she held the world by the tail. She'd been dead wrong.

Despite the shadows of late evening concealing her face, she went over to sit on the sofa, needing distance between her and Creed. The last thing she wanted was for him to see the ghosts in her eyes. "What?" she asked when she realized he'd been speaking to her.

"I said," Creed enunciated carefully, "he was probably soaking up the energy in those places. Desperation is a heady emotion for demons."

"They prefer anger, jealousy, hatred, and distrust."

With a nod, Creed crossed his arms over his chest and asked, "What did he do while you were in the clubs? Drink? Dance?"

Rubbing her thumb over the rough edges of the crystal,

Maia closed her eyes and tried to visualize a typical night. "Nothing alcoholic," she murmured. Her human circle had teased both of them about their beverage choices. A flash of sensation hit her, the sense of her body sliding against Seth's as he moved within her. She barely stopped the grimace. "Mostly, he liked to watch people, to listen to them."

"Which clubs in the Twin Cities would he gravitate toward?"

"I have no idea."

"Come on," he growled.

"I'm not being coy. I don't know. I haven't gone to any since I moved here." Maia hadn't done anything reminiscent of that time in her life.

"Can you ask someone?" The question was nearly snarled.

"Yes, but the people I know now don't have enough money to waste at places like that."

He muttered something she couldn't make out and settled on the coffee table in front of her. Their knees bumped and Maia shifted hers to the side, not wanting to touch him. "Just talk to them, okay? Maybe someone celebrated an anniversary or a birthday at a club like that, or maybe someone dated a man who could afford it. People can surprise you."

"I'll ask," she said, an edge in her voice despite her attempt to sound neutral.

Creed nodded and leaned forward, resting his hands on either side of her legs. "What else can you tell me about the demon?"

Maia was aggravated enough that she wanted to say something deliberately shocking, like maybe what Seth's favorite position had been, or what he liked to do after they came. Those memories were unobstructed, maybe even deliberately sharpened, but she reined in the impulse before she surrendered to it. The last thing she wanted to do was share her sexual history with Creed.

"Instead of badgering me," Maia suggested as a sudden idea occurred to her, "why don't you do a demon summoning? You know Seth's name now and it would be easier than going through this."

Because of how close he sat to her, she could plainly see the fierce scowl he directed at her. "Didn't you learn anything as an apprentice? The stronger demons can't be summoned against their will, and Seth is infinitely more powerful than even the darkest branch."

She frowned right back at him. "First of all, not everyone receives the kind of demon training that you and Ryne got. Apparently, my magic was never great enough to make me a candidate for a rover. Second, maybe we don't know how to summon the strong branches now, but that doesn't mean our ancestors didn't. There were larger numbers of powerful demons roaming loose then, including Seth and his kind. Have you thought about looking for something like that in your journals?"

For an instant, he appeared startled, then a thoughtful expression crossed his face. "That's not a bad idea," Creed said slowly, "but since I can't count on finding anything, or depend on finding it in time, tell me more about Seth."

"Why don't you try asking more specific questions?" Maia suggested. "Maybe that will jog my memory."

"You said you saw Seth's full power once. Which of the elements did he show an affinity for?"

Tilting her head back, Maia closed her eyes and tried to think back to that night. Like the Gineal, demons worked with the four elements, and like her people, they usually preferred one over the others. "The information on Set is that he was a fire god, but I can't bring to mind anything firsthand."

Creed's hands pressed harder into the couch, making the cushions beneath her move. Maia knew he was frustrated, but she was, too. It wasn't easy to have pieces of the past stolen, to sometimes wonder what was gone.

He straightened, resting his forearms on his thighs. "Did the demon hang out with certain types of people?"

Before Maia could say anything, she heard a thud against the side of her house. "What was that noise?"

"Don't try to avoid the question."

"I'm not. I heard something." She made a move to stand, but because of Creed's nearness, she couldn't get to her feet. "Move out of the way."

There was a second thud and Creed's demeanor changed, going from dismissive to alert. He was up and on his way through the kitchen by the time she stood. Maia chased after him, racing out the open utility room door. She caught a glimpse of his back as he rounded the corner of her house and headed for the front. Shaking her head, she followed him.

Creed slowed, hugged the side of the structure. He stopped at the front corner, and just as she neared him, he began drawing power from the earth.

Maia identified the two shapes standing on the sidewalk about the same time Creed pulled back his hand. Terror seized her vocal cords. *Oh my God!* Heart in her throat, she leaped the distance between her and Blackwood, grabbing his arm. He got the shot off anyway.

She clung to his biceps and held her breath. Luckily, the lightning bolt sailed over the boy's head, but only because the kid had bent down. Creed started to draw more power and Maia gave his arm a yank. Terror morphed into fury. "What are you doing?" she yelled at Creed.

The two boys began running and Maia called out, "Jimmy Taylor, Austin Hughes, I see you. You stop right where you're at or I'll be on the phone before you're halfway home." She hoped only she heard the waver in her voice.

They went still so fast, it would have been amusing if she wasn't so angry at Blackwood and horrified over his actions.

"Get back over here," she ordered the teenagers, trying to exude authority although she was shaking with fear and rage over what had almost happened. Giving Creed's arm another yank, she demanded in a hot whisper, "What the hell is wrong with you?"

He looked at her, but didn't answer.

Without a backward glance, she went around the side of the house and down the front steps until she was standing in front of the boys. Something squished and crunched under her sandal. She looked down and saw egg yolk and broken shell. "You were egging my house?" Maia asked even though she knew they were.

"No, we'd never do—"

"You were not only going to vandalize my house, but now you're going to lie to my face?"

The boy dropped his gaze and she looked at Austin. "It's not vandalizing, Ms. Frasier," he said.

She felt Creed at her back and stiffened before she said to the teen, "You might think egging is only a prank, but do you know how difficult it is to get dried eggs off a house?" He shook his head. "I guess you'll be finding out tomorrow."

That jerked Jimmy's head up and they both gaped at her. "We ain't gonna—"

"Oh, yes you are."

"You can't make us," Austin jumped in.

At five-foot-ten, Maia was taller than both fifteen-year-olds and she used the height advantage as she stared sternly at them. She didn't ease up until they shifted uncomfortably. "I might not be able to *make you* do anything, but you have a choice. Either you come here tomorrow and clean up all the eggs, and I mean thoroughly, or I'll be on the phone with your families. Austin, your grandmother has been working two jobs for years so that you can go to college. What do you think she's going to say when she finds out what you did tonight?"

The boy's lower lip actually quivered before his head dropped.

"And Jimmy, at the last neighborhood block party, your father was bragging you up, talking about how you'd become such a responsible young man. He was proud of the example you were setting for your younger brothers and sisters. Do you think he'll be proud when he finds out what you did tonight?"

"No, ma'am." He hung his head, too.

Creed shifted behind her and Maia turned to glare at him. He held both his hands up in surrender. She focused her attention on the teenagers again.

"I'm being generous by offering you a choice. I could call both your families right now or I could contact the police to report your actions and let *them* call your families. Instead, you have a chance to keep this between us. What's it going to be, boys? Is my house going to look pristine by the time I get home from work tomorrow evening or should I get the phone?"

"We'll clean it up," Jimmy said.

"Yeah, it'll be perfect; you don't have to call my gram," Austin added earnestly.

Maia nodded. "Good. I'd recommend starting first thing in the morning because it'll be easier. Once the sun has had a chance to bake the eggs, cleanup will be much harder."

After some more assurances that of course they'd take care of it right away and that her house would look better than it had before their nighttime foray, Maia gave them permission to leave. Neither teen wasted any time getting out of her vicinity.

Only when they were out of earshot did she relax the tight grip she had on herself. Her knees buckled, but Maia locked them and took a deep breath. When she was back in control, she pivoted to face down Creed. "What in the name of hell were you thinking?" she demanded, so furious her voice was shaking. "You could have killed those boys with that lightning bolt."

"I fired over their heads."

She curled her hands into fists to hide her shaking. "You think you're going to lie to me, too? I saw it, Blackwood. The only reason your shot missed Jimmy was because he bent down. If he hadn't, that boy would be dead right now. So I repeat, what the hell were you thinking?"

Creed's shrug held a complete lack of concern. "There was a threat; I answered it."

"You overreacted," Maia pointed out. "Some problems don't require magic or force."

Stepping around him, Maia headed back to her house. She had more she wanted to say, but she didn't think she could keep her fear under control. The Gineal *protected* humans. Blackwood, however, had not only endangered those two kids, he didn't seem to care.

How deep was he? And sweet heaven, how could she trust him to save her sister?

* * *

Creed sat slouched in the chair on Maia's patio and stared out into the yard. She'd gone straight to her bedroom after she'd dealt with the boys, and although he needed more answers about the demon, he hadn't gone after her.

What in the name of hell were you thinking?

He didn't have a fucking clue. One minute he'd been moving to the front of the house in order to assess the situation, the next he'd seen that lightning bolt streaking through the night. It scared the shit out of him, because he had no memory of firing it. None. After Maia had left him to confront the boys, he'd even checked around, looking for who had been responsible, but there'd been no sign of anyone.

She said he'd been the one to shoot and Creed had no reason to doubt her. Maia had been directly behind him. Another memory lapse. More than a lapse. He hadn't just lost time and awoken somewhere strange this go-round.

Every day he was losing more control.

It didn't matter. He wasn't going to fall. Like he'd told Maia, he couldn't. The Gineal needed him; they needed all their troubleshooters right now and for the foreseeable future.

Most of his people didn't like to talk about Twilight Time, they didn't even want to think about it, but nearly all societies on Earth had an end-times prophecy. Theirs dated from before the Gineal had a written language, passed along from generation to generation. After reading a number of accounts, he'd decided that it had been remembered with great accuracy.

Terrifying accuracy.

Uneasily, he shifted in his chair. Twilight Time was often referred to as the final battle between the dark forces and the light, and God knew, the troubleshooters would be on the front lines. If they won, there'd be a thousand years of peace and enlightenment. If they lost, Earth would descend into a nightmare of hellish proportions.

They had to prevail. The alternative didn't bear thinking about.

Too many troubleshooters had been lost in the last twenty years. They'd fallen to the dark like Anise MacAlister, or they'd died in the line of duty—and then there was Maia, who'd ceded her powers. Their ranks were more depleted now than they'd been in hundreds of years, and he'd almost diminished their numbers by one more by withholding information from Ryne.

Creed scrubbed both hands over his face. He didn't blame her for not trusting him. Not only could he have gotten her killed, he'd done it for no other reason than he'd been feeling vindictive. He'd had plans for her, damn it, and she'd fucked them up royally.

And if he were being fair, he couldn't blame her for that either. He'd had six years to make a move before she met Summers, and Creed had never so much as kissed her. The *why* wasn't a mystery—he hadn't wanted to. And in his arrogance, he'd assumed she'd welcome him when he finally got around to it.

Idiot.

He grimaced. Maia would be calling him a hell of a lot worse than that if she ever learned that he'd coldly and dispassionately decided to develop a true soul pairing with her sister. He'd wanted the extra power and the edge in holding out against the lure of the dark forces.

They whispered to him, cajoled, and enticed. And sometimes he didn't know if they came from outside or if they were already within.

That thought brought him full circle.

The Gineal needed Ryne, and yeah, even Summers,

untrained though he was. Creed snorted. By the time the man was ready to fight, the war would likely be over. But Summers anchored Ryne, and she was probably the most important of them all.

It was almost laughable. Creed knew he had a reputation for being the strongest, baddest troubleshooter, but Ryne was more powerful. Their test scores were supposed to remain confidential, but he'd gotten a look at them, and she was off the charts. The only reason she wasn't a rover already was that no position had opened up since she'd finished her training.

He grimaced, impatient with his thoughts. *Seth,* he reminded himself. If he did nothing else, Creed had to stop the threat that demon posed. Had it been *his* influence tonight that had him shooting at those kids? "Shit."

Straightening in his seat, Creed ran down what he'd learned from Maia. Seth liked nightlife. That gave Creed a place to start. Even if he didn't know specifically which clubs were the upscale type that the demon preferred, he could hit downtown Minneapolis and check a few of them out. Who knew? Maybe he'd get lucky.

Her idea about looking for a summoning spell wasn't a bad one either. That would eliminate the game of hide-and-seek—if he could find an incantation that would work on that demon—but she'd also had another good point. Once, long ago, the demons who'd been worshipped as gods had lived on Earth and the Gineal troubleshooters had likely had a few run-ins with them. If an enforcer had fought one, it was on record. Somewhere. His people had been diligent about documenting everything. It was one of the reasons they couldn't find things now when they needed them—the sheer volume of information.

Decision made, he sent out a telepathic request. It

only took a moment for a transit to open and a young woman stepped through. "Cousin Fia," he said, trying to sound friendly, "thanks for coming."

She looked suspicious. "How can I assist you, laoch solas?"

Fia's use of his title indicated she wasn't going to be a pushover. "I need some research done," Creed said, opting to cut to the chase. "It's critical."

"Then you need to follow procedure and put in a formal request. I'm not on duty tonight." She pivoted and started toward the transit.

"You'd turn your back on family?"

That halted her in her tracks and she swiveled back to level a glare at him. "Your grandfather and mine were second cousins or something," she said. "We have a connection, but we're hardly family."

"Second cousin or not, my grandfather saved your grandfather's life and you wouldn't be here today if he hadn't."

She growled and Creed would swear he heard her grind her teeth. Looked like Fia had done some growing up since the last time he'd talked to her. "I'm certain," she said at last, "that your grandfather received proper thanks."

"There's a demon on the loose," he said, picking up on the slight note of resignation in her voice. "He's dangerous and he's after one of our troubleshooters." She opened her mouth to speak, but Creed kept going, not giving her a chance to shore up her weakness or argue with him. "I received intel that his name is Seth aka Set aka *Sutekh*."

Fia gasped. "Those demons left Earth millennia ago!"

"That's what I said, too, but if my source is right, at least one of them is back. Do you get how important this is now?"

"For something this critical, you should talk to our head librarian and have Galen assign a senior dìonachd to the task."

"I can't go through channels," Creed said and he carefully took hold of her shoulders. "If I do, it will be logged, and you can imagine the reaction of our people to such news. And it might not be Set, anyway. What point is there in alarming others over information that might not be accurate?"

"But—"

"I need to know everything you can find out about Set under any of his names." He bulldozed over her protest. "I also want you to discover if one of our ancestors recorded a summoning spell powerful enough to pull one of the god-demons—if that's who this turns out to be."

"You can't be serious."

"I am serious. He has to be stopped, and if I can't hunt him down, I need to bring him to me."

She shook her head. "You're insane."

Creed managed a grin that felt real enough. "That's in the job description." Giving her shoulders a gentle squeeze, he released her. "I know I'm asking you to give up your free time, but families—no matter how distant—stick together. Don't they?"

Fia sighed, and with obvious reluctance said, "Okay. What else can you tell me about him?"

"Not much. He's apparently been around for the last seven-plus years, but his whereabouts during most of that time are unknown. I'm more interested in when he was deified in the past; it's unlikely he would have hidden his powers then. This is a general search, so I'm looking for anything you can find. I can have you focus in on a particular area later if needed."

"You assume much, laoch solas."

"It's one of my endearing qualities."

Shaking her head again, she said, "I'll consult with Dìonachd Galen about where to start and get back to you shortly."

"No. You alone, Fia, do you understand me?" That was all he needed. Only when she looked at him oddly did Creed realize how hard and cold he'd sounded. He softened his tone. "Galen is bound to follow procedure and that means a log, but you researching as a favor to family doesn't require the paperwork. I'll need your word that you'll remain quiet."

Her hesitation lasted long enough for Creed to worry, but at last, Fia gave her promise. She repeated his request, making sure she had the details right, then walked through the transit. As it winked closed behind her, he heard a gasp.

Mrs. Olson stood behind him, clutching her cat, and even at this distance in the dead of night, Creed saw her shocked expression.

Shit.

10
CHAPTER

She'd quit her job.

Maia knew she should be panicking, not calmly driving down the street. There were bills to worry about—not the least of which was her mortgage—and health insurance. Her hands should be shaking, she should be in such a state that she needed to pull over and regain control.

What she felt, though, was free.

It was as if a thousand-ton weight had been lifted from her, and for the first time in years, she could breathe again. If she pulled over, it would be to get out of the car and do a little jig, that's how excited she was.

The traffic light in front of her turned yellow and Maia glided to a stop. Her boss had told her she couldn't take vacation. He'd called her into his office and said he only granted time off if the request was made two weeks in advance. Her explanation that it was a family emergency hadn't swayed him. The rules were the rules. That was when she'd felt panicked. Ryne was in danger and this man didn't give a damn about anything except his own bureaucratic nonsense.

So she'd quit.

It had taken less than fifteen minutes to clean out her cube and turn in her badge. The boss had blustered, said she had to give notice, but she'd ignored that and visited HR. She'd filled out the paperwork to convert her vacation to cash and walked out the door. Maia smiled. She couldn't help it.

As the light turned green, she moved her foot to the accelerator and replayed the look on her boss's face. The smile became a laugh. That alone was worth the months of macaroni-and-cheese dinners she'd be facing if she couldn't land another job quickly.

She'd worry about a new position later, though; the most important thing right now was keeping her sister safe. This was all her fault. Blackwood might say Seth hadn't used Maia to find Ryne, but it didn't matter—she knew the truth. Seth had promised he'd take his revenge.

Maia nearly drove past the store, but then she saw *it* in the window. She had to brake hard, earning her a honk from the driver behind her. Her cheeks heated at her carelessness. With a short wave of apology, she turned into the parking lot and pulled into a spot just to the left of the door.

As soon as she had her car turned off, she was out and headed for the front of the building. For a long moment, she simply stared at the display.

The pyramid was at least three feet high and each block was a different color. Its shades graduated so smoothly, though, that they seemed to flow from one piece into the next with no end. Maia sighed softly, amazed by the artistry.

It was more than its beauty that held her in thrall, however. Seth had loved anything with ties to ancient Egypt. How could she have forgotten that? Maia hadn't understood it when she'd believed him to be human, but when she'd learned the truth, it made sense. Why wouldn't he be attracted to items that reminded him of the time when he'd been considered a god? If Seth had seen this, he would have had to stop and look at it.

Would he have gone inside the store? Maia stepped back in order to see the sign on the building's facade—it was a New Age shop. She pursed her lips as she considered.

Seth hadn't liked being around humans that vibrated at a higher resonance than most, and the majority of the people who would come to a place like this fell into that category. She'd seen him recoil once when they'd been out and run into someone who had been particularly enlightened.

But New Age stores also attracted customers who weren't on the light path—maybe enough of them to counteract the energy of those who were—and his fixation on Egypt hadn't been something Seth had been able to control. They'd spent evening after evening at the Luxor because he couldn't stay away. If they'd been near enough for him to see the hotel, it was as if he had an itch that he couldn't ignore.

That decided it, as far as she was concerned. She walked to the door and opened it. A musical chime sounded, and the first thing Maia noticed was the sweet, smoky scent of sandalwood incense. She grinned. Was there a New Age store that didn't burn sandalwood incense?

Still smiling, she looked around. There was a section with tarot and other divination cards, and the corner had shelving filled with books. As if real magic spells could be found in mass-market paperbacks. There were glass cases near the register filled with jewelry—some of it quite beautiful—a few drums hanging from the walls, a row of smudge sticks, candles, aromatherapy gear, and of course, the incense. She didn't spot any fetishes or other items she associated with black magic, and Maia relaxed.

The store was light, airy, and uncluttered—not what she'd expected. Granted, she hadn't been in many places like this, but the few she had gone inside had been cramped. They'd all had wood floors and tall, darkly stained shelving units looming over the customers. In that atmosphere, the sandalwood had seemed cloying, and she'd escaped as quickly as possible. Here, though, it didn't overpower.

The pyramid was accessible from the inside of the shop and she went to have a closer look. Do Not Touch. The sign was small, but its placement ensured it couldn't be missed.

Sunlight hit the pyramid, sending a rainbow of color dancing in the beams. The urge to run her fingers over the smooth side had her curling her hands. Her attraction had always been to paintings more than glasswork, but she couldn't deny the beauty of this piece.

"It's stunning, isn't it?" a voice asked.

Maia shifted to look at the woman standing behind her. To her great relief, the employee was about her own age and professionally dressed. Maia had expected gypsy skirts, flowing scarves, and long white hair. What she saw was creased navy trousers, a pale yellow polo top, and deep auburn hair cut in the same casual chin-length bob that Maia wore.

Her response must have been apparent because the

woman laughed and said, "My caftan and love beads are at the cleaners."

"Was I that obvious?"

"Not really, but you're not the first person to be surprised. I'm good at reading it."

Deciding to change the subject, Maia gestured toward the pyramid and said, "This is incredible work. Who's the artist?"

"Her name is Shona Blackwood, and thank you; I'm blown away by her talent every time I see one of her pieces."

"Blackwood?" Maia heard her voice climb three octaves, but this shock was the biggest one yet today.

"Do you know her?"

Maia had to clear her throat. "No, I don't." Her reaction seemed to require some kind of explanation, so she added, "I recently met a man with the same surname, and since it's not the most common, the coincidence shocked me."

The woman's gaze sharpened. "I don't believe in coincidence," she said.

Neither did Maia, but it had to be nothing more than some fluke. What else could it be? Before she could come up with something to say that would deflect the scrutiny, the woman nodded as if she'd reached a decision. "What?" Maia asked warily.

"My name is Caitlin Ramsay." She held out her hand.

"Maia Frasier." This formal introduction had her uneasy, and with great reluctance, she shook hands. She broke contact as soon as she could, but something in the other woman's eyes made Maia believe it was too late.

"You're not one of my regular customers, and given your surprise when you came in, I'd say this is your first visit. It's a weekday and you're dressed for the office."

Although she knew what she had on, Maia looked down at her cream-colored crochet dress anyway. It was the kind of outfit a woman wore either to work or to a baby shower; it wasn't casual, I-have-the-day-off clothing.

"I'll add a couple more assumptions to the list—this is your regular route to and from your job. The store's been here three years and that means you've driven past it at least a thousand times, probably more, and I bet you never saw it until today." Caitlin arched one eyebrow. "I put the pyramid in the window about an hour ago. How did I do?"

The uncanny accuracy made part of Maia anxious enough to want to walk out the door and forget this stop. After all, if the glass pyramid had just been placed in the window, Seth wouldn't have had a chance to see it yet, but she couldn't give in to this cowardly side. There had to be a reason why everything had happened as it had. Maia needed to learn what it was. "You're right on the money," she admitted.

"But you wish I wasn't."

"No kidding." Maia smiled ruefully.

"Do you want to find out why you were drawn here?"

"Not really, but I suppose I better."

Caitlin nodded and said, "I'll give you a reading; that will probably tell us what you need to know."

The woman started off, but Maia didn't follow. Everything inside her balked at the idea of having some kind of psychic reading done. Most of her reasons against it were personal, but the one that mattered was protecting the existence of the Gineal.

Caitlin was halfway across the shop before she realized that Maia wasn't behind her. "What's wrong?"

Maia hesitated for only an instant, then said, "As of

today, I don't have a job. I can't afford to spend money on this." It was something a human would understand and it should get her out of things neatly.

"I'm not going to charge you."

There went easy. "Look," she said, deciding to level with the woman, "there are things about me I'd rather no one know. No offense, but that includes you."

Caitlin walked back to stand in front of Maia. Voice pitched low, she said, "If it's because you're worried I'll find out you're Gineal, you can relax. I know. I sensed it when we shook hands."

Maia didn't know how to react or what to say. Humans weren't supposed to be aware of their presence; concealing themselves was the only thing that had saved her people from being wiped out centuries ago. She couldn't admit anything, but she didn't think the woman would believe a denial. Maia remained silent, the only thing she could do.

With a shrug, Caitlin explained, "I'm a hereditary magic user and my family's history is filled with stories of living side by side with a group much more powerful than us, of learning from them, and of being persecuted along with them. I've always known of the Gineal. We've kept the secret since your people chose to go underground."

She couldn't figure out what to say, and Caitlin took her elbow, steering her toward the back of the shop. Maia let herself be guided. She'd have to tell Creed this information and have him pass it on to the council. The decision on how to handle these humans belonged to them, not her.

"Amy," the woman called, "I have a client. Please watch the store."

They stopped in a small room, barely larger than a

closet. There was a rectangular table for two and a pair of chairs that looked comfortable, but not much else. There were no windows, no incense, and no beads or chimes. Soft instrumental music was playing and Maia recognized the artist. She listened to his CDs whenever she wanted to meditate. On the table next to the wall were a variety of crystals. As familiar as she was with stones, even Maia couldn't identify all of them, but she was willing to bet they helped people open up psychically. There was also a tape player—she'd have to make sure that was off during her reading. On the far side was a cabinet with six drawers of various sizes and she wondered what was stashed inside there.

Caitlin closed the door and dimmed the lights before gesturing toward the seat closest to the exit. She lit a smudge stick, cleansed the space, and tamped it out in a ceramic bowl atop the cabinet. Only then did she take the chair opposite Maia.

Closing her eyes, Maia took a few deep breaths to center herself. If she was going to do this, she was going to do it right—even if she did feel slightly bulldozed into the reading. She heard the other woman opening and closing drawers for a moment, then heard Caitlin begin shuffling cards.

She let herself be lulled. The rhythm of the music, the soft rasp of the cards, and the scents of sage and cedar from the smudge stick all worked to relax her.

"Cut the cards into three piles for me," Caitlin said quietly. Even that soft request jarred.

Maia opened her eyes, checked to make sure the recorder remained off, then reached out. She stopped short of the deck. She'd guessed tarot, and she was right, but this was no mass-produced deck. "You do readings with these cards?" Maia asked, unable to believe the woman wanted any stranger's energy seeping into something as special as this deck.

"Not normally, no." Caitlin's lips curved. "You're an extraordinary case."

Nodding, Maia took the deck. The cards held power, she could feel it as she touched them, but it was different than the Gineal. That had her wondering just who—and what—Caitlin Ramsey and her family were.

When she was finished, the woman laid out ten cards in a standard Celtic cross spread. Maia stared at the faded pictures, trying to do her own divining, but nothing came to her. She'd never had talent along these particular lines, though, and she'd never attempted to use tarot.

"You've known great pain," Caitlin said. "It wasn't your fault."

Maia nearly rolled her eyes. Everyone had a time in their life where they'd known great pain, and everyone wanted absolution, assurance that they were blame-free. The Gineal viewed things differently.

"You're a nurturer, someone who needs to be needed, and you've felt at loose ends lately." There was a pause. "She'll always need you, Maia, but in a different way than in the past. You've worried about that for no reason."

"Who?" Maia asked, wanting verification. Maybe the woman did have some talent.

"Your sister, who else?" Caitlin's hand hovered over one of the cards, then she said slowly, "A man has entered your life."

And Maia had told the woman that herself not more than ten minutes ago when she'd been stunned about the name of the artist. Brilliant use of offered details. "Let me guess," she said with light sarcasm. "He's tall, dark, and handsome."

"Both men fit that description." Caitlin looked up, the green in her eyes seeming a deeper shade in the dim room. "Be careful who you trust. They're both potentially dangerous to you and your family."

A shiver went down her spine; this was cutting a little too close. "I'd never trust—" Maia cut herself off before saying "Seth."

Caitlin shrugged. "Maybe your past with him will help you avoid that. I see percentages, possibilities, but you know the future isn't carved in stone."

"Free will," Maia agreed. There were few specifics. A Gineal seer would have laid out a lot more detail, including names, pivotal events, and what choices the seeker would face when he reached one of life's crossroads. The human had spoken nothing except generalities and most of those were easily guessed or loose enough to apply to anyone. Mostly.

"You're a skeptic."

Maia remained quiet, not wanting to insult the woman.

"I can't blame you; this isn't the best reading I've ever done." Caitlin looked down at the cards she still held, ran her thumb over the edges. "I'd offer to switch to the deck I usually read with and try again, but I don't think that will make a difference. It's as if there's some obstruction within you that stops me cold."

While she'd still had her powers, Maia wouldn't have cared much about hurting a human who thought she could compete with the Gineal in any respect. She'd been arrogant in her youth. But now she knew what it was like to live without the magic she'd taken for granted and she understood it wasn't easy. For that reason, she suggested, "Why don't you continue? Maybe the block you're running into will give way."

A determined look settled on Caitlin's face and Maia

resigned herself to sitting through this for a while longer. She could afford a few more minutes.

"Life-altering events have started to happen to you and they'll continue to occur."

Like maybe no longer having a job? Maia had told Caitlin that herself, but she kept quiet now. She wanted to get this over with and get out of here without the other woman feeling too bad about her abilities.

"Your parents were star seeds and didn't have a soul connection to anyone else on Earth. That's why they were so easily able to ignore you and your sister. They incarnated here to help the transition at Harmonic Convergence, and with that done, they left."

Maia barely swallowed a gasp and struggled to keep her expression blank. There was no way that was a lucky guess. There were different theories on what convergence was, but the most popular among humans was that it was a time of worldwide awakening to unconditional love. While the Gineal had hoped that was true, the event itself wasn't part of their belief system and her parents had lived for years after convergence. So was Caitlin right? Maia hadn't revealed anything about her family, but why would her parents have a role in the event?

Caitlin tapped the deck with a finger, then slowly laid out three more cards off to the side of the spread. She gasped and Maia looked down, trying to see what had caused that reaction, but nothing made sense to her. "You're the one," the woman said, raising her head until her gaze met Maia's. She appeared absolutely shocked—beyond shocked.

"The one?" Maia asked.

With shaking hands, Caitlin gathered up the cards on the table and bundled them back with the rest of the deck. Several fluttered to the table and it took her a few tries to retrieve them. "It explains why I couldn't read you. You're Gineal, but not Gineal. Human, but not human." She wrapped the cards in silk and rested them on the table. "I didn't believe you existed. I'm staring right at you and I still can't believe it."

Maia shifted in her chair, uneasy with this turn of events.

"You don't know what to say; I apologize." Caitlin's entire body trembled as if she were freezing and her voice shook. "A debt of honor has been passed down in my family from mother to daughter, generation after generation. I'm finding it difficult to grasp that it's my duty to see it fulfilled."

"I don't know what you're talking about."

"I know you don't. Will you wait here?" Caitlin didn't pause for an answer. "I live above the store and I'll be back in no more than a couple of minutes. Will you wait?" she repeated.

Her curiosity aroused, Maia nodded. The woman all but ran out of the room and Maia could hear her footsteps pounding on the stairs and then overhead as Caitlin moved about her apartment.

"Stranger and stranger," she muttered, but some sixth sense she hadn't quite lost had her cells buzzing.

A loud bang made her jump, then the sound of more running. Caitlin burst in the room, out of breath, her face flushed, and there were tear tracks on her cheeks. When she saw Maia sitting where she'd left her, she smiled tremulously. "Good, you're still here. I wondered if you'd take the opportunity to escape. I had to get this." She held up a book before clutching it to her chest.

Although most of the thick tome was concealed, Maia knew it was old and that there was a protection spell around it strong enough for even her to discern without her powers. "Where'd you get that?" Maia asked, sounding almost choked.

"From my mother. We've been guardians of this book for hundreds of years; it seems odd to have it finished." Caitlin jerkily placed the text on the center of the table and sat again. She stared at it for a moment, then raised her head. "I believe it's meant to be yours. Open it and let's see."

Maia reached out, and this time, it was her hand shaking. She half expected the spell around the tome to zap her when she tried to touch it, but nothing happened, and hesitantly, she lifted the cover, turning a couple of pages. The language was Cànan, something the Gineal hadn't used in a very long time, and the book was handwritten. More than just a few hundred years old, she realized. "When will we know if I'm the right person?" Maia asked.

"We already know." Caitlin's voice was thick and her eyes were bright with unshed tears.

"How?"

"Close the book again."

Maia did as she requested. Caitlin took the volume and tried to raise the cover. It didn't budge. She used both hands, pulling with all her strength to try to open it, but she couldn't. Placing it back on the table, she said, "Only one person can read it; the woman who's supposed to claim it. *You.*" A tear ran down Caitlin's cheek and she rubbed at it impatiently. "I'm sorry," she apologized. "I don't know why this is such an emotional moment, especially since I never really believed the story my mother told me when she passed the responsibility along."

"Perhaps it's because you've filled one of your destinies and it's time to move to the next one."

"Perhaps." Caitlin smiled shakily. "I guess we know why you were attracted to the store today."

Maia murmured an agreement, but she was worried. Why now? She *had* driven past this store every weekday that she'd gone to work—there had even been times she'd gone this direction on the weekends—and she'd never even noticed the shop. Yet at a time when her greatest, most dangerous enemy was in town and threatening her sister, she stopped to claim the book.

It was too neat, too convenient. She believed Caitlin about the text being passed down in her family for generations. What she wondered was who had given them the book to begin with—a Gineal who was untainted? Or was it one who'd turned to the dark forces and was acting in concert with demons?

Fifteen minutes later, as she turned into her driveway, the doubts still nagged at her. As she waited for the door to go up, she spotted a package on her front steps and frowned. She didn't remember ordering anything.

After pulling in, she went to the front door. The box was light and the return address was from some clothing company. Her skirt. It had to be the skirt that had been on back order since May. The name of the business didn't sound right, but it was probably some subsidiary. She took it to her kitchen, got a knife, and slit the packing tape, but instead of the cute melon-colored skirt she'd expected, Maia saw black cloth. Ignoring it, she lifted the envelope that rested on top. Her hands shook as she pulled the card out.

I've never forgotten you, my precious.

She dropped the card as if it were a cobra. *Seth.* Dear God, it had to be Seth, because only he had ever called her his precious.

Almost afraid of what she'd find, Maia gingerly

removed the fabric from the box. It felt like some kind of cotton knit and she shook it out. A black T-shirt. She turned it around to see the front and felt the blood drain from her cheeks at the taunt: *Come to the dark side. We have cookies.*

11

CHAPTER

Seth was bored.

He'd been in the hottest clubs from London to New York to Tokyo and this didn't compare. Not only was it a pale and inferior imitation of those elite places, but the music annoyed him. He thought about disabling the sound system and ending his misery, but it felt like too much effort.

Looking around, he took in the has-beens, the wannabes, and the never-will-bes and sighed. Desperation, jealousy, and other delightfully petty emotions swirled through the mass of humanity, but he didn't care.

Seth leaned his elbow on the bar and wondered if it was the club that bored him senseless or if ennui had finally overtaken him. He'd lost track of how many thousands of years he'd existed, but that hardly mattered; time passed differently on Earth than in his dimension anyway. When was the last time he'd felt truly entertained? The answer came easily—Las Vegas. Maia. His thoughts drifted. Had she liked his gift? He wished he'd been present to observe her reaction.

His amusement quickly faded. He'd instructed the elementals living in the grass around her sister's home to notify him if she left, but he didn't expect to hear anything. She was a boring homebody—unlike Maia. At least the Maia he'd known.

Perhaps he should lower the cloak that kept him invisible and see about finding a woman for the night. Seth looked around the club again, but the groupies there to bag an athlete didn't interest him. Tuesday night apparently brought out only the woefully pathetic. He wasn't *that* bored.

In an effort to amuse himself, Seth decided to toy with the humans. He spotted a woman more conservatively dressed than most and studied her. Classy, he judged, and from her mannerisms and movements, very much a lady.

Seth found the most disreputable male in the place and took control of his mind. It was child's play to walk him over to the woman. After an instant of indecision, Seth decided not to waste time on subtlety—he had the man reach out and cup the woman's sex. Her shriek of outrage made him smile, as did the sound of her palm meeting the man's face.

But as the bouncers rushed over to see what the uproar was, Seth was left feeling unsatisfied. It seemed as if nothing here would entertain him tonight. With a shrug, he straightened and transported himself out of the club. Maybe something interesting was happening at the mall.

Maia strolled across the skyway from the parking ramp, in no hurry to reach the club. Even in her party days, this wouldn't have been the type of place she'd choose, but it sounded like somewhere Seth might enjoy. In fact, it was on the top of her list.

It had taken hours of frustrating online searches to come up with the names of a few bars that she thought would attract Seth. This one had been the only one with its own Web site. From there, she'd learned the hours it was open and that it had a dress code that was strictly enforced. Except Maia had read a few reviews on other sites that talked about how some people in jeans were allowed in while others properly attired were denied entrance. She'd known exactly what that meant: the rich and beautiful received preference.

Her money had disappeared along with her job as an enforcer, but she still had her looks, and she was using them to ensure she wasn't turned away. The burgundy halter dress she wore showed off her body perfectly and left most of her back bare. Wrapping the two-tone straps around her waist had accentuated its narrowness and called even more attention to her breasts.

Maia glanced into the skyway window. The interior lights made it reflect like a mirror and she was able to assess her appearance. With the style of the dress and how she filled out the bodice, she'd had to be generous with the fashion tape to prevent it from slipping and turning her into an unintentional exhibitionist. The silk jersey clung to her hips and thighs despite the fullness of the skirt. She sighed. Between the material and the air-conditioning, it was readily apparent that she wasn't wearing a bra.

The look would have been better if her hair was still as long as it had been the last time she'd worn this dress, but there was nothing she could do about that now. Maia raised a hand and arranged her bangs until they fell across her eyes in a sexy kind of way. That would have to be good enough.

Her stomach knotted as she got closer to the club. She didn't want to do this. If Maia had her way, she'd be home, reading that book Caitlin had given her today, but nothing was more important than her sister. Nothing.

Maia tried to find the mindset she'd had when she'd lived in Vegas. Amazing how a few years could change a person. Once, she'd loved to party, and going to a club alone had been no big deal. Of course, then she'd had magic to deal with the creeps who wouldn't back off, but as Creed had reminded her, she'd been trained in martial arts.

Speaking of Creed. Where the hell was he? She'd waited for him until it grew late enough that she'd had to leave. As it was, she hadn't parked her car until after nine. She had to believe that most people wouldn't be out till all hours on a Tuesday night, even if the club was open until two-thirty, and Seth wouldn't hang around if it was only sparsely populated.

Block E. Alone. At night. Martial arts or not, heavy police patrols or not, Maia wished Creed were with her. His presence would make her feel safer. At least physically.

She hesitated at the end of the skyway, tempted to turn around and go home. There was nothing she wanted more than to wash off all the makeup, change into her pajamas, and curl up in her bed with that book. She could give the names of the clubs to Creed and let him handle his assignment without her interference.

Except this was her sister's life at stake, damn it, and she couldn't trust Blackwood.

What was she so afraid of anyway?

The answer popped into her head and surprised her.

Maia clutched her purse a little tighter. She was worried that she'd fall back into the party-girl lifestyle.

After she'd ceded her powers, she'd gone cold turkey. It had become easier after she'd moved to Minneapolis. She hadn't known anyone here except her sister, and God knew Ryne would rather walk barefoot over blazing coals than hang out in a club. Hell, half the time, it had been all Maia could do to get Ryne to go out to dinner and a movie. This would test her resolve, though, and Maia wasn't sure she'd pass. She couldn't become the woman she'd been when she'd lived in Vegas.

But as much as she hated regressing, Maia hated the thought of anything happening to her sister even more. That was the bottom line. She pushed open the skyway door. Nothing was stopping her from protecting Ryne.

The queue to get in was short, and the guy guarding the entrance took one look at her and practically began to drool. Way back when, she'd taken that as her due—now it made her uncomfortable. But she'd dressed this way for a reason. Maia put a hand just above her left hip and shifted all her weight to that leg. The pose stuck her breasts out just a fraction more and made the silk jersey outline her hip.

She was allowed in the club in minutes.

The place was crowded, surprisingly so for a weeknight, and while Seth would like that, it would make it more difficult to find him. It didn't help that there were a lot of big men present and she couldn't see around their shoulders. Jocks. One of the reviews she'd read said the place attracted athletes.

Maia moved deeper into the bar, ignoring the leers and the "hey, baby" comments tossed her way. She'd been concerned before leaving the house that she might be dressed too sexily, but it turned out to be a needless worry. There were women whose necklines plunged much more deeply than hers and some had dresses that looked painted on. There were also women in stylish pants or wearing more modest dresses.

Good. All the Web site had said was *fashionable* and that covered a lot of ground. She'd hate to stand out by being too conservative or too suggestive. It seemed as if she'd landed right in the middle.

A woman's scream jerked her to a stop and quieted the voices. The music continued on, though, and gradually the murmur of conversation resumed. Maia stood aside when two burly men wearing club T-shirts came through. They each held the arm of a third man between them, clearly escorting him out of the bar. She relaxed. Security had taken care of the problem.

She continued wandering around, trying to spot Seth or feel his energy, but after half an hour she hadn't covered very much ground, thanks to the crush. At this rate, she wasn't going to make it halfway through the place before it closed. Although, once it thinned out, it wouldn't be so difficult. Maybe then, she could even see what the bar looked like. Her lips curved.

A man blocked her path, and Maia stepped to one side. This time, though, the guy moved with her. She went left again, and again, he followed. "Excuse me," she said sternly, making sure there was no weakness, no invitation, in her voice.

"Hey, baby, let me buy you a drink."

"No. Thank you, but I'm with someone." She moved to get around him, but he stood in her way again. Maia sized him up in case she had to put him on the floor. He was about her height, but he was broad and very heavily muscled, making her think he did a lot of weight training. She wouldn't have an easy time taking him down. Looking beyond the obvious, she noted the style of his blond hair and the clothes he wore. A self-proclaimed ladies' man, she'd bet her bank balance on that.

"Where you running off to?" he asked and grabbed her arm. Maia tried to pull loose, but he tightened his hold.

"Let go. You're hurting me." And the slur in his voice worried her. Drunks weren't easy to reason with. He started pulling her toward him, and Maia gave her arm another yank as she repeated more loudly, "I said, let go."

"Take your hands off her," a deep voice drawled behind her.

"I saw her first," the drunk said. "Find your own woman."

"She told you she wasn't interested, now let the little lady go and don't bother her anymore." His voice, even with the soft southern accent, brooked no argument.

The drunk knew it. He released her. "She's too old for me anyhow," he said. "You're welcome to the *little lady*." And with that, he swaggered off, as if he'd been the one to turn her down.

Maia had found the *little lady* comment a bit amusing herself. In heels, she was about six feet tall, but when she turned to thank her rescuer, she realized that to him, she probably was tiny. He had to be a good seven or eight inches taller, and the width of his shoulders was easily double hers. "Thank you for the assistance," she said.

"It was surely my pleasure. Why don't you let me buy you a drink and you can thank me properly."

Out of the frying pan and into the fire. "Sorry, but like I told that other guy, I'm with someone."

"He can't be very smart if he let a woman who looks like you out of his sight."

"A lady has to powder her nose sometime."

Her rescuer smiled, transforming his face from pleasant to downright attractive. "Now, see, if I were here with you, I would have escorted you to and from the restrooms. I'd understand that a man protects someone precious like you."

Maia went on alert. *Precious.* Could Seth have transformed himself? Or worse yet, had Seth possessed this man? Strong demons could indwell without much effort. Carefully, she reached out with her senses, probing, but he read completely human to her. That didn't mean much, though, since she'd been fooled before. "Seth?" she asked, leaning forward.

"No," the man said, "Rand Donovan." He paused. "You don't know who I am, do you?"

"Should I?" Maia asked, still suspicious.

"I guess you don't like football."

"I don't like to watch any sports. Why? Do you play?"

"Ouch! I reckon you put me in my place," Rand said. "My mama would tell me I deserved it for letting my ego get too big. Do I look like this Seth?"

Obviously, if she'd thought he was a dead ringer for another person, she would have called him that name immediately—and she hadn't. Maia scrambled to come up with a plausible explanation; after all, she could hardly tell Rand that she thought maybe he might be possessed by a demon.

"Uh, Seth is someone I met online. In a chat room," she improvised. "He mentioned that he likes to hang out here, and when you referred to me as precious, I thought . . . well, that's what he always called me, so I wondered."

"This boyfriend of yours know you hang out in chat rooms?"

Maia smiled. "We're dating, not living together."

Rand shook his head. "You should stay out of those places; some of the people there are downright strange."

"I know, and Seth is probably the strangest of them all."

There was no reaction from the man opposite her, not so much as a flicker in his eyes, and Maia decided Seth couldn't be indwelling. No matter how much control he'd tried to exert, he wouldn't have been able to resist responding in some way to her jab. "Thanks again for the rescue," she said.

"You're welcome. Are you sure I can't buy you a drink?"

She was tempted. Here was this appealing man, a sports star probably, since he'd said his name as if she should know who he was, and he wanted her. For seven years, she'd been no one, she'd been nothing— *nothing*—but tonight men were looking at her as if she were important. *This* man was looking at her as if she mattered. The admiration in his eyes was like water falling on land parched from drought and it was as heady as a drug.

That sobered her. It was a false high, just like using the dark forces. There wasn't a male in this club who cared about Maia Frasier. Not the person. All that mattered to them was that she was beautiful and they'd like to have sex with her.

"I'm certain. You're a nice guy, Rand." And he was. He'd had no reason to intervene when she'd been dealing with that drunk.

"You tell anyone that and I'll deny it," he said with a smile.

Reaching out, Maia gave his hand a quick squeeze, then continued making her way through the crowd. Where had that moment of pathetic neediness come from? Did she desire validation so much that she'd put aside her mission? Maybe she hadn't learned as much the last seven years as she'd believed.

When she realized she was focused inward to the point that she wouldn't recognize Seth if he came up to her and said *boo,* Maia forced aside the introspection. She'd have plenty of time to evaluate her life after she saved her sister.

Time after time, though, she caught herself preening over the masculine attention she was garnering, strutting like she had when she'd been a cocky twenty-year-old troubleshooter. Maybe she *was* needy. Maybe after seven years of being an outcast among her own people, she was hungry for any attention she could get.

With the downstairs covered, she headed to the second level. It was every bit as crowded up here and Maia resigned herself to another long, slow trek as she checked for Seth. He might not be here, or he might be concealing his presence from her. No doubt he had that ability, but she'd cover this whole place anyway.

She didn't see the man until his hand rubbed her rear end. Maia froze, knocked aside the offending arm, and turned to deliver a frosty glare. That's when she saw the drunk guy from the first floor.

"Looks like you're a liar, baby. You're not here with anyone." His words were drastically slurred now.

"Of course I—"

He cut her off. "No, you're not, so there's no reason you can't show ol' Paul a good time."

"Except for the fact that I don't want anything to do with *ol' Paul.*"

Before she could react, he grabbed her. She'd never expected a drunk to move that quickly. He gripped her arm just above her elbow and Maia tightened her lips to keep from gasping at his painful hold. As he pulled her near, she drew back her fingers, preparing to use the heel of her hand to deliver a sharp blow. She never had the opportunity.

Abruptly, the man's hold slackened and his face went pale. Someone just behind her had twisted ol' Paul's hand back far enough to cause him pain. Maia looked over her shoulder, half expecting to see Rand, but it was Creed rescuing her.

His hair was slicked back into a queue, and with a black shirt, black slacks, and an ice-cold expression, he looked more like a Mafia hit man than a Gineal troubleshooter. As his eyes met hers, Maia saw contempt and she knew he was going to give her grief about taking care of herself. Her chin went up. She'd been about to handle it; was it her fault he'd jumped in? But despite the crap she was going to have to face, she'd never been so glad to see anyone in her life.

Creed felt his temper become more and more precarious as he moved through the throngs of people in the nightclub. He assumed the owners had the air on, but with all the bodies jammed together, it was hot and he was sweating. Even with the sleeves of his shirt rolled up, it was uncomfortable.

It wasn't the heat, though, that had him irritable. His damn mind shield was slipping. He could feel the emotions of these humans buffeting him and it was giving him a headache of epic proportions. It had to be the demon. Seth had gotten behind his mental protection more than once, and now he was trying to dismantle it. He was succeeding, too.

Without warning, he felt a sharp pain in his arm, and Creed knew immediately the hurt belonged to someone else. He zeroed in on it, sending his mind along the line to the source. The last person he expected to see was

Maia. In an instant, his temper hit the red zone. *No one* manhandled her.

He crossed over to her, people parting before him as if he were Moses. Creed pried the man's fingers from her arm and bent the asshole's hand back. He was going to break every bone in the fucker's body and he'd do it nice and slow.

"Creed," Maia said, "the guy's drunk. He didn't know what he was doing."

"Like hell," he growled. Satisfaction filled him when the asshole cried out.

"You're hurting him."

He ignored her—until she rested her hand on his forearm and ran her fingers up and down the bare skin there. That easily, the haze covering his mind lifted. Releasing the man, he turned to Maia. "Are you okay?"

"I am. I was going to take care of him," she added. Her tone was defensive, but her bottom lip wobbled.

Damn, he wished she hadn't done that.

Running the back of his index finger from her jaw to her chin, Creed tilted her face to his and lowered his mouth until their lips brushed. He'd meant the kiss to be nothing more than a quick reassurance, but he'd wanted a taste of her since that first afternoon when he'd turned from watching *Jeopardy* to find her glaring at him, and hell, she was kissing him back. They barely touched— only their lips, his hands at her face, and her hands on his forearms—but he couldn't remember anything ever feeling this erotic before.

Creed ran his tongue over the corner of her lips and she opened for him. Sweet. She tasted so damn sweet. The club receded and he might have forgotten about their audience entirely if the drunk hadn't picked that moment to shove him.

Pissed at being interrupted, Creed raised his head and turned an icy stare on the man. He was too inebriated to register Creed's mood.

"I saw her first," the asshole said.

Before he could reply, Maia jumped in. "I told you I was here with someone; this is him."

Creed nearly growled at her, but reined in before showing his aggravation at the comment. "It doesn't matter if you saw her first and," he added pointedly, "it doesn't matter if she's here by herself or with the entire starting lineup of the Chicago Cubs. The bottom line is that she isn't interested, and you not only wouldn't take no for an answer, you hurt her."

It didn't take any great perception to know that the blond man was far too drunk to get what Creed was saying. Frustrated, Creed ran through the incantations he had memorized, came up with one he found appropriate, and silently chanted the words. When he closed the proclamation, he put his hand on Maia's bare back and steered her toward the stairs.

"Hey," the asshole called after them, "we're not finished."

Creed glanced over his shoulder, wondering if the man would follow them and cause more trouble, but a pair of bouncers converged on the drunk. Trusting that they had the situation in hand, or would shortly, he turned his attention back to Maia. "What the hell are you doing here anyway?" he demanded.

Maia answered with a hotly whispered question of her own. "What was the spell you cast on him?"

He thought about stonewalling her, but decided not to bother. "From now on, whenever he tries to strong-arm an unwilling woman, he'll be dealing with an impotence problem." Creed's lips quirked up. "And a burning pain in his cock that will last about forty-eight hours."

She laughed. "Ol' Paul isn't going to like that."

"No, but he'll learn to keep his hands to himself."

"Eventually."

They reached the stairs. "Let me go first," Creed said. "That way if you lose your balance, you'll fall into me and not down the entire flight."

She looked startled, but nodded, and Creed led the way. He swore he could feel her heat at his back even though she wasn't touching him, and it raised his body temperature even higher. It was a relief to reach the bottom of the stairs—at least it was until she looked up at him and he remembered her mouth under his.

Swallowing a groan, Creed moved them out of the flow of traffic and against a nearby wall. "You never answered me. What the hell are you doing here?"

"What do you think?" she snapped.

"Okay, stupid question." Someone bumped into Maia from behind and Creed gathered her closer until her breasts pressed into his chest. He sucked in a sharp breath. Closing his eyes, he fought for control, but he couldn't locate his peaceful center. He gave up on that and started running through multiplication tables.

"What's wrong?" Maia asked. He ignored her until she said his name with a thread of concern.

Creed met her gaze. When she gasped, he suspected his eyes held all the heat his body felt. "You're not wearing a bra," he said, voice so thick it was nearly unintelligible.

"So? I don't need one; there's no sag yet." Her tone was defensive.

She thought he was complaining? He pulled her even nearer until his cock pressed against her hip. Her eyes widened and Creed stared pointedly at Maia before he eased her back. "Give me a minute, okay?"

Maia being Maia, she didn't. "This is sudden," she said suspiciously.

"What is?" Couldn't she give him a chance to get the blood back to his brain before holding a conversation?

"Your interest in me. Is this some kind of trick?"

"You think I'm faking it?" He laughed without amusement. "Angel, if my control wasn't so damn good, I would have had you up against the wall last night. Tonight, well, that dress—and your body in that dress—is more dangerous than zortir poison."

Her lips parted slightly and Creed tightened his hold on her hips, fighting not to pull her against him, fighting not to kiss her. The music, though, had a beat that was sexual and he seemed to throb in rhythm with it. They couldn't do this. *He* couldn't do this. It wasn't like he could fuck her and walk away without repercussions.

Unless he severed all ties to Ryne forever.

When Creed realized he was considering jettisoning a six-year friendship for sex, he worked harder to cool his blood. Yeah, Ryne had messed up his plans, and yeah, she didn't want anything to do with him now, but when Seth was caught and she realized he'd saved her, she'd forgive him. And God knew he didn't have enough friends to go carelessly tossing them aside for a roll in the sack.

"I'm guessing you didn't find Seth," he said when he had his self-command back.

"No, but with this crush, it would have been easy to miss him, particularly if he was concealing his presence. What about you? Do you even know what Seth looks like?"

Creed shook his head. "I was going by sense. I know

how his energy feels, but like you, I was having a hard time searching with all these people around. How far did you get?"

"I covered the first level and had just started the second."

"I began upstairs and went through the two private rooms, the VIP lounge, and the balcony area."

"So between the two of us, we covered the entire club." Maia sounded discouraged.

"Sounds like it. Do you think there's any point in making a second run through the place?"

"I doubt it. It's the kind of club Seth would come to, but I don't think he'd like it much. It's too . . . I don't know, too frantic maybe." Maia shrugged and Creed fought to keep his gaze off her breasts and on her eyes. "And he'd absolutely loathe the music. He always preferred quieter, smokier stuff like blues."

"Do you think he'd show up later? Demons are nocturnal and it isn't even midnight yet."

"He could," she said, sounding doubtful, "except I've never known him to put in an appearance anywhere after 11 P.M."

That was a fact about Seth that he never would have known if Maia hadn't told him. With their obsessive natures, demons tended to stick with a routine, and while they might change it from time to time, it wasn't easy for them. It was a trait Creed had used more than once to find and defeat one of those beings. "We might as well leave and try again tomorrow."

"I'm ready to get out of here," she agreed.

"Are you in the parking ramp across the street?" She nodded. "I am, too. I'll walk you to your car and then follow you home."

Once they were out of the club, it was a short distance to the skyway. As Creed held the door for Maia, he had enough light to notice that she didn't have any tan lines on her back, and since he could see most of it thanks to that dress, that meant she either sunbathed topless or she was damn conscientious about moving the straps of her suit around. He felt his control slip.

It disintegrated further when they entered the well-lit skyway. He almost groaned aloud. Most women looked better in the dim surroundings of a bar, but not Maia. He'd known she was beautiful, but he'd had no idea just how killer her body was until now, not when she usually hid it under boring clothes.

"Are you okay?" she asked as they crossed the street in the enclosed hall of glass.

"Yeah." He didn't want to know why she was asking. Before she figured out just how she affected him, Creed decided to put her on the defensive. "I thought I told you to stay out of my demon hunt."

"And I told you that I wasn't going to sit on the sidelines when my sister is at risk."

"You're powerless; you can't do anything but get in the way."

"I know Seth." Maia came to a stop and he did, too. "I don't recall everything I know, though. Today, I was driving past a store and I saw a pyramid in the window. That's when I remembered his attraction to anything from ancient Egypt. There will be other things that come to me like this." She stepped closer. "I'm protecting my sister, period. It's up to you whether I do it with you or on my own."

Creed gritted his teeth. "Sit back and trust me to do my job."

"I wish I could."

What did he say to that? He didn't blame her for not trusting him—sometimes he wasn't sure he trusted himself. "He can use you against me."

"I'm only leverage if you allow me to be."

"What the hell are you saying? That if he threatens you, I should let him kill you?"

Maia reached out, put a hand on his arm. "If you have to choose between saving Ryne or saving me, you save my sister."

"You can't ask—"

"I'm not asking; I'm *telling* you. You save Ryne." She resumed walking, leaving him where he stood.

"Great," Creed said. "An ex-enforcer with a death wish. Just what I need."

"I don't have a death wish," Maia said over her shoulder. "I'd prefer to stay alive, but if you have to make a choice, the decision is made."

Creed went after her, drew her to a halt, and looked down into her eyes. He could tell she hadn't made the choice lightly. "Why?"

"I love my sister, can you understand that?" Maia asked, voice raised. "I'd kill to keep her safe or be willing to die trying. I even ceded my magic so she wouldn't have to live with the guilt of hunting me. Ryne is the only person on this Earth who loves me. Not my body, not my face—*me!* She's seen me at my best and at my worst; we've bickered like sisters will and I've irritated her with my nagging, but I've always known that Ryne would walk into hell for me without thinking twice. I'd do the same for her." Maia looked away, took a deep breath, and when she met his gaze again, she was completely calm, as if her outburst had never happened. "And no matter how much you deny it, I know Seth is after Ryne because of me."

"Why do you think that?" Creed asked cautiously, unwilling to deal with the other emotional land mines.

"The last thing Seth said to me was that he'd get revenge for what I'd done." Her smile held no humor.

"You see, he was just the teensiest bit enraged the night I ceded my powers because I grabbed a part of his as well."

"You can't be saying—"

"I am. I stole some of Seth's magic and sent it away with my own. *That's* why he wants Ryne's power."

12
CHAPTER

Creed scowled as he reread the spell. Maia had warned him that it could only be used while a Gineal was ceding his powers, but he'd wanted a look at it anyway. She'd been twenty-five when she'd given up her magic and might not have had enough experience then to know for certain it couldn't be altered. Besides, anything that took strength away from the demon had to be examined; Seth was dangerously strong.

But after reading through it half a dozen times, Creed couldn't find any way it would work outside of the few minutes between the start of the proclamation to cede magic and when the incantation was closed.

Maia amazed him. That she'd had the presence of mind while deep into the dark forces to not only find a spell that would take power from Seth but actually use it was remarkable. Almost as remarkable as ceding her powers was to begin with. Creed reached for his coffee mug, found it empty, and his frown deepened.

He couldn't imagine giving up his magic, not for any reason, but Maia had done it because she loved her sister. A love like that, deep and unselfish, was rare. Creed got up, grabbed his mug, refilled it, and returned to the kitchen table. As he sipped his coffee, he paged through the other spells in the text, hoping to find some helpful incantation. Everything else he saw, though, was either something he'd read in another book or not particularly useful.

Rubbing his forehead, he stared at the book. His damn mind shield was still faltering. There wasn't enough protection around Maia's house to block human thoughts, and the constant static was giving him a headache he couldn't shake. He'd considered why Seth wanted his mind open, and had only been able to come up with one reason. If Creed's personal defenses were down, it made the whisper of the dark forces inside his head all that much louder. All that more seductive.

"Judging from the look on your face, I was right about the spell," Maia said.

Grateful for the distraction, Creed closed the tome and looked up. She was back in her usual modest clothing—tailored red shorts that hit her knee and a white blouse—but it didn't matter. He could envision her body far too easily after seeing her in that damn dress. When he realized she was waiting for a response, he shook himself out of the fog. "Yeah, you were right."

With a nod, she poured herself a cup of coffee and joined him at the table. "So what's on our agenda for the day?" she asked after taking a sip.

"You're assuming we're working together."

"Aren't we?"

Grimacing, he silently chanted the proclamation to return the text to the Gineal library and changed the subject. "What do we have for breakfast?"

She gave him a look, shook her head, and said, "I think it's called brunch at this time of the day. There are eggs in the fridge and I have bagels and instant oatmeal—take your pick."

"What about a sandwich?"

"I have chicken or roast beef."

"I'll have chicken."

Maia arched both eyebrows. "Bread is in the refrigerator and the chicken is in the meat drawer. If you want butter, the knives are next to the stove."

"You make your guests cook?"

"Guests are invited. Freeloaders have to fend for themselves."

That took him by surprise and he smiled before he was aware of it. Damn, when was the last time he'd been honestly amused? Creed let himself enjoy the moment as he pushed back from the table. "Can I get you something?" he asked, because she was right, he hadn't been invited to stay here.

"If you wouldn't mind toasting a bagel for me, I'd appreciate it."

"Butter?" He looked over his shoulder and she nodded.

Neither one of them talked while he worked, but it was a companionable silence. Although Creed would never admit it, he liked that she insisted he take care of himself. In an odd way, it made him feel as if he belonged here. Besides, he got tired of being fawned over, treated like a legend and not a man. He put her bagel on a plate, buttered it, and placed it front of her.

"Thanks," she said as he sat to her right. He'd finished about half his sandwich when Maia asked, "So what *is* the plan for today?"

Creed sighed. He'd never agreed to let her tag along,

but she'd read him accurately enough to pick up on his capitulation. "I thought we'd drive over to the Minneapolis Institute of Arts. According to their Web site, they have a small collection of ancient Egyptian artifacts on display. Maybe Seth paid a visit and maybe I can pick up a trace of his energy and follow it."

"Do I have time to check on Mrs. Olson before we leave? I haven't talked to her for a couple of days."

For an instant, he was tempted to tell her no, but that would just be delaying the inevitable. "Yeah, you can check on her." Creed glanced at his plate. "I guess I should probably warn you that I had to wipe out a few minutes of her memory."

"What?"

Maia's voice went up an octave on the word, but he'd guessed she wouldn't be happy with him. "It wasn't a decision I made lightly." There was nothing he took more seriously than erasing events in someone's mind. "I was talking to one of our librarians about researching Seth and your neighbor caught her leaving through the transit. I couldn't let the memory stand."

"Where were you when she saw this?"

"In the backyard. I know," Creed said, cutting off whatever rebuke Maia was about to deliver, "but it was late enough at night that I didn't think she'd still be awake, and all your other neighbors within viewing range have privacy fences up. I thought it was a safe enough risk to take."

"I trust you'll be more careful in the future," Maia said, voice devoid of any emotion.

"You know it."

She nodded and began clearing the table. It didn't take much to put a couple of plates, mugs, and a knife in the dishwasher, and in minutes, she was headed out. "I won't be long," Maia promised, but before she could leave, his cell phone rang. It was on the island next to the door and she picked it up, glancing at the caller ID screen as she did. "Looks like you have a call-out," she said as she handed it to him. The phone rang again. "I'll take my keys and lock up. Guess I'll see you when you're done."

He nodded and decided there were definite advantages to Maia being a former troubleshooter. She understood his job and that he could be put to work at any time. He opened his phone. "Yeah?" Creed said as he heard the door close behind her.

"When I hang up with you," Taber said without preamble, "I'll be calling Ryne to give her an assignment. The council wants you to back her up."

"She won't like that."

"Then she can complain when the mission is over," Taber said sharply. "We do not allow any laoch solas to dictate to us."

"Yes, ceannard," Creed said, trying to sound repentant. He ruined it by adding, "I'm surprised the council believes she needs backup, not when she has Summers."

"The true soul pairing offers many advantages, but Deke is a new apprentice, and while he's learning quickly, he doesn't even understand all the basics of magic yet. As for Ryne," Taber added with what Creed thought was affectionate exasperation, "she believes that anything can be defeated if she hammers at it long enough. In this case, she'd be wrong."

"She's still young."

"That she is." Taber was quiet for an instant, then said, "The mission isn't urgent, at least not just yet. A tracker is keeping us informed of the creature's actions, and at the moment, it's in a field with no humans nearby. The council decided this was a good opportunity for Ryne to gain experience with something she's never fought before, and since you've had a recent run-in with one, you're being sent in to ensure she isn't injured before she figures out that a direct attack isn't going to win."

Only his self-command kept him from groaning. He understood the council's position on continuing to educate their enforcers. Creed also understood that it was crucial Ryne be broken of the might-solves-all-problems habit she'd picked up from her mentor—with her incredible power, she was going to be pivotal in the battles of Twilight Time—but damn it, why did they have to choose now? "What are we facing?" he asked instead.

"Zortir."

One word, no inflection, but Creed felt his stomach roll. Son of a bitch. "Ryne told you?"

"No, she didn't. I see we'll be having a talk with her as well as you in the very near future."

Great, another reason for Ryne to be pissed off at him, but if she hadn't given him up, how did the council know about his visit to the forbidden— "Wait a second. Zortirs can't jump dimensions. How the hell did one end up in a field here?"

"Something for you to figure out," Taber said, and from his tone, Creed knew the conversation was over. Without being told, he opened for the mental transmission of intel on the situation.

"I got it," Creed said when Taber was done. Without another word being spoken, the call was disengaged.

Flipping the phone closed, he stood and rubbed his palm over one of the scars he had courtesy of his last meeting with a zortir. "If at first you don't succeed," he muttered and then did the spell to open the transit.

Creed spotted the tracker immediately, but he kept scanning until he located the zortir as well. Once he had the creature's position fixed, he crossed to the other man. "Creed Blackwood," he said, holding out a hand.

"Zane Conners. I thought they were sending Ryne."

"She'll be here."

"And not happy about having help," the tracker guessed.

Creed smirked. "I take it you know her well."

Before the other man could comment, a transit opened and Ryne and Summers were there. Creed was a little surprised she brought her apprentice with her to face a zortir, soul pairing or not, but he shrugged. She was doing the training.

Her professionalism was total and she didn't give away her displeasure by so much as a flicker of an eye. The first thing she did was ask Conners for a situational update, something Creed wouldn't have bothered with, but Ryne was the lead on this. Everything they heard had been transmitted by Taber before they'd arrived and was a total waste of time. At least it was until the tracker said, "This is only my impression, but Ryne, I think the zortir is confused. It seems unsure of where it is or what to do."

"Why do you think that?" Creed asked before he remembered this was Ryne's show.

"It was wandering in circles when I arrived," Conners said, "smelling things and staring at them." The man shrugged. "The creature just acted lost."

Interesting, Creed thought.

"Anything else we should know?" Ryne asked.

The tracker hesitated. "I had an odd sense from time

to time like there was another presence in the field, but when I'd try to zero in on it, I couldn't find it."

"How sure are you about this?" she asked.

"Not very. It was a vague sensation at best and could have something to do with the zortir—I've never tracked one before."

"That makes us even; I've never fought one before, but Blackwood has." Ryne turned to him. Creed waited for some dig, but instead she asked, "How did you approach it? What did you do that worked and what did you do that didn't work?"

"Taber told you that a frontal attack would fail?" Ryne nodded. "Wish I'd known that before I tried." Creed rubbed his side. "I didn't get a chance to go to plan B."

Summers spoke up. "What if we magically created a pit and drove the zortir into it? Once it was contained, we could deal with it."

Creed glanced over at the man, but his expression was serious, his eyes flat. "Won't fly," Creed said. "They have enough magic to get out of a pit. What if—"

"Not to interrupt your conversation," Zane Conners drawled, "but the zortir is moving, and this time, it isn't aimless."

"Crap. Okay, here's what we'll do," Ryne said. "We'll get in a triangle at a far enough distance that it can't get to any of us easily. Whoever has its back, fires. They're not supposed to be too bright, so let's confuse and maybe weaken it until we can take it down."

Her strategy was reasonable, but it wasn't going to be successful. Creed almost told her that, but swallowed the words. The council wanted Ryne to learn, and sometimes that meant the hard way. "Where do you want me?" he asked instead.

Although Creed was unfamiliar with the area,

Ryne's mental imagery was good enough to give him the location. Creed opened a transit, but before he stepped through, he saw Summers reach for Ryne's hand and the two of them shared a glance that spoke volumes. The exchange only lasted a split second, but it was long enough.

Jealousy stabbed through Creed, followed closely by anger. As he crossed the transit to his own post, he struggled to tamp down the emotion. Ryne should have been his, damn it. He should have the power that came from a soul pairing, not some fucking outsider who didn't even know what to do with his own magic.

Though fury continued to bubble within, catching sight of the zortir cooled his surface temper. He studied the creature. It reminded him of a dinosaur in a way— not a sleek one like T-Rex, but an awkward species that lumbered on four legs. In this case, looks were deceptive. The thing was incredibly fast.

Its coloring was an odd translucent blue, as if someone had dropped it in a vat of indigo dye and pulled it out before the job was finished. The two horns on either side of its forehead were a pale orange color from the venom running through them, and the frill around its neck was better than armor. Shit, the entire body was scaled, even the eyelids. He'd found that out when he'd aimed his shot at what he'd assumed was a weak area.

It looked like they were in a fallow farmer's field, but there was a line of trees around all four sides. They didn't provide much cover, but it was better than nothing. Creed located Ryne—she stood diagonally across from him—and Summers was to his left.

As he waited for the zortir to come closer, Creed found it harder to keep his emotions in check. It didn't matter if the creature was twenty feet away or twenty yards, their shots would have the same effect. Zilch. The council should have put him in charge—Ryne didn't have a damn clue what she was doing.

They'd done it because she was magically stronger, he knew. The dark forces whispered then, promised that he'd be more powerful than Ryne if he embraced them, and Creed almost snorted. Yeah, he wanted more power, but not because of ego. He wanted more so that he could better defend his people during the battles of Twilight Time. His reasons were selfless.

Creed ignored the amusement he sensed.

Taking a deep breath, he tried to contain his impatience. He was a veteran troubleshooter, he shouldn't be edgy. The zortir continued to narrow the gap and Creed's scars seemed to tingle. He fought the need to rub at them, knowing that movement would give away his position. Why the hell were they standing here, doing nothing? He wanted to send that question to Ryne, but was pretty sure he remembered reading that zortirs could pick up telepathic messages.

Summers, of course, probably knew exactly what was going on. Because of his connection with Ryne, they shared thoughts without needing to send them. Creed scowled.

While the zortir wasn't wandering aimlessly, it also wasn't in a hurry to get anywhere. Even at this leisurely pace, though, Creed felt the ground shaking with every step it took. His hands tightened into fists.

Fucking shoot already.

The zortir stopped and long pointed ears separated themselves from its head. Shit, he hadn't sent that thought, but it must have sensed something anyway.

Creed worked on keeping his mind calm. After a

moment, the creature resumed its plodding, but its ears remained out, twitching from time to time. The awareness might cost them the advantage of surprise. Advantage. Yeah, right. Like catching it unaware was going to change the outcome. This plan was stupid and dangerous.

Ryne's tactics were weak. He'd been a troubleshooter twice as long; she'd learn more as his backup.

Creed ignored the internal voice reminding him that he didn't have any better ideas. Hell, at least he'd be doing something more than standing.

The burning at his two scars intensified and it was all he could do to keep from scratching them, trying to ease the fire. He looked down and saw two glowing orange circles through his faded gray T-shirt—exactly where his scars were from the earlier attack.

Panic clawed at his belly, but Creed forced it aside. He was a troubleshooter, damn it—no fear allowed. Drawing power from the earth, he prepared to blast the zortir. If Ryne was going to sit idle, he'd take over.

He pulled his hand back, then paused. When this mission went to hell—and it would—she was taking all the heat. Not him.

Creed watched the zortir stroll toward them. He waited for Ryne to shoot. And waited some more. His body was tight, ready for the fight, but she held her fire until the creature was past her, then she let loose. Damn it, what the hell was she thinking? The zortir's roar confirmed that he wasn't injured, just pissed off, and Creed seethed. What a fucking joke.

The zortir reared onto its hind legs, shifting into a two-legged creature and sprouting wings that were so black they glistened blue in the midmorning sun.

A shiver went through him—this was something he

hadn't seen before. Damn, he hoped the thing couldn't fly or they were in a shit-load of trouble. Eight feet of armored muscle packed with poison on the ground was bad enough; if it took to the air . . .

Ryne fired again and the zortir bellowed its displeasure as it turned to confront her. He and Summers shot at the same time, both of them hitting their target square in the back. The roar became a screech of absolute fury.

They continued taking turns blasting away, whoever had its rear being the one to shoot. Creed switched from fire to lightning, but it didn't seem to make any difference. All they were doing was spinning the zortir in a circle as it turned to face down whoever had hit it last. They were damn lucky it was low on brain power.

It spread its wings, flapping them angrily, and Creed decided it couldn't get airborne, not with that small wingspan. Although magically—

The zortir stopped rotating and looked directly at him. Its horns curved forward. Creed dodged clear as venom spewed from one of them. Smoke rose from the spot where it landed.

Summers shot the thing, turning it back toward him, and Creed glanced down. The orange puddle was maybe the width of a baseball and it sat like some kind of gel on the earth. The grass around it was black. That could have hit him. It could have hit him and it would have been Ryne's fault—after all, this was her genius plan.

There was another screech as the creature directed its toxic waste toward Ryne, but its aim was off and the shot fell harmlessly off to her side. She'd always had more luck than brains.

He should have had her power—he'd know what to

do with it. Creed mindlessly shot at the creature when it was his turn. Hell, Ryne couldn't even take care of a no-mind zortir and the council expected her to lead their people through Twilight Time?

Creed sidestepped another dart of poison. She wasn't merely incompetent, she was a danger. Anyone who followed her was at risk.

Taking her out would protect lives.

He could do it. Look at them now, vainly shooting at something that had enough armor to be immune to their attack. The zortir apparently had an inexhaustible supply of venom, and they were using up power faster than they could replenish it.

He was done wasting magic on this idiocy. Ryne wanted Summers—let the two of them handle this. Creed stopped firing, leaned against a nearby tree, and watched. The zortir continued to spin, shooting poison like a lawn sprinkler. Its aim, he noted, was more accurate when it directed the venom his way than when it attempted to hit either Ryne or her apprentice.

Why aren't you helping? Ryne's voice sliced through his head.

Because all we're doing is making the zortir dizzy.

Ryne began to give him an earful, but Creed blocked it. He was supposed to listen to her? Not a chance in hell. In his years as a rover, he'd learned a lot more than she had as a regular enforcer, he'd faced things she'd only read about, and he'd come out victorious.

She thought she was hot shit because she had more power than he did. She thought that gave her the right to lord it over him, to give him orders. She thought she was so much better than everyone else. Her attitude was a liability.

Ryne was a liability.

Wasn't he a guardian of his people? Hadn't he taken a vow to defend them no matter the cost?

She wasn't protected from him. All her shielding was going toward the zortir. Creed could solve this problem with one easy shot. He began to draw power from the earth, but something inside him balked.

You've done difficult things before to protect the Gineal.

Creed had, lots of times.

Would you allow hundreds, perhaps thousands to die because you lack the fortitude necessary to eradicate a danger?

Ryne wasn't only another troubleshooter, though, she'd been his friend as well. Could he do this?

Is she your friend? She turned from you quickly, did she not? And why? Because you didn't mention a small detail about soul pairings. Is that true friendship? She was using you, trying to milk your knowledge, your power.

Always asking him questions.

A user.

Yes, a user. A parasite. She contributed little and took much—not only from him but from the Gineal as well. They couldn't afford such a drain on their resources, not now.

A globule of zortir toxin landed less than an inch from his foot. Creed looked down at it, watched it sear the grass.

Her incompetence had nearly cost him. If that had hit him, the pain would have been excruciating. And she was costing the earth—the creature's poison was destroying the land around them.

What happened if a human wandered by?

She probably hadn't thrown the spell to keep others

away, and a human would be easy prey for the enraged zortir. How much longer would he stand here, allowing her to risk his life? The lives of the Gineal and of innocents?

He'd never shied away from necessary tasks before.

Creed drew his arm back, pulling energy from the earth, and aimed at Ryne.

13

CHAPTER

Maia closed the door sharply behind her, tossed her keys on the counter, and snarled, "Blackwood!"

No answer. It was a letdown to come in spoiling for a fight and have the man you wanted to throttle be absent. She huffed out a loud breath and leaned her hips against the kitchen cabinets. His little stunt with Mrs. Olson's memory had repercussions he couldn't have guessed— those missing minutes made the woman believe she should be in a nursing home.

She blew out another long breath. Honesty forced her to admit that it wasn't all Creed's fault. The woman's family took part of the blame.

Mrs. Olson's idiot sons and their families already paid too little attention to her. Christmas, Easter, Mother's Day, and birthdays were the only times the older woman could count on seeing them. It was Maia who visited every couple of days to make sure she was okay. Maia was the one who took her grocery shopping and went over on the weekend to help her sort her medicines into the pill container marked with the days of the week. Maia didn't mind doing it, but she knew it would mean so much more if it were a relative.

She was pretty sure she'd convinced her neighbor to wait and see if she had a repeat episode before making any hasty decisions, but Maia wanted to skin Creed alive for scaring Mrs. Olson. Sure, he'd promised to be more careful in the future, but he should have been careful to begin with. Gineal children were trained from the time they were tiny not to use their power where a human could see it.

Maia tightened her hands into fists. One of the symptoms of using black magic was carelessness. Not always, of course. Sometimes it was simply a mistake or not thinking things through or a human appearing where he wasn't expected. So which was it with Creed—miscalculation, as he'd claimed, or the dark forces?

Until she was sure, she was hanging close to him. It was the only way to ensure her sister was protected.

Pushing away from the counter, Maia paced the kitchen about half a dozen times before she decided it was a waste of energy. Creed would show up when he was finished, and that could be awhile depending on a few factors, including whether or not the council wanted a debriefing at the end of it.

With time to kill, she headed for her bedroom. She might as well do something productive, and she'd wanted a look at that book from the instant she'd touched it.

When she reached her bedroom, Maia shut the door behind her. If Creed returned and barged in—and he might—the few seconds it took him to open the door would allow her to close the text. That should keep it private.

She settled on her bed, propping up the pillows behind her, and reached for the book. Almost fearfully, Maia lifted the cover.

The first page was blank, maybe as a way to protect the information on the next page. Like thousands of other volumes in the central library, it was written in the ancient language of the Gineal. It had been seven years since she'd read anything in Cànan and Maia wondered how well her ability to translate had held up. Looked like she was going to find out. She tilted the book to a more comfortable angle and began.

Dear shorn woman—

Shorn woman? She scrunched her brow. That didn't sound right. Maia reread the word, ran through some possibilities, and figured it out.

Dear short-haired woman. There, that was better. *I am called Eithne, my father is . . .* Maia skimmed through the familial associations. Maybe one of the Gineal archivists would go into raptures over the names, but they meant nothing to her, and it wasn't as if she could ask anyone.

I'm certain you've many questions, but first and most pressing is why you were given this book. You will . . . Maia squinted as she tried to make out the word. She didn't recognize it, but whether that was because of the writing, the spelling, or a lapse in her language skills, she couldn't say. From the context, she thought perhaps it was "not believe." *. . . what I tell you and I do not blame you for your skepticism. You exist in a time with much evil around you and must always be wary.*

Last night as I sewed by the fire, my grandmother came to me. Since she's been dead for nigh on a score of years, it startled me and I pricked my finger. I add this to assure you that I was not dreaming. My grandmother's message was a simple one; I was to record in one place the knowledge acquired during my family's studies of those who have ceded their magic.

Maia sat up straighter. She hadn't realized anyone had wasted time looking into what happened to a Gineal who gave up their powers. Her excitement didn't last long. She'd been without her magic for seven years now and she doubted there was much this book could teach her that she didn't already know.

When I asked the whys of it, she replied that I would know some of the answers when the timing was correct and she bade me leave the first number of pages blank, that I would know what to write on them later. This message to you is the final item . . . Maia stumbled over the next word. Inserted, maybe? *With her instructions given, my grandmother departed.*

She was a wise woman, my grandmother, much esteemed in her lifetime, and I promised to fulfill her request. For the past three years, I have devoted myself to this project, diligently gathering generations' worth of notes and transferring them here for you. Tonight, my work ends.

I have doubts, concerns over what I chose to include and what I deemed less important. I could not fit everything we learned into one volume nor could I afford the time to copy more for you. I am an old woman, my hands ache so badly that I can hardly write these words. I persevere because I must, because tonight I saw why you need to have the information in this book.

My gift of far sight has been sporadic, more of a— Maia ran her finger under the line of text, trying to decipher the word. It was illegible. *—than a talent. I saw enough, however, to know that you are in a dangerous situation.*

When I close this book, I will put a spell around it to protect it, and a second so that only you will be able to open it. If I leave it in my home or to another of our people, it will be lost to you, but there are humans who farm nearby and they are kindred, magic users in their own right. They will help me. Then it will be up to fate. I pray that this book reaches you at the right time and that you are able to use the knowledge here.

Maia turned the page, but there was no more to the letter, damn it. She closed the text, and set it aside. Her head was spinning and she didn't know what to think.

Almost every Gineal who'd had access to paper and pen had recorded anything that had struck his or her fancy—kind of like current-day humans with their blogs—but simply because it was in black and white didn't mean the information was accurate. The spells were easier to evaluate because they had an energy to them, a power that could be felt, but discernment became much iffier with other writings.

And for an extra layer of difficulty, not only was the veracity of the message in question, so was the character of the writer. It wasn't just troubleshooters who were in danger of turning to the dark forces—any of the Gineal could turn. Anyone. While an effort had been made to quarantine texts left behind by someone who had fallen, some had likely slipped through the cracks—and Eithne had made certain that this tome had circumvented the few safeguards that were in place.

Maia picked the book up and ran her hand over the leather cover, trying to sense the intent of the woman who'd created it. Nothing.

Tossing the text back on the bed, Maia slumped against her headboard. Why couldn't anything ever be easy?

How many times had she asked that question of her mentor? Each time Taber had patiently replied, "If it were easy, we'd have no need of troubleshooters." A bit of an exaggeration—as long as human nature and Gineal tendencies remained as they were, there'd always be a need for the enforcers—but Maia understood. Life wasn't black and white, but a trillion shades of gray, and choices weren't always clear cut.

Like last night. Creed's kiss had made her go all molten, and she, who didn't like public displays of affection, had forgotten they were in a club. She'd never had that happen before, not even with Seth.

If things were simple, Maia would date Creed, get to know him better, and discover if his kisses always elicited that kind of heated response from her. But it was complicated. She'd ceded her magic and was considered an outsider. A relationship with Creed meant she'd be involved with someone who could never share his life with her, and she'd loathe that. She already hated the secrecy between her and Ryne; it would be nearly unbearable with a lover.

Then there was the question of how deeply Creed had delved into black magic. Had he turned? If he had, he was far more dangerous than she could deal with.

Maia crossed her ankles. She couldn't forget Ryne in this equation either. Her sister was mad as hell at Creed and didn't trust him. She'd constantly be interfering if Maia started something with him.

Part two of the Ryne factor was the persistent rumor that Creed had been romantically interested in her sister. Could she tolerate being the consolation prize because the woman he really wanted was taken?

It all might be moot, though, if Creed wasn't interested in a relationship. She knew he wanted her. Even if she hadn't felt his erection last night, she would have known from the hungry way he'd kissed her, but she needed more than sex, and that might not be part of the deal. Gineal didn't form long-term bonds with the powerless, period, and she wasn't settling for a fling. Been there, done that, and Seth had sent the T-shirt.

A shiver went down Maia's spine. Instead of worrying about her personal life or about a book that might not have any new information to impart, she better keep her mind on one particular demon. Seth wasn't just dangerous, he was lethal, and he was gunning for her sister.

Fucking son of—

At the same instant as he released a stream of fire, Creed jerked his arm and prayed.

The shot missed Ryne by inches. If she'd moved . . .

Her defenses went up instantly, but her focus remained on the zortir. Creed half expected Summers to come after him, but she must have warned him to stick to business. For now.

Creed started shaking as reaction set in and he tensed his muscles, trying to regain control. He'd nearly killed a friend.

Why the hell hadn't she protected herself completely? She should have enough experience to know better. But Creed couldn't hold on to the anger. Despite everything, she'd still trusted him enough not to shield herself against him. That was a mistake Ryne wouldn't make again.

She'd kept quiet about his withholding important intel, but she'd report this to the council. The ceannards would call him in, question him, and no matter what excuses he gave, they'd monitor him closely. Creed couldn't afford that.

Somehow he had to prevent Ryne from ratting him

out. Taking a deep breath, he forced his muscles to relax and tried to come up with something. He knew her. She followed the rules, but she was loyal to her friends. They were on the outs, but maybe six years would count for more than the last four months. What could he say, though, to convince her it was an honest mistake?

The scars on his torso itched, and with a hand that wasn't entirely steady, he scratched at one, then the other. Wait a second. When the burning intensified it meant—

Creed barely managed to leap clear of the zortir's shot of venom. Instead of thinking, he'd better fight. Somehow they needed to take out this thing, and they needed to do it before they ran out of magic or someone got hurt. He pushed aside the reminder that he'd nearly done more damage than their quarry.

Ryne and Summers were still stuck on their original tactic. Creed shook his head, but he understood her method—wear 'em down and get 'em—only that wasn't working. The only plus on their side of the column was that the zortir hadn't charged.

He looked around. Taking a tree down on top of it wasn't going to do much, he decided, not with the armor it had. Rocks ran into the same problem. Zortirs had enough magic to get themselves out of a pit, they could avoid a flood of water, and they were able to go without breathing for long periods of time, which left asphyxiation out of the mix.

Looked like they were stuck with Ryne's plan. Creed shook his head. There had to be two dozen softball-size patches of toxin searing the earth and who knew how many more would be added before this ended?

The zortir dropped back to all fours and ran at Summers. Ryne let loose with the most intense and lengthy blast of fire Creed could remember seeing. It worked. The thing turned back toward her and spit more poison.

Since he had the perfect angle, Creed shot a bolt of lightning, hitting his target in its right flank. His healed wounds became inferno hot and he gasped—he couldn't prevent it. The zortir stared intently at him, its blue eyes glaring holes into him. Ryne swung the creature back toward her and Creed gasped again, this time in relief as the burning eased. He looked down and saw that the two circles looked like flashlights being held to the fabric of his shirt.

He wanted this thing done. Creed gathered himself, drew all the power he could, and chanted a spell to send the zortir back to its dimension. The spell might not work; it could have enough magic to overcome this, too, but this should have been the first thing they tried. Stupid that they hadn't.

It ended up being a nonissue—nothing happened when he closed the incantation.

What are you doing? Ryne sounded suspicious.

After he explained, he added, *Spinning the zortir in circles isn't doing much. Got any other ideas?*

When she closed the connection between them, Creed guessed she didn't. Neither did he, not at the moment. If they could figure out how it traveled to this dimension they might be able to come up with a countermeasure, but trying random spells and hoping one worked was a good way to burn through magic.

Creed ducked as a shot of venom sailed high. The damn thing was up on its hind legs again. As far as the zortir's defenses went, he far preferred dodging poison gel to getting gored.

Defenses. Wait a second. Why did any creature develop venom? To either capture food or to defend itself, right? And the zortirs' toxin was strong stuff, maybe strong enough to take out another zortir. This thing was shooting the poison out of its horns, which led Creed to believe that was a standard ploy when it was in battle.

The globs of orange gel sat where they landed and Creed telekinetically gathered them together. He started with the ones near him, rolling them toward each other until they formed a bigger ball. Once that was accomplished, he drew in the ones that were farther afield.

More darts of poison were directed at him while he worked, but the zortir remained unaware of what Creed was doing. Maybe it didn't care. Maybe the level of toxicity declined rapidly and all he had was orange gelatin, but it was worth a try.

He waited until the creature had its back to him, then Creed mentally lifted the large ball of poison. As the zortir whirled back in his direction, he gave it a strong magical push.

Despite its evasive maneuver, the venom hit it squarely in the face and chest. As the zortir shrieked, Creed quickly shot lightning at it, catching it where the toxin had hit. It staggered.

Drawing more power, Creed shot again and again.

Ryne and Summers both caught on, and as the zortir reeled, they hit it with fire. With the three of them working together, they were able to let loose with a continual barrage.

The zortir fell.

It shot one last desperate round of venom, but it landed on the creature. The whimper sounded pathetic.

Creed had the best angle, and he delivered the death blow.

The three of them met over the body. "How did you know to do that?" Ryne demanded.

He shrugged. "It seemed logical."

She scowled at him before scanning the dead zortir. As she started the chant to transform the zortir into pure energy and send it out into the universe, the scars on his belly began to burn again. He crossed his arms over them before anyone could see them glow.

Summers looked like he wanted to take Creed apart, but he was still tethered. That wasn't going to last long. Once they wrapped things up here and the mission was officially over, it was going to get ugly.

Ryne began a second proclamation and Creed interrupted her. "Don't mess with the poison. You don't know what you're doing."

"And you do?" she asked.

"No, but the Gineal have experts in cleaning up magical toxic waste. Rather than risking more damage, it's better to have them handle this."

For a moment, she looked as if she wanted to argue with him, but then she nodded and moved on to a different subject. "You want to explain," Ryne growled, as she crowded him, "why the hell you shot at me?"

He'd known that question was coming, and with Ryne, that it would be sooner rather than later. Unfortunately, he hadn't come up with any good lies. Creed cast a quick glance at Summers, but the man looked like he wanted to rip Creed apart with his bare hands.

"Well?" she demanded, moving even closer.

With his arms crossed, it threw him off balance, and though it displayed weakness, he was forced to take a step back. Ryne followed. He started to lower his arms, but the burning sensation meant those scars were still lit up like— Inspiration struck. "It was an accident."

"Bullshit. You were aiming right for me."

"Wrong. If I'd wanted to hit you, I would have. I was taking a shot at the zortir and something distracted me."

"You expect me to believe that?" Ryne asked incredulously. "Everyone knows Creed Blackwood is cool under fire."

He made certain his hesitation was noticeable, then he raised his T-shirt, letting both Ryne and Summers see the glowing orange scars on his sides. "This was a new one for me."

"Holy crap," Ryne said, and the anger was gone from her voice. "What the hell is that?"

"I don't have a clue." And that was the truth. "It started with a burning sensation, and the longer the battle went on, the more it intensified." He let the shirt drop.

"And you want us to believe," Summers said, sounding more than a little skeptical, "that in the middle of shooting, you glanced down, saw those things, and just kept firing without looking at what you were trying to hit?"

Creed had hoped, but he'd known it would be unlikely. "It wasn't like that. I felt something different, more than the burning. It came on suddenly and made me jerk my arm. That's what had me looking down."

It sounded plausible, and because of their positions, no one would know any different. Creed cleared his throat before adding, "No one was more upset than me when I realized how close I came to hitting you, Ryne."

That brought her gaze back to his and she studied him intently. This last statement, though, was baldly honest and she wouldn't discern anything except sincerity.

Ryne reached for his arm, gave him a reassuring squeeze. "Creed, it's—"

"Babe," Summers said quietly, "don't forget that pretty boy left out a crucial piece of information about the soul pairing thing last April. Today's the second time he nearly killed you."

She withdrew and stepped back until she was side by side with Summers. "That's right," Ryne said. "You never answered me before when I asked this question, but why didn't you tell us that Deke and I could share power?"

Ah, fuck. Creed scrambled. Usually, the most convincing lies had a bit of truth in them; time to mix things up and see how well he did. What the hell—at this point, he had nothing to lose. "I planned to tell you, but Galen showed up and it all became chaotic as I left."

"Blackwood," Summers drawled, "you're full of shit. You could have said something to me while Ryne was letting Galen in or you could have spoken up and gotten our full attention. Instead, you waltzed out the door and left her hung out to dry."

"Ryne had been chasing Anise for six years at that point. I had no way of knowing there wouldn't be another opportunity to mention it." Creed hooked his thumbs through his belt loops.

"And you were feeling malicious," the other man suggested.

Time to throw in some truth. "Was I happy Ryne had hooked up with you? No, you know I wasn't, but I would have passed the information on later. Things just happened too fast." At least he liked to think he would have passed it along. Creed wasn't sure himself any longer. Summers continued to stare at him. "Whatever else did or didn't happen," Creed added, "Ryne's been my friend for six years. That means something to me."

Their expressions didn't change, but something shifted, Creed felt it. Maybe, just maybe, they wouldn't report his actions today to the ceannards.

"We better get out of here," Ryne said. "I need to

contact the council so they can send someone over to clean up."

Creed nodded. Her voice had been carefully neutral and he didn't know what she was going to say in her report, but he couldn't ask. Any push, no matter how slight, could tip his house of cards and it was precarious enough as it was.

He opened a transit when they did, but after Ryne and Summers departed, Creed stayed where he was and slowly looked around the field. The sun was shining, the breeze was gentle, keeping the humidity from feeling too cloying, and he heard birds singing in the distance. The scene was nearly idyllic, but he'd always associate it with the most terrifying moment of his life.

What happened today was scarier than the blackouts. Much scarier. He'd been aware of what he was doing, but it was as if he were a bystander and had been watching someone else. Someone he was unable to stop.

The tremors began anew and Creed jammed his hands into his pockets as he took deep breaths. It was too easy to see Ryne dying. To see her dead.

Part of him had stood there and coldly, resolutely prepared to kill his friend. Another part of him had been howling, wailing, begging that other half not to do it, but that side hadn't been in control. He'd been powerless to stop his own actions until the very last instant, and that was one of the most frightening things of all.

It didn't top the list, though.

He couldn't deny the truth any longer, couldn't pretend. No matter what he'd told himself in the past, what happened here had shown him the truth. Creed drew in a shaky breath. He'd fallen to the dark forces.

14
CHAPTER

Maia walked alongside Creed to the entrance of the Minneapolis Institute of Arts. He'd been pensive since his return from the call-out, and though she knew better than to ask, she was curious about what had happened.

"I've got the admission fee covered," he said as he opened the door for her.

"It's free, but thanks."

"Free? Every Wednesday?"

"No, every day," she said. The dedication to the arts, and the belief that they should be available to everyone, was one of her favorite things about living in the Twin Cities, although she rarely took advantage of it. Maia tried to remember the last time she'd been to the museum, but drew a blank. More than a year, though, easy.

Going to places like this was a bittersweet experience for her; maybe that was why she didn't put herself through it too often. She loved art, could lose herself in it for hours, but it hurt to know that she'd never be part of it, not as anything more than an observer.

If she'd been smart, she would have gone to college while she'd been working as a troubleshooter, but back then, Maia hadn't seen the point. What good was a degree in art when she'd spend her life working as one of the council's enforcers? It had been simpler to read on her own, and she didn't have to worry about tests that way. Now, of course, she fervently wished she had that little piece of paper.

Creed stopped by the information desk and picked up a map of the museum. They moved out of the flow of traffic before he opened it. "Second floor," he said, tapping a square on one of the three maps. "Egypt and Ancient Near East."

They went up the stairs side by side, their hands brushing a couple of times. The third time it happened, Creed reached for her and linked their fingers. Maia was taken so off-guard that she nearly tripped and had to grab the railing to steady herself. Surreptitiously, she cast a glance at him, but his face gave nothing away.

Something had definitely happened today, because Creed wasn't a hold-your-hand kind of guy. The way that he was hanging on to her, though, made her think he needed comfort or maybe to be anchored to another person. For the first time, she wondered if he felt alone like she did. Sure, he had friends, but how often could he see them when he was working? The council kept the rovers busy, they always had. In the five days he'd been with her, Creed had taken two assignments, and from what she could see, neither job had been easy for him. She remained quiet until they reached the next level, however, then with as much nonchalance as she could muster, Maia said, "You were gone on the call-out for a long time."

His hand tightened around hers. "I had to go see a healer afterward."

"You were hurt?" He hadn't told her that.

"Old injury." Creed's left hand came up and rubbed his side—about the area where the zortir had wounded him.

"I thought Ryne healed that."

"So did I."

"Let me get this straight," she said, keeping her tone even with effort. "After making me promise not to get you a healer while you were on death's door, you just decide to stop off on your way home from a call-out?"

His lips curved slightly at the corners. "It turned out the council already knew about my visit to that other dimension."

He didn't say more, and even though she had a million questions, Maia changed the subject. She pointed to the sign in the archway up ahead. "We must be getting close."

It was either a very wide corridor or a very narrow room, but it was lined with round white pillars and exhibits. Track lighting made the space bright and each of the cases had its own interior light. She was tempted to slow down and take a longer look at the displays as they walked through, but this wasn't a fun outing, it was a mission. If she wanted to immerse herself in what was here, she'd have to come back some other time.

Thinking of works of art had her glancing to her left again. Creed had taken a shower and changed clothes when he'd come home. He'd stayed in the bathroom for a long time, another indication that something had happened today. She'd never seen him in a shirt with a collar before, but the aqua polo showed off his tan and the muscles of his biceps. He hadn't bothered to do more than towel dry his hair, and between that and the thick humidity, it had curled more than usual.

"What?" he asked, catching her staring.

"I was just thinking that it was nice for once not to be the prettiest half of a couple."

Creed snorted. "Are you fishing for compliments or do we need to find a mirror to remind you what you look like? Trust me, I'm not the one getting leered at."

"Hah! You need to pay attention. Women are more subtle than men when they ogle."

He made a grumbling sound, but Maia thought she detected some extra color in his cheeks. "This is it," he said as they turned the corner. "Can we focus on what we're here for and leave appearance out of it?"

"Sure," she said easily. But her goal was accomplished—Creed didn't seem to be brooding anymore.

She'd expected him to release her now that they'd reached their destination, but he didn't. Instead, he tugged her with him to an alabaster wine jar. They stood, seeming to stare at it for a really long time, but she knew Creed was trying to pick up any traces of the demon's presence. Maia wished she could help with this. After all, she could still sense things, but unless Seth had been there within the hour, she'd read nothing.

"It's not a large collection," Creed said as they moved to a model boat with figures. The wood had been eaten away in places, but considering it was over four thousand years old, it was in remarkable shape.

"No, it isn't," Maia agreed. "With Seth's obsession, though, it would take only one piece to attract him. You're not sensing anything?"

Creed shook his head. "Not yet."

Maia remained quiet and let him concentrate. It seemed to take forever before he moved to the next piece, but from his demeanor, she knew he'd come up empty again. The same thing happened over and over.

Had Seth somehow managed to overcome his fixation with ancient Egypt?

Everything they stopped at was beautiful, but Maia caught her breath when they moved to another display. She wanted to reach out and touch it, but of course, she couldn't. The granite carving of the pharaoh Amenhotep wasn't even a foot tall, but the details on it were exquisite, right down to the stripes and cobra on his headdress.

They stood in front of the pharaoh a lot longer than they had at any other exhibit and Maia looked at Creed. He had a furrow between his brows, but she wasn't sure if that meant he was sensing traces of Seth or if he was frustrated because he was coming up blank.

The room was empty now, although that was unlikely to last long, and Maia looked around. Something in another display caught her attention and she stared at it intently, trying to make out the features. At this distance it was difficult to be certain, but if she was right and Seth had been to the museum, he would have made a beeline for it. "I hate to interrupt," she said, voice low, "but if you're not getting anything here, I suggest we take a look at that bronze."

"We might as well," he said.

Maia nodded in satisfaction when they reached the piece; she had been correct, it was Isis. She didn't know how accurate Egyptian mythology was, but from what she'd read, Set had been tied to this goddess as well as to Osiris.

According to the information card, the piece was from the Roman period, a little later than Seth's area of interest, but she didn't think that would matter to him, not when it was Isis. The fine details on this statue were even more perfect than on the carving of the pharaoh, but before Maia had a chance to really appreciate it,

Creed's hand tightened around hers. He immediately relaxed his grip and said, "Got him."

They moved slowly as Creed followed Seth's path through the museum. The demon had apparently wandered through most of the second floor and Maia wondered at his interest in Asian art. A few times, Creed hesitated, and she knew without his needing to say a word that he was having trouble staying on the trail. It probably meant that Seth had been here days ago and that a lot of humans had come through since, muddying the energy. She'd known it was a long shot that they'd find him staring at an exhibit, but she was disappointed anyway. Maia wanted this over.

Wordlessly, they exited the building and crossed the street to a park. The grass was green, there were a lot of trees for shade, but she had a hard time imagining the urbane demon wanting to spend time here. They went up a gentle rise and Creed stopped near a tree that had a bench positioned in front of it.

"His trail ends here," he announced.

Maia nodded. "Seth wasn't into the outdoors, not even manicured nature like this. He was probably trying to find somewhere discreet to use magic in order to leave."

"Could be," Creed allowed, "but I was hoping to find a hint of where his lair is. You know he's holed up somewhere."

Tugging her hand free of his, Maia crossed to the bench and sat down. She'd hoped to have more to show for this excursion, too. Creed sprawled beside her, close enough for her to feel his heat, but far enough away that they weren't touching. "Have you checked all the five-star hotels in town?" she asked.

"And the four-star, as well."

Seth must have found somewhere private to stay then, maybe a condo or a mansion. Maia sighed; it would be too time consuming to try to track that down. Their best hope was finding a trail that led to where he was living, but he'd had a lot of years to hone his survival instincts.

"Seth isn't going to be easy to find."

"Or easy to take down," Creed said. "How'd you hook up with him anyway?"

Maia gave no outward reaction to the question, but her heart began to pound rapidly. There were a number of noncommittal answers she could make, like reminding him that Seth had blurred her memory, but she remembered this with absolute clarity. "Do you want the long version or the short one?" she asked.

It wasn't an offer Maia made often, but she was hoping if she showed a willingness to share that she might get more information out of him. Besides, this wasn't all that sensitive, and some of it he'd guess at on his own anyway.

"What's the short version?"

"I was using black magic for years by the time Seth showed up, and you know that like attracts like." It didn't get much shorter than that.

Turning his head to meet her gaze, Creed said, "Give me the long version."

"It's really long," Maia warned him. If she provided details, he needed the background, too. She wanted him to understand why she'd made the choices she had.

"My afternoon is yours," he said. "Shoot."

She didn't speak immediately; instead, Maia stared at the leafy top of one of the park's trees and took the time to organize her thoughts. "I grew up," she said quietly, "with parents who didn't pay any attention to me. I'm not telling you this for sympathy, but simply for context. I was never physically neglected, but emotionally? Yeah. There were times I wondered if my parents remembered they had children."

"How could they forget?"

Maia shrugged. "Who knows? Too lost in each other and their jobs as troubleshooters, maybe? I'd pretty much given up trying to get their attention by the time Ryne came along. I'm five years older," she tacked on in case Creed didn't know that. "I tried to give my sister what our parents couldn't, but that didn't allow me to be a child. And," she admitted, "there were times I resented it. Not Ryne," she clarified, "the situation."

She paused, but Creed just waited patiently. "When I was twelve, I left home and went to live with Taber and his wife. I thought I'd have more freedom because I wouldn't have to take care of my little sister any longer, but you remember what it's like being an apprentice troubleshooter."

"Yeah, I know," Creed said. "It's like going to two different schools, each of them full time, and we're expected to excel at both, no excuses."

"I wanted to join the drama club, but I couldn't. Same for dance line and the yearbook staff and the tennis team. There was no time to do anything for fun; it was all studying and work and tests. Maybe if I'd had a younger mentor, he would have remembered the need to simply be a kid now and then, but Taber was in his seventies and at the tail end of his career as an enforcer when I was sent to him."

"He was among the best troubleshooters the Gineal ever had," Creed pointed out, "and he's been an outstanding councilor."

"I know. My intent isn't to insult Taber. I'm aware there were apprentices who would have given anything to trade places with me. I'm only explaining that it was all business with him. I didn't get to go to parties or out on dates. I woke up in the morning, went to school, came home, and studied the things that the Gineal expected me to know. There was never a break."

"There's a lot to learn."

"Did you get time off occasionally?" Maia countered. She really did know how lucky she'd been to have Taber as a mentor. She could have ended up with someone like her sister had. Anise had already turned to the dark forces before Ryne had gone to live with the older woman, though no one had known it at the time, and her sister had been messed up in a lot of ways. Ryne was still dealing with some of the fallout.

"Yeah," Creed admitted, "but I didn't get to participate in extracurricular activities either." He smirked. "I like to believe I'd be playing in the major leagues if I'd only been able to join the baseball team."

For a moment she couldn't speak, amazed that he'd offered any personal information, no matter how benign, then she said, "You'd have companies lined up, wanting endorsements from you whether you were a star or not."

"Is that another allusion to my looks?" He didn't give her time to answer. "You keep it up and I'm going to start mentioning your appearance."

At that moment Maia realized that Creed didn't center his attention only on her beauty. Most people couldn't see beyond her face, but Blackwood didn't judge her by that criteria. Yes, he liked her appearance, she knew that, but it wasn't his *sole* focus. Maybe it was because he was gorgeous himself that he looked deeper than her exterior. Maia shifted on the bench, adjusting her bracelet to buy some time; she wanted to figure this out. He didn't allow her to think very long, though.

"So Taber worked you to death and . . ."

"I wasn't complaining," Maia said between gritted

teeth. "I just wanted you to understand that from the age of five or six until nineteen, I had to be an adult before I should have been."

"I get it, angel. Now can we move past your teenage angst?"

Maia went rigid. "Don't—"

Creed cut her off. "I'm sorry," he said, putting a hand just above her knee and squeezing her leg. "I have a headache and it's making me short-tempered. I didn't mean to piss you off, but you're a long way from answering the original question."

She could feel the heat of his fingers searing into her thigh and it was all she could do to keep from squirming. When she noticed he was waiting for her to accept his apology, Maia considered what he'd said and decided he meant it. "I'm sorry, too. I know I get defensive when I talk about anything having to do with Seth and black magic. I can't seem to help it."

"Understandable."

"So I was nineteen, I'd finished training, and I was immediately assigned to a territory. I'd expected to guard the library first like most troubleshooters do, but I guess I was deemed more mature and ready for the job than the others who were unassigned at the time." She shrugged. "I went from Taber's supervision and an apprentice's stipend to being on duty in Las Vegas and having the salary of an enforcer literally overnight."

"It went to your head."

"Oh yeah, though not at first. I started out just as serious as I'd been during training, but then it dawned on me that there was no one to say I couldn't go out and see the strip."

"You got hooked on gambling."

"No," Maia shook her head, "I didn't. It was shopping. Clothes and shoes and jewelry and art for the home I lived in. Of course, I had to show off all this stuff some-where, so I started going to clubs. Gradually, I ended up with an entourage and we'd barhop together."

"You must have had a lot of call-outs in that territory," Creed said neutrally. "That had to cut into your partying."

"Not as much as you'd think. I'd handle the job, change clothes, and catch up with the group. It was somewhere in this time frame that rumbles reached me about how strong Ryne was. People started saying I was the pretty one and my sister was the powerful one. She was only fifteen years old and hadn't even come into her full magic yet."

"You resented that?"

A breeze fluttered her hair and Maia pushed it out of her face before saying, "I'm not sure resent is the right word; I never begrudged Ryne her power. Did I wish I had it? You bet—name one Gineal who wouldn't—but I was glad for her."

"I resented her," Creed admitted, taking Maia by surprise again. "She calls me the biggest badass trou-bleshooter, but she usurped that title a long time ago, and I didn't appreciate it."

"How'd you end up being friends then?"

Creed's thumb began to circle on the outside of her knee and Maia shivered despite the heat. "I met her. You know how straightforward she is; it's hard not to like that."

"What did you do that made her distrust you so much?" She didn't think he'd answer, but damn it, she wanted to know.

"Ask Ryne. If she tells you her side of the story, I'll tell you mine."

"Nice evasion, Blackwood," Maia groused. "You know how hell-bent she is on following the rules."

"Yep," he said, sounding so damn smug, Maia nearly

growled. "Now, you were in Vegas playing party girl, and . . ."

She wanted to press him, but knew it wouldn't do her any good, just like it wouldn't get her anywhere to push Ryne on this subject. Reluctantly, she moved on. "And I was pretty much out of control. I was shopping most days, out every night, and it took a toll. I knew exhaustion weakened our powers, but I was young enough that I still felt invincible. It was a rude awakening to find out that I wasn't, and to keep from getting killed, I dropped dark. Really dark. I vowed I'd never do it again, it was a one-time thing and I'd learned my lesson, but . . ." Maia let her voice trail off, uncertain how to explain how easy it was to forget all her good intentions.

"But you'd had a taste of the dark forces," Creed said. "Hell, you'd used them without losing control, and if you went that deep once without a problem, you could do it again."

Maia smiled sadly. "Yes, and this way I could continue to go out and have fun. You'd be surprised how easy it was to slide just a little bit farther each time."

"No, I wouldn't. It's a battle every troubleshooter wages over and over during their career."

The grimness in his voice made her pause for a moment. "I lost. Of course, I didn't realize that, and by the time I was twenty-five, I was fully into black magic and blind to the fact. And then Seth showed up."

Creed gave her leg another squeeze, but it was almost as if he were taking comfort as much as giving it. Maia could only shake her head at what a fool she'd been. Why had she ever believed that she'd be the one to master the dark forces when others had not?

"He was smart," Maia said when Creed cleared his throat. "For one, Seth hid that he was a demon. All I sensed from him was human energy. And for another, he didn't come at me directly. He befriended my neighbor, and when Justin introduced us, I didn't think anything of it."

"Seth made himself one of your hangers-on?"

"He joined the group and never left. Somehow, he usually ended up sitting next to me, and he was charming, funny, and movie-star handsome."

She frowned, remembering how easy she'd been for Seth to manipulate. It sickened her to recall that time. Even though she knew Gineal didn't fall for outsiders, she'd been in love and thinking about forever. She'd been the only one. For Seth, she'd been a convenience, a way to get off when he was randy. Maia cringed at the thought, but she refused to soft pedal the truth to make herself feel better. Though it mortified her, she knew it had been her power and her body that had attracted him, not her.

"He knew exactly how to play me," she confessed. A lump formed in her throat and Maia swallowed hard to get rid of it.

"He's a demon who's been around for thousands of years; of course he knew how to play you."

It was the note of impatience in Creed's voice that made what he said register. How *could* she beat herself up for falling for Seth and his lies? She'd been twenty-five, a baby compared to him.

"He knew how to play everyone," Maia said slowly. "Seth never put a foot wrong himself, but he stirred things up, and when I finally did realize what he was, I figured out that he influenced people around him to act. I can't tell you how many times he'd make a woman flash her breasts or lift her skirt, and that was just for starters." She shook her head. "There was nothing he enjoyed more than setting things in motion and watching the tempest that followed."

"Chaos demon," Creed said grimly.

"Yes, exactly."

"How did you learn who and what he was?"

Maia sighed softly. "He slipped. It made me wake up and see how far gone I was."

That was one memory she wished wasn't clear. They'd been in bed, and for a split second at the moment of his orgasm, he'd dropped the shield that made his energy appear human. The lassitude she'd been enjoying after her own climax had been ripped from her as she'd sensed what Seth really was for the first time, sensed just how fetid and ugly a demon he was. And with that knowledge had come disgrace and the realization of how far she'd fallen.

By the time he'd recovered, she'd had a mask firmly in place. For nearly two months, Maia had struggled to hold that instant of clarity as she'd desperately searched for an out, some way to keep her powers. She hadn't found one.

It hadn't been easy to hang on—she'd dropped into black magic again and again—but she hadn't lost her awareness. At least not totally. Most important, though, she found a spell she could use when she gave up her magic that took part of Seth's. Maia had known that at some time in the future, one of the Gineal would be fighting the demon, and she'd wanted that enforcer to have the best chance possible.

Feeling the weight of Creed's stare, Maia turned—and found him closer than she'd expected. For an eternity, neither one of them moved, then he ran his fingers along her jaw line, tipping her face to his. The kiss was gentle, soft, but in it Maia found comfort, understanding, commiseration, and beneath that, a banked heat that she longed to set free.

Before she did something stupid, Creed pulled back,

putting space between them, but he didn't take his hand from her thigh. Despite that, his expression was remote again, the way it had been when he'd first come to town, and she regretted that.

The silence now seemed awkward, and to try to dispel some of that, Maia said, "Once I became aware of the fact I'd gone too far to ever turn back, I realized I had to give up my power. I knew the council would send Ryne, and I couldn't let her hunt me."

Creed's hand tightened on her leg, then he released her and leaned forward, resting his forearms on his thighs. He shifted, seeming to reach a decision, and said, "The council knew you'd turned." She gasped, but he kept right on talking. "They didn't assign Ryne to bring you in, though. They gave that job to me."

15
CHAPTER

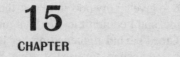

"What?" Maia asked softly. She realized she sounded as bewildered as she felt, but she couldn't seem to shake herself out of it. "That's not possible."

Creed continued to meet her gaze, and as she stared at him, it dawned on her that she wouldn't have needed to cede her magic. She could have allowed an enforcer to kill her because it wouldn't have been Ryne. "That's not possible," she said again, but this time her voice was stronger, almost accusatory. He had to be lying. "The council always sends the enforcer closest to the one who turns. *Always.*"

"Not this time."

"Why?" He looked away from her and Maia saw red. "Damn it, you tell me why they were sending you!"

She heard him sigh and wanted to smack him. This was one topic Maia wasn't going to gracefully drop because it was troubleshooter business. She needed answers. "Why you and not Ryne?"

Creed muttered something she couldn't quite hear and then straightened, but he stared out at the park, refusing to meet her eyes. "I was in Peru when I was contacted. I expected a call-out, only I was summoned to the council chambers instead. I remember racking my brain, trying to come up with what the hell I'd done that would get me in trouble, but I'd been good lately."

He paused and Maia fought the need to tell him to keep going. She had to curb her impatience and let him explain this his way or she might not get any answers at all, no matter how determined she was.

"All nine ceannards were there when I arrived and I figured I was in really deep shit this time." Creed shifted, putting some more space between them on the bench. "Nessia had only been council leader for a few months at that point, and she gave me the assignment. I'd been a rover for eight years by then and I'd never been asked to bring in one of the Gineal before; my missions always involved demons."

"So you wanted to know why you and not Ryne."

"Not quite. I didn't know who you were, and while I'd heard of Ryne, I didn't know she was your family. My question to them was, why the hell can't you find someone else?"

"Worded that way?" Maia couldn't imagine talking to the council with such a lack of respect.

"Yeah." Creed shifted again, this time turning toward her. His lips had curved slightly. "Now you know why I was trying to figure out what I'd done to get summoned. I was in trouble a lot back then." He sobered. "Instead of reprimanding me for my tone and language, though, Nessia answered and I heard more than I expected. You said something the other night about giving up your magic because you didn't want to force your sister to kill you; that's the same reason the council gave me. They didn't want to lose Ryne as a troubleshooter."

Maia tried to make sense of what he said, but she couldn't. There was no reason on earth why the council would think that she had a prayer of taking down her sister—even if Maia was far enough gone to shoot at her. "As strong as Ryne is, there's no way the council would have lost her."

"You don't think so?" Creed raised his brows. "Then you need to think a little harder."

It only took an instant to come up with the answer. "Killing me," Maia whispered, "would have destroyed her." She'd been aware of this, but she hadn't realized that the council had understood it as well.

"She'd finish the assignment because that's the kind of person she is, but she'd never be useful again. They were concerned that would be the case even if she managed to bring you in without a fight. The ceannards weren't sure if Ryne could live with being responsible for you being stripped of your magic and your memory. At the time, I thought they were exaggerating or worrying about nothing, but after getting to know her, I got it. She's tough in a lot of ways, but not when it comes to you. Shit, Maia, she fucking worships you."

"I know," she said quietly. This time, Maia was the one to look away.

Her relationship with her sister was more complicated than that, of course. The hero worship had lessened as Ryne had gotten older, but it had never gone away entirely, and when Maia had admitted to ceding her powers because of black magic, not a human male, the news had knocked the slats out from beneath Ryne. There'd been disillusionment, a lot of it, but that had faded over time and Maia had a feeling she'd been cast in the role of noble hero, sacrificing everything for her younger sister.

Maybe she hadn't tried as hard as she could have to talk Ryne out of that scenario, but was it so wrong to want her sister to respect her? And in a way it was true, it had been her promise to protect Ryne that had given Maia the strength to relinquish her magic—even if there would have been no need for any sacrifice if Maia hadn't fallen.

She recalled some of Creed's comments and the fact that he'd been aware of her use of black magic, something that had never been common knowledge among the Gineal. "That's why you know things about me, isn't it?"

"Yeah. The council filled me in on you."

She nodded, unsurprised by his response. The councilors would have given him everything they had on her when he'd received the assignment, and the ceannards held extensive information about all their enforcers. Maia debated whether or not to ask the next question, then decided she wanted to hear the answer no matter how uncomfortable it left her. "How far along were you with the job?"

Creed stared at her for a moment and she knew he was measuring her. She must have passed because he said, "Preliminary recon. I felt it when you gave up your magic, reported it to the council, and they recalled me."

Reconnaissance meant he'd been trailing her, trying to get a feel for her habits. Maia barely hid the grimace. He'd seen her with Seth then and had observed the bar-hopping firsthand. Her only consolation was that Creed must have been around close to the end, and Maia had been fighting to rein in her behavior then. She'd done far more outlandish things before she'd realized how deep her involvement with the dark forces was. "I never noticed you," she admitted. "How long were you following me?"

"Four days. I tracked your energy signature at a distance so you wouldn't know I was there."

"You were close to confronting me, weren't you?"

He shrugged, but Maia knew she was right. It had taken so much energy for her to hold on that last week that she hadn't done anything spontaneous. Creed would have learned by then that her routine was set in stone and begun to make his plans.

"You had to have seen Seth then, gotten a feel for his energy. Why the difficulty with him now?"

Creed tapped his fingers against his thighs and she knew he was deciding what to say. He stilled, then said, "I scanned the people you came in contact with once and that was it. All I read was human energy and a few demons from weaker branches."

"Seth fooled you, too." She barely kept the pleasure out of her voice. It hadn't only been her or some deficiency she'd had; a rover had been taken in as well. The grumbling noise Creed produced expressed his frustration and Maia sighed. "Did Seth know you were there?"

"You know him better than me. Would he be aware?"

After a moment's thought, she said, "I have no idea. He hid a lot from me and blurred some of what he didn't conceal. My memory—"

"Is compromised. I know. It's a bitch, though."

"No kidding." *He* didn't like it? Maia snorted. Blackwood should try living with it. Her irritation didn't last long, though. He was trying to catch Seth and protect her sister; she couldn't fault him for that. Stretching her legs out in front of her, she let the green of the grass, of the trees, soothe her.

A question popped into her head about the council.

"Why the special treatment for Ryne?" Maia asked. "I don't recall the ceannards making an exception before." Although she was damn glad they'd done it this time.

After a minute, Creed said, "She's one of the strongest ever recorded. Not among the most powerful living now—the most powerful ever. Nessia said our people couldn't afford to lose her, that she'd be the spearhead in the battles to come."

"Which rankled you further," Maia suggested.

"No shit." Creed's lips turned up again. "Until then, I'd had fantasies of being the one to lead the Gineal in the wars of Twilight Time. I had to switch to daydreaming about hitting the winning homer in the final game of the World Series."

He was making light of it, but Maia didn't think he'd been amused seven years ago. It had to be hugely humbling to go from believing he was the strongest of the enforcers to learning a twenty-year-old girl could kick his ass. Maia started to offer some subtle sympathy, but then she remembered something he'd said the other night. A true soul pairing allowed troubleshooters to share—no, *increase*—their magic. Things fell into place.

She curled her hands into fists. "Is that why you were romantically interested in Ryne? Did you think if you had a soul pairing with her that you'd be the biggest badass again?"

Hiding his emotions was ingrained, and Creed figured that was the only thing that kept him from reacting. Damn, he'd said more to Maia than he'd realized if she was able to reach this conclusion. "Why would you think I had a romantic interest in your sister?" he asked, stalling.

"It's been the talk among the troubleshooters for years. I might be an outsider and not privy to Gineal secrets any longer, but gossip was considered safe conversation."

Creed wanted to bring a hand up and rub his throbbing temples, but she might read too much into that. He just wished, though, that he didn't have to tap dance in this mine field with his head feeling as if it were about to explode.

"You'd believe idle speculation?" he asked. Without giving Maia time to answer, he continued. "I've known Ryne for six years, and in that time, I've never asked her out, never kissed her, hell, I've never even held her hand. If I were interested in her, don't you think I'd have done something?"

Maia looked dubious. "Well, yes," she reluctantly admitted, "but—"

"But what? Do you really think I'm *that* lame with women?"

Her fists uncurled and Creed relaxed. He was out of the woods—for now, at least—but if Maia ever had a conversation with Summers about this, his ass would be back in the sling. Ryne had been oblivious, but her lover sure as hell wasn't.

"No one could possibly be that backward," Maia said, "especially not someone who looks like you."

He gave a mock groan. "There you go, bringing up my appearance again. Tell the truth—you're hot for me."

"Blackwood, no matter how good you look, your personality offsets it." But she was smiling as she said it.

"That's one sharp tongue you have."

"Somehow, I think you'll bear up."

Creed opened his mouth, then shut it again. He was

bantering. Him. Shit, he hadn't done that since his first year as an enforcer, and he was enjoying it.

That sobered him. He couldn't feel. It was too dangerous. He needed to be stoic, in control. That was the only way he'd survive, the only way he could avoid falling deeper into black magic. Now he raised his hand and massaged his forehead.

"You should see a healer about those headaches; you've had a lot of them," Maia said.

The concern warmed him, and that was another damn emotion he couldn't afford. "I will after we catch this demon," he lied. He couldn't let a healer know that Seth had gotten behind his mind shield, that he'd weakened it bit by bit until it was as thin and insubstantial as the wings of a butterfly. No one could realize he'd fallen to the dark forces, not when his people needed him. A bead of sweat trickled down his nape and Creed ran a hand across the back of his neck. "You ready to leave?"

She nodded and got to her feet. As they walked along the park's pathway, he thought about the Maia he'd followed around Vegas. Her hair had been long then, going halfway down her back, and he'd had moments when he'd fantasized about her trailing it over his naked body. Creed hadn't liked it then, and remembering it left him uncomfortable—and not because it made his cock twitch to think about it.

No, what had him uneasy was the fact that he'd been attracted to a woman deep into black magic. He'd known at the time that she was sleeping with someone, and even that hadn't fazed him. Neither had the contempt he'd felt. Creed jammed his hands in the front pockets of his jeans to keep himself from reaching for her hand. Damn, maybe he was shallow. While he respected Maia more than he had back then, there were

times he still wanted to growl at her. He hated the oh-
woe-is-me-I'm-powerless shit, and as far as he could
tell, she'd done nothing with her life except wallow
since she'd ceded her powers.

He still wanted her.

They turned onto the sidewalk. She came with more
strings than a marionette, Creed knew that. What scared
him was that it mattered less and less every day. So did
the reasons to keep his distance. She was powerless.
He'd made his own descent into black magic. She'd
heard he'd been interested in her sister. He wanted the
extra power a true soul pairing could give him. The list
could go on and on.

But when they kissed, it was hotter than hell.

"You're awfully quiet," Maia said as they reached the
parking garage.

"Just thinking. You said you had some other clubs in
mind that Seth might like more than the one we were at
last night?" Creed asked. If she thought he'd been lost
in thought about his job, well, he couldn't help it if she
jumped to conclusions.

She dug her keys out of the tiny purse she wore
across her body and pressed the button to unlock the
car. Creed opened the driver's door for her, then went
around to the passenger side and climbed in. "After seeing you in Vegas, I still can't believe you're driving this
thing," he said as he fastened the seat belt.

For a moment, she looked sad. "I miss that car."

"That wasn't a car, it was a *Ferrari 360 Modena Spider*. Midmounted 3.6-liter V8 engine; zero to sixty in
about four seconds. You can't call that a *car*, it's a fucking work of art."

Maia backed out of the parking spot and started toward the exit. "Don't forget it was red."

"Women," Creed muttered. "You don't appreciate the right things about a vehicle."

"I appreciated it just fine, especially how I looked behind the wheel. Back then, it was all about the image."

Creed stayed quiet until she merged on the expressway, then he asked, "What happened to the Spider anyway?"

"I sold it." Maia's voice was flat. "Just like I sold my jewelry, paintings, and furniture." She shook her head, but didn't take her eyes off the traffic. "I even went through my clothes and sold what I could through a consignment shop."

"You were in debt." He should have guessed that.

"I was okay as long as the troubleshooter salary was coming in, but with that gone, I didn't have a prayer of making even a minimum payment on my credit cards."

"Ryne—"

"You think I was going to ask my baby sister to bail me out?" Maia demanded. "I wouldn't. Besides, she'd barely been working a year at that point and didn't have the kind of money I needed."

He thought about asking just how much debt she'd managed to accumulate, but it was more out of curiosity than any need to know. Maia hadn't owned the home she lived in back then, the Gineal Company had, and that had limited her resources. "Do you still owe money?" he asked.

"That is absolutely none of your business."

Instead of apologizing, he said, "I bet you don't. In fact, I bet you paid it off as soon as possible and that's why you're cautious with your finances now—you never want to be in that kind of situation again."

"Blackwood, how would you like it if I started quizzing you about your life?"

"Go ahead and ask." Creed leaned back and closed his eyes, hoping that blocking the sun would ease his headache. The car's AC was still blowing warm, but there was a hint that suggested it wouldn't be long before the cool air filled the space, and that might help, too.

Maia didn't say a word—too much damn pride—but he started talking as if she had asked him something. She had to feel at a disadvantage since he'd been thoroughly briefed on her; this would even things up a little. "I live near Chicago, only because that's where the Gineal Company and our illustrious council are headquartered, but I average about four or five call-outs a week, so I'm almost never there. For that same reason, I don't own a car. If I have to drive, I just rent something."

Dead silence, but he knew Maia was listening and probably intently, at that. Creed didn't bother to open his eyes and check. If she didn't want to hear, she'd tell him to zip it.

"I apprenticed in Sydney and I still get back there as often as I can. Hell, maybe I should live there; God knows the climate is better, and since I don't have a territory, it really doesn't make a difference where I call home."

Still nothing from her side of the car and he'd run out of things to say. With a mental shrug, he tried to make himself more comfortable, but he was six foot four and her vehicle wasn't made for a man of his height. Creed let the motion of the car and the sound of the engine lull him.

"Creed," she said as he was beginning to drift.

"Yeah, angel?"

"You said something back at the park about Nessia believing that Ryne would spearhead the Gineal during the battles of Twilight Time. Does the council really think we're that close to the time of prophecy?"

That shook him out of his lethargy, but Creed kept his body loose and relaxed. "I can't speak for the council." He heard her huff of frustration and added, "But I think they do believe that. The evidence is there to support it."

"What kind of evidence?"

Now he opened his eyes; Creed needed to know why Maia was asking. She'd slipped on a pair of sunglasses, but he could see enough of her face to know she was concerned. Hell, it made sense—her sister was on the front lines. "The number of call-outs has quadrupled in the last twenty years. Our enforcers in the big cities can barely keep up, and we're facing stronger and stronger creatures on a more regular basis."

"It seems like every hundred years or so, someone has claimed it was Twilight Time."

"Yeah, I know. Maybe I'm wrong; I hope like hell I am, because we're damn shorthanded."

Maia frowned. "How many troubleshooters have we lost since I revoked my powers?"

"About half a dozen." It was Creed's turn to scowl. This was one of the reasons why he had to hang on—the Gineal couldn't afford to lose another enforcer, especially one as powerful as he was. "What?" he asked when he realized she looked stunned.

"That's a lot to go down in a short period."

Shit, he was talking manpower with an outsider. He knew better than that, but it was easy to forget that she wasn't one of them any longer. Creed changed the subject. "What time are we heading out tonight?"

With a soft sigh, Maia said, "Ten or so, I guess. Seth wouldn't start his evening too early."

"How many clubs are there around here that he'd be interested in?"

Maia switched lanes, and as she got on the exit ramp, she said, "I don't think there are too many. Minneapolis isn't New York or Las Vegas. It's not even Chicago."

"You said Seth wouldn't like the bar we were at last night; would he go back there anyway?" Creed asked.

"It depends on the other places. If he doesn't like any of them, he might return. Unless, of course, he decides to pop out of town for a night of fun." She cast a quick glance at him.

Creed shook his head. "Demons are obsessive, and Seth wants Ryne. I don't think he's leaving town as long as she's here."

"She's not going anywhere; at least she's not planning on it, anyway. Ryne makes a point of letting me know if she's leaving." Maia turned onto her street. "Oh hell."

"What?" Creed immediately went on alert.

"The lawn service didn't show up to cut Mrs. Olson's yard."

"So? They'll come tomorrow then."

Maia pulled into her driveway and turned off the car. "It doesn't matter; Mrs. Olson will be out there cutting it this evening if I don't beat her to it. She can't stand it when her yard doesn't look neat."

"But—"

"Don't try to make sense of it," she said. "My neighbor lady is as obsessed with her grass as Seth is with Egypt. It just is."

He met Maia in front of her car and led the way up the stairs. "I'll cut it," he volunteered. "I'll change clothes as soon as we get in the house."

"You will?"

Creed took the keys from her and unlocked the front door. "Consider it a thank-you for letting me stay here and an unspoken apology to Mrs. Olson for messing with her memory."

Maia smiled at him and Creed hated to take his eyes off her face to walk in the house. His good mood disintegrated in a hurry. *Uh-oh.* "You have company," he told her.

And Ryne looked pissed.

16
CHAPTER

Maia shifted to peer around Creed's shoulder and sighed. *Uh-oh.* Ryne looked seriously angry.

"What are you doing with my sister?" Ryne growled.

Maia tried to get around Creed and calm Ryne down, but there wasn't enough room to slip past, not without getting a lot more intimate with the man than she wanted to right now.

Blackwood, idiot that he was, put his hands on his hips and antagonized her further. "I'm testing the market to see how much I can get if I sell her to the bouda—you know how they like to consume the flesh of good-looking women."

"Oh, for God's sake." Maia shoved Creed hard enough to allow her to move past him. "I took him to the museum, okay?"

"You can't trust him," Ryne said, looking past her to Creed.

"Hey—" he began, and from the tone, Maia knew she wasn't going to like what she heard.

"You," she whirled to glare at Creed, "keep your mouth shut if you're going to be an ass."

"But—"

"No buts. If you can't play nice, change your clothes and go mow like you promised. I can talk to my sister without your interference." Maia met Creed's stony expression with one of her own. She was damned if she was putting up with this in her home.

"Fine," he said shortly and brushed past her to go to the guest room. He'd capitulated far too easily, but she'd have to find out what that meant later.

"What the hell do you—" Ryne started.

Maia interrupted her, too. "You don't get to use that tone with me, Ryne Frasier. Creed was in the wrong because he deliberately goaded you, but we walked in to find you foaming at the mouth. If you can't be civil, you can leave."

Ryne gaped and Maia felt oddly smug. It was a rare day when her sister didn't have a comeback. She left the entry area and joined Ryne in the living room. "Where's Deke?" Maia asked.

"At home on the phone with his business partner." Ryne sounded slightly subdued.

"I'm surprised you left him; the two of you are like a pair of conjoined twins."

"We're not *that* bad." Maia just stared until Ryne shrugged. "Okay, maybe we are; we'll get over it in a while. It's going to be a long call, something about merchandising rights in Europe, and I didn't want to wait to make sure you were okay."

"Why wouldn't I be all right?"

Before Ryne could answer, Creed returned wearing a

pair of faded cutoffs and a tank top. Maia's knees went weak. She locked them, but Lord, that man had muscles.

He walked up to her, looked her dead in the eye, and said, "I'll be back in about an hour, angel."

And then the bastard put his arms around her and bent down to kiss her. Maia was too stunned to react, and by the time her brain was functioning again, he was closing the front door behind him. Almost afraid of what she'd see, Maia looked at her sister. If she thought Ryne had appeared shocked earlier, that was nothing compared to the look on her face now.

It was the calm before the storm, Maia was certain of that. "He did that deliberately to set you off," she said, hoping to avert the fight. "Don't let him push your buttons, sweetie."

"I know why *he* did it. You're the one I'm trying to figure out."

"Me? I was as surprised as you were."

"You leaned into him, Mai. You closed your eyes and leaned into him when he kissed you."

Maia couldn't read her sister's tone. It wasn't accusatory, it wasn't bewildered, it wasn't jealous—but knowing what it wasn't didn't help her identify what Ryne was thinking. "That doesn't mean anything; it was reflex."

"I know. How many times has he kissed you already?"

Closing her eyes, Maia counted to ten, and then said, "You have no business asking questions like that."

Ryne took a step, ran into the coffee table, and muttered, "I can't even pace in here." More loudly, she said, "I know it's none of my business, but I'm concerned. You can't trust him; I'm not joking about that."

Settling on the couch, Maia patted the cushion next to her and said, "Let's sit down and talk about this."

She didn't want to do it, that was clear, but Ryne grudgingly joined her on the sofa. Maia expected her to launch into more about Creed, but her sister remained quiet. It wouldn't last—Ryne was never shy about speaking up—but Maia was grateful for the momentary respite to collect her thoughts. Her sister's intensity was part of who she was, but there were times it wore Maia out.

With her mind calm, she decided to face this head-on. "What happened today?" Maia asked and immediately held up a hand. "Don't say nothing did; I know better than that. The last time we talked, you were resigned about Creed staying here, but this afternoon it's a different story. Why the change?"

A look of absolute frustration crossed Ryne's face and Maia felt her own irritation rise. Whatever had occurred was Gineal business and her sister didn't feel like she could share it with an outsider. That chafed. Creed wasn't as closemouthed with information, although Maia knew there were instances where he'd censored himself, and it made Ryne's silence seem like an even bigger slap in the face. Maia balled her hands into fists to keep from saying something she'd regret.

"I called you at work today," Ryne said. "They told me you quit and that you didn't even give them two weeks' notice. The last time we talked about this you were adamant about not leaving, so I came over to check on you, and you weren't here."

"And you'd worried yourself sick by the time Creed and I got home and you lashed out."

Ryne grimaced, gave a shrug. "Maybe that's part of it, but it was seeing you with him that upset me the most. You need to tell him to leave. He can't stay with you anymore."

Maia shook her head. "That's not happening."

"What?"

"You always do this, issue orders and expect instant compliance, but it doesn't work that way. If you want me to tell Creed to leave, you better provide some damn good reasons, otherwise he's staying."

"He's turned. Is that a good enough reason for you?"

Maia's stomach nosedived and twisted into knots. "Have you reported this to the council?" she managed to ask. Ryne shook her head and Maia felt some of her tension ease. "Then you're not certain, are you?"

Ryne mumbled something.

"What was that?"

"No, I'm not sure." Her sister pushed to her feet so fast it was like an explosion of motion. Ryne paced a few steps away before turning and coming back. "He's got plausible explanations for his actions, but my gut says they're lies." She sank back on the couch and put a hand over one of Maia's fists. "Believe me, you need to tell him to leave."

Maia only needed a couple of seconds to make her decision. "No. He's staying."

"I probably shouldn't say this because it's only going to make you mad," Ryne began and Maia braced herself, "but you don't have the best track record in the world when it comes to men. Remember Justin? Maybe you didn't give up your magic for him like I thought, but he still dumped you to marry another woman."

It took more strength than Maia thought she possessed to keep control. She was more than mad, she was downright furious. As she took deep breaths, she fought the urge to strike back. "You don't know what you're talking about," she said tightly. "I was never involved with Justin."

"You introduced us when I went to Vegas."

"He was my neighbor, nothing more." Maia tensed her muscles, trying to stop the shaking.

"Then whose clothes were in your closet?" Ryne countered persistently. "You told me they were his."

Maia's breathing hitched. Ryne had made one weekend visit while Maia had been in Las Vegas, showing up without any warning. It had been a struggle to hide from her sister how far into black magic she'd been, but Maia had pulled it off. Maybe it had been so easy because of Ryne's age or because she trusted her older sister. The problem arose when Maia decided to take Ryne out to a show and they'd gone into her closet to find something her sister could borrow. Ryne didn't own anything dressy, but since they were the same size and height, they could share.

Seth had left some clothes at her house, a fact Maia had forgotten until her sister had spotted them and started asking questions. Maia hadn't known he was a demon at that point, but some instinct had told her to never let Ryne meet Seth. Justin had come over then—the timing couldn't have been better—and he'd gone along with the charade without hesitation.

"Those clothes belonged to another man," Maia said, shaking herself out of the memory. "Someone I didn't want you to know."

"How bad could this guy be?" Ryne asked and Maia remained quiet. "That bad, huh? Is this where I say I rest my case when it comes to your judgment?"

"You're overstepping. Did I say anything hurtful when you spent weeks crying over Deke?" Maia continued talking over the top of Ryne. "Did I say anything when he showed up and suddenly all was right in your world? No, I didn't. I could have pointed out that he'd broken your heart once and you were an idiot to allow him a second chance, but I bit my tongue and let you make your own decisions. I expect the same respect from you."

Ryne's fingers spasmed around hers before her sister withdrew her hand. She appeared more than stunned; she looked downright stricken. "You're siding with Creed over me?"

"It's not a matter of choosing sides," Maia insisted, but in a way, it was. She *was* choosing to believe Creed's assertion that he was still okay over her sister's claim that he was using black magic. And as Ryne had so thoughtfully pointed out, Maia had been wrong before.

Creed silently opened the utility room door and poked his head in, but everything was quiet. His scan had told him Ryne was gone, but he hadn't been able to trust that, and he needed his ears to verify it.

He wiped his feet on the mat and noiselessly shut the door behind him. It was anyone's guess what kind of reception he'd receive from Maia. Creed was fairly certain Ryne wouldn't tell her sister what had happened today, but he couldn't be entirely sure. If there was one thing he'd learned in his thirty-five years, it was that women were unpredictable.

Maia entered and he froze, but she spotted him anyway. "There you are," she said. "I thought I heard the mower stop about half an hour ago."

Damn, he couldn't read anything from her tone. "Mrs. O made lemonade," Creed said as he left the utility room and joined her in the kitchen. "And she wanted to talk."

"She's lonely; I'm glad you sat with her for a while."

He relaxed. Maia didn't sound like she wanted to carve out his heart with a butter knife, and as protective as she was of her sister, she wouldn't be able to hide her fury this long. "I enjoyed talking with her. She's an interesting lady."

"She is, and she has great stories. How do you feel about chicken stir-fry?" Maia asked, changing the subject.

"You're not going to make me provide dinner?"

She laughed and Creed allowed himself to close the rest of the distance between them. "If I leave food up to you, I'll have clogged arteries by the end of the week."

"Stir-fry sounds fine," he said as he came up beside her. "Do you mind if I take a shower instead of help?"

"No offense," she said, wrinkling her nose, "but I'd prefer you take a shower. You smell."

"That's from honest labor," he said and wrapped his sweaty arms around her in a bear hug.

"Ugh! Blackwood!" But she was laughing as she twisted, trying to free herself. All Maia succeeded in doing, though, was to rub her body against his and Creed felt his blood flow south.

He knew the instant she realized he was getting hard because she went dead still. Moving his hands from her waist to her hips, he tugged her more tightly against his body. Maia didn't protest. Instead, she wound her arms around his neck and pressed her breasts to his chest. She was the one who pulled his head to hers.

Her lips met his tentatively, as if she were unsure, and Creed reined himself in. He should step away—they shouldn't be doing this, not after his actions today—but instead, he let her set the pace.

Soft. So soft, so feminine, and she fit against him exactly right. Creed nibbled at her lower lip, taking it as slowly as he could. Keep it easy, he warned himself. He couldn't let this go too far, not after what had happened the last time he'd tried to have sex.

She eased back and their lips clung before separating. Maia stared, trying to see deep inside him, but before Creed could become anxious, she went back up on her toes to kiss him again. She was done teasing; Maia opened her mouth beneath his, inviting him deeper.

The kiss went from zero to a hundred faster than her little red Ferrari on a straightaway. Putting his arms around her again, Creed turned, pressing Maia into the refrigerator. She met him kiss for kiss, her tongue sliding against his as he tasted her.

Creed rocked his hips into hers, letting her know just how much he wanted her. She met his next thrust forward. Control slipped further from his grasp.

He was starving, dying for her, and Maia was every bit as hungry. Creed slipped a hand between their bodies, found the button at her waist, and worked it free. The zipper went down with a gentle rasp. It wasn't as simple to lower her shorts with only one hand, but he managed that, too, using his knee to help when he had them down far enough.

Never taking his mouth from hers, Creed caressed her bare flank before moving his hand around to the juncture of her thighs. Her panties were damp and he moaned quietly as he worked his fingers underneath the fabric.

Maia sucked in a sharp breath as he circled his finger over the center of her pleasure, then pushed him away. "No," she said, voice thick.

Creed thought about begging—his cock was hard enough to ache—but he released her and stepped away. She stared at him for a moment, her brown eyes dilated and heated, then bent to get her shorts. He choked. Maia froze, looking at him in question, and Creed shook his head. She was wearing a red, lacy thong that hardly covered anything, and damn it, her ass was perfect.

As she pulled up her shorts, she said, "You believe in heading straight for the goal, don't you?"

"I can do foreplay. Join me in the shower and I'll show you how good I am with a bar of soap."

"That offer is oh so tempting, but I think I'll make dinner instead." She zipped her shorts. "You might want to go heavy on the cold water, though, when you get in the shower."

Creed smirked. "Cold shower, my ass. Angel, I'm going to stand under some nice warm water and fantasize about you bent over the kitchen table while I have you from behind. It should take me less than half a dozen strokes to come, then I'll wash up and rejoin you." He took a couple of steps forward, brushed his lips over hers, and headed for the hall. "Think about it," he said over his shoulder before he exited.

He heard her cursing him, and Creed smiled, his heart lighter than he could remember it being in years.

Maia now knew she'd come a long way from her party days in Vegas. It was Thursday, and after bar-hopping for three nights, she decided she'd rather be home reading that book Caitlin had given her. She was tired. Yesterday they'd gone to the museum, then hit the bars, and today they'd spent hours combing the area around Nicollet Mall. And come up empty.

Tonight they were checking out a club called Ground Level. This enormous building was their second stop, and probably their final one because it would take them a lot of time to cover it. The place was industrial in appearance, but stylish, and it was crowded. Creed had his arm around her waist as they moved through the crush and the gesture was purely possessive. Maia wasn't sure how she felt about that, but she had no desire to break his hold. That wasn't good.

To keep from thinking about his touch, she looked around at the people. There were all kinds of fashions here from goth to casual to fancier clothing, but her close-fitting, sleeveless red dress was a little too much for this nightclub.

Someone bumped into them and Creed cursed, his arm tightening around her. "How many more fucking people can they jam in here? Isn't there a fire code?"

Maia grinned up at him. "Don't be such a stick-in-the-mud. Everyone's having a good time—look how full the dance floor is."

"The whole building is packed. How are we supposed to find Seth in this mess?"

That wiped the smile off her face. She turned into him and leaned close so she could talk more softly. "You can't separate the different energies to locate him? You did it earlier tonight and every other night this week."

He shook his head. "There were less people at those places. This bar is overwhelming."

"And that's the very thing that Seth would love about it."

Creed grimaced and that's when she noticed that furrow was back between his brows. "You have another headache, don't you?"

Ignoring the question, he used his shoulder to open space for them between two groups of people. If Creed couldn't sense Seth, that meant they were going to have to visually check the bar, and the most efficient way to do that was break it into quadrants. Of course, that would be shot to hell if Seth moved around—either deliberately or inadvertently—playing some sort of cat-and-mouse game with them.

A mob of people milling about forced them to come to a halt and Maia used the opportunity to ask, "Can Seth sense us in this throng?"

"I don't know," Creed admitted gruffly. "The damn thing is that because demons like Seth have been gone from this dimension for millennia, there are no living Gineal who've fought them. If we have any knowledge, it's buried inside our library."

Maia nodded. Unfortunately, she was probably the best resource on Seth, and while she knew his likes and dislikes, she didn't know most of his abilities. "Have you heard anything from the librarian researching Seth yet?"

"No. I guess I better move following up with Fia higher on the priority list."

The crowd thinned momentarily and Creed used the opportunity to move forward. They couldn't get through side by side, though, and he released her waist, taking her hand instead.

As they slowly fought their way to the back of the club, Maia kept her eyes open, but finding Seth was going to be next to impossible if Creed's ability to scan wouldn't work. That wasn't the only problem she had, and Maia was looking for more than Seth. Creed was tugging her along when she finally spotted what she needed—the ladies' room.

"I'm going to use the restroom; I'll be right back," she told him. She raised her voice to be heard above the din, but hopefully not loud enough for those nearby to hear.

Creed tightened his hold on her hand. "Why didn't you go before we left the house?"

She rolled her eyes. Like she was a preschooler who didn't know better. "I did, but that was more than three hours ago and I have to go again. I don't see a line so I won't be gone long."

"I'll go with you and wait outside."

"Not a chance in hell. We're nearly to the back of the bar; why don't you go all the way to the far wall and return? I'll meet you here."

He didn't want to leave her unescorted, that was obvious, but he reluctantly nodded. Maia ran her palm over his cheek and turned to make her way through the crush. It was a novel experience having someone who wanted to watch over her. She'd always been the protector, the caretaker.

There was a short line inside the women's room, but it had plenty of stalls and she made it out almost as quickly as she'd thought. After washing her hands and freshening her makeup, she walked into the hallway.

Something was wrong.

Maia hesitated. If she went to her right, she'd be back in the bar, but to her left, the corridor made a sharp turn. After a brief hesitation, she decided to take a quick peek. Odds were this was nothing; she'd check it out, reassure herself, and find Creed.

It wasn't nothing. She stopped short before he saw her.

The powaqa was in the middle of sapping a human's life force; that was the only reason she was able to identify what he was. If he hadn't been feeding, she would only have seen a man standing close to another man. Maia began to leave and get Creed, but realized she couldn't walk away. If she did, the powaqa would have time to drain his victim completely and a man would lose his life. She had to act now.

For a moment, she wavered, then squared her shoulders. She was damned if she was going to run from a powaqa—they had very little magic—and she refused to listen to Creed deride her again for cravenness. No one who'd been a Gineal troubleshooter was a coward, damn it.

All it took was a brief touch of the human's shoulder to break the mental hold the psychic vampire had on him. That drew the powaqa out of his blissful state. "Leave us alone," he growled.

The man looked between the two of them and scurried away without a backward glance. That made things easier.

"Don't feed from humans," Maia snarled right back at him. "The Gineal don't like it." And with that, she pivoted, heading back for the bar.

The powaqa grabbed her arm as she reached the end of the hall and spun her to face him. "Not so quick. You deprived me of my sustenance, so you will take the human's place," he announced and started to drag her back down the corridor. His mind butted against hers, trying to gain a lock on her, trying to put her into the same kind of hypnotized state that the human had been in.

She easily rebuffed the probe.

Maia looked over her shoulder, saw Creed trying to make his way through the crowd, and relaxed. He'd save her—and give her a ton of grief for not taking out this creature on her own.

Like hell.

Pulling her fingers back, Maia struck the powaqa with the heel of her hand. Blood spurted from his nose as she scored a strong hit. Before he could react, she drove the stiletto heel of one of her pumps into his foot. His shoe saved him from serious damage.

She could sense Creed's frustration as he tried to muscle his way through the throng and she felt him mentally chanting a spell—one to ensure humans wouldn't see or hear anything.

The powaqa twisted her arm and she turned with it, propelling the elbow of her free arm into his belly. Air rushed from his lungs. If she weren't in heels, Maia would have delivered a strong kick, but she couldn't risk losing her balance.

She sensed Creed beginning a second incantation, this one to protect her, and she gave a quick shake of her head. Her telepathy had been lost with her powers, and she damn well shouldn't know he was working magic.

While the powaqa was still bent over, trying to regain his breath, she locked her hands together and brought them down on the back of his neck. He went to the floor.

As he made a grab for her leg, Maia took the chance on compromising her stability and kicked. It was solid, powerful, and connected with his temple. That ended the fight.

Adrenaline continued to surge through her body. It was an old sensation, one she used to experience regularly as a troubleshooter. One she'd missed. Maybe she was little more than human now, but she'd handled herself and taken out the powaqa. Her lips curved in satisfaction.

Creed finally reached her side and she turned on him. "Don't you ever tell me again that I've embarrassed the Frasier name, you hear me?"

"Yes, ma'am," he drawled, clearly unimpressed by her ferocity. Before she could do more than snarl, Creed added, "Let me get him out of here. I don't want to keep the spells in place longer than I have to."

Maia nodded. Even if Seth couldn't read their energies, he might be able to pick up on the use of magic. The longer Creed held the proclamations, the greater the chance the demon would discover it if he were around. Her stomach churned. This was exactly the kind of place Seth loved. Lots of people, lots of energy, and the music they'd played here tonight wouldn't bother him. As she'd told Creed, there were a limited number of trendy, upscale nightclubs in Minneapolis.

Creed crouched down and held his hands over the powaqa. Again, she felt him calling on his magic and then the creature disappeared. Since the energy vampire wasn't dead, she suspected he'd sent it to another dimension, but she didn't ask.

"Anything hurt?" he asked as he stood.

"I'm okay, but I broke his nose. Do I have blood on me?"

"Yeah." He held his hand in front of her and rubbed his thumb against his fingers as he worked some magic. "There. It's gone." Creed offered her his elbow. "Let's go, so I can lift the barriers I threw."

He did just that when they were about twenty feet away from the hall and Maia shook her head again. She shouldn't be able to sense when Creed was working or releasing magic—not without her abilities—and even if she still had them, she might not pick up anything. Not if he was shielding his use of power, and she suspected he might be in order to conceal it from Seth.

Creed tugged her sharply to the right, saving her from getting someone's drink all over the front of her dress. "Watch it," Blackwood growled at the young man. With a quick nod, the guy disappeared into the mob.

"Thanks for saving my dress," Maia said with a smile.

Creed ignored that. "We'll sweep in sections," he told her. "Up, down, and up again until we've covered the club."

It took more than half an hour to make it about midway to the front and Maia was starting to get as irritable as Creed was. The place was hot and sweat trickled between her breasts and down the nape of her neck. She spotted a large group blocking the way up ahead and wanted to groan. Somehow, they were going to have to make their way around them.

Before they got there, though, the DJ segued into a new song and a shout went up through the bar, including the troupe blocking their path. In a split second, they were running for the dance floor and it opened up a path for her and Creed.

That's when Maia saw someone near the front of the bar that caught her attention. She didn't want to take time to speak, so she nudged Creed with her elbow and pointed. He looked at her, raising an eyebrow in question, and she nodded. With determination, he set off, tugging her along in his wake.

It might be Seth—maybe—and he was with a woman. She wore a skimpy minidress and her dark hair was pinned atop her head.

They didn't make it far before the gap in the crowd was filled with more humans. The crush made it a fight to get anywhere and she heard Creed snarl a couple of times when people got in their way.

It took an eternity to reach the club's entry area. "Do you have a lock on him?" Maia asked breathlessly.

"I lost it a few minutes ago. He was headed out of the club when it happened."

"It was him?"

Creed shrugged. "I think so. Come on, let's look outside."

The street, though, was empty, not even a car driving by. They went back inside and finished checking the bar, but Seth had disappeared, and so had the woman he'd been with.

17
CHAPTER

Seth scowled as he looked down at the naked woman kneeling in front of him. Her blow job was among the worst he'd ever received. She fastidiously licked at his head while keeping both hands wrapped around his shaft, guaranteeing she held control. He'd prefer an enthusiastic virgin.

"Open your mouth," Seth ordered.

The woman smiled up at him in a sexy way, but shook her head. His temper began to climb. He'd been revered as a god, and it had been deemed an honor to be allowed to suck his cock, yet this mortal showed her disdain, her very distaste for the act she'd initiated. She should be worshipping him.

He moved his hips forward, but she leaned back, tightening her hold on him. Seth reached out, buried his hands in her dark hair. The pins holding it up ripped free and she mewled her pain. He ignored it, drawing her head to him. The crown of his cock penetrated her open mouth, and in retaliation, she bit him—not hard, but enough.

Seth reached the limit of his tolerance. He used his powers to force her arms to her sides and lock them in place. Since he liked the subservience of her kneeling as he stood before her, he froze her in that position.

"What—" she began, but Seth stopped her voice.

"I gave you an opportunity to treat me as I deserve," he told her, "and you chose not to take it. Now you will pay the consequences for your decision."

Because it pleased him to do so, Seth used his hands to adjust her face. He forced his thumb into her mouth and she bit him once more. Grabbing her hair, he gave her a yank strong enough to make her cry out. He smiled with satisfaction.

"You will not have the chance to use your teeth a third time," he told her. It took little for him to arrange her mouth, lips, and tongue in a pleasing configuration and cast magic to hold them that way. He looked down into her blue eyes and saw the fear. Good, those who angered the gods should know terror.

"I didn't expect you to go down on me," he said conversationally. "That was your idea, but you arrogantly assumed your beauty made you master. You were wrong."

She made a gurgling noise as she tried to speak, but Seth ignored it. Her protests meant nothing.

Taking hold of his cock, he slapped it against her full lips. "You've lorded it over men for years, haven't you? You used your face, your body to get your way. You teased, giving only what little you felt like sharing. This time, however, you chose the wrong male. I've known others far more beautiful than you, females lauded by poets and troubadours as the ideal of femininity." Seth began to strike her cheeks, leaving streaks of clear fluid behind. "Even in this age, I'm acquainted with women whose appearances surpass yours. You overrate yourself."

Tired of denying himself, Seth pushed his penis past her lips. Her mouth needed a slight adjustment to increase the pressure he felt and he took care of it with a flick of his fingers. He stroked lightly at first, then grabbed her hair again and began to fuck her face, going deeper with each thrust.

The woman choked, but that didn't appease Seth's anger. She would take all of him before he quit, every last centimeter. He went deeper, harder until the head of his shaft hit the back of her throat. Her gagging massaged his cock and he groaned his pleasure. When he pulled back, saliva streamed from his length. He continued, ignoring the noises she made. It was his right to take her in any manner he pleased, and he did so.

As he reached orgasm, Seth pulled back, coating her tongue with his essence. When he was at last satisfied, he withdrew, allowing her to swallow.

She spit out his seed, pushing it from her mouth. As he watched it drip from her chin, Seth's gratification turned to fury. He drew his hand back, and as he slashed it forward, morphed it into a claw with razor-sharp talons. They bit into her flesh, blood spurting as he tore through her arteries and veins.

With his strength, it took but one slice to sever her head from her body.

Friday afternoon and she was standing side by side with a man preparing dinner. She really knew how to live it up. But Maia's lips curved—she liked this better than searching through Ground Level and there was something soothing about chopping vegetables, occasionally bumping hips with Creed as they worked.

Oprah was on television, but Maia only listened with half an ear. The sky to the west had become ominously dark and she wanted to see the five o'clock news to find out what was headed their way. Considering the heat and humidity, she wouldn't be surprised if they were hit with severe weather.

Maia finished the bok choy and reached for the stalks of celery lying to her right. "Are you okay?" she asked Creed.

"Yeah, why?"

"You've been pretty quiet." Not that Creed talked very much anyway, but today he'd been particularly reticent.

He put down the knife he was using and leaned his hip against the counter as he turned toward her. "I'm frustrated. We almost had him last night, but that damn crowd impeded us and he disappeared, and today, nothing. Not a damn trace."

Putting down her own knife, Maia rested her hand over his on the counter top. It seemed natural to offer comfort, and that disconcerted her for a moment. "I know you were getting impatient, but though it seems odd, I thought there was a chance he'd visit a zoo here. We went to the one in Vegas a few times."

Strange for a demon or not, Seth had loved animals. She'd seen him go out of his way to aid dogs, cats, coyotes, birds, and even snakes. When she'd believed him to be human, Maia had found it sweet. Once she'd learned what he really was, though, she hadn't known what to think. It was simply bizarre.

"Demons have quirks," Creed said, as if reading her thoughts. "And I wasn't irritable because I believed we were wasting time at the zoo. It was the damn crowd at both places."

"The headaches."

Creed pulled his hand out from under hers and returned to slicing carrots without a word.

"Creed," Maia persisted, "you need to call a healer about those things."

"There's nothing they can do," he said gruffly.

"Of course th—"

"They can't restore my mind shield."

She nearly asked if he was joking, but she saw from the look on his face that Creed was dead serious. No wonder he had headaches. He was picking up the psychic energy of everyone around him and the noise had to be incredible. "Has this happened to one of the Gineal before?"

With a humorless laugh, Creed said, "Yeah, but what caused her problem and what's causing mine are two different things."

Something about the way he'd said that made her curious, but Maia didn't question him about it. He was the one that was important. "How do you know? Maybe the circumstances are more alike than—"

"I think the demon dismantled mine," Creed interrupted again. "I started to lose it after I arrived in town and was in closer physical proximity to him. The other person's problem had nothing to do with any type of demon. And yes, I know this for a fact," he added before she could ask.

Maia thought about Creed's conjecture for a moment. "Seth never took down my mind shield."

Creed stopped chopping. "Maybe he didn't feel the need because of how deep you were into black magic," he suggested.

There'd been a note of kindness in his voice, an empathy that kept Maia from becoming angry. She watched the closing credits roll on the talk show and gave his theory some consideration. "It's possible," she conceded, "and Seth wasn't always predictable."

"Demons are impulsive and their emotions sometimes prompt them to act before intellect can kick in. Those factors play a role in the choices they make."

"I learned that, too," Maia said, "but Seth had better control than I'd been taught demons had." She realized belatedly that Creed had shifted the conversation away from his issue. "Back to your shield. Isn't there anything that can be done to shore it up? If not a healer, some type of spell?"

A low rumble of thunder sounded in the distance. "I don't know. There might be, but I don't have time to look for some obscure incantation. The headaches haven't left me incapacitated, and as long as I'm careful about crowds, I should be able to function. I have to take care of Seth."

"How are you going to do that?" Maia countered. "You said yourself that it was difficult to take down that groige demon, and while that's a deadly branch, Seth is much stronger."

"I know that," Creed said, "but he can't be allowed to roam loose. Who else is going to deal with him?"

That stopped her cold. Creed was undoubtedly the strongest of the roving troubleshooters, which meant he had the best chance. "You're right," she admitted. "I know that, but I don't want anything to happen to you." It was the truth, but the revelation made her uneasy. Fortunately, the news started and Maia shifted her attention to the TV.

The opening graphics and introductions only took a moment. "We have some rough weather coming in," the anchorwoman said, "and we'll tell you about that in a minute, but first police in Minneapolis are investigating a grisly homicide. Twenty-six-year-old Erica Sorenson was found dead in her home this afternoon."

A picture of the victim came up on the screen and Maia gasped. "What?" Creed asked.

Maia pointed to the television, not wanting to miss a word. While she couldn't be completely positive, Erica Sorenson looked like the woman Seth had left the bar with last night. The anchor continued giving the facts, and when she mentioned Sorenson's head being severed from her body, Creed cursed. The potentially severe thunderstorms seemed almost anticlimactic after that.

"It might not be the same woman," Creed said. "The bar wasn't well lit and we didn't get a great look at her, but the severed head makes it possible it was a demon kill."

"It's the same woman," Maia said grimly.

"How can you be so sure?"

"Because except for some minor differences, she looked a lot like I did when I knew Seth."

"I don't see any great similarity." Creed sounded skeptical.

Maia didn't understand how he could miss it. "You followed me in Vegas, so you should know."

"I never got that close, remember? I trailed your energy signature from a distance."

Yeah, he'd told her that, but still . . . "Get on the Internet and pull up the story with the woman's picture; I'll join you in a minute."

Maia went to her bedroom and dug through a box on the floor of her walk-in closet. She found the photo album she wanted and pulled out one of the pictures. For a moment, she stared at the woman smiling in the photograph. She looked far different today than she had at twenty-five.

When she'd known Seth, her hair had been long,

falling halfway down her back, but the differences went further than that. Her makeup now enhanced her appearance, but seven years ago, it had been much more dramatic, and she'd used it as a mask. The clothes she'd worn then were different, too—sexier, more revealing—and another way to hide her true self. If people were checking out her body, they weren't looking deeply enough to see her weakness.

With a grimace, Maia crossed the hall to the guest bedroom and found Creed sitting at the desk in the corner checking his e-mail. When he saw her, he logged out and switched to the television station's Web site. There was an image of the murdered woman on the screen, and without preamble, Maia held her own picture next to it.

"Holy shit, angel, she could have been your twin."

Creed handed the last plate to Maia and she loaded it in the dishwasher. They'd finished preparing dinner and had eaten in near silence. Conversation had been beyond him while his mind had been stuck on the fact that the demon had killed a human. That increased the urgency of finding Seth and taking him down, and maybe that's what Maia had been worrying about, too. While they'd heard it their entire lives, it had become a mantra from the ages of twelve to nineteen while they'd trained to be troubleshooters: humans must be protected.

Rain beat down on the roof, on the windows, and the sky was dark enough that they had the lights turned on. The gloominess of the weather fit his mood.

"Creed," Maia said as she pushed the button to start the dishwasher, "did you ever contact your researcher?"

"No, and you're right, I should talk to her." He'd

even mentioned doing that the other day, but he'd never gotten around to it. "You want to sit in?"

"Of course."

His lips curved at Maia's momentary surprise. "Just don't get all bent out of shape if Fia squawks at your presence, okay?"

"She's not going to be happy to see me, huh?"

"I doubt it, but then, she won't be happy to hear from me either," Creed admitted. And a few minutes later when he sent out the telepathic request to Fia, he got exactly the kind of response he'd expected.

It's Friday evening. The complaint was clear in Fia's message.

What? You're out on a hot date?

Well, no, but—

Put the movie on pause. You can pick up where you left off after you fill me in on what you've learned about the demon.

"I wasn't watching a movie, laoch solas," Fia said after she came through the transit into Maia's living room. "And I could have had plans. It *is* the weekend."

Creed might not be up on everything that was passed along his extended family grapevine, but he had heard the concern about Fia's lack of a social life. It wouldn't have mattered to him, though, not given the gravity of the situation. "Even if you were out on a date, I would have insisted you give me a report. Seth killed a human last night."

That stopped Fia's grousing and she waved her hand to close the transit she'd used.

Crossing his arms over his chest, Creed leaned his shoulders against the wall and said without prelude, "Tell me what you learned."

Fia looked over to the couch where Maia sat, then

met his gaze again. "I can't talk in front of her; she's an outsider."

"Maia was working as a troubleshooter while you were still playing with dolls," Creed snapped. "She was training to be a troubleshooter before you were old enough to go to school." He gritted his teeth, took a deep breath, and added, "She's helping me find Seth; everything you tell me, I'll turn around and fill her in on anyway. All you're doing is adding a step for me."

"But laoch solas, the rules—"

"Sometimes you have to screw the rules."

A flash of lightning made the lights flicker and a crack of thunder punctuated his words. Fia stared at Maia, maybe measuring her. After a long moment, she said, "I haven't found much on Set and haven't located any spell that can be used to summon him. I've spent nearly all my free time looking."

Creed had figured as much. With the god-demons gone for so long, the unneeded information on them would have been lost amid the millions of books the Gineal library had. No one knew everything that was housed in the tasglann, not even the librarians who researched regularly. "Give me what you've got."

Fia took a seat on the opposite end of the sofa from Maia. "I guess I'll start at the beginning. Set was considered the god of chaos and destruction in ancient Egypt and was associated with the desert. It was thought he controlled sandstorms, and for a while, he was viewed as a hero. There was artwork showing Set being one of the gods who crowned the pharaohs, but when he fell out of favor, they were redone to show Thoth in his place."

"How could he be considered a hero?" Creed asked.

Fia shrugged.

"Seth can be very charming," Maia said so quietly, he barely heard her over the storm. "He's wily, knows how to bide his time, and it would be easy for him to hide his true nature—for a while at least."

Fia brought up a three-dimensional image of Set in the animal form that Egyptians used to depict their gods, then she changed him to a human appearance. Maia pointed out a few errors and Fia corrected them until Maia said, "That's what he looks like now."

With a nod, Fia dissolved the image and continued. "He was one of five brothers and sisters—Osiris, Isis, Thoth, Nephthys, and Set. According to legend, he killed Osiris and battled Isis and her son, Horus, for control of the living." Fia bit her lower lip. "I think the god-demons have a council much like we do. At least that's what I inferred from what I read. There was something in one of the books about Set being banished by a council ruled by Re."

Creed straightened away from the wall. "Set was outcast by his own kind?"

Fia nodded. "He was locked in a battle with Horus that lasted eighty years. During one of their skirmishes, Seth lost some body parts, including his testicles, and he put himself together with pieces from animals."

"That's not true," Maia said. "Seth's body had no scars, no indications of any kind of battle wounds."

"Maybe you didn't see them," Fia suggested.

Maia looked at Fia and repeated, "He has no scars on his body, so unless he was able to magically heal all of them, that story isn't true."

"The books talk about the scars, not just Set's, but those of Horus as well. That leads me to believe that they were unable to make them disappear entirely." Fia shrugged.

He should be concerned about whether or not the

intel his young cousin was passing along was correct, but instead Creed was fighting jealousy. Fia might not have understood what Maia had said—not at first—but he had. She'd slept with the demon.

His reaction was stupid—he knew it—but Creed hated that he could put a name and face to a male from her past. It made it too easy to picture that bastard touching her, taking pleasure from her, and that was something he didn't want to imagine. When he closed his eyes, the only man he wanted to see with Maia was himself.

"Are you going to rejoin the conversation, Blackwood," Maia asked, "or should we go ahead without you?"

The irritation in her voice was barely noticeable, but it was definitely there, and that led him to believe that she had an idea what was bothering him. With effort, he forced his emotions aside. "If the books were wrong about the scars," Creed said, addressing Fia, "then there's no way to know if anything you've told us is accurate."

"No, there isn't, especially when the next fact I was going to mention was that some stories say Set was gay."

Maia tried to hide a smile and that pissed Creed off again. Damn it, he didn't want her remembering another male or thinking about Seth sexually.

"I don't think he's gay," Maia said. "Maybe bisexual."

"That would fit in with the other accounts I read that mention several wives."

"Wives, plural?"

"His sister, Nephthys, and two goddess-demons named Anat and Astarte," Fia said, shifting to face Maia. "There might be more, but I only found those three names."

The rain had eased up at some point and the thunder

had grown more distant, the lightning less frequent. He stood near the window, and while it was only open a crack, a cool breeze gusted through the screen as he listened to them debate the demon's sexuality. Creed began to feel as if he were the intruder in a conversation between the two women. Aggravated over being excluded, he interjected, "The victor writes the history."

"What?" they said in unison.

"How much of the information you found on Seth was from firsthand accounts by the Gineal?" he asked.

"None, laoch solas," Fia said. "It was all retellings of human tales."

"Then everything you read was filtered by the humans who followed Horus, and do you think they're going to make themselves or their god of choice look bad?"

"I don't know," Fia said. "The things I read about Horus didn't make him sound much better than Set. The only real difference was that he had justice on his side. Allegedly."

Creed shook his head and moved closer to the sofa. "Horus would have been a demon, too; of course he wasn't any better than Set. Look at the spin they put on his actions, though. Set was evil and he'd killed Osiris. That meant that anything Horus did was justified, right? He was avenging his father."

Fia looked confused and Creed sighed. Damn, she was young; he tended to forget that because she was so smart.

"What Creed is saying," Maia interpreted, "is that the information on Set is suspect. The men who followed Horus probably threw in any accusation they could that would discredit Set in their society's eyes. That's not to say he's innocent, because he *is* a demon after all, but that some of the so-called facts about him were skewed or are entirely made up."

"Politicians and mudslinging," Fia equated.

"Exactly. That means the only information we can trust completely are eyewitness accounts from Gineal," Maia said.

"If there are any," Creed pointed out.

There was a long silence, broken only by the gentle patter of rain and the hum of the dishwasher. Creed seriously needed more information on Seth, and it was looking like he wasn't going to have any—at least not anything he could trust. How did he fight something that was an enigma to him?

"Is there any point in my searching further?" Fia asked, breaking the quiet.

"There is," Creed told her. "We might not have had any plans of getting involved in a war between demons, but you can damn well bet the Gineal who were around back then collected everything they could find about Set, Horus, and the rest of the gang. The council couldn't risk being ignorant."

"Information like that won't be easy to find," Fia said glumly.

"That's why I contacted you. You're an expert at research."

"I suppose that means you want me to go back to work?"

Creed tried a smile. He figured saying "hell, yes" would only annoy Fia and he wanted her giving the project her all, not dogging it because she was pissed off at him. "Please."

With a sigh, Fia stood and opened a transit, hiding it from the windows by placing it at the entry to the hallway. "I'll let you know if I find anything." She nodded at Maia, then walked through the glowing gate. In an instant, it disappeared.

Suddenly feeling tired, Creed scrubbed his hands

down his face, then walked the rest of the way to the couch. He sat beside Maia and put his feet atop the magazines on her coffee table. She leaned back beside him, her shoulder pressing into his.

"Do you think there really was a war between demons? Or is that information suspect as well?" she asked.

"I think it happened. There's that famous quote from a human historian, 'Power tends to corrupt, and absolute power corrupts absolutely.' We see it at play with the Gineal."

"Yeah, it's why some of us fall to the dark forces—the quest for more power." Maia sounded dispirited, but before he could come up with something reassuring to say, she continued, "It looks as if we'll be flying in the dark for a while longer with Seth."

"Finding anything in our library was always a longshot." He put his hand on Maia's thigh, but her pants kept him from her skin and he cursed the fact she wasn't wearing shorts. "I just thought we might be due for some good luck." And they needed it. Seth had to be defeated.

"So what do we do now?"

Creed closed his eyes. "We keep hunting and hope we find him before he attacks."

"That hasn't worked real well for us so far."

"We almost had him once, we'll find him again."

He knew from the way her muscles tensed under his hand that she hadn't liked that answer. "That seems too iffy when my sister's life is on the line. How long is Seth going to mess around? My bet is not too much longer, he's not patient, and while he might think of it as a game right now, the instant he grows bored, he'll go after her."

"Ryne's protected inside her home," he reminded her, "and she doesn't leave often."

"Can the wards hold against a demon like Seth? We can't assume that they will. She also isn't the hermit she once was. She and Deke do get out. I can't tell her to stay inside; she'll want to know why."

"We're doing everything we can to find Seth."

Maia was quiet and Creed let himself relax. Her skin was soft and warm, her scent enticed him, and the even rhythm of her respiration soothed something inside him.

"I have an idea we might try to smoke Seth out."

"What's that?"

Maia stopped his fingers before he could slide them higher up her leg and said, "Use me as bait."

18
CHAPTER

Creed didn't need time to think about her scheme. Exploding to his feet, he demanded, "Are you out of your fucking mind?"

"Don't you swear at me, Blackwood," Maia snarled as she stood and squared off with him.

He almost asked her how the hell she was going to stop him if he wanted to curse, but swallowed the words. No way did he want to sound like some grade-school kid saying *make me*. Control, he needed control. Creed curled his hands and took some deep breaths. Troubleshooters were trained to hang onto their self-command and he knew he couldn't afford to lose his.

"Sorry." He had to force the word out.

She nodded. "Time's running short and we can't count on getting any information from the Gineal library that will help us."

"I know that." It's why he'd planned to use *Ryne* as bait—he needed to lure out the demon—but he'd never found a way to work it, especially after he'd nearly shot her. The difference was that if things went to hell, Ryne could defend herself. Maia couldn't. "But your scheme won't fly." Creed relaxed. He'd managed to sound calm and rational. Yeah, Maia would want reasons, but he'd lay those out and the problem would be resolved.

"Why not?" she asked, just as he'd expected.

"Seth wants Ryne for her power. Going after you doesn't get him anything."

Maia stepped around the coffee table and walked over to where he was standing. "Yes, he wants power, but he wants revenge, too."

"Which he gets by going after Ryne." Creed shifted his weight to his right leg and crossed his arms over his chest to keep from reaching for her. He wanted to pull her body against his, not discuss her harebrained scheme. "Anyone who knows you would realize your sister is your Achilles' heel."

"Just like *I'm* Ryne's weak spot. He might think that he can use me to get to her."

It was a decent argument and Creed stopped to consider it. Seth was supposed to be cunning—Maia herself had referred to him as wily—but if they set a trap, he'd probably spot it and avoid it. The demon could try to turn it to his advantage, however, and that would leave Maia vulnerable. Creed wasn't putting her at risk. "He's not going to bite for you."

"He already has."

"What?" Creed felt his command of the conversation start to slip away.

Reaching out, she rested a hand on his forearm. Her touch jolted every cell in his body and left him distracted. "Do you think it was coincidence that the woman he killed last night looked almost exactly like I did when I knew him in Vegas? He might want to keep his attention on Ryne, but he's not finished with me—and his victim proves it."

"It proves nothing," he ground out.

"If he doesn't want to get back at me directly, then why pick her up in that bar?"

"Opportunity." Creed took a step away, breaking her hold on him. "She was there, so why not? Or how about the fact that he might know you're working with me and he chose her to send a message to you to back off."

"So we give him another opportunity," Maia said insistently. "I'll dress the way I did then and sit at the bar by myself. Seth won't be able to resist, and when we leave, you follow us."

Creed took a deep breath and tried to explain again why her reasoning was wrong. "Murdering that woman wasn't a direct attempt at you. Let's face it, if he'd wanted you, he would have had you. Remember your trip to the restrooms? I never could have gotten there in time if Seth had appeared, not even if I'd opened a transit and used it to cross the club."

"He might not have known I was there," she said quickly.

"Second," he continued as if she hadn't interrupted him, "you don't think he's going to figure out something's up if he sees you by yourself?"

"Probably, but Seth always was a gambler and the higher the stakes, the more he liked it. Plus, he's arrogant enough that he won't care even if he does know it's a setup; he'll think that he can prevail no matter what, and rub our noses in it."

Closing his eyes, Creed pushed both his hands through his hair and stifled a groan. This was why he liked to work alone. The other person inevitably thought his—or in this case her—role was that of partner rather than subordinate, and that led to ludicrous suggestions like this one. Of course, if he told her flat out what he thought of her idea, she'd get her back up. It would be much easier to be diplomatic, though, if his head hadn't been pounding all day. He'd have to give it a shot anyway.

He uncrossed his arms, took her hands, and said, "I appreciate that you want to catch Seth and that you're concerned it's taking too long, but I don't think this is the answer."

"You're writing my idea off without giving it a fair shake," Maia argued, her expression part irritation and part plea.

As he looked down into those big brown eyes, Creed wanted to grant her whatever she asked of him. His gaze dropped to her lips. They were set in a firm line, but despite that, they were full and he wanted to taste her, to explore until Maia forgot about her brainstorm.

Kiss her, a voice inside his head urged. *You know you want to, and she'd like it, too. Remember her response in the kitchen.*

"I'm saying it won't work after weighing the variables," Creed said, voice tight. "I don't think you've considered them, not completely. The danger to you alone is enough—"

"I understand the risk and I'm willing to accept it. I'm not some human or a Gineal who's been on the sidelines of battle. I was a troubleshooter."

She said that with a pride he hadn't heard from her before and Creed almost hated to burst her confidence. "And now you're not."

"No, but I'm accustomed to being under attack, I know how to handle myself in stressful situations, and I'm not going to fall apart or be so overwhelmed by adrenaline that I do something foolish." She invaded his personal space again. "You know how I was trained; we'd be on the same page."

Before he could stop himself, Creed freed his hands, reached for her hips, and tugged her to him. She looked startled, and he couldn't blame her—he was kind of surprised himself. Her spicy, sexy scent teased him and he leaned forward, wanting more.

Take more. She's winding her arms around your waist—is that the action of someone uninterested?

Shaking his head to dispel the inner prodding, he said, "You're forgetting a critical piece in all this—I don't know if I can take down Seth. If I can't, you'll be at his mercy."

"I didn't forget," Maia said soberly. And as he looked into her eyes, he realized she understood the situation completely.

"Ah, damn," he murmured as he nuzzled below her ear, "what's the point in both of us dying? You can stay safe if you keep out of this. I don't think the demon will waste time going after you if you're not a player."

"Maybe," she agreed, angling her head to give him freer access, "but I can't let you or my sister die without doing everything I can to prevent it."

How can you not kiss her after that?

Yeah, how could he resist? Creed turned and brushed his mouth over hers.

Ravish her.

Creed ignored the thought. Maia was the first person who'd expressed concern about his well-being since the death of his grandfather. Everyone else viewed him as some kind of invincible legend, but she saw the man. He sipped at her lips, showing her without words how much her concern meant to him.

"Creed, we're having a discussion," Maia said, but she spoke between kisses and didn't turn from him.

"Uh-huh."

She fit against him just right. With his height, standing

while kissing a woman was usually awkward, but Maia was tall and it wasn't uncomfortable to hold her this way. He shifted his arms—one at her shoulders, the other low on her waist—and drew her closer.

He nipped at her bottom lip and licked away the sting. Maia, though, opened her mouth just enough for the tip of her tongue to touch his. Creed shuddered and fought the need to taste her.

In an effort to regain his self-command, he pressed his lips to the corner of her mouth, to her chin, and strung a line of kisses along her jaw line. He traced her ear and nibbled at the lobe until she gasped, her hold tightening at his waist. Exploring her throat, he bit at her pulse point and her collarbone, and enjoyed the way she rocked into him.

Maia released him and used her palm to turn his face back to hers. Impatiently, her tongue trailed over the seam of his lips, demanding that he open for her. Creed resisted. Once the kiss went deep, his control would be gone—and he wasn't going to rush. Not this time. He tried to break loose, but she buried both hands in his hair and held him to her.

With a low groan, he capitulated.

When she realized she no longer had to hang onto him, her hands stroked him—his hair, his shoulders, his back—and her body undulated against his. Maia tugged his T-shirt from his jeans and ran her hands under the cotton.

"Slow down," he murmured against her lips, but she wasn't listening. Creed broke the kiss, but before she could do more than moan a complaint, he reached for the hem of his shirt and yanked it over his head. Maia was back in his arms before it hit the floor.

Her hands caressed his bare chest. Creed struggled to rein in—the last thing he wanted to do was put her on the floor and fall on top of her—but he was getting to that point fast.

She bit at his pec and he groaned more loudly, his head falling back. Shit, he cursed silently when he managed to open his eyes again, they were standing in the middle of her front windows and the interior lights were on. They had to move this somewhere else.

She'll tell you to stop if you allow her time to come to her senses.

Yeah, she would, and he was loving the way she teased his nipples with her tongue and lips. He didn't want this to end.

Don't say anything. Do you care if you're entertaining the neighbors?

No, he didn't. If they wanted to watch, let them, but it would bother Maia. She'd be mortified if this went any further while they were standing in full view of the street, and if he didn't say anything, she'd remember this interlude with shame once their need was sated.

Creed felt his stomach clench at the thought.

"Maia." She ignored him. "Maia," he said more loudly, "look at me." She did, her pupils so dilated her eyes appeared black. "Let's move this to the bedroom, okay?"

"What?" she said, not quite comprehending him.

He pointed to the windows. "We need privacy."

That registered, but instead of pulling away and calling a halt, Maia smiled, took his hand, and drew him along with her. The lamp on her bedside table was on and there was a book beside it that caught his attention, but he forgot about it when she wrapped her arms around him from behind. She kissed him between his shoulder blades and Creed's world narrowed to one woman.

Since he didn't want to risk another interruption, he

checked the windows. The room-darkening blinds were down and no one was going to see them, even in silhouette.

Creed turned to face Maia and ran the backs of his fingers down her cheek. "You're beautiful," he told her. "Not only the outside," he added before the disappointment he observed in her eyes could deepen, "but inside, too."

He wanted her to know that in the same way she saw beyond the legend to the man, he saw beyond her face and body to the woman. "The way you care about people," Creed said as he tipped her chin until their gazes met, "the way you nurture and protect them—that's special. *You're* special." He shrugged, suddenly feeling uncomfortable. "Just so you know."

"And you're sweet." She traced her index finger over his bottom lip.

Capturing her hand, Creed drew her finger into his mouth and laved the tip before he gently bit the pad. "You know," she said slowly, "for a man who dropped my shorts after a couple of minutes of kissing, you're moving pretty slow tonight."

Creed gave her finger one last kiss before taking her hand in his and tickling her palm with his tongue. "I had to prove I knew what foreplay was somehow, since you wouldn't join me in the shower."

Her chuckle caressed his skin as smoothly as her hands had earlier. "You proved your point, Creed, now pick up the pace."

He grinned, and after another slow, deep kiss, he tugged her shirt free of her purple capris. Her sleeveless blouse was white and cut low, putting the first button just above the swell of her breasts. He let his fingers brush her as he opened each one. She caught the shirt before it fell to the floor and tossed it on her dresser.

Her bra was flesh-colored, and God help him, it plunged dramatically. Her nipples were hard, outlined clearly by the nearly sheer lace, and he lightly pinched one, his hand shaking.

Then she was in his arms again and this kiss was wild, completely unrestrained. Creed unhooked her bra. Maia opened the button of his jeans and lowered the zipper. He pushed her pants off. For a long moment, he stared. Apparently, she believed in wearing the tiniest thongs that it was possible to manufacture. This one matched the bra. "Turn for me," he choked out.

Slowly, teasing him, she did just that. Creed groaned when he saw her back. Maia looked over her shoulder. "You must be an ass man."

He shook his head. "I'm a *you* man."

Sweeping her up in his arms, he brought her down to the bed and followed her. The only things between them were her panties and his briefs, and if he had his way, they weren't going to impede him long. But instead of stripping her, Creed cupped a breast and kissed her.

"Why so slow?" Maia asked, her hand stroking his erection through the cotton.

"I'm hoping to find control," he admitted. "I don't want to go off too fast; it's been about seven months since I last had sex."

Maia squeezed him gently and said, "It's been seven years for me."

She'd managed to shock him and that helped him bank the fire. He almost said something about not believing a woman who looked like her had been celibate for so long, but he knew she wouldn't like the reference to her appearance. Then he realized that seven years ago had been Seth. Creed felt another kind of heat start to build and tried to smother it.

Maia released him. "I'm sorry I said anything," she said, sounding hurt.

"I'm the one who's sorry." Creed leaned over her and brushed the hair off her face. He fumbled for words and settled on one. "Why?"

"How many reasons do you need? How about the fact that I'd have to hide a big portion of my life from a human and the Gineal pretty much shun me? Or how about the fact that the last male I was with was only using me and that I've doubted my judgment ever since? Or—"

"I meant, why me? I'm not exactly some white knight who rescues damsels from their towers."

Her smile was weak, but he was relieved to see it anyway. "You're gruff and abrasive and the farthest thing from charming that I've seen in a while—and I trust that. Besides, we click."

Yeah, they did, like a lit match to dry tinder, and he wanted to fan the flames. Which was why it sucked like hell that he had to stop.

Nooooovo! She's willing; you can't walk away from a willing woman. Creed ignored the inner voice and the way his cock ached. There was no other choice.

He climbed out of bed, retrieved his jeans, and stepped into them. Maia propped herself up on her elbows and watched as he began to gingerly zip them. "Why are you getting dressed?"

"We can't do this."

"What?" She looked at him as if he'd lost his mind. He probably had. What sane male walked away from someone with a body like Maia's?

"I want you—one glance should tell you how much— but this isn't right, not for you."

Slowly, she sat up. "Isn't that my decision to make?"

Shit, Maia wanted to discuss this while she was half

naked. He looked around, found the blouse she'd discarded earlier, and tossed it at her. She caught it, but didn't move. "For God's sake," Creed growled, "put that on." She did, but didn't bother with the buttons.

You can rejoin her on the bed. She'd welcome you still.

Maia would; he could see she remained aroused and she wasn't mad, simply puzzled. "You're right, it's your decision, but you're forgetting something—I'm a troubleshooter and you're powerless." She lost some of her languidness. "You waited seven years to have sex because you didn't want a casual relationship, but you and I, we can't have more."

That knocked most of the passion out of her and she clutched the blouse closed. "And you stopped," she said, a note of near-wonder in her voice.

"I had to, angel. I might not be some knight, but I'm not a complete bastard." Creed shrugged. "Not yet, anyway. If you were the kind of woman who went for no-strings-attached sex, I'd be in bed with you right now, but we both know you're not."

"No, I'm not," she agreed softly.

Creed gathered the rest of his stuff. "I need some space before I do something we'll both regret. If we're not done talking about this, we'll have to pick up later." He escaped without waiting for her response.

He quickly changed into shorts and a white T-shirt, then Creed bolted from the house and went for a run. The rain continued to come down, but he welcomed it.

It took a good mile before he felt his need of her begin to subside and another mile before his mind cleared. What the hell was wrong with him? He knew better than to mess around with Maia.

But it hadn't felt like *messing,* it had felt like more.

Creed picked up his speed. It couldn't be anything

except casual. She didn't have magic any longer and he wanted a soul pairing with another troubleshooter. More than wanted it. The Gineal needed him and he'd fallen, but with a pairing, he could hang on indefinitely— maybe he could even walk away entirely from the dark forces—and beyond that, he'd have more power. That could only help when Earth entered Twilight Time.

The light was against him at the intersection and he turned right instead of crossing. There were other reasons for pulling back with Maia—like the fact that the last time he'd nearly had sex, he'd felt the dark forces start to swamp him.

How had he forgotten that? Especially with his inner voice encouraging him to do things he knew weren't right.

Shaking his head, Creed pushed himself harder. Somehow, he had to hang on. He needed to conquer Seth and have enough strength of character to walk away from Maia.

Of the two, the latter suddenly seemed the more difficult.

19
CHAPTER

The rain had ended half an hour ago, but the pavement remained wet, and in the gleam of the streetlights, it shone as if it were created of polished onyx. Tonight, however, Seth couldn't appreciate the tiny fragment of urban beauty.

This section of the city was largely deserted and that suited his mood. To ensure he wasn't disturbed, he'd cloaked his presence from humans. He had much to think about and there were plans and decisions to make.

Seth had nearly had Blackwood tonight, but at the last instant he'd swerved off course. It was endlessly frustrating to be forced to use another as his instrument, but Seth had no option. The spell was clear; he could acquire a Gineal's power at only one moment—when his soul was out of his body, but before he died—and to make it more difficult, Seth could not be the one responsible for the injuries. It was a ridiculous limitation, but years spent studying the incantation had not provided an alternative.

Once he'd accepted that the covenants of the spell could not be broken, Seth had sought the most powerful of the Gineal as his prey. He'd found Blackwood in London and had followed him for more than three months, exerting whatever influence he could on him and waiting for a moment when Blackwood was severely injured. It was bound to happen, since the man regularly fought the strongest of the remaining demons. Before he could be wounded, however, he'd led Seth to the true prize—Ryne Frasier.

The instant he'd felt her power, Seth had adjusted his plans—he'd take her magic instead. Unlike Blackwood, however, she was too protected to be swayed, and it was improbable that she'd easily be wounded in battle—not with the added shield that her partner gave her.

So Seth had concocted a scheme.

A faint smile crossed his face at the memory. He would continue to work on controlling Blackwood, and when the timing was right, he'd compel the man to attack Ryne. In the ensuing battle, one of them would be the loser and he'd take the magic of whichever it was. He preferred the woman, but Seth would settle for Blackwood's power—it would be enough.

He stopped and watched a police cruiser drive by, but of course he remained unnoticed. When the car was out of sight, he resumed walking.

What he truly needed, however, was complete control over Blackwood, and that had been within his grasp earlier tonight. So close! Seth shook his head. How could any male pass on an opportunity to have sex with a woman who looked like Maia?

The hair at his nape prickled and Seth whirled to confront whatever was behind him.

The streets were empty and a thorough scan of the area with both his senses and his magic verified that no one was close at hand. Had he lost too much power to know if Horus was out there? He shivered, realized that the weather had turned cool after the storm, and adjusted his body temperature to compensate.

Last night, he'd made an error when he'd killed that human woman, and now, time was running short.

His magic had been equal to the other demons of his branch until Maia had stolen some of his power. It hadn't taken long for word of his weakness to travel through the group and he'd been hunted by his enemies ever since.

Seth, though, was clever—far more clever than his foes—and he'd been able to stay one step ahead of them. Until last night. The uncontrolled emotion combined with his use of power and the method he'd used to kill the human had been as good as hoisting a neon sign miles high with an arrow and a message proclaiming *Seth is here*.

Crossing against the light, he walked more quickly. He needed to leave town, to disappear, and he couldn't. Not when he was so excruciatingly close to acquiring more power. Instead, he'd have to go to ground and manipulate things from a distance. It should keep him safe—for a while.

Either Ryne's or Blackwood's power would make Seth stronger than his fiercest opponents. Yes, once he had Gineal magic, he would vanquish his enemies forever and rule the living. He'd been born for it and been deprived for these many millennia. The time of reckoning, though, was at hand.

All he needed was to take the power before Horus tracked him down and killed him.

* * *

Things could have become unbearably awkward between her and Creed the last four days, Maia knew that, but they hadn't. In fact, since he'd called a halt to their lovemaking, they'd developed a comfortable routine. They'd even started jogging together every morning before they set out looking for Seth.

Today, however, their plans had been put on hold after his cell had rung. Maia had learned pretty quickly that he never received calls unless he was being given an assignment, and that saddened her. He should have friends that picked up the phone to razz him about the Cubs blowing another game, or to ask him if he wanted to go boating over Labor Day weekend. All he received were call-outs.

Maia put the last cereal bowl into the dishwasher and closed the door. She looked around, but the kitchen was clean and there was nothing here to keep her mind off her questions. Where was he? What kind of demon was he fighting? Was he okay?

The house seemed oddly empty without him, and that was bad news. He wasn't staying permanently, she knew that. If he survived the showdown with Seth, Creed would move on and she'd be alone again. Maybe more alone than she'd been before.

Deciding she didn't want to think about that or about Creed possibly getting hurt, Maia went to her bedroom. She kicked off her sandals, settled on the bed, and reached for the book Caitlin had given her. Despite the days canvassing the metro area and the nights spent at clubs, Maia was nearly halfway through the tome. As she'd suspected, she had yet to read anything she didn't already know, although some of this information would have come in handy seven years ago when she'd first given up her magic.

She understood why Eithne had made the text impossible to open by anyone except Maia. There might not be anything new here for her, but there was plenty of information about the Gineal and about those who'd ceded their magic. If this book fell into the wrong hands, humans could cause an incredible loss of life among her people—and they'd done a damn good job of that without help.

Although she was largely bored by what she was reading and tired of translating handwritten pages, Maia kept going. There just might be something here if she persisted.

It didn't take long for her thoughts to wander. Friday night she'd been on this same bed with Creed and they'd both been almost naked. The memory was enough to make her thighs clench. It had been difficult enough to tell him no that day in her kitchen when he'd been in such a hurry, but when he was taking it slow, the man was nearly irresistible.

He was gorgeous, with a face pretty enough to get him on the cover of magazines and a body ripped with muscles, but Maia had been around plenty of good-looking men and none of them had affected her like he did. She wasn't sure why. He had little charm or tact, but she'd reached a point where she hardly noticed it anymore. Creed could be stubborn, he liked to be in charge, and when he gave an order, he expected instant obedience. All things she hated. Normally.

But beyond that gruff exterior was a man she could trust, a man who saw beneath the surface. Maia had grown so tired of people judging her by her appearance, of wanting her body without knowing who she was, but

Creed had looked deeper, and that meant everything to her.

Maia blinked and refocused her attention on the book. She made it through the section on how she could still read energy—more stuff she knew—and turned the page.

What really got to her, though, was the way Creed had stopped. Twice. The first time so they weren't putting on a show for the entire block, and the second time because he knew her well enough to understand she couldn't have a casual fling. No one would have blamed him if he'd kept going—heaven knew she wouldn't have—but he'd shown more kindness, more compassion than most men would have.

That kind of protectiveness was rare, and it had to mean Creed had feelings for her. Didn't it?

God help her, she hoped it did, because she'd done something stupid. More than stupid, moronic. Maia didn't know why she hadn't figured it out earlier—a woman didn't break seven years of celibacy without a good reason—but when he'd walked away from her because it was the best thing for *her,* she got it.

Like an idiot, she'd fallen in love with Creed Blackwood.

There was nothing but heartache on that path—that was a no-brainer—and now she had to decide which would hurt worse—Creed leaving after becoming her lover, or leaving without her ever knowing what it was like to feel him deep inside her.

She couldn't keep mooning over Creed. Tightening her hold on the book, Maia looked down and made herself read each word. It took a while, but she found something that grabbed her attention. The section talked about how some Gineal who'd surrendered their powers had begun to practice magic the way humans did. She hadn't realized that was a possibility. How much could she do if she tried that?

She didn't have an opportunity to find out before she heard movement in the living room. Quickly, she shut the book and tucked it in the drawer of her nightstand. Just in time, too. Creed walked in, stepped out of his tennis shoes, and without a word, crawled in beside her on the bed. He lay on his back, groaned softly, and dropped his arm over his eyes.

"You look like hell," Maia said.

"Then I look better than I feel."

Scooting lower, she turned on her side and rested her weight on her elbow, allowing herself a good look at his face—at least the part that wasn't covered by his arm. She wanted to ask what had happened, but instead she lightly stroked his cheek.

"The demon knew I'd lost my mind shield," Creed said.

"What branch?"

"Breug."

Not as dangerous as a groige, but it didn't miss by much. She ran her hand over the shoulder of his forest-green T-shirt and said, "You need to find out how to get that up again."

"You don't think I know that?" he snapped, and then immediately groaned. "Shit."

Instead of growling back at him, Maia rested her hand over his heart and rubbed. He was irritable enough after a day around humans who weren't mentally attacking him; she couldn't even guess how much he must hurt right now.

"Why don't you put your head in my lap and I'll send you some healing energy."

"You'd do that?" Creed asked, lowering his arm.

There were lines of pain at the corners of his eyes, and a furrow between his brows.

"Sure," she said. Maia hated performing healings because they reminded her too much of everything she'd lost, but for Creed she'd handle it.

When they were settled—she with pillows propped against the headboard to cushion her back, and him with his head squarely in her lap—Maia put the palms of her hands over his temples and called for healing energy.

When she'd still had her magic, she'd been able to see the green flow come out her hands and enter the person she was helping, but those days were long gone. Maia felt the pain that came with the reminder, but instead of eviscerating her as it normally did, this was only a pang. A hard one, yes, but it was so much less than her usual reaction and almost bearable.

A peace came over her as she sat silently working on Creed. It was good to have him here, safe, and if not entirely well, at least not badly injured.

Her hands went cool, but neither one of them moved. Since the healing had ended, Maia began to stroke his hair. She couldn't believe she found his shoulder-length mess sexy, but she did, probably because it was his. "Your hair is longer than mine, Blackwood," she pointed out matter-of-factly.

"You jealous?" he asked, one side of his mouth quirking up.

"No, I'm merely making a comment."

"I don't like my hair short." He cracked an eye open. "You're not going to nag at me about getting it cut, are you?"

"Nope, it's your hair, do whatever you want with it. Why would you think I'd nag, anyway?"

Creed opened both eyes and tilted his head back to look at her. "My grandfather used to ride my ass pretty hard about keeping it short, and so did my mentor when I was training."

Maia nodded. "Your mentor would have been concerned about the length hindering you in battle."

"Yeah? Were you told to get your hair cut?"

"No," she admitted, seeing where he was going with this.

"And you used to wear it much longer than me, so that means it's not a legitimate concern."

"Since you're suddenly feeling feisty, your head must be better."

He grinned and sat up. "It is better, thanks."

Creed shifted to his right, lay back down, and patted the mattress beside him. It was an invitation, pure and simple, and one she didn't waste much time resisting. He put his arms around her as she lay beside him and she wrapped her own arm over his waist. This was nice. He wasn't putting any moves on her and he didn't expect anything. He just wanted her close to him, and Maia liked that. A lot.

"When did your grandfather die?" she asked quietly, unable to contain her curiosity about his family.

"I was twenty-two." Before she could ask, he volunteered, "The man was stubborn and refused to visit a healer once a year. It turned out he hadn't seen one since my grandma died—she'd probably pushed him into going." He paused and said softly, "It was a sudden heart attack."

Maia hugged him more tightly, almost feeling his pain although she couldn't see his face.

"He raised me," Creed said. "My grandma, too, of course, but she died when I was nine, and from then on it was my grandfather and me."

Creed had talked about his grandparents once before

and had mentioned that his grandmother had been a troubleshooter. "Did she die in the line of duty?"

"Yeah."

One word, no inflection, and it told Maia an ocean's worth of information. Creed had been devastated by the loss of his grandmother. She lightly stroked his side, wanting to offer comfort. "Both my parents were troubleshooters," she offered even though he already knew. "They died together when I was nineteen." Her words came out choppy, but it was difficult to talk about, even if she wanted him to know that the sharing went both ways. "It was line of duty for them, too. Another Gineal who'd turned."

"I'm sorry, angel," Creed said, gathering her closer.

"Condolences aren't necessary. I never had much of a relationship with either one of them and neither did my sister—or do you know that already?"

"No, Ryne never talked about your parents. Do you want to tell me about them?"

Definitely not, but she would anyway. "I don't know what to say. They were so into each other that half the time I don't think they even remembered they had children. Someone told me it was because my parents were star seeds, here for a single purpose."

"Star seeds?" Before she could explain, she saw the confusion clear. "You mean they reincarnated on another planet and had never had a life or a connection to anyone on Earth before, right?"

Maia released a long sigh. "Yes, and that included Ryne and me."

"You don't sound angry or bitter. I'd be both in your place."

"I used to be." Until recently. She wasn't sure when the change had occurred, but Maia was glad to have the weight of negative emotion lessened. "I guess it's hard to hold on to that kind of anger, though, when it really wasn't their fault."

Quiet reigned once more. Maia was curious about his parents—Creed had never said a word about them—but she didn't ask because she didn't want to tread on sacred ground. But there was something else she'd been wondering, and she saw no reason not to bring it up while he was being forthcoming. "You don't happen to be related to a Shona Blackwood, do you?"

Creed's entire body went rigid and his arms tightened almost painfully around her before he relaxed them and popped off the bed. "Where the hell did you hear that name?" he demanded.

Slowly, Maia sat up. "She's a glass artist and I saw one of her pieces at a store in town. Who is she?"

Without a word, he turned and left the room. Maia jumped off the bed and chased after him. "Oh, no you don't. If you don't want to talk about her, you say, 'Maia, it's none of your business,' but you don't give me your back and walk out, do you hear me?"

He stared out the window of her living room, not responding in any manner. Maia wanted to push, but she'd never seen Creed quite this way before. She hadn't meant to hurt him or stir up bad memories. Hesitantly, she went over to him and ran her fingers down his back. "I'm sorry, I didn't mean to upset you."

Again, there was no response, but she stayed where she was and continued to stroke him. Sunlight streamed in the windows, a robin hopped across her lawn, and she could watch the cars go by on the street, but while she was aware of all these things, it was in a peripheral way. Creed held her attention.

After a long while, he bowed his head and said, "Shona Blackwood is my sister."

Maia's hand stilled before she resumed caressing his back. "I didn't realize you had a sister."

"Neither did I," he said, voice devoid of emotion again.

The other night, she'd wrapped her arms around him from behind as a way to let him know she wanted him. Today, Maia did the same thing, even pressed a kiss between his shoulder blades again, but this time it was meant as comfort. She hadn't wanted to plunge into potentially dangerous water by asking about his parents, but somehow she'd ended up there just the same.

Creed's hands covered hers where they met at the front of his waist. "You have questions."

"I do, but I'm not going to ask them."

His muscles loosened. "That's one of the things I like about you," he said. "You're sensitive enough to realize when something's touchy, and caring enough to back off."

Maia's heart trembled at his words. How foolish could one woman be? It was a simple statement that he might make to any friend, not an avowal of love, and yet she acted as if he'd handed her the moon. "I know what it's like to have areas of your life that you'd rather not talk about."

"That didn't stop me from quizzing you," Creed reminded her.

"You needed information about Seth." She really was a sap. He'd been obnoxious as hell prodding her for more details, and here she was excusing it away—but Seth had to be stopped, especially now that he'd killed a human.

Creed toyed with her fingers for a moment, tracing them with his own, before he said, "Shona is nine or ten years younger than me and I've only seen her once, from a distance."

Biting her lower lip, Maia tried to think of a way she could ask for clarification without churning up waves. There was more going on here than he'd said, that was obvious. He'd mentioned that his grandmother had died when he'd been nine. His sister's age suggested his mother and father had still been fine when Creed had been sent to live with his grandparents. The question she really wanted the answer to was why hadn't he remained with his mom and dad, and she could almost bet asking that would stir up a tempest.

"Not a tempest," Creed said and Maia stiffened. "It is hard to talk about, though."

He'd read her mind. He must have, because Creed had replied as if she'd spoken aloud. She'd lost her telepathy with her magic, so how had he known what she was thinking? That was something she'd worry about later, though. Right now Maia had bigger concerns. "What happened? If you don't mind telling me about it," she tacked on.

His hands stilled, then he broke her hold on him and turned. "Come on," Creed said, "let's get comfortable for this one."

Tugging her to the couch, he sat and pulled her onto his lap. He tucked her head under his chin and Maia bet he'd done it to hide his face and eyes from her. She didn't know what he was going to tell her or even if it would be the full story, but it would definitely be something that left him ill at ease.

Creed remained quiet and Maia lost herself in the soothing rhythm of his breathing, in the warmth of his body against hers. He had a hand on her knee, and as she waited, she traced her index finger along the veins of his forearm.

"In general, wouldn't you agree that everyone is cautious with where and when they use magic?" he asked.

"Of course."

"My parents weren't," Creed said, his hand giving her leg a brief squeeze. "They didn't give a damn where they were or who was around; if they wanted to use their powers, they did, and they never cleaned up after themselves."

Maia stiffened in surprise. She knew Creed felt it because he froze for an instant, but then he began gently stroking her leg and continued talking.

"Most of their transgressions escaped the notice of the council, but the bigger events didn't, and they were warned to be more circumspect. The ceannards talked to them three times; the fourth time, they took me away from them, stripped them of their magic and their memories, and set them up in a new life."

"How old were you when that happened?"

"Six."

"And the council didn't let you go with them." Obviously, but she had difficulty believing they'd separate a child from his parents.

"I'd already been tested and they'd known I was going to be a troubleshooter. They couldn't afford to lose me." He shrugged. "And I hadn't done anything wrong, so why should I be punished, too?"

Maia nodded. It made sense that he'd gone to live with his grandparents, but it couldn't have been easy on Creed. She knew him well enough to figure out what he'd done later.

"And how old were you when you went to see your mom and dad?" She tried to shift in order to see his face, but he tightened his hold, preventing her from changing positions.

"Nineteen and fresh out of troubleshooter training."

There was something in his voice that was mocking, but Maia knew he was denigrating himself and the young man he'd been. She took his hand from her knee and linked their fingers. "What happened?" she asked, although she could guess.

"They didn't remember me. I knew they wouldn't consciously, but I thought that on some level, they'd have to recognize me even if they didn't understand why."

"And they didn't."

"No. I discovered that I strongly resemble my father. There was no way they should have looked at me and not wondered if I was related, not asked questions, but they didn't."

And that must have hurt. "Did you ever go back?"

His hand tightened around hers. "No point in it, but that's how I discovered I had a sister. She was playing in the yard when I drove up. I did some investigating when I returned to Chicago and found out who she was."

Maia turned her head and kissed his throat. "Do you want to see the work of art Shona created? She's hugely talented." Maia didn't make the offer lightly; she understood it would be a risk, but she was willing to gamble on Caitlin's silence in order to give Creed this.

"Yeah," he said, voice thick, "I'd like that."

Maia brought his hand to her lips and kissed his palm. There were layers to the man, so many of them that it would take a lifetime to explore them all. Why couldn't she have found him earlier, before she'd fallen to the dark forces?

Except, she realized, if they had met then, Creed probably wouldn't have liked her. Hell, she hadn't liked herself. She'd been emotionally needy and had looked outside herself for validation. And because she hadn't wanted to peer into her soul, discover who she was, and do the hard work to fix what made her unhappy, she'd shopped without restraint and partied the same way. Both activities had kept her from thinking.

The lifestyle had led to her downfall. She'd begun to use black magic, which had attracted Seth and accelerated her slide until Maia had noticed how far she'd gone.

Giving up her powers had been the hardest thing she'd ever faced, but she was glad now that she'd done it. Her sacrifice had kept Creed from needing to kill her, and she'd grown so much in the last seven years, filling the emptiness within herself bit by bit. Maia had become someone she did like—most of the time. The only remnant of the woman she'd been was her fear of walking away from a job she hated, but she'd done that, too, and had found a new freedom. She snuggled closer to Creed.

Life, even without magic, was a miracle. She was wrapped in the arms of the man she loved, and everything that had occurred before had brought her to this moment.

Maia kissed his throat again. This place in time was special and worth the pain she'd experienced in order to reach it. It was even perfect enough to make up for the agony she'd go through when Creed walked away at the end of his mission.

20
CHAPTER

Creed pulled to a stop in front of their home. Maia was dozing beside him and he put a hand on her knee, lightly shaking her awake. At 2 A.M. the roads were deserted and the houses dark—with one exception.

"Mrs. O's place is all lit up," he said and turned off the engine of his rental car.

"I better check to make sure she's all right." Maia reached for the door handle and Creed rushed to get out. He made it around the hood in time to offer her a hand. Her body-hugging maroon dress hampered her movements and she needed the help, although he knew she'd manage on her own. The instant she was on her feet, she hurried down the sidewalk and he trailed behind her as she went up the stairs to her neighbor's home.

Maia rang the bell, knocked, and then pounded. "Mrs. Olson, can you hear me? Are you okay?"

There was no answer and Maia went around the side of the house. Before she reached the back door, they spotted the elderly lady standing in the middle of her yard wearing a housecoat. "Mrs. Olson!"

The woman turned and met them partway. "Maia," she said and Creed frowned, concerned over the way she gasped for air. "Mister Jenkins . . . He's loose." Mrs. O grabbed Maia's arm. "Hissing . . . and growling. Maybe . . . feral . . . raccoon. I'm . . . scared."

"Where is MJ? Near where you were standing when we rounded the house?" Maia asked. Mrs. O nodded. "Okay, I'll go see what's going on."

"No," Creed interrupted. "You stay here and let me check it out."

"But—"

"Your heels are going to sink into the grass and I think someone needs to stay here. Just in case," he added.

She met his eyes and nodded, expression grave. Creed returned the nod and went to see what had the cat so upset. He hoped for something simple like a raccoon, but with a demon in the vicinity, he couldn't count on anything that benign. As he walked across the lawn, he heard Maia talking to Mrs. O, trying to get her to calm down and breathe easier.

When Creed neared the spot where Mrs. O had been standing, he heard the damn cat snarling and carrying on. He slowed and tried to sense what was out there, but he'd spent more than five hours checking out bars and his head couldn't hurt worse if someone used a sledge-hammer on it. Not being able to scan left him flying blind.

He hesitated long enough to cast a spell that strengthened his protection, then went to see what had the hell-cat in a lather. Cautiously, Creed rounded the side of the privacy fence, and once out of view, he cast another incantation, one that allowed him to walk through the wooden slats. His lips quirked at the sight of Mrs. O's pet confronting a leopard with a substantial height and weight advantage.

The base fur was tawny brown with darker shadowed markings edged with black. Its long tail flicked lazily as the clouded leopard sat, watching the hellcat.

"Quinn, is that you?" Creed asked in a loud whisper.

The big cat stood, stretched, and shifted into a man. Not Quinn, but Keir. The house cat screeched, but after a pointed look from Keir, MJ turned tail and raced away.

"You need to learn how to read markings, Blackwood, then you wouldn't always be asking who we are."

"Sorry." Creed glanced over his shoulder. "We only have a few minutes; I'm going to have to chase down the hellcat before his owner comes looking for him."

Keir smiled and crossed the remaining distance with all his natural feline grace. "I sent the fierce warrior back to the one he watches over. It is well."

With a nod, Creed cast a spell to screen the area. If he didn't, the way his luck had been running lately, one of Maia's neighbors would wake up, look out the window, and call the police. Then Creed would have to explain what the hell he was doing talking to a naked man in the dead of night.

"Your mind shield is gone," Keir said.

"Yeah, I know."

The man shrugged and turned his face into the breeze. In the distance, Creed heard Mrs. O fussing over MJ, and a minute later, the sound of a door closing. Maia had probably gone inside with her neighbor, and that gave him a window of time to talk to Keir. Somehow, and he didn't know why it had happened, Creed had become the contact point between their societies. Whenever it was necessary to exchange information, he was the one the cat people came to see.

"We prefer 'Otherkind' to 'cat people.' Even the Gineal can pronounce that."

Creed tucked his hands in the front pockets of his trousers and inclined his head. "I meant no offense. Your language is difficult for us," he admitted, "and 'Otherkind' doesn't come naturally to mind."

"No offense is taken," Keir replied. "I merely point it out for your edification."

"Edification?" Creed asked, raising both brows. "You're lapsing in and out of some pretty formal speech tonight."

"I've spent the last few months with the elders, and they don't like to use English." Keir ran a hand over the back of his neck. "I'm still thinking in our language and translating."

There were a lot of questions Creed wanted to ask, but he swallowed them. For one thing, Maia would be checking on him shortly—he didn't have much time—and for another, the cat pe— er, Otherkind, were secretive.

"For the same reason the Gineal conceal their presence," Keir said, clearly reading Creed's thoughts. "Survival."

"Do you think a large jungle cat roaming the suburbs is inconspicuous?"

"It's easier to track you as a leopard." Keir shrugged and changed the subject. "The matriarch sent me to find you. We have information for the Gineal."

"What kind of info?"

"The barrier between this dimension and the one the Gineal have labeled forbidden wavered."

"Shit," Creed muttered. "How long was it down?"

"A mere microsecond."

Maybe that was how the zortir had gotten through to that farm, although he didn't like the coincidence of it showing up so close to where he was working. "Has it done anything odd since?"

"It hasn't been normal from the time it faltered. Whatever happened thinned it. The matriarch is concerned that a second flicker would make it disintegrate entirely, and she fears what will cross into this world."

"Or who might inadvertently wander into that one." Creed pushed a hand through the top of his hair. "I'll pass the message along to the council," he promised.

"There's more."

Creed braced himself. "Shoot."

"The guardian told our matriarch that when the barrier faltered, great evil crossed into this world. She referred to them as the demon gods."

"Gods? Plural?" Fuck.

"Creed? Are you okay?" Maia called from nearby. Before he could reply, she rounded the fence at a run, not drawing to a stop until she was beside him. He knew the instant she noticed Keir. "Wow," she breathed. "Hello."

The Otherkind's posture changed. "Hello, beautiful woman."

With a scowl, Creed put his arm around Maia's waist and drew her to his side. Cat people mated for life, but he knew Keir was unattached. "At least you had enough sense not to run in those shoes," Creed groused at Maia, "but you should have stayed inside. What if I was in the middle of a fight?"

"I'll leave you two to your argument," Keir said, taking a step back.

"No," Creed said quickly, "I need more info. Do the Otherkind know how many of the demon gods came through? How can your guardian be certain they *were* the demon gods?" He wanted to ask what the hell a guardian was, too, but figured his odds of getting that answered were around nil.

Keir looked at Maia, then back at him. He must have decided it was safe to talk because he said, "The guardian reported three, but was uncertain. As for how it was known which demons they were, we sense things much like the Gineal do."

Maia opened her mouth and Creed squeezed her waist, warning her to stay quiet. He questioned Keir further, but the cat man didn't know anything beyond what he'd said.

"If we learn more, I'm certain the matriarch will send me, or another, to you with the information."

Creed nodded grimly and thanked the man. Keir didn't bother to conceal himself before morphing back into leopard form. With one nod, he turned, slinking off into the darkness.

"Cat people really exist," Maia said, sounding dazed. Since he didn't feel as if he could tell Maia more about the Otherkind than what she'd already seen, Creed steered her back the way he'd come, and switched topics. "How's Mrs. O? The way she gasped for air scared the shit out of me."

"Yeah, me, too," she said after giving him a sideways glance. "I think she's okay. I'll check on her when I get up in the morning."

Creed crouched down, retrieved Maia's heels from the middle of the yard, and continued to her house. "Are you alert enough to have a conversation?" he asked once they were inside with the doors locked and the lights on.

"About more of the strongest demons coming through?" Creed nodded. "Yes, I'm definitely awake enough for that," she said dryly. "Can I change clothes before we talk?"

"Go ahead."

She took her heels from him and went down the hall.

Creed followed her into her bedroom. "Blackwood," she growled.

"What?"

"Never mind." Shaking her head, she went into the closet, put her shoes away, then dug through a drawer and disappeared into the bathroom. The door closed sharply behind her.

He sat on the bed and waited. It wasn't long, though, before she came out wearing an oversize T-shirt and carrying her dress. That, too, went into the closet. At another time, he would have expressed his disappointment that she didn't sleep in a sexy little nightgown, but not tonight. Creed waited until she sat beside him before he spoke. "We need to catch Seth, ASAP. You heard Keir, three god-demons came through and it makes me wonder if they're here to get revenge—on Seth."

Maia crossed one bare foot over the other. "If what Fia reported about the war among them is true, there might be old scores to settle, but maybe we should let them take out Seth—after all, they have enough power to do it."

He shook his head and clasped one of Maia's hands between his. "Do you really want humans to be caught in the middle of a grudge match between these demons? Their last skirmish lasted eighty years, and the stories have survived as myths for thousands of years. And back then," Creed reminded her, "no one had video cameras and phones that took pictures. If they're here because they want Seth, our best bet is to eliminate him first."

"Easy to say, Creed, but if they couldn't kill him way back when, how are you going to do it?"

"I don't have a fucking clue, but I do know that the only way to protect humans is to stop a demon war before it starts. The problem is that it's been five days since we've had a trace of Seth."

"I think he's lying low after the murder."

"So do I, but we need to flush him out." Maia looked at him, but he couldn't read her face. Taking a deep breath, Creed forced the question out. "Are you still willing to act as bait?"

21
CHAPTER

Seth knew he shouldn't be out tonight, not when Horus and his allies hunted him with such determination, but he'd been bored out of his head and desperately needed a diversion. He'd cloaked himself as thoroughly as possible, doing what he could to protect himself, but that would only slow his pursuers, not stymie them. The risk was worth it, he decided. Already he was enjoying himself at this jazz club far more than he'd expected.

He had a clear sightline across the bar to Maia. Her dress said "fuck me" yet her expression warned, "keep away." Unfortunately for her, men weren't looking at her face. Seth had watched her fend off at least two dozen admirers and there'd be more judging by the interest he saw displayed.

Leaning against the wall, Seth gazed beyond Maia. Poor Blackwood looked miserable, most likely because so many men were fantasizing about the woman he wanted. Clearly, the troubleshooter had never learned to share.

On another night, he might have felt insulted over the obviousness of their ploy to snare him. Did they think him that foolish? No doubt they counted on his anger at Maia making him reckless, but they were wrong.

Seth chuckled softly. He intended to use their plan to initiate a scheme of his own. It was the perfect opportunity to turn things in his favor.

Another man approached Maia. She hardly looked at the human as she dealt with him. That gave Seth an idea—one that would allow him to get close without putting her immediately on guard—and he changed his appearance and clothing. Then, using a little magic, he helped himself to a bottle of beer. He needed the prop to complete the image.

Tail between his legs, the human walked away from Maia's table. Seth would give her a few minutes to wind down, then he'd head over and stir things up.

Maia believed every woman should own one sleazy dress and she was wearing hers—for the third time. It was black Lycra with spaghetti straps and cutouts that started at the top of the bodice, went beneath her left breast, and around to the back. A bra was an impossibility and so was bending over—it was much too short.

When she'd walked into the living room the first night, Creed had gawked. Maia had felt oddly smug as she'd watched him start to get hard merely from looking at her. Without a word, he'd gone to the guest room and donned a blazer before returning. He'd worn one every night since.

But while she enjoyed Creed's reaction, she wasn't quite as thrilled about the attention the dress garnered her from other men. It seemed as if they were all on the prowl this Friday night and she'd had to deal with too many already. Maia ran her fingers around the rim of her glass of mineral water and tried to send out "keep away" vibes.

Creed believed her presence would lure Seth out of hiding, but Maia didn't think she would be the determining factor. For Seth, it would be a combination of boredom and his need to take risks that would get him back out on the town. It had been eight days since he'd killed that woman, eight days since he'd started to lie low, and by now, he had to be climbing the walls. Yeah, he'd chance it. The only question was when and where he'd make his appearance.

Maia sighed and took a sip of her water. She was torn between wanting Seth to show up and hoping he stayed away; she didn't want anything to happen to Creed, and that demon was strong. Dealing with dark-force beings, though, was Creed's job—it used to be her job, too—and she had to let him do what he'd been born for without acting like a ninny.

Putting the glass back down on the table, she shifted and tugged at the hem of her dress.

"I was enjoying the view," a male voice said from behind her shoulder. Before she could comment, he brazenly took the seat opposite her and placed his beer bottle on the table. "Hey, baby, can I buy you a drink?"

"I have one," she said, pointing to her nearly full glass.

"How about a dance then? They're playing our song."

"No, thank you," she said coolly. "I'm waiting for someone, so if you don't mind?" She made a shooing motion with her hand.

"Baby, you shouldn't be so unfriendly; you're breaking my heart." He clutched his chest.

Maia shook her head and said, "The theatrics aren't going to change my mind."

"Maybe this will." He morphed right there, changing from a twenty-something dude to the Seth she'd seen in front of the library. Along with dark hair and darker eyes, he had a light mustache and a tiny soul patch beneath his bottom lip and something about the look made him appear as evil as she knew him to be. People! Quickly, she looked around, but no one seemed to have noticed what he'd done.

She tried hard to appear unfazed by his quick-change routine, but it was difficult. Maia hadn't sensed that it was him, and that frightened her right down to the toes of her kitten-heel shoes.

Seth leaned forward and ran a finger lightly over her hand. "Hello, precious. Did you miss me?"

"Not even a little," she said with calm she didn't feel. Slowly, not wanting to show how disconcerted she was by his touch, Maia moved her hands to her lap.

"Really? Then why have you been looking for me? You even dressed with me in mind."

"My clothing has nothing to do with you."

He made a tsking sound. "You really shouldn't prevaricate. Isn't that one of the reasons why you gave up your power? You said you were tired of being a liar, but if nothing's changed, you could have held onto your magic."

A wave of despair welled up. Seth was right—if she hadn't changed her ways, what had been the point in surrendering her magic? Now she was powerless and still— Maia's eyes narrowed. "Stop playing with my mind."

"As you wish." Seth leaned back, sprawling in his chair. "Did you cut your hair because I liked it long?"

"I cut it because it was easier for me."

"And perhaps because this new length mars your beauty?" Seth suggested. "Do you think that's why your Gineal friend opted not to share your bed?"

Maia tried not to react, but when Seth smiled, she knew he'd picked up something. "That's beneath even someone like you."

"Your repartee was more entertaining in the old days."

"Of course, I live for no purpose other than to amuse you," she said, but her hands were clenched into fists as she struggled to deal with her rising emotions. Part of her was repelled by the idea that she'd slept with Seth for months on end, that she'd allowed him to know her so intimately. Another part of her remembered the pleasure he'd given her, and though it shamed her to her soul, she responded to him.

"It's natural for your body to ready itself for me," he said, leaning forward again, and his eyes held a heat that made her tingle. "I gave you orgasms that made you scream."

He was reading her mind, damn him, but she couldn't deny what he'd said. Those were some of the memories Seth had left untouched. "Stay out of my head," she warned. "And sex without emotion is empty and meaningless."

"Being the high-minded individual you are, you have no interest in that, right?" The table was small and Seth didn't need to stretch in order to pinch her distended nipple. She gasped, but before she could move out of range, he gave it a little flick with his finger and eased away.

Maia couldn't stop herself from glancing over at Creed. If he'd seen that, he'd be halfway to her table already. He remained in his seat, however.

"Don't worry; he won't be joining us."

"What did you do?"

Seth shrugged. "I merely froze him in place. So what do you say? Once more for old time's sake?"

"Why? So you can kill me like you killed that woman last week?" Maia realized she shouldn't have said that a beat too late, especially since Creed was no longer able to help her.

"I doubt you'd anger me the way she did." The playfulness was gone from Seth's voice. "You savored my cock. If I recall correctly, and I'm certain I do, I believe you mentioned that sucking me off was your favorite thing."

Maia felt the blood drain from her face.

Seth noticed even in the dim lighting of the bar and smiled. "I see you remember that as well."

"That wasn't me," she gritted out.

"Oh, but it was you, Maia-mine. The dark forces did nothing save lower your inhibitions. Why does it mortify you now to have enjoyed giving sexual pleasure to another?"

"Maybe because you were using me and my body. Tell me, Seth, did you care about anything besides my looks and the fact that you wanted to take my magic?"

He laughed. "You figured that out at last, have you? I wondered if you would."

She shifted and impatiently tugged the hem of her dress back into place. "I was already using black magic—I can't blame you for that—but over and over again, you lured me deeper."

"I did," he admitted without a visible shred of conscience. "At the rate you were going, it would have taken years before you sank far enough for the Gineal to notice your misdeeds."

Maia didn't understand why Seth cared if her people had known, but she didn't ask. He'd never tell her the truth, not unless it worked within his own agenda. "Is that why you picked my sister? Because I foiled your plans?"

"You overestimate your importance. I chose your sister for only one reason—she has more power than any other Gineal."

Her fingers spasmed in her lap, but she didn't think he noticed. "You need that magic, don't you? Your enemies are looking for you and you're weaker than they are now."

Seth picked up his beer bottle and rolled it between his hands before he looked at her from beneath lowered brows and said, "You ruined a lot of things for me, precious. Not only did you give up your magic, negating the months of work I'd invested in you, but you took some of my power. That's inexcusable. But even that wasn't enough for you. You cast me into some strange dimension, and by the time I found my way back to this one, nearly six years had passed." He returned the bottle to the table with a loud thunk. "I don't believe in forgive and forget."

"What demon does?"

His smile returned. "Exactly."

Taking a deep breath for courage, Maia said, voice low, "I want you to leave the Gineal alone, especially my sister, her fiancé, and Blackwood."

"Ah, you'd like to open negotiations."

"Yes, what will it take?"

Propping his arm along the back of his chair, Seth appeared to give her question some thought. "What would you say if I asked for your body to do with as I wanted for a full day? Would you agree to empty, meaningless sex?"

Maia felt the mineral water she drank start to come up and swallowed hard. While it might cost her dearly, it was far less than she'd expected him to ask for. "That's all you want in exchange for leaving my people alone?"

"No," Seth said, voice intractable, "that's what I want to open negotiations, otherwise I'm not willing to discuss this with you. Just think, it would be a guilt-free way for you to have me again. As you screamed your pleasure, you could reassure yourself that you were only lying with me to save others. Such a martyr."

"You expect me to agree to have sex with you simply to talk? I don't think so."

"I hold all the cards, Maia-mine, but I'm not unreasonable. I'll offer a good-faith gesture in exchange. You satisfy me sexually and in return I'll vow not to kill your sister. See? I can be reasonable."

Maia felt her blood turn to ice. "You wouldn't. If she's dead, you can't take her magic." It was a bluff since she had no idea how his spell worked.

Seth grinned at her and leaned toward her again, squeezing her chin between his thumb and forefinger. "I'm a demon, worshipped as the god of chaos and destruction. Do you really think I care how I take her powers as long as I replace what you stole?"

"But you'll promise not to kill her if I have sex with you?" He nodded and Maia felt her stomach flip again. That didn't leave her with much choice.

"That's the idea," Seth said and his mouth covered hers. He didn't give her time to accept or reject him, he simply took from her, his tongue plundering, demanding her surrender. "Kiss me back," he ordered before taking her lips again.

She did, but Maia felt cold inside. There wasn't the desire she used to feel when Seth had kissed her all those years ago. She found herself comparing his selfish taking to the way Creed kissed her. He was often greedy himself, but there'd never been the total self-absorption that Seth displayed. He cupped her breast, palmed the nipple, and even though her body responded, her mind recoiled. This was wrong.

Seth broke the kiss, took her hand, and drew her to her feet. "Let's move this somewhere else, shall we?"

Maia only had time to scoop up her evening clutch before he pulled her away from the table and through the bar. She didn't want to do this, she wanted Creed, not Seth, as her lover.

She dug her heels in when they reached the entry of the jazz club. "No, I'm not going to have sex with you."

"Your decision, precious," Seth said and released her. "You go back to your table and I'll take a drive by your sister's house. Maybe I'll see if her lilies are still blooming. They're very unusual for a northern climate, aren't they? They look tropical, yet they mustn't be."

Maia tuned out the rest of his words. No matter how nonchalantly he spoke, Seth's meaning was clear—there would be repercussions if she refused him. She bit her bottom lip. How the hell had their plan gone so wrong?

"You both underestimated me," Seth said, reading her thoughts again. "You of all people should have known better."

Yes, she certainly should have. She'd been an idiot.

"Shall we?" Seth asked, offering his elbow.

Feeling as if she wanted to vomit, Maia reached for his arm. Seth's smile of satisfaction disappeared almost immediately and his body went rigid. Maia felt the tension in his arm before he shook her off.

Her confusion turned to alarm an instant later when she finally sensed what he had. Everything seemed to go still, as if the world itself were holding its breath.

Something evil was coming and it was as powerful as Seth had once been. Horus! It had to be Horus.

Heart hammering wildly, she looked for somewhere to hide, but she was caught, as vulnerable as a rabbit in an open field. Some ridiculous instinct had her moving closer to Seth, the demon she knew, for protection.

Ever the gentleman, Seth waved his hand and disappeared, saving his own rear. That left Maia alone to face a demon with energy that was darker, more vile, than anything she'd ever felt before—and that included Seth in his heyday.

As soon as he could move, Creed was killing that fucking demon. Seth had pawed Maia's breast as if he had the right. Creed still felt as if someone had driven a dagger into his heart when Maia had turned to his table, fear in her eyes, and he hadn't been able to help her.

He strained against whatever magic the demon was using, but Creed couldn't break the paralysis. When he exhausted himself, he settled down, drew energy, and worked on gathering his power for another attempt.

Creed watched them chatting away, looking very intent. What the hell was she talking to Seth about anyway?

Old times, perhaps? Remember, she'd been his lover.

Like Creed could forget that. The jealousy bubbled up. Seth knew her in ways Creed didn't. The demon knew whether or not she liked slow, easy strokes to begin. He knew what her favorite position was and whether she liked direct or indirect contact during oral sex. If he could have moved, Creed would have clenched his hands, but he was frozen.

In disbelief, he watched Seth lean over and kiss Maia.

She's not merely accepting the kiss, she's returning it.

Yeah, she was. He growled low in his throat. The snarl increased in volume when Creed noticed Seth had his hand on Maia again. He had no right to touch her that way.

You could love her well enough to make her forget the caress of any other male.

He could. That idea tempted him. Maybe he couldn't be Maia's first, but he could show her how good they'd be together.

She was leaving the bar with Seth! The frenzy seething within shot off the scale and Creed fought against the demon's magic again. He refused to let anyone else have her. Maia was his and he was claiming her.

Yes, tonight. Claim her and show her who she belongs to. Prove to her that no one else can make her feel half as much as you.

Yeah, he would. Maia was his, damn it. Creed yanked with all his might against the hold and nearly fell over the table when it released. Without hesitation, he ran through the bar. He had to be in time, had to be. He wouldn't allow Maia to leave with Seth.

Creed came to an abrupt halt when he saw her standing alone in the entry. She appeared shaken. "Where is he?" he demanded.

Maia shrugged, her breasts moving with the motion. "He took off when one of his demon friends made his presence felt."

He closed the remaining distance. "Horus? Where is he?" Creed opened his senses further, trying to discern the god-demon.

"Probably chasing Seth." Maia bit her bottom lip. "The other demon appeared for less than a nanosecond, then took off. I think he realized Seth wasn't here any longer, and luckily, he had no interest in me."

With demon senses being at least as sharp as the Gineal's, it was a logical supposition. Creed returned to what was eating at him. "Why the hell were you leaving with Seth anyway?"

For a moment, she studied him, then she said quietly, "He threatened Ryne. I had to cooperate." Her eyes filled with tears, but she blinked them away. Then, with a shaky smile, Maia stepped into his arms and wrapped her arms around his waist. "God, Creed, I didn't want his hands on me again, but what choice did I have?"

Slowly, Creed gathered her against him.

She needs you to erase his touch from her skin. Will you give her new memories? Ones that don't make her ill?

Yeah, he'd make sure Maia had some new memories. "Come on, angel," Creed murmured against her ear, "let's go home."

22

CHAPTER

Maia wasn't sure what was going on with Creed; he hadn't been able to stop touching her on the ride home. That itself wasn't too unusual—he seemed to almost always have his hand on her leg. But this was different—tonight he was touching her with intent. Even now, as they walked from his rental car to the front door, his hand rested at the small of her back, a gesture that was purely possessive.

It had only taken a couple of minutes for Maia to make her decision—she wanted to make love with Creed. If he didn't call a halt, she wouldn't either. Although she was curious why he'd changed his mind when he'd been the one to stop the other day, she wasn't going to ask. It might shake him out of this amorous mood and that was the last thing she wanted.

After a brief pause to unlock the door, they were inside, and to her surprise, she felt oddly nervous. What if she was reading him and the situation all wrong? Maia took a deep breath; she'd know soon enough.

Before they'd left, she'd turned on a small lamp in the living room, and the glow made the space feel intimate. As he closed the door and locked it, Maia crossed to the end table and put her black clutch down next to the lamp. When she straightened, Creed was behind her.

His hands went to her hips and he nestled his groin against her bottom. She leaned into him, shifting her weight in order to caress him with her body.

"You know," Creed said, his mouth next to her ear, "we've been to all those clubs and we've never danced."

Maia shivered. "We don't have any music."

"I can fix that. Be right back."

She turned in time to see him disappear into the guest room; a minute later, music softly played. It was slow, sexy, and the beat was erotic.

Creed returned without his blazer. He stood in front of her, drinking her in with his eyes. It was so sensual, she nearly squirmed. There was no question in Maia's mind that he was looking at *her*. Not her body, not her face, but the person she really was deep inside where it counted. He held out a hand, and when she took it, he pulled her into his arms.

What they were doing couldn't be called dancing; they moved just enough to arouse each other. Maia wound her arms around Creed's neck and leaned into him.

His hands weren't still. They stroked her hips, her thighs, her back. He adjusted their positions slightly, and with each little motion, his erection rubbed against her. Every so often Creed would hit exactly the right spot and her hands would tighten as she reveled in the sensation.

The music segued from one song into another, one even more primal. Creed slid a hand under the short skirt of her dress and cupped the bare cheek of her bottom. His groan was low and long.

"How tiny is the thong you're wearing?"

"You'll have to discover that for yourself," she teased.

Maia didn't expect him to tug her dress up around her waist then and there, but that was what he did. Creed stepped back and choked. "Holy shit."

Pleased with his reaction, she made a slow rotation. "Ultra mini. I wore it for you."

"You might as well have nothing on," he said and drew her back into his arms.

"I thought about it." Maia tried to lower her skirt again, but Creed captured her hands and put them around his neck.

"Leave it. Please."

She did. There was something downright sexy about dancing with a man who was fully clothed while she was, in essence, half dressed. Maia didn't think he could get any harder, and with every sway, his bulge pushed at the little strip of material that went down the center of her mound. It was even more delicious when he stroked the bare skin on either side of the strip.

Creed's fingers traced patterns on her exposed cheeks, occasionally slipping between her legs to tease her. She'd gone beyond damp, and she was dying for him to find out just how wet she was—how ready for him.

Maia ran her hands over his shoulders, down his chest, and pulled his shirt free. Slowly, eyes locked on his, she opened each button. When she reached the tail, she made certain the backs of her hands brushed against his erection. Running her hands up his torso, she shoved at the shirt, wanting it off him. She growled her frustration when she realized she'd forgotten to get the buttons at his wrists, but she felt Creed call on a little magic and the shirt fell to the floor.

He took her back into his arms and the only thing between her breasts and his chest was the top of her Lycra dress. She turned her face into him and nuzzled his shoulder.

Another song started. This one had lyrics, but instead of breaking the mood, the breathless singing added to it. Creed lowered his head, his lips next to her ear, and in a low baritone, he sang the words.

French had never sounded so sexy before. She didn't speak much of the language, but she knew enough. Creed was singing about want and desire, about exploring fantasies.

A shiver coursed down her spine. He had his hair pulled back in a queue and Maia freed it from its band. She ran her hands through it, letting the shoulder-length strands glide through her fingers. She trailed her nails across his nape and his shudder sent a stab of desire through her.

This wasn't enough, not anymore. She wanted him naked, wanted to be naked herself, but at the same time, she didn't want to end this. Maia felt treasured, desired as she never had before. "Creed," she murmured, needing to say his name.

She wouldn't have noticed when a new song began except that she lost the serenade. Her pang of disappointment didn't last long. Creed nipped at her earlobe.

Maia gasped, her nails digging into his shoulders. "Enough."

He ignored her, kissing his way around her throat and up to her lips. He kissed her softly, but with such great hunger Maia had no doubt how much he desired her. She opened her mouth beneath his, wanting him to taste her. When he hesitated, Maia went after him, dipping inside Creed's mouth and tracing the inside of his lips.

Lowering her arms, Maia reached for the waist of his pants. She unhooked him and slowly lowered the zipper. They stopped moving and he raised his head. His eyes held so much heat, she thought she'd go up in flames from a mere glance.

"Bedroom," Creed growled, stopping her from pushing his pants over his hips.

"Yes."

Neither one of them wasted time getting down the hall. He left the door of her master suite open, and the music flowed in here just as seductively as it had into the living room.

"Are you sure, angel?"

"Oh, yes. Are you?"

"Yeah." He reached for the gather of material at her waist. "Raise your arms."

She did and he lifted the dress off her. For a long moment, Creed did nothing but stare, and Maia's nipples puckered further under the fire in his gaze.

Before she could undress him, though, his brows drew together. "What the hell is that?"

Maia looked down and laughed. She couldn't help it. "Fashion tape." She reached for the edge of a strip and peeled it off her torso. "They kept the dress in place. I didn't want it sliding and showing anything I didn't want the world to see."

Creed took hold of another piece of the tape. "You mean I hoped in vain all night that one of those cutouts would shift?"

"Sorry, but there was no way that was happening." He continued to help her until she suggested, "Why don't you lose those trousers while I finish getting the tape off?"

He nodded, reached in his front pocket, and tossed a couple of condoms on the bed before bending down to get rid of his shoes and socks. Only then did he shed the pants. All Creed had left were his briefs, but they did more to emphasize his erection than to hide it.

"Did I miss any?" she asked, holding her arms out to her sides.

"Huh? Oh. No, I don't see any more."

Creed crossed to her, drew her against his body, and her breasts pushed into the hard planes of his chest. Her moan was almost inaudible over the pulsing beat of the music, but she knew he heard it. The corners of his lips tilted up and he took hold of her hips, his fingers flaring over her bare bottom. "Will you get bent out of shape if I tell you you're beautiful?"

Maia shook her head. "I don't mind it from you."

"Good, because you are beautiful; you take my breath away." He gave her a short kiss, then raised his head. "Will you get bent out of shape if I say, hot damn, you don't have any tan lines and the idea of you lying outside naked turns me on?"

She laughed and hugged him. "Will you get bent out of shape if I tell you I go to a tanning salon and there's no chance of anyone seeing me without clothes?"

"Another fantasy busted."

That sobered her. Twice now he'd mentioned displaying herself and that wasn't something she would ever do, not even for him. "You don't expect me to be an exhibitionist, right?"

He shook his head. "No. I don't want anyone else to see you, I just like the idea that *I* might be able to sneak a look."

Her smile returned. "Yeah, but you don't have to sneak; you can see all of me whenever you want."

His hands tightened, but when he lowered his head

to kiss her, Creed's lips were gentle. He didn't take, he gave, and with a soft sigh of pleasure, Maia clung to him. Maybe he was gruff and abrasive, but he was also sweet and tender, and she'd fallen in love with every facet of him, from the badass troubleshooter to the lonely teenager to the kindhearted man who looked out for others.

Maia stroked his back, explored each of the hard muscles there. She longed to touch his chest, too, but didn't want to give up the feel of his hair teasing her nipples. Instead, she moved lower and tugged at the elastic of his briefs. He didn't stop her and she pushed them down, baring him.

When they were at his upper thighs, Creed lost patience and drew her back against him. The moist head of his erection pressed into her belly, his flesh so hot she thought it might sear her. "Hurry," she urged him, wanting more than kisses.

"Not yet. I've barely started."

Taking his hand, Maia brought it to the front of her thong. "I'm ready," she told him, and she was—what little fabric she had there was sodden.

He shook his head and repeated, "Not yet." Creed stepped away from her and pushed his briefs the rest of the way down. Maia reached for the waistband of her thong, but he stopped her. "Leave it on."

"Why?" Maia could hear the frustration in her voice.

"Because when I take you, I'm just going to tug that scrap of material aside. I want you in what you're wearing now."

Her panties and her heels—she wasn't sure whether to laugh or moan.

Creed grabbed the condoms from the bed, tossed them on the nightstand, and yanked back the comforter and blankets. He didn't have to gesture to the bed for

Maia to know what he wanted. She climbed in, lay back, raised her knees, and let them fall open invitingly.

From Creed's agonized cursing, Maia guessed the view was as provocative as she'd hoped. She felt the bed give and raised her head. He settled between her thighs and braced himself above her. "You're making it hard for me to wait."

She ignored the obvious opportunity his words had given her and asked, "Why do you want to?"

"I want to savor you, Maia, to touch every inch of your body, then I want to use my mouth and lips on you until you're begging me to make you come. And even then, that might not be enough. I want to remember this night if I live to be a thousand and I want you to remember it just as long."

Maia arched her hips, but much to her annoyance, Creed went up on his knees, moving out of her range. "Damn it!"

"I haven't even had a chance to do this yet." Creed reached out and lightly circled her nipple with his finger. And he did exactly what he'd said—teased her with his hands before using his mouth on her. Maia was damn near senseless before he moved from her breasts.

He made better time down her torso, stopped to trace her navel with his tongue, then continued on. Everything inside Maia went still as he tugged the thong out of his way. Was he finally going to—

Instead of sliding inside her, he ran his finger between the lips of her sex, and when her eyes were locked on his face, he licked it clean. Her groan was loud and long.

Creed didn't use his hands; he went down on her, bringing her to the brink again and again, but not letting her come.

After the fourth time he did that, Maia wrested control. Before he had time to react, she put Creed on his back and straddled him. She thought about taking him inside her now, but decided instead to torment him the same way he'd tortured her.

Maia kissed him, telling Creed without words how deeply her feelings for him ran. This wasn't just sex; for the first time, she was truly making love.

She ran her hands over his arms, kissed his palms, took his fingers into her mouth and laved them. His gaze was on her, watching as she explored his chest. Maia almost hated to break eye contact, but she lowered her head and lightly bit his nipples. There was a hitch in his breathing, but otherwise Creed didn't react. She took that as a challenge.

Licking her way down, she traced his abs with both her fingers and then her tongue. Maia shifted, and kneeling at his side, she curled her hand around his erection and stroked him.

Damn, Creed was beautiful—long and thick. His head was already red and she hadn't even— Maia stopped as she bent to kiss him there. Would he think she was a slut if she went down on him? Seth had implied that, and she had to face it, he'd been right when he'd said she loved fellatio—she did. There was something about it that drove her arousal off the scales, but she didn't want Creed to think badly of her.

"Maia," he said, voice almost unintelligible. She looked up and met his eyes. "There's—" Creed cleared his throat, started again, then gave up and *sent* the message. *There's no one else in this bed except you and me. Whatever we want to do, it's right. Anything you want, angel, any* way *you want it.*

After studying him for a moment, Maia decided he was telling the truth. She got off the bed and patted the edge of the mattress. He understood. Creed sat where she'd indicated.

Kneeling in front of him, Maia widened his legs and kissed her way up the inside of his right thigh. She reached his penis, and gave him a quick lick, then teased her way down the inside of his other leg.

When she got to his knee, she sat back on her heels and looked up at him. Creed had his eyes glued on her. Maia waited until his gaze met hers, then she ran her tongue over her lips.

She trailed her fingers over his shaft before holding it. Leaning forward, Maia pressed a kiss to his tip. He jerked in her hand. Starting at his base, she licked him to the crown a few times, then cupped his sac, lightly caressing him with her thumb.

Tired of the teasing, Maia swirled her tongue around his tip, and took just the head in her mouth. She moaned as she finally got a taste of Creed.

Letting him slip slowly out, she stroked her face with his erection, letting him see how much she loved this part of him. How much she loved him, period. As she took him back into her mouth, Maia put a hand between her legs, touching herself as she went up and down on his penis.

Maia didn't know who enjoyed this more, her or Creed. When she saw the way his hands were curled into fists at his sides, saw the way he was struggling not to come, she loved it. She could have told him not to worry, if she didn't get to have an orgasm, there was no way in hell he was getting one, but she refused to take her mouth off him to speak.

Long before she was ready, his hands went to her hair and eased her back. "Creed!"

"Too close." He helped her to her feet and tugged her back on the bed.

Creed reached for a condom, and since he never took his eyes off of her, Maia put her hand back between her legs. There was no mistaking how much he liked that.

When he joined her on the bed, she held her arms out in welcome. He brushed against her opening, then with a long, slow kiss, Creed sank into her. Her moan was a keening wail. Forever. She'd been waiting for this man forever, and at last she'd found him. At last he was right where he belonged, right where she needed him.

Creed struggled for control. It wasn't only his need to come, it was the dark forces. He was wrestling with them, fighting to keep them at bay. They wanted to take him over, and they would if he wasn't careful.

"Mine," he said when he reached as deep as he could go.

"Yes," she agreed and he nodded, satisfied.

He took a minute to gaze down at her. Some of her hair was falling in her face, and he brushed it aside. Her eyes told him how aroused she was, and her lips were parted as she breathed quickly. Creed flexed his hips at the memory of her taking him in her mouth. Seeing how much she'd loved it had turned him on.

His good humor faded. That had been the beginning of his problems. The urge to grab her hair and drive his cock down her throat had almost overwhelmed him. It wasn't something he'd do, and the fact that he'd thought about it scared him.

She arched her hips, encouraging him to move, and Creed held her tightly. He knew she didn't understand, and he couldn't tell her. The last thing he wanted Maia to know was how close he was to being swamped by evil.

Remaining frozen, however, was a losing proposition.

His body demanded he move and end the unbearable tension he felt. Every cell cried out for completion.

Maia tightened her muscles around his cock, and with a groan, Creed surrendered. It was inevitable.

He began slowly, letting her get accustomed to him moving inside her, but as she met his thrusts, he stopped worrying. His strokes became firmer, but even as he drove for orgasm, Creed continued fighting to hang on. Maybe he'd already fallen to the dark forces, but he couldn't let them control him.

Looking down, he saw the thong pushed to the side while his cock drove into her, and something slammed into him so fast he didn't have time to fend it off.

It became all about getting off. She was a vessel for his pleasure, and that was as it should be. Was he not worshipped? Adored? Feared?

He pushed her legs up, opening her further and taking complete command. Her face was suffused with arousal and a side of his mouth quirked up. Just like old times.

Almost.

She looked up at him with love in her eyes and for a moment, he faltered.

Creed reclaimed control. He shouldn't have even begun to make love with Maia, he'd known how dangerous it would be, but it was too late now. As much as he wanted to pull out and stop, he couldn't—not when he needed her so much. Slowing, he stroked into her more gently. He couldn't hurt her, he wouldn't.

For years he'd fought evil and won, he could win now, too. He had to; there was no other choice.

The tension built and Creed worked on bringing Maia with him. It was important to him that she enjoy this every bit as much as he was. And when she cried out, her body tightening around his, he relaxed and drove for his own climax.

316 • PATTI O'SHEA

It hit him like a speeding locomotive. Self-command was gone, and in its place was ecstasy. Maia, sweet Maia . . .

As his orgasm ended, he dropped on top of her, allowing her to take his full weight. It was a small enough price to pay for the way she'd stolen his magic. He was fortunate it had only been a minute portion—she'd tried to take all of it. His temper mounted and he fought it back. Now was not the time, not when his plan was close to fruition. While one part of him remained prone, another part opened a portal and brought an acais through to this plane.

Her hands stroked over his shoulders and that brought him back to the here and now. Breaking away from her, he disappeared into the bathroom, rid himself of the condom, and cleaned up. She was still lying where he'd left her, legs splayed, and he fought back a sneer.

Instead, he picked up his briefs from the floor and pulled them on. "Creed, what are you doing?" she asked. As if it weren't obvious.

"Leaving," he said.

She sat up and her breasts caught his attention. Even after all these years, her body remained incredible. He shook off the thought and collected his remaining garments from the floor.

"Come back to bed." Maia held out her arms and smiled. "We can cuddle a little while you gear up for round two."

"I have other things to do."

Uncertainty crossed her face. "You can't just walk away."

"What? Do you require some praise before you let a man leave? You were good. There? Does that make you happy?"

She looked stricken and it was all he could do not to smile as he sauntered from the room. When he reached the guest room, he turned off that horrendous noise and grabbed a pair of jeans. His taste in clothing was as questionable as his taste in music.

He'd barely finished tying his shoes when Maia stormed in, barefoot and wearing a robe. After nothing more than a glance, he fished his wallet and keys from the trousers.

"Where the hell do you think you're going?"

Ignoring her words, he tried to move around her, but she shifted with him, blocking his escape.

"Oh, no you don't, Creed Blackwood. You don't get to make love to me and walk away as if nothing happened."

"Make love?" He snorted. "We fucked. Don't try to pretty it up." That shocked Maia and he managed to brush past her. He only made it as far as the front door, though. Reaching around his body, she put her palm flat against the wooden portal and pushed it shut.

"If you leave now, don't come back, do you hear me?"

"Don't worry, I won't be back. I have what I came for."

He pulled open the door again, but she didn't stop him, and he went down the stairs with a spring in his step.

It was time to kill Ryne.

23

CHAPTER

Maia brushed at a stray tear as she hung the towels up in the bathroom. While the shower made her body feel cleaner, nothing would eradicate how sullied she felt inside. With one hand, she rubbed at her chest, trying to ease the pressure there, and she turned off the light with the other.

She gathered clothes, needing to be fully dressed despite the hour, but Maia hesitated when she reached her lingerie drawer. Shaking her head, she grabbed a pair of high-cut panties instead of her usual thong. There was no way she could wear one, not right now, and she hated that she was letting Blackwood affect her choice of clothing. She grabbed a pair of jeans from the shelf in her closet. Okay, so they weren't something she wore often, but denim was thick and she felt as if she needed armor between her and the world right now.

Standing in the middle of her walk-in, Maia got dressed, right down to a pair of sneakers. It was stupid, she knew that; nothing was going to protect her from what had already happened.

As she exited the closet, she was confronted with her rumpled bed. A sob escaped before she could stop it, but Maia grabbed hold of her emotions. She wouldn't cry over him—at least not more than she had already.

There wasn't any possibility that she could sleep there, not now, and she crossed to it, yanking off the blankets. Her hip knocked the nightstand and the book fell to the floor, opening up when it landed. Maia stopped, looked down, and frowned. That shouldn't happen. She was supposed to be the sole person who could lift the cover. Her frown deepened. Why was it out anyway? She'd put Caitlin's text away because she didn't want Blackwood to spot it. She returned it to the drawer and went back to stripping the bed.

Her sister had warned her—don't trust him, she'd said—but Maia had dismissed Ryne's words. She'd been so sure she'd known Creed better. What a foolish decision. Her sister had been friends with the man for six years and if she'd withdrawn her support of him, Maia should have taken heed.

More tears fell and she impatiently scrubbed at her cheeks. With all the bedding in a pile on her floor, Maia went to the hall closet and retrieved fresh linens.

Her nightstand drawer was open and she shut it with her knee. She thought she'd closed it and it aggravated her that she was upset enough to forget what she had and hadn't done. Shaking out a sheet, she began making up the bed.

What had Ryne said? Something about her not being a good judge of men. Maia had shrugged that aside, too. After all, Seth didn't count, not when she'd been under the influence of the dark forces. Looked like her baby sister was right. Blackwood had snowed her. She'd made excuses for him nearly every day, explained away the things she didn't want to examine.

Idiot.

Maia tucked the edges of the blanket underneath the mattress and stood staring at the bed, the site of her latest downfall. She'd made love with him, and he'd— She couldn't even think the word he'd said. For the first time ever, she'd held nothing of herself back, hadn't tried to protect herself emotionally. It was a mistake she wouldn't make again.

He'd used her. Temper reared up, ripped away the pain and she welcomed it. She deserved better. A lot better, damn it. Damn *him*! The bastard had seen she distrusted men who were only interested in her looks, and he'd deliberately complimented her on other things. He'd played her like a master.

Gathering up the pile of bedding, she stalked to the utility room off the kitchen and loaded the washer. She needed that son of a bitch's scent off her sheets.

With the laundry going, she headed back down the hall. Maia wanted his stuff out of her house tonight, too, even if she had to pack it herself. But when she reached the doorway, she faltered and those damn tears welled up, overflowing again.

She couldn't touch his things—not yet.

Whirling, Maia went to her own bedroom. It wasn't even midnight yet; there was plenty of time to bundle up his belongings and put them out on her doorstep. Or better yet, drop them off at a charity for resale.

She stopped short just inside her door. That damn book was on the bed—open.

Heart pounding, Maia looked around, but she didn't see or hear anyone. She ran through the possibilities. The house was secure—she'd locked the door after Blackwood had left—and who would break in and put a text on her bed anyway? Same went for her sister or one of the Gineal using a transit to enter. And aside from the one the bastard had, there were no extra keys to her house floating around.

With the likely explanations gone, Maia went with the less plausible—maybe there was some kind of spell on the text beyond the two that protected it. She couldn't come up with a guess why Eithne had bothered or what had triggered it now rather than yesterday or tomorrow or next week, but it was either that or her house was haunted, and she'd never sensed a ghostly presence.

Hesitantly, Maia approached the bed. The book was turned to a page near the end, a bit further than she'd managed to read.

Maia picked it up and thought about jamming it back in the drawer, but with a sigh, she gave in. She had a feeling that the tome would keep appearing until she read it. Using her finger to mark the spot, she went into the living room, put on a brighter lamp, and sat down with the book.

Dear short-haired woman: if you've read this far you are either frustrated or amazed; I know not which it will be. If it has been many years since you surrendered your power, you will find the earlier words uninteresting and likely be impatient. If you are recently without magic, then you've no doubt learned much. What I pen in these next pages, however, is the sole purpose for this text.

Your magic is gone, this you know, and there is no method to reinstate it. You know this as well. What you do not know is that you retain power over the demon.

Her head jerked up. What? That wasn't possible.

You doubt me, I see it in your face. As you no longer have access to the spell you invoked to take a portion of the demon's power, I include it here for you. Study it with great care.

Maia did, perusing each line, each word, thoroughly. She had to be reading it wrong—there was no way this could imply what she thought it did.

The incantation you used was not capable of taking the amount of power from the demon that you wished, but it allows you to continue to perform spells that affect him. You might have believed you failed when you did not neutralize him as you wanted, but you are not finished. I've included the proclamations you will need to complete your task.

Paging ahead, she glanced at some of the handful of spells. There was one to track Seth—or a part of Seth—to any location at any time. One— Maia clutched the book harder. One would end the demonic possession of a Gineal.

Creed.

She hadn't been wrong about him! It had to be Seth who'd had him saying the things he had and doing what he'd done. The uncertainty crept back, but she pushed it aside. She couldn't be making excuses for him again, it had to be real.

Why would Seth want to indwell in Creed, though? It didn't make sense. Only a portion of the demon would be controlling Blackwood, the rest of him would be in his own body, and that left Seth vulnerable if the other god-demons attacked him.

Unless it was part of his plan to reach Ryne. Her sister might not entirely trust Creed any longer, but he could still get much closer to her than Seth could. And Seth wanted Ryne's power because it would make him stronger than the demons who hunted him. He might think the reward was worth the risk.

Maia didn't understand how she could still do magic—even if it only affected Seth—without powers, but she didn't need to have answers right now. Maybe

Eithne was lying, maybe Seth had stood behind the woman's shoulder and told her what to write and this would lead to Maia's death, but she had to take the chance. If Creed was possessed, both he and Ryne were at risk.

Clasping the book tightly to her chest, she grabbed the clutch containing her wallet and her car keys and raced to the garage. Maia didn't waste any time opening the door and starting her sedan—she had to make it before Seth could hurt anyone she loved. Turning on the overhead light, she took a deep breath and recited the spell that allowed her to track Seth.

As soon as she closed it, a blue, glowing line lit up the street in front of her house and headed off in the direction Creed had driven. Maia put the car in gear and followed the trail. She had to be in time.

If Seth were testing the speed of the Gineal response to a threat for a future attack, he'd be heartened right now. For quite some time, the acais had been wandering loose and no one had arrived. Unfortunately, he wasn't gauging the timing for another ambush, he was waiting for a troubleshooter and her absence was angering him. Did they think he had all night?

It had been millennia since he'd indwelled and it felt odd to have his consciousness present in two bodies simultaneously. There were also limitations he'd forgotten, and that was why he wanted his chosen target to hurry. If Horus found him while he was split like this, he'd be at a distinct disadvantage and he might have to release Blackwood, especially since Seth was expending extra energy to keep him cloaked. After the months it had taken to reach this point, the very idea infuriated him.

He looked around and measured the area through Blackwood's eyes. Seth had chosen another fallow field for this assault, although this one only had trees along a single side. That's where he was concealed. With total control of this Gineal finally his, there'd be no last-minute reprieve for his prey, not as there'd been the previous instance.

The acais meandered aimlessly, but it mattered not. They were stupid, powerless creatures, though dangerous enough to get a troubleshooter dispatched. The moonlight made the acais's parchment-color skin look eerie and he idly wondered if a human happened along, would he believe he'd seen a ghost or an alien?

Here we go. He came to attention as he felt the arrival of one of the Gineal. Only a tracker, but his chosen troubleshooter was sure to follow. Less than five minutes later, she did.

She remained at a distance, no doubt being briefed, and he carefully worked to make the small copse he stood in seem forbidding. He wanted a clear shot at her, not a game of hide-and-seek among the trees, and his trick should work since she had no reason to feel she needed a great deal of protection. She appeared then and took cover behind a thigh-high boulder, the man who was her lover and apprentice beside her.

Raising his hand, Seth called on Blackwood's power and tried to supplement it with his own. His seeped away, though, leaving him with only what his host had.

If he put more of himself in Blackwood . . . But Seth didn't dare, not when he had old enemies to worry about.

He shrugged. What he had to work with should be enough, and if it wasn't, he'd help himself to Blackwood's magic after Ryne Frasier had taken care of him. Seth preferred the woman since she was stronger, but he'd settle for his puppet. He readied himself to fire and nearly cursed when she shifted, presenting him with an angle that made a direct hit difficult.

Patience. He had to wait for the optimal moment to shoot.

Her shields were up, but not at full strength. He'd counted on the Gineal's instinctive need to conserve magic, and it appeared as if he'd won that gamble, but he'd only have one shot before she fortified them, and it had to be a good one.

It was the apprentice that fired at the acais, catching it in the center of the chest. Interesting that he'd been the one, but it made sense given the weakness of their opponent.

The creature bellowed, sounding like a wounded elephant, but with the natural shielding it had, Seth doubted it was hurt. That would buy some time, though it shouldn't take overlong before they vanquished the being. He needed a clear shot and he needed it soon. Seth measured the situation and his aggravation rose; he saw no handy method to make her move, not without giving his presence away.

He hadn't gone to this much trouble to fail.

The anger, the frustration, the impatience swirled inside Seth and he took deep breaths. He couldn't allow his emotions to get the upper hand—that had been the downfall of many a demon, and he refused to be added to that number.

Seth reassessed the situation with a calmer mind and decided that luring the acais to a certain position would get his troubleshooter of choice in line for his shot.

Her apprentice continued to attack. The creature roared its displeasure again and again, but it moved as Seth directed, and then it happened—the sight line opened up.

He let loose with all the firepower Blackwood had.

Direct hit.

Her knees sagged and she would have gone down had her lover not grabbed her.

Seth popped Blackwood into a new position, unworried about how much energy he expended. It wasn't his magic, after all, and using it wouldn't diminish the strength he'd acquire if he were forced to settle for his host's powers. The move came just in time as both troubleshooters unloaded with streams of fire where he'd been standing.

Despite the show of force, her defenses were weaker than normal. He felt it and smiled.

The man shielded her with his body. As if that would stop Seth for long. There was a temptation to hurry—he'd been waiting and planning for so long—but he restrained himself. Haste could cost him his prize and he wasn't losing it.

It was a simple thing to maneuver the acais again, but the duo didn't move with the creature this time—they were too busy looking for the threat.

If it wouldn't have given away his position, Seth would have laughed. The Gineal were so predictable. Instead of retreating to regroup or call in reinforcements, they stayed on the field of battle and were going to slug it out. That was to his advantage and he planned to use it.

He directed the acais to charge them and it did, drawing up their attention back to their original job. Gathering up the power, he readied himself for another shot. Blackwood struggled to regain control of himself, but Seth easily held on.

His second shot winged her, but it was enough to cause further damage to her protection.

Again, he changed positions. Since they were focused

on the trees now, he moved behind the couple, using nothing except his ability to cloak to keep himself hidden.

Beautiful! She was wide open.

He fired again, long and powerfully, hitting her square in the back. Before her apprentice could turn, Seth returned to the trees. He nearly chortled with glee. This was going well, and it was only a matter of time now until he was victorious.

And to think it was his precious Maia who'd enabled him to indwell inside Blackwood. He'd have to send her another gift.

The troubleshooter's next shot came a bit too close for comfort and Seth put aside his elation to focus on winning. He could celebrate later.

He continued to manipulate the acais, using it to divide their attention. As long as the creature remained a threat, they couldn't focus solely on him, and that gave him a nice advantage.

As if realizing that very thing themselves, the troubleshooter and her apprentice instigated a concentrated assault on the dumb creature.

In an effort to split their notice, he rushed to let loose with a rope of fire.

It was a mistake.

His aim was the slightest bit off and he hit the student. The magic ricocheted back at him and he barely evaded the blast. It could only be mirror protection, which meant he had to be careful not to catch the man again. As Blackwood would say, that fucking sucked.

No matter what he did, they kept most of their attention on the acais. Seth managed to clip the woman a few more times, but they weren't good, solid hits.

His frustration bubbled back, threatened to overwhelm him, and that only increased when the creature fell. It didn't stay down long, pulling itself back to its feet and staggering toward the pair, but it wouldn't take much more to end it.

Be patient, he reminded himself, but he fired anyway. Again, he hit the apprentice and that damn bulwark of his sent it sailing back. This time Seth wasn't quite fast enough, and Blackwood's body took a hit. Because he hadn't been putting much power behind his protection, the glancing blow caused more damage than it should. Seth had no choice save to reinforce the shield.

In the few seconds this required, they took aim at the acais once more, and this time when it went down, it stayed down.

That ended his diversion.

With the firepower he'd leveled at the woman, she should be finished already, but she wasn't. It mattered not. She was reeling, having difficulty keeping her feet.

Seth decided to risk it. He put more of himself into Blackwood. This time when he tried to combine his power with that of the rover, it worked. With careful deliberation, he lined up his shot and let loose with all he had.

That put her on the ground, and even in the moonlight, he could see her body convulsing.

With a smile, Seth raised his hand to finish the job.

24

CHAPTER

Maia spotted Creed's rental and skidded her sedan to a stop on the deserted country road. It was pulled off to the side and she parked in front of it. Grabbing her book, she jumped out and followed the glowing blue line on foot.

It disappeared into a small wooded area, and after a brief hesitation, she waded in. The going was rough, with grass and weeds that reached her knees, and uneven ground beneath that. She proceeded slowly and cautiously, but when she saw the flash of fire, Maia picked up her pace. She'd hoped to reach Creed before anything happened, but she was too late, the battle had already started.

She felt as if she weren't making any progress, not when she had to fight for every inch. Maia stepped in a hole, tried to catch her balance, but went down anyway. Briars scratched at her arms as she attempted to regain her feet, but she clutched the book tightly, ignored the sting, and fought her way upright.

Her ankle hurt, but another flare brightened the sky and Maia hobbled on. She'd taken care of Ryne from the time her sister had been a toddler—she wasn't failing now—and this time there was someone else involved. Creed. She wanted to protect him, too.

Maia reached the end of the trees and scanned the area. With the only light coming from the full moon, it took her a split second to realize that the dead body didn't belong to a person. Thank God. For a minute she'd thought—

There wasn't time to take a deep breath. At the instant her eyes found Ryne, her sister was hit with a blast that dropped her to the ground.

A scream welled up inside Maia and her knees started to buckle, but she regained control. Battle calm descended. She'd been a troubleshooter, damn it, and she knew how to handle herself. She wouldn't embarrass the Frasier name.

Deke was crouched in front of Ryne, protecting her with his body. He had no idea, though, where the threat was because Creed had popped into a new position. If only she still had telepathy.

"Behind you!" she called. The last thing she wanted to do was give her position away, but she'd enabled Deke to shift and cover Ryne. With the angle cut down, the blast went wide and her sister was safe.

Instinct had Maia hitting the dirt. The energy ball hurtled over her head and took out a tree, sending large splinters flying.

Clasping the book to her chest, she rolled out of the way of a second shot. This one was close enough that dirt kicked up and rained down on her hair and neck.

Creed turned his attention away from her when Deke

laid down a barrage. Cover fire, she realized, and leaped to her feet. Maia scurried for a small trench dug into the earth not too far from the trees and lay on her stomach. It didn't offer her much security, but the copse was too dangerous, and she couldn't go to the boulder where her sister was. Deke might try to protect both of them and Maia wanted him only thinking about Ryne.

While the two men were occupied with each other, she opened her book and paged through it, looking for the incantation that would force Seth to leave Creed's body.

Damn, why hadn't she taken five minutes to memorize the spell? Trying to read the spidery handwriting in the dim lighting was almost impossible. She continued scanning until she found what she wanted. Softly, voice not even a breath of sound, Maia repeated the words of the proclamation.

She was maybe halfway through when Creed shouted and the book was telekinetically yanked from her hands. Maia made a lunge, trying desperately to catch it, but it sailed off into the field. Peeking over the edge of the irrigation ditch, she saw him level a rope of fire at the text. The intensity forced her to duck her head, but when it ended, the tome was unharmed.

Creed and Deke became engaged in another shoot-out and she cringed. It might be Seth who was causing all the trouble, but it was Creed's body taking the hits. She needed that damn book. Once the demon was expelled, they could fight him without hurting Blackwood.

Maia eyed the distance between her and the text, and decided retrieving it wasn't going to be easy. She'd have nothing to shield her, and with no magic of her own, one blast from Creed would kill her.

Seth. It wasn't Creed who was fighting Deke. It wasn't Creed who would kill her. It was Seth.

With careful deliberation, Maia crept out of her hiding

place, but before she reached the top, Seth spotted her. The shot had her diving back into the trench and lying flat. Small rocks, dirt, and pieces of foliage pelted her body and she covered her head with her hands to protect it.

The night grew still, but Maia didn't move right away. Seth might simply be waiting until she thought he was occupied and the instant she showed her face, he'd zap her.

Sounds reached her that had her lowering her arms. She couldn't place them and slowly she peeked above the rim of earth. Her breath caught when she saw what was out there—creatures, at least a dozen of them. Ryne hadn't moved, Creed was possessed, and that left Deke to face them on his own.

She'd been a troubleshooter for six years and she didn't recognize most of what Seth had called forward, not even from pictures. The few she could identify were deadly, but lacked magic. That puzzled her, but she didn't have time to wonder long—the dark-force beings were converging on her sister.

Deke began blasting them with fire, but as she'd suspected, it did nothing—they had too much natural protection. He didn't give up, though, and Maia could only shake her head. That method was so Ryne, but without her sister's experience, he had to be burning through his reserves of magic fast.

For now, he was managing to keep the creatures at bay, but once he drained himself, he and Ryne would be sitting ducks. Maia couldn't allow that to happen.

She looked around, picked up the glowing blue line, and followed it to Creed— er, Seth. He leaned against a tree to her left, arms crossed over his chest, and his lips were curved. It was the smile that worried her the most.

Her options were limited. Even if she could communicate telepathically, she didn't know anything that would help Deke fight and win. Battling the beings herself was suicidal, and with Seth standing there, watching the proceedings, he'd notice and stop her if she tried to reach the book.

She could only think of one idea that might work. Demons were extremely emotional; all she had to do was infuriate him enough to get him to act on impulse. And hopefully not level his power at her.

"Seth," Maia said in a normal voice. Even though he was in Creed's body, he'd still have the heightened senses of a demon, he'd hear her. "When did you become such a coward?"

That wiped the grin off his face.

"You're among the most powerful beings to ever live," she continued, "and you're afraid of an apprentice troubleshooter?"

I'm not afraid.

He sent the thought into her head, and while it wasn't unexpected, Maia didn't like it. "No? From here, it sure looks like you're scared. What is it about Deke that has you hiding behind these dark-force creatures?"

This time he didn't respond, but she was certain he was listening.

"No wonder it was Osiris who was named ruler of the living and the succession went to Horus and not you. Who would want such a craven lord?"

Seth straightened away from the tree and leveled a glare in her direction. He could make her be quiet—permanently—but he didn't raise a hand. Maia swallowed hard. There was no question he was mad, just not enough to throw aside his plan.

"You couldn't even fight Osiris face to face. You had to fool him in order to kill him. What a brave demon you must be, Seth," Maia mocked.

Shut up!

"You were no more courageous as you fought Osiris's son. How many dirty tricks did you pull? Yet despite your cowardly methods, Horus won and you were the one disgraced; you were the one banished by Re." Damn, Maia hoped this much was true or he'd probably laugh at her and she'd lose the progress she'd made angering him.

"I said shut up!" he roared and this time he did raise his arm.

She threw herself to the bottom of the ditch in time to avoid getting hit by an energy ball that had to be as big as a watermelon. He hadn't needed half that to kill her. It didn't end there; he continued to fire over her head and that irrational reaction told Maia that Seth was as furious as she wanted.

While the demon was throwing his tantrum, Maia projected her thoughts. On several occasions, Creed had responded as if he'd read her mind. She was counting on being able to reach him.

Creed, you have to take control away from Seth. I know it won't be easy, but I need a couple of minutes. Try, okay?

Maia eased up as high as she dared and waited. She'd mentally mapped out her path and all she needed now was for Creed to overpower Seth. He wouldn't be able to hold him at bay long, not since he was already possessed, but she knew how strong—how stubborn—Blackwood could be. It might be a longshot, but she was betting he did it.

Seth stopped shooting, and Maia didn't wait—she scrambled up the side of the trench and ran for the book.

If she was wrong, if Creed hadn't gained control and Seth had reined in his temper, she was dead. With every running step, she anticipated being hit. It didn't happen.

Scooping up the text, she pivoted and dove back into the trench. She was down from her original position, closer to Ryne and Deke, and this section was muddy. Maia didn't check to see what was going on with Seth and Creed; there wasn't time.

Flipping open the book, she paged quickly to the spell to summon Seth. Demons couldn't be in close physical proximity to the one they possessed, and once he was here, he'd be forced to leave Creed. The proclamation was written in such a way that Seth wouldn't be able to take Creed over again—added insurance—and it would hold him in the area for a short period. Maia began the incantation again, whispering as fast as she dared. She couldn't chance mispronouncing or missing one of the words, but she needed it finished and closed.

Creed lost the battle with Seth before she reached the end, and Seth was even angrier now. He yelled threats at her and shot over the spot where she'd been, not where she was now.

Afraid he'd scan for her energy signature and figure out she'd moved or worse yet, discover the book was gone and jerk it away from her again, Maia intoned the phrases just a shade more rapidly. She reached the end, closed the spell, and took a deep breath.

The voice shouting imprecations changed, became Seth's and not Creed's. Maia stuck her head up and saw Blackwood was prone on the ground and the demon was beside him. To say he was enraged would be understating it.

Deke was still firing at the creatures that had been called forth and Maia shook her head. "Deke, shoot at Seth!"

She ducked to avoid another blast from the demon. He wasn't happy with her at all. Too bad. Now that

Creed was no longer an unwilling host, Seth could be attacked full out.

Maia opened the book again. There was one more spell she wanted; this one would take all of Seth's magic and that would solve the entire situation they were dealing with. Well, almost. It wouldn't get rid of the dark-force creatures, but without the demon's power to prevent it, Deke should be able to transport them back to whatever dimension they'd come from.

This incantation was long. Maia hurriedly scanned it, but she didn't see any obvious places where she could omit phrases. She was just going to have to start it and pray that Seth forgot about her long enough to enable her to finish it.

The handwriting here seemed even paler and harder to read than the other. She tipped the book, trying to catch as much of the moonlight as possible, and while the battle raged on around her, Maia softly intoned the words of the incantation.

Mud seeped through her jeans, but she didn't let the clamminess slow her down. Seth could read energy, and since spells affected it, he'd know she was up to something if he paid attention. She had to finish in case that happened. Had to. Keep him busy, Deke, Maia thought, keep him busy.

A cloud covered the moon and she barely swallowed a curse. It was difficult to make out the words now and she paused for the sky to clear, but it wasn't happening.

It was risky, Maia knew that. If she messed up, God knew what the incantation would do, but she couldn't wait any longer.

She read on, trying to be accurate, but she had to use the context of the sentence and her knowledge of spellcasting to guess at a few of the words. If she'd only taken a few minutes to read through the proclamations, she'd at least be familiar with them, but she hadn't. Maia pushed aside the regret and doggedly continued.

The moon returned when she was near the end, but she didn't have a chance to feel relieved—the book went sailing from her hands. Seth had felt her using the energy.

Before she did anything else, she whispered a short verse to append the spell she'd been reciting. She had no idea if it would kick in or not since she didn't have her magic, but she didn't want to start that damn proclamation from the beginning again, and if this worked, she could pick up where she left off.

Maia peeked up over the edge again. From her angle, she could see Ryne sitting up, leaning against the boulder—Deke was still using his body to shield her—and her hand was tucked in the waistband at the back of his jeans. It was a huge relief to see her sister upright. The added bonus was she'd be able to tell Deke what to do even if she couldn't do it herself.

A couple of the creatures were down and some were wounded enough that they weren't going to be a threat. Maia didn't know if Deke had somehow managed that or if Seth hadn't been on target when he'd returned fire, but it didn't matter. It helped things at least a little bit.

She ID'd Seth's position and then scanned for the book. With the protection spells around it, Maia was certain it was still in the vicinity and in one piece.

When she spotted it, she groaned quietly. It was going to be damn difficult to reach it. If she had telepathy and could make Deke and Ryne aware of where she needed to go, they might be able to level some cover fire for her, but as it stood . . .

Maybe Seth wouldn't shoot at her if she made a run for the text. Sure, he'd fired at her, but he hadn't hit her and if he'd really wanted her dead, there were probably a dozen ways he could have killed her without expending much effort. He could put a poisonous snake in the ditch with her or fill it with water, and those were just the two she came up with off the top of her head.

Don't be stupid, Maia, she told herself. *Seth used you; do you really believe he has enough feeling for you not to kill you?*

Yeah. It was just as likely that he hadn't bothered with her because he believed she wasn't any real threat. Forcing him to stop indwelling in Creed would have irritated Seth, but overall, it wasn't a big deal.

And if it weren't for that text, he'd be exactly right. Here she was hiding in a ditch while Deke, Seth, and assorted dark-force creatures fought it out. She had to do something. Creed was down and she didn't know his condition, but Ryne was sitting and Maia could still save her sister—maybe Creed, too.

Her tennis shoes slipped against the muddy sides of the trench as she tried to climb out. Again and again, her feet went out from under her, but at last she found a toehold and made her way to flat ground.

Maia crouched at the top, heart pounding, and paused to see if she'd need to dive back in, but Seth didn't shoot at her. Staying low, she crept carefully toward the book.

She stayed as close to the ditch for as long as she could, but finally she had no choice except to move away from its safety. Maia hated her rapid breathing, her racing pulse, and the sound of blood roaring in her ears. Maybe no one else was aware of how scared she was, but she knew and it mortified her.

From the corner of her eye, she could see the flashes of the shots Deke and Seth were exchanging, and Maia risked a glance over her shoulder at the demon. What she saw froze her. Seth wasn't trying to hit Deke or Ryne.

His volleys came close, sending chips of the boulder flying or tearing up the earth, but Maia had never seen a demon that was such a poor shot. Seth was far too arrogant to let himself be this ineffectual. Something had to be going on that she didn't understand.

A soft grunt had her turning to look behind her.

Uh-oh. Maia didn't know what this was, but it walked on two feet, had longer-than-average arms, and its skin was orangish, making it look like a giant Dreamsicle. Either it had magic or Seth had used his powers to move it. One thing was certain, it hadn't snuck up on her.

Maia wiped her hands off on her pants, but that just made them muddier. Shaking her head, she assumed a defensive posture.

Offense, angel.

Creed?

It'll wear you down if you only react. A frioghan has a lot of stamina. Weak spot is under the armpits. Stab it there.

Ducking the first swing, she tried to come up with an action plan. Although the area had only that one wooded place, Seth's rage had left splinters scattered over half the field. She had to get a long shard, preferably one with a pointed end.

After blocking another strike, she delivered a thigh kick and a couple of quick jabs to the kidneys—or where kidneys would be if the frioghan were human.

It lashed out and its reach was longer than she expected. The force of the blow drove Maia to her knees. She rolled to her right, snagged a tree fragment, and came to her feet in one continuous motion.

The frioghan caught hold of her and she spun, forcing it to release her. She needed a maneuver that would make it reveal its vulnerable area.

With a quickness she hadn't expected, the creature

put her into a loose clinch. She raised her arms, turned to the left, and tried to wrench its elbow. The position momentarily exposed its weak spot, but she couldn't get the wood around in time to drive it in.

Maia danced in close and whipped it in the neck with a back forearm shot. The frioghan grunted and grabbed her by the hair. Even with her hair cropped to chin length, the thing got a good hold on it and jerked her to the ground.

Damn, no one had pulled her hair since she'd been in grade school and she'd forgotten how much it hurt.

Rolling out of the way of a kick, she got to her knees, and without letting go of her stake, dove at the creature. It was the last thing it had expected and Maia yanked it off balance.

When the frioghan went down, she was on it. Before it could react, she pulled her arm back and drove the splinter of wood into its left armpit with all the force she could muster. Blood spurted, covering her hand, and Maia let go of the wood.

She didn't hang around to see if her opponent died or not. Only one thing mattered. Maia ran for the book before anyone or anything else could get in her way.

Grabbing it up, she quickly flipped through, found the spell and the place where she'd left off. It took her less than a minute to finish the incantation and close it.

As far as she could tell, nothing had changed. Damn, she hadn't been able to pause the proclamation and that meant she had to start over from the beginning. She eyed the throng of combatants and hoped she'd have enough time to repeat it.

Maia paged backward and began it again, but before she could get far, everything went still. Even she felt it. Something powerful was coming. Very powerful.

She didn't want to be in the line of fire for this showdown, but before she could think about finding cover, Seth waved an arm and disappeared. One by one, the dark-force creatures—wounded, living, and dead—vanished as well.

Creed. Ryne had Deke to watch over her, but Creed was alone. She ran across the field, needing to reach him.

The figure began to materialize before she'd covered half the distance. Maia froze, wondering what this demon would do when he realized Seth had bugged out, but he never fully appeared. Instead, after scanning the area, he faded out and left. The sounds of the night returned—crickets, owls—and she walked the rest of the distance to where Creed lay.

Settling beside him, she reached out and stroked his arm. "How are you doing?" she asked quietly.

"I'll make it." But he didn't open his eyes.

"Deke," Maia called, "you better request some healers."

"I'm on it," he replied and she relaxed.

It was going to be smooth sailing from here on out.

It was a fucking three-ring circus.

Creed tried to shake off the healer working on him, but she pushed him back down easily enough that he decided he might need a little more attention after all. Maybe he should look at this time as a respite from the inquisition that was coming.

There were three members of the council present, half a dozen trackers, and four healers. Everyone was working, trying to come up with answers about the god-demons that had been here tonight. The chief information the ceannards wanted was where the hell they'd gone, but he didn't think the trackers were going to have much luck coming up with that.

He propped himself up enough to search for Maia. He spotted Ryne first. Three healers continued to tend to her and his gaze moved on until he found Maia standing to the side with Summers. The conversation they were having looked intense and he lowered himself back to the ground, draping an arm over his eyes.

Maia's injuries had been minor, thank God, but he'd refused to let a healer touch him until the woman had taken care of Maia. His angel had saved the day while he'd been possessed by Seth. Creed grimaced. Yeah, he was a legend all right. What a joke.

For months he'd believed that the flashes he received from his mysterious demon were inadvertent and that it only went one way. Instead, what he'd received had been deliberately sent and Seth had known every move Creed made or planned to make. He'd been maneuvered like a marionette and hadn't even realized he had strings attached. Maia had called him an idiot more than once and she was exactly right. He was the biggest fool around.

Only now that the demonic influence was completely gone could he see just how pervasive it had been. The blackouts, the missing time, the vindictive behavior—all Seth. And despite his conduct, Creed had still been stupid enough—blind enough—to believe that he'd been in control.

The healer shifted and held her hands directly above his chest. He could feel the heat of the energy she sent into his body and he opened to it, let it fill him.

When her hands cooled, she withdrew them. "After some sleep, laoch solas, you should be fully healed," she said.

"Thanks." Creed stood and helped the older woman to her feet. She walked over to the councilors, but there was no way he planned to head that direction. They'd find him soon enough.

The only thing less appealing than facing the cean-nards was dealing with Summers, but that's where Maia was, so Creed took a deep breath and joined her. He wasn't surprised when the conversation came to an abrupt halt or that Summers's hands balled into fists at his sides. It was a testament to his control that he didn't take a swing. "How's Ryne doing?" Creed asked, sliding his arm around Maia's waist.

"She's going to be fine," Maia said.

"No thanks to you," Summers added coldly.

"It wasn't Creed," Maia defended him immediately. "Seth possessed him and dictated his actions."

"So you've said."

Creed squared his shoulders. "Look, I'm sorry." It irked him to apologize to Summers, but it had to be done, and when Ryne was on her feet, he was going to have to repeat these words for her. "If the demon hadn't been involved, I never would have targeted Ryne. Not today, not with the zortir, and I wouldn't have withheld the information she needed last spring."

"You expect me to believe that you were possessed for four months?" Summers's skepticism was obvious.

"No. Influenced. He was working on indwelling inside me for about eight months from what I've figured out."

"The ceannards are headed this way," Maia interjected.

They stopped talking and turned to watch the council leader and two other members bearing down on them. Creed stiffened and he knew Maia felt it because she put her arm around his waist and gave him a squeeze. That one simple gesture eased the knot in his chest and he could breathe again.

Nessia came to a halt. After scrutinizing each of them in turn, she addressed Summers. "The healers are finishing up with Ryne now. We'd like the two of you to make a report before the council tonight, but we won't keep you long." She didn't wait for agreement. "Maia, we've already spoken with you at length; if more questions arise after our investigation, will you be willing to continue working with us?"

"Of course," Maia said.

The councilwoman inclined her head. "You're free to leave whenever you like."

"I'll wait for Creed."

"No, you will not," Nessia told Maia and her tone brooked no disobedience. At last the woman leveled a stern look at him. "Laoch solas, I speak for the entire council when I express my disappointment in you. We expected better."

Creed nodded, unsurprised by her words. He'd broken rules left and right with little regard or consideration of the possible consequences.

"You will stand before us and answer for your actions. After we have heard the facts, we will decide your punishment."

25
CHAPTER

Creed prowled the small room outside the council chambers and tried to control his impatience. The ceannards were going to ream his ass, and most people in his position wouldn't be chomping at the bit to face the music, but he wanted it over and done. Putting it off wasn't going to make it any easier.

They were saving him for last, though, so they could get a full accounting of his sins before giving him his sentence. Ryne and Summers were in there now and Creed could just imagine what they were telling the council.

He paused in front of an uninspiring black-and-white print of the Golden Gate Bridge, shook his head, and resumed pacing. No matter how many times he came to Gineal Company headquarters, he was always struck by the ordinariness of it. No human walking in here would spot anything he wouldn't see outside the executive offices of any other Fortune 500 company. Corporate gray. Corporate bland. Yet this conglomerate claimed a board of directors who were all former troubleshooters and could still throw a mean fireball if the need arose.

Despite the gravity of his situation, Creed couldn't stop his lips from curving at the thought. CEOs for other companies who believed they were hard-nosed would whimper like babies if the Gineal council went after them.

The amusement didn't last long. He was in the deepest shit of his career, and if the council leader's demeanor meant anything, the ceannards were not going to be lenient.

Creed felt a brush against his mind and it calmed him. Maia had no clue about the connection they shared or that she could reach out to him, and he planned to keep it that way for now. If he told her they shared a true soul pairing, she'd think he wanted to stick around for all the wrong reasons. Hell, that had nothing to do with anything. It wasn't like he'd get most of the benefits anyway, not when she was magicless.

He dropped into one of the chairs in the waiting area. It appeared as if eventually they'd be able to communicate mentally, even though she'd lost her telepathy, and he suspected the bond would help him block out the whispers of the dark forces and their enticements. That was about it, though. Staying with Maia meant giving up his plan to gain access to more power by developing a pairing with a full-fledged enforcer.

It was a sacrifice he was willing to make.

At least now he knew why his mental protection had faltered and then failed. It had nothing to do with Seth and everything to do with Maia. Before the new, stronger mind shield went up—one that encompassed both halves of the couple—the old one had to come down.

Reaching for a magazine on the table next to him, Creed flipped through it, but he was too tense to read and he put it down quickly. Damn, he wished the council would get this over with and let him go home to Maia.

As if the universe heard his wish, the door opened and one of the aides stood there. "Laoch solas, the ceannards will see you now."

He stood, crossed the floor with a nonchalance he didn't feel, and entered the lion's den. The council was in what he called their V-formation, their table open like the wings of a stealth bomber. Each of the nine council members was present and staring stonily at him.

Bowing his head to show deference, Creed said, "Ceannards."

They left him standing there for a long time before Nessia, the council leader, said, "We'll hear your report about the events of tonight and what led up to them. Leave nothing out, laoch solas, do you understand me?"

How much did they know, and how much could he omit and get away with it? From their forbidding expressions, Creed decided if they hadn't already had a monitor with retrocognitive ability check into this situation, they would after he left, and things would go much worse for him if he held anything back. Reluctantly, he began, starting eight months earlier when he'd first had the microsecond flashes of the demon.

The questions he fielded were sporadic until he started to recount his arrival in Minneapolis and the events that had happened, then he was bombarded. Every councilor grilled him. Creed, who'd always considered himself cool under fire, actually had sweat trickling down his spine before the ceannards were satisfied with his account. The silence seemed foreboding.

They could have asked him to leave the room or

communicated with each other telepathically and made their decision without him knowing who was arguing what position, but that wasn't what they did. With a flick of her hand, Nessia created a wall that separated him from the ceannards.

Creed worked on taking some deep breaths as he waited. Even though he felt as if he'd been put through the wringer, when they returned, he wanted to appear calm. Troubleshooters were trained to always maintain control, but his was shaky right now.

What was the worst that could happen? He didn't think they'd strip him of his magic, not over this, but he couldn't be completely certain, and that's what had him on edge. After all, his own parents had lost their powers.

The wall disappeared before he was ready.

"Laoch solas," Nessia said sternly, "As I told you earlier, I speak for the council as a whole when I say we're very disappointed in you. We've always allowed our rovers more autonomy than the other enforcers, but in your case, that was a mistake."

He couldn't agree, but it was politically unwise for him to disagree. Creed settled for inclining his head once more.

"Since we can no longer entirely trust you, we have new rules that you'll follow. They'll remain in effect until we either regain our confidence or lose our faith in you entirely and remove you from your position."

Creed stiffened, but remained silent.

"You will give a full report to the council after each and every mission. It doesn't matter how simple it was or how easily you handled it, we will hear the full summary of events."

Nessia paused, but when Creed stayed silent, she continued. "Point two. You will not handle anything you happen across without the council approving your participation."

"But if someone's at risk—" he started.

"If it's a life-or-death situation, you will be allowed to take care of it and then report to us, but we don't anticipate that happening often." She leveled her most forbidding scowl on him. "That's precisely what occurred this time, is it not, laoch solas? You felt a demon and instead of telling us and letting us make the decision on how he was to be dealt with, you took matters into your own hands. This is what we wish to avoid in the future."

"Yes, council leader," Creed said evenly.

"Third, when you give your reports, you should be prepared to justify every action you did or didn't take. Whether the strategy was successful or not, we will question you and your answers had better be appropriate."

Whatever the hell that meant, but Creed knew better than to say that aloud.

"And last, you will be given random checks by a monitor with the ability of far sight. He or she will tap into your life without warning and report to us what was seen."

The last point, and the lack of privacy, angered Creed, but he kept his voice neutral when he spoke. "Isn't this steep for one transgression, ceannard?"

"One transgression?" Nessia asked archly. "You had many opportunities over the past eight months to report what was occurring and yet you failed to do so. If we count one error per day for that time period, you have almost two hundred and fifty marks against you." Several of the other councilors nodded.

Creed hid his grimace. When it was put that way, it sounded much worse than it was—in his opinion.

"Have you any further arguments?"

About a dozen of them, but they were all excuses and wouldn't go far with the council. "No, council leader."

"You accept our conditions?"

"Yes, council leader," he said respectfully. What choice did he have? But the indefinite time frame left him uneasy. He'd much prefer a set length to his sentence.

With his punishment meted out, he waited to be dismissed. It didn't happen, and from the glances flying around the table, he suspected they were having a silent conversation. That couldn't bode well.

"We have one more concern," Nessia said. "You not only told an outsider things she shouldn't have heard, but you involved her in troubleshooter business and endangered her."

Maia. They were talking about Maia. Creed went rigid. "I shared nothing with an outsider," he disagreed coolly.

"You dare to lie?" Nessia demanded with barely concealed anger.

"I don't lie. Maia is Gineal and a former troubleshooter. She knew the risks and willingly chose to save her sister."

"Maia Frasier ceded her powers, and according to our laws, that makes her an outsider. Or do you forget the tenets you've sworn to uphold?"

"I forget nothing, council leader," he said coldly, "including why that law was enacted centuries ago. There were Gineal who feared for their lives from human factions, and hoping to save themselves and their families, they gave up their magic. There were some who also shared information with our hunters, buying their safety with the blood of our people."

"The council does not require a history lesson," Nessia said sharply.

Apparently they did, but Creed didn't say that either. "Maia ceded her powers to save her sister the trauma of hunting her because that's who she believed would receive the assignment. She didn't give them up to protect herself. She didn't give them up because of persecution by humans. She gave them up out of love—a completely different motivation."

He looked at each ceannard in turn, daring them to argue with him. None did. "In the last seven years, has Maia even once given you cause to believe she would sell out the Gineal? Has she done anything to deserve the ostracization she's been subjected to? No, she hasn't," he answered for them. "All she's done is try to adjust to a life without magic and continue to nurture her sister."

"Be that as it may," Nessia said, "the law is clear and we do not want you associating closely with her."

Creed's temper hit the red zone. He closed the remaining distance between his position and the council table. Resting his hands on either side of the point, he leaned forward and nearly went nose-to-nose with Nessia. "No."

She sputtered, but Creed cut her off.

"You can force me to report to you after every five-minute job, but you do not get to dictate who I can and can't be involved with in my personal life. I'll continue to see Maia and I'll continue to use my discretion as to what I tell her."

Nessia gave him a jolt of magic powerful enough to back him off a couple of steps. "You forget your place, laoch solas."

"No, council leader, you and the other ceannards are the ones who've forgotten," Creed shot back. "Your oath of office states that you will govern wisely and fairly, that you will judge each situation on its merits and without blindness or prejudice. Where is the wisdom or the fairness in simply using the law as a blanket? Where is the discernment and common sense that you're asked to bring to each decision?"

He started to take a step forward, remembered Nessia's reaction, and decided to stay put. "Ceannard Taber, you were Maia's mentor. Given the reasons behind why she ceded her magic, do you believe she's a threat in any way to the Gineal?"

"No, I don't," the old man said firmly and Creed realized that he'd won an ally.

"Do you believe after seven years that she'll suddenly start informing humans about us?"

A few more of the councilors shook their heads.

"She was a troubleshooter," Creed continued more quietly. "All of us know the temptation the dark forces pose to us more than any other group. Over the centuries, many have fallen. How many have given up their magic to protect another?"

No one answered.

"How many of those who've turned have other troubleshooters been forced to hunt? How many of our enforcers died trying to bring one of them in?"

He paused, letting what he'd said sink in. "Tell me why we should shut Maia out of everything having to do with the Gineal?"

There was another silence, but this time Creed let it stand. They were mentally talking among themselves now, he was certain of it, and he didn't want to do or say anything to interfere with their discussion.

"Your points are well made," Nessia said at last, and to her credit, there was no reluctance in her voice, merely thoughtfulness. "We will not insist you end your association with Maia, but we will monitor her for a time to ensure the safety of the Gineal."

Creed nodded his agreement. He didn't like Maia losing privacy either, but the council was responsible for the well-being of their people, and as far as he knew, there had never been another situation where a troubleshooter in thrall to the dark forces had ceded her magic. It made sense that they wanted to play it cautiously.

"If everything is agreed upon, you may leave, laoch solas."

As he walked out of the council chamber, Creed felt the rest of his adrenaline leave him. Worn out, he opened a transit and went to the one person and place he thought of as home.

Maia found Creed on the back steps of her house. He sat leaning forward, his forearms resting on his thighs, and he appeared exhausted. The sunrise was beautiful, but from the angle of his head, he was staring at either his hands or the cement between his feet. She'd been half afraid he wouldn't return, but just because he was here now didn't mean he would be for long. He'd left his things in her spare room and it wasn't going to take much time to pack everything.

She drew a deep breath to calm her racing heart, then reached for the doorknob and joined him outside. The stoop wasn't wide and their hips pressed together, but Creed didn't look at her. "How'd it go with the council?" she asked.

"About as you'd expect," he said with a grimace.

That didn't tell her much. Nessia's attitude had made it clear they were angry at him, but there were extenuating circumstances. "They chewed you out?"

Creed straightened. "And put me on a tight leash."

"How tight?" She rested her hand on his thigh, stroking lightly along the inseam near his knee.

"Reports after every mission. No handling things that crop up without informing the council and receiving their blessing to take care of it except if it's an extreme emergency. I was also warned to be prepared to justify any decision I made because they wouldn't hesitate to call me on something they deemed questionable. Oh yeah, and I shouldn't try to leave anything out when I fill them in because they're going to have a monitor check up on me at random intervals."

For an instant, Maia was too stunned to react, then she became angry. "Didn't they understand that it was Seth's fault, not yours? How dare they—"

With a grin, he put his arm over her shoulders and tugged her closer to his side. "That's one of the things I love about you, angel—your loyalty." He kissed the top of her head. "But the council's point was legitimate. If I would have said something eight months ago when I first felt flashes of the demon, the whole indwelling probably could have been averted. Seth wasn't controlling me at the start."

One of the things I love about you? That couldn't mean . . . Maia decided she was reading too much into what he'd said, that he was using it as a figure of speech. "There are no guarantees that they could have stopped Seth."

"No, but they have resources at their disposal that I don't have."

Maia nodded. The ceannards could have assigned the entire corps of librarians to research Seth and the other god-demons, they could have warned the monitors to watch for that kind of energy pattern, or they could have put a group of enforcers on it, maybe even all the rovers. But she didn't blame Creed—who would have predicted that a troubleshooter could be possessed?

"It happened when we were in bed, didn't it? Seth took you over when you came."

"My defenses were down and he stormed right in." Creed frowned. "I guess I should apologize for the things I did and said after we made love."

"The things *he* did and said," Maia corrected.

"Yeah, but you didn't know that at the time. I'm sorry you were hurt and I'm sorry our first time together will always be colored by what happened afterward."

Her hand tightened on his thigh. "You'll just have to give me some new memories to erase that one."

Creed smiled slowly. "I'm taking you up on that."

"I'm counting on it."

Neither of them made an effort to start anything, though. Maia had showered off the mud as soon as she'd arrived home and changed clothes, but she hadn't gotten any sleep and neither had Creed. Besides, she still had questions.

"Why did Seth possess you? Why did he have you shooting at Ryne? None of it makes any sense."

He sighed, but didn't speak.

Maia felt her nerves pull taut. She'd hoped that somehow they'd come up with reasons for Seth's actions. At least with that, they could possibly defend against future attacks, but if no one knew, then Ryne remained at high risk—probably Creed, too—and that was unacceptable. "Doesn't anyone have a hint?" she asked, voice choked.

"I know why," Creed said softly. "He made no effort to hide anything while he was indwelling. I told you Seth has a spell where he can take the power of a Gineal—as it turns out it's only under certain circumstances."

Creed went quiet again and Maia straightened, shifting so she could look at him squarely. "Do I have to yank it out of you? What are the circumstances?"

Raising an eyebrow, he stared at her, his gaze all but daring her to try and force it from him.

"Blackwood," she growled, "I'm not asking out of idle curiosity. This involves people I love."

He studied her for a moment longer, then said, "First, Seth can only do the spell while we're between life and death. If we're fully in our body or dead, he's out of luck, and second, he can't cause the injuries that leave us nearly dead."

Maia scowled. "That can't be right. If he shot at Ryne while possessing you, that means Seth would have been responsible for whatever injuries she sustained."

"I agree with your logic, but it has to be wrong as far as the incantation goes. Seth spent a lot of years working to get more power; he wouldn't have risked his chance." Creed leaned forward again, assuming the pose he'd had when she first came outside.

Maia was forced to concede the point. Seth had the highly emotional nature of a demon, but he had planned to use this spell for more than seven years. He would have examined everything thoroughly before acting.

"Ryne had a near-death experience about four months ago," she said. "Why didn't he take her magic then?"

"Shit," he muttered and blew out a long breath. "You're going to keep asking, aren't you?"

It was a rhetorical question and Maia remained silent. Now that she felt certain he wasn't going to try evasive tactics, she could wait for his reply.

Creed turned his head, but he didn't sit up. With a grimace he admitted, "Because the demon wasn't aware of her then." The hesitation was almost unnoticeable. "I led him to her a week or two after that."

His tone didn't change, but Maia understood Blackwood—he was blaming himself for putting Ryne in jeopardy. There was nothing she could say, though, that would lift his guilt, and instead, she ran her hand over his back, stroking him lightly. It was the closest thing to absolution that she thought he'd accept.

"I'm surprised you're not pushing me down the stairs," he said wryly. "It's my fault your sister was in danger."

"Did you lead him to her on purpose, or out of carelessness?"

"Of course not."

"Then I don't have any reason to kick your butt. Things happen that we have no control over, I know that."

He sat up slowly and she put her hand back in her lap. It didn't stay there long. Creed reached over and took it, linking his fingers with hers. "Thanks," he said gruffly.

"Of course, I can't promise that Deke won't kick your ass."

Creed's chuckle was silent. "He can try, but Ryne's the one who scares me."

Maia smiled because Creed had laughed. He was usually so grim. With good reason, she had to admit, but it was nice to see him more lighthearted.

His humor didn't last long. "She's not going to be as forgiving as you are," he said.

"You broke faith with her and you'll have to regain her trust. She'll come around, Creed. You were one of her best friends for a long time," Maia said, squeezing his hand. "It just might take Ryne a while to forgive and forget."

He grunted and rubbed his thumb over her skin. Maia moved on to her next question. "So Seth was hanging around you, you went to see my sister, and he decided she was a better prospect for power. Was he gearing up to possess you from the beginning or did that come later?"

"As far as I know, he came up with it later. My guess is he studied Ryne after he became aware of her, realized he wasn't going to be able to count on her getting killed in the line of duty, and started working on alternatives."

"That's what he was doing with you," Maia said slowly. "He was following you, waiting for you to get hurt badly enough in battle that he could swoop in like a vulture."

"And in my case, his odds weren't bad."

"But why have you kill Ryne? Why not another demon or some other dark-force creature?"

He closed his eyes for a moment, then looked at her again. "His plan was to have Ryne and me fight it out and he'd take the loser's power. That way he came out a winner no matter what happened."

That sounded like Seth. "How do we stop him from going after Ryne or you or another Gineal? He's not going to give up."

Creed turned toward her and stared at her strangely. "What are you talking about? That incantation he wanted to use can only be invoked by someone or something with the power of a god-demon, and after what you did to him last night, that takes Seth out of the picture forever."

"What do you mean, what I did to him? I didn't do anything." No matter how much she wished she had.

"Like hell. You drained his magic down until he's no stronger than an average troubleshooter. He doesn't have a prayer of using his spell."

She had? "Really? I didn't sense anything."

"Trust me. Seth might have been forced to stop indwelling, but he still held a connection with me when you closed whatever proclamation you invoked. I felt his powers go." He scowled again. "Which leads to my big question—how were you able to do that? You ceded your magic."

"I know." Maia smiled weakly. "It seems that when I took that little piece of Seth's power seven years ago, I didn't send it to the universe like I believed." Maia had finished the book while she'd waited for Creed and discovered a few things that she hadn't known.

"What did you learn?" he asked.

"Did you just read my mind?" She tried to jerk her hand free, but he refused to let go.

"Yeah, I did, now what was it that you learned?"

Maia thought about pressing him, but decided from the avid look on his face that Creed was too interested in what she had to say to allow her to steer the conversation another direction. "That dollop of magic? It's inside me. Unfortunately, I can only work spells on Seth and there are also a limited number of them that can be performed—less than a dozen—so it's an almost useless ability."

"It wasn't useless tonight."

"No," she said, "and his missing power explains why Seth cut out so fast. He must have felt the approach of Horus—or whoever that was."

"I'd guess Horus, but it's impossible to be sure. It was one of the god-demons, though." Looking dour, Creed shook his head. "Sometimes it's a bitch to be a troubleshooter."

"You're thinking you'll end up hunting that demon?"

"Maybe not me," he said with a self-deprecating twist to his lips, "but someone's going to get the assignment sooner or later, unless we get lucky and he leaves without causing any problems."

Maia could tell from Creed's voice that he thought it was unlikely, but then the man had said a few times that he believed they were in the shadows of Twilight Time.

With that mindset, it was no wonder he didn't have a positive outlook. She didn't want to spend time on this, though. At this moment, the sun was shining, birds were singing, and everyone she cared about was safe—that's what mattered.

"Do you want breakfast? I'll cook," she offered.

"Later. Sit with me a while longer, okay?"

"Sure." Maia didn't react outwardly, but something inside her started to tighten. He wasn't through talking yet, and the only subject she could think of that needed addressing was them. She could guess what he was going to say. He was a Gineal enforcer, she was powerless—more or less—and they couldn't develop anything serious.

For her, it was too late. She'd fallen in love with him, but she didn't hold any illusions about Creed's feelings for her. Maybe if she still could do magic he'd be interested in something more, but their society discouraged relationships with anyone who lacked magic, no exceptions.

She dug deep and found more strength. Maia knew she'd need it when he explained why she shouldn't expect anything more than sex from him. It would rip out her heart, but even so, she wasn't ready to give him up. If that made her a fool, so be it.

Creed didn't say anything, though. Instead, he sat quietly and played with her fingers. At first, she considered it a reprieve, but as her nerves pulled taut, Maia changed her mind.

When she couldn't stand the suspense anymore, she spoke up. "Come on, Blackwood, just spit it out already. It's not like you to dodge the tough stuff."

"Yeah, you're right." He sounded reluctant. "You haven't known me when I wasn't influenced by the demon and you've got to be wondering how much was me and how much was Seth." He shrugged. "The truth is that even without the extenuating circumstances, I'm abrasive and stubborn."

"And overbearing," Maia suggested.

He cast her a sideways look. "That, too. If you're expecting a miraculous transformation, it isn't going to happen."

"I wasn't expecting you to change." And that was the truth. "My guess is that what I saw while you've been here is basically who you are with a few facets exaggerated by Seth. Those will probably scale back to normal, but I doubt they're the parts of you that I'd like to see toned down." Maia nudged his shoulder with her own. "It's okay. I can handle you. I'm used to arrogant troubleshooters—I used to be one myself. Besides, I doubt you can touch Ryne when it comes to intensity."

"Yeah," he said sounding happier. "You do deal with her edginess, don't you?"

"Constantly."

Creed nodded and went quiet again, only this time he seemed to be considering things. Not that the idea eased her nerves, but it was better than his earlier moodiness.

"Here's the thing," he said. "I'm difficult even when there aren't demons involved and I'm a roving troubleshooter, which means a lot of time away from home. That's for openers. Then there are the laws the Gineal have about sharing with outsiders. While I'm willing to bend that rule a lot, there will be times I won't tell you things no matter how much you persist. Is that something you can live with?"

Her heart started pounding fast again, sounding as loud as a runaway train. This wasn't the speech she'd been expecting. "Will I like it? No. Do I understand? Yes. Will it cause friction? Sometimes. I can't say that it won't, but yeah, I can live with it."

"Things happened fast between us—probably too fast," Creed said, "but you've gotten under my skin. I can't imagine not sparring with you or kissing you, not being able to talk to you whenever I feel like it or getting razzed about my age."

She opened her mouth, but he raised his free hand and put the pad of his index finger over her lips.

"Let me finish. We both need time to get to know each other under normal conditions. Okay, at least as normal as life with a troubleshooter gets." He smirked, but almost immediately became serious once more. "I want that time. I love you, Maia."

Again, she tried to speak, but he pressed his finger just a shade more firmly against her lips.

"I'm not saying that to pressure you or because I expect you to feel the same. Like I said, I know things happened fast. I want you to understand that I'm not taking things lightly and that my next suggestion isn't coming because I want some fun and games."

Maia reached up and captured his hand. "What suggestion is that?"

"Let me move in with you." He shook his head, cutting her off. "I know, I'm presumptuous, but hell, we're long past dating and being careful around each other. If that's what you want, though, I'll do it. I don't want to lose you."

And Creed, bless his heart, actually looked the slightest bit scared. "Well?" he prompted.

Maia ran through a host of different responses before she settled on the most straightforward. "I love you, too. Even if you do make me crazy half the time."

His grin returned. "Yeah?"

"Yeah."

He leaned forward and kissed her, a slow easy caress that spoke as much as words. "I don't really have a home—I haven't had one since my grandfather died—but angel, with you, I finally feel like I belong somewhere."

She'd been doing well holding the emotions at bay, but that did it. Maia felt tears well up. "Me, too. Me, too."

Another kiss, then, "I know I'm probably pushing my luck, but what do you say about the living together part?"

"I say the council is going to go berserk at the mere thought of it. You know Gineal don't have serious relationships with the powerless."

"Fuck the council," he snarled and Maia gaped at him. Creed shook his head and sounded calmer when he explained. "That's more of a human-Gineal problem; we shouldn't have any big issues."

"Why do you think—"

"A relationship with a human opens a can of worms." The growl was back in his voice. "Including how we deal with integrating one into Gineal society. Since you already know we exist and what we can do, it's a nonissue. And second, we'll be okay because if we have children, they'd still have magic. They'd be dormants, but that's easy enough to take care of. Not so with a human-Gineal pairing, which is why it's heavily frowned on."

Children? It was definitely too early for that topic. "The ceannards aren't going to object then?"

"No. Now will you answer the question?"

With a shrug, she put aside her concerns. If the council said anything, she'd deal with it later. Instead, Maia considered living with Creed and realized that if they did the dating thing, he'd probably be spending most of his nights here anyway. What was the point in pretending otherwise? And that's all saying no to his moving in would be—a pretense. She was committed to him and he would never have used the "L" word if he didn't mean it. "Let's give it a try," Maia said at last and ignored Creed's whoop. "Just be aware that I expect you to pull your weight."

"Yes, ma'am."

Splaying her fingers through his hair, Maia tugged him to her and gave him a long, slow kiss. "You want to try to make up for your behavior last night?" she asked.

"Hell, yeah." Creed helped her to her feet, but he stopped her before she opened the door. "There's one more thing you should know."

"What's that?"

He hesitated, then said, "Meeting you is the best damn thing that's ever happened to me."

He was such a sweet talker, but that was Creed Blackwood, and while the eloquence wasn't there, she knew he'd always be sincere. "Even though I don't have magic anymore?"

"Power doesn't matter, not really. What matters is here." And he put her hand over his heart, covering it with his own.

Maia felt the last knot of tension left inside her melt away. Everything was going to be okay between them; she knew it.

Epilogue

SEVEN MONTHS LATER

Maia stepped out of her heels the instant they were inside their suite at the Beverly Hills Hotel and let out a deep sigh of relief. "I'm beat," she told Creed.

"It was a long day," he said. "You held up well, though." He shrugged out of his suit coat and tossed it over one of the chairs. "Your eyes got misty a couple of times during the ceremony and once when they danced at the reception, but no real tears until Ryne and Summers drove off to start their honeymoon."

She made a face at him and sat on the sofa, slumping back. "I don't know how parents deal with their children leaving the nest. I feel lost right now."

It was silly, Maia realized that. Ryne had been self-sufficient for a long time, not to mention the fact that Deke and her sister had been living together for nearly a year already. It was hardly as if the wedding were some turning point that signified tremendous change.

Creed sat on the coffee table in front of her and patted his leg. "Give me your feet," he said.

She did, resting them in his lap, and he immediately began to massage one. Her groan of pain quickly changed to pleasure as he worked out the soreness, and Maia closed her eyes to enjoy the attention. Damn, the man was good with his hands.

"You know," Creed said as he kneaded her instep, "I never would have imagined Ryne going for a traditional wedding with all the hoopla."

"Tell me about it." Maia smiled fondly. "If I'd had to guess where she'd get married, I'd have put my money on a beach in Hawaii. Wearing a sarong," she tacked on. "Ryne in a formal dress? Incredible." She paused while Creed switched to her left foot, then added, "She's softening toward you."

He snorted. "I don't know why you think that."

"Because she wrote your name on the invitation, not *Maia Frasier and guest.* Six months ago, my sister didn't even want you at the wedding. It helps a lot that you managed to square things with Deke."

"Summers and I are hardly friends."

Maia sighed in bliss as Creed rubbed a particularly painful spot. "He'll stay cool until Ryne comes around, but you can bet he's working on her behind the scenes."

"If he is, it's because of you, not me."

Creed was right about that. Deke was determined that nothing drive a wedge between her and Ryne, and that included Maia's relationship with Creed. The whys didn't matter, though, just the results, and her sister *was* coming around, whether Blackwood noticed it or not.

They were silent as Creed continued to massage her

foot and she felt herself start to drift. Ryne had looked beautiful and Maia couldn't have been more proud. Her sister had handled the room as if she'd been doing it all her life, even though she'd had to interact with a lot of different types. Not only had there been the celebrities Deke knew because of his television show, there'd been some of Hollywood's biggest movers and shakers present—along with Deke's old friends from the police force and people he'd worked with as a private detective. The groom's guests had almost made the Gineal seem ordinary.

Her amusement faded. Taber had talked to her at the reception and told her a few things that Maia hadn't known. Namely, that the council *had* objected to Creed's relationship with her and that he'd fought them in order to continue it. According to her old mentor, Blackwood hadn't argued half as strenuously in his own defense.

Of course, he hadn't told her that, but if she'd had any doubts about how much he loved her, that would have settled them. Maybe Creed didn't say much, but he showed his feelings in other ways, and she always felt cherished by him, even when they were in the middle of a knock-down, drag-out argument.

He ran his hand from her foot up her calf to her knee. "Finals at the university end mid-May, right?"

"Yeah, why?"

"I was thinking that when you begin summer break, we'll take a vacation. You have a week built up at your job by now, right?"

Maia nodded. She had another clerical position, but this time things were different. For one, it was semi-interesting. For a second, she knew it was only until she finished college. The third thing, though, was the most important—her new employer created a pleasant work environment and treated their people well. "Getting time off won't be a problem," she added.

"Good." Creed cleared his throat and squeezed her foot briefly before he relaxed his grip. "There's an art show in Seattle that we could start with and then maybe hop up to Vancouver."

Opening her eyes, Maia met his gaze. "Shona's having a show?" she asked quietly.

His nod was jerky. "It opens May 20, but I thought we'd hit it a few days later. I don't want to talk to her— I know better than that—I just want to see some more of my sister's work."

"That sounds like a plan; let's do it."

That earned her another rough nod, but Maia was familiar enough with Creed's moods that she knew now wasn't the best time to talk about Shona or his family. She'd bring it up later, though, when he was more receptive, and see if she couldn't do something to ease this burden for him.

Maia changed the subject slightly. "Vancouver has companies with Zodiac boats that take tourists out whale watching. Maybe we could do that while we're there."

"Yeah, why don't we." He moved her feet from his lap to the table and shifted to sit beside her on the couch. His hand went to her knee and he lightly stroked her. "There's this incredible suspension bridge that I'd like to see, too."

Bridge? Must be a guy thing. "Okay," she agreed. "We'll have to make a list before we leave of what we want to do."

That got her a grunt and she hid a smile. Creed liked to pretend that her penchant for organization was a pain in the butt, but it wasn't true. He'd never admit it, but she'd picked up his thoughts on this topic, and he liked how smoothly things went when they were planned. She let her eyes drift shut again as the silence lengthened.

"You know," he said awhile later as he ran his hand from her knee up her thigh, "you look sexy as hell in that dress."

"Thanks." Maia opened her eyes and turned her head toward him. "You looked damn fine today, too." She'd practically had to lasso Creed to get the man to shop for a suit to wear to the wedding, but it had definitely been worth the effort. "When do you think I can talk you into wearing it for me again?"

"How about when we get married?"

Her heart lurched, but she teased easily. "That long, huh?"

"Not long. I thought if you put your organizational genius on the project, we could do it before your fall session starts."

"You're joking, right?" Maia couldn't prevent the incredulity from permeating her voice.

Creed grimaced. "That wasn't the response I was hoping for."

There was a flare in his eyes that told Maia just how serious he'd been. Something inside her eased—it was going to be okay. "Blackwood," she told him, putting her feet flat on the floor. "If you expect me to say yes, you need to ask me to marry you, not throw out an offhand comment to test the waters."

"You want the pretty words," he grumbled.

"Afraid so."

He took a deep breath, bracing himself, and Maia had to glance down until she had her amusement under control. He acted as if he were girding himself for battle.

"I love you, Maia," Creed said gruffly. "Coming home to you is like returning to a sanctuary, one where I'm welcomed for who I am rather than what I can do." He shrugged, looking uncomfortable, but he took her hand and continued to meet her gaze. "You complete me in a way I never expected. It's like I'm more with you than I'll ever be on my own, and I hope I give you at least part of what you've given me." He took another deep breath. "I want forever with you, angel. Will you marry me?"

Talk about leaving her misty-eyed. She was so choked up, she could barely talk, but Maia read his anxiety and forced out one word. "Yes."

That earned her a relieved grin. "Don't I get some pretty words in return?"

Maia laughed. "I tell you how I feel all the time, but if you want to hear it again—I love you, too." Her voice was still thick. "I can't imagine living my life without you."

His hand cupped her cheek, and he kissed her slowly, reverently, before easing back to meet her gaze again. "I never thought," Creed said quietly, "that I'd love anyone as much as I love you. It's terrifying—and I wouldn't give up the fear for anything."

Maia understood exactly what he meant. "You said once that you feel as if you belonged with me. I feel the same way, Creed. I'd been alone in a lot of ways for a long time, but then you barreled into my life, turned it upside down, and when I regained my equilibrium, you'd made a place for yourself in my heart."

It was her turn to become uncomfortable. Her family had never been physically or verbally demonstrative, but she wanted Creed to know how important he was to her.

"All my life, I'd been looking for something; I'm not searching anymore," Maia said. "With you, I have everything I need."

TOR
ROMANCE

Believe that love is magic

Please join us at the website below for more information about this author and other great romance selections, and to sign up for our monthly newsletter!

www.tor-forge.com